Agent of Influence

A Thriller

By

Russell Hamilton

Reviews for Agent of Influence

"Hamilton delivers a taut political thriller that moves with speed and agility. A fast-paced thriller with an imaginative premise." Kirkus Indie Reviews.

"Agent of Influence is an action-packed mystery/thriller that is certain to entertain." City Book Reviews.

"This is one roller coaster ride readers won't want to get off." Foreword Clarion Reviews

"Hamilton has written as tightly plotted an international spy story as you are going to find in this genre." Bookreview.com

"Crackling with insights and rife with adventure." Chuck Morse; talk radio host, former candidate for the US House of Representatives, and author of The Nazi Connection to Islamic Terrorism.

Agent of Influence
A Thriller

Copyright 2009 Russell Hamilton

ISBN: 978-0-6156-6227-5 (sc)

Library of Congress Control Number 2009905108

Printed in the United States of America

Agent of Influence – the simplest and most direct method of affecting a foreign government's actions. An agent whose task is to influence directly government policy rather than to collect information.

(From *Silent Warfare, Understanding The World Of Intelligence* by Abram N. Shulsky and Gary J. Schmitt Copyright 2002, Potomac Books Inc. Third Edition)

"That the Turks should be deprived of Constantinople is, in my opinion, inevitable and desirable as the crowning evidence of their defeat in war; and I believe that it will be accepted with whatever wrathful reluctance by the Eastern world. But when it is realized that the fugitives are to be kicked from pillar to post and that there is to be practically no Turkish Empire and probably no Caliphate at all, I believe that we shall be giving a most dangerous and most unnecessary stimulus to Moslem passions throughout the Eastern world and that sullen resentment may easily burst into savage frenzy."

Lord George Curzon, Foreign Secretary of Great Britain, speaking to the Western powers at the peace conference in Paris in 1919. (From *Paris, 1919* by Margaret Macmillan, Published by Random House)

"I am more and more convinced that man is a dangerous creature; and that power, whether vested in many or a few, is ever grasping, and, like the grave, cries, 'Give, give.'"

Abigail Adams, wife of the second President, John Adams, in a 1775 letter to her husband

Prologue
Cairo, 1967

Streaks of white flames flashed across the night sky, followed immediately by thunderclaps of explosions that rattled the building every few minutes. A few of the windows were shattered due to the violent explosion of a missile that landed only a few blocks away.

Ayman al-Zawahiri stood at the threshold of one of the jagged holes where a window used to be and looked down at the dusty street below. The roads and alleyways were deserted except for the occasional military vehicle that tore down the street with a load of soldiers being rushed to the front. Anyone with common sense was huddled in their home, trying to hide from the ring of fire the Israeli Air Force was raining on the city.

The Jews have proven to be an effective and dangerous enemy, Ayman grudgingly admitted to himself as he stroked his black beard in a thoughtful manner. He gazed out over the ancient city, and pondered once again what the tiny man waiting patiently behind him had said. It was an audacious plan, that he fully admitted, but could it actually work? Ayman's brothers within his organization already told him to refuse the man. Apparently he was developing quite a reputation as a troublesome and annoying interloper.

"My friends believe you to be crazy," Ayman said as he adjusted his white robes. "They say if Sayyid lost faith in you, why should we be put our trust in you?"

"Sayyid spent many years in jail being tortured by Nasser's animals before he was hanged. It was only a matter of time before he turned on us. A man can only sustain himself for so long. And what about you, Ayman? If my idea is so crazy then why did you agree to this meeting?" Aziz said softly as he walked up and stood beside Ayman at the open window. "You know my idea has merit, Ayman. You are a smart man. You have risen to your position because you are an intellectual, and can see through the obvious."

4

The smell of cordite wafted into the window as they both stood with their hands clasped behind their backs. They watched the city several stories below them slowly begin to come back to life. The last bomb exploded a few minutes earlier, and it appeared the bombing raids were ceasing for the moment.

"Your plan is intriguing. I admit that. You have already gotten further than I thought possible. But you are years away from your plan bearing fruit. Possibly even decades," Ayman retorted. "My brothers feel they cannot waste that amount of time when there are so many pressing problems here to deal with. Killing the apostate Nasser being the most prominent."

"If you kill him he will simply be replaced by another; and the other may be worse. My friends in the government have told me some of the people under him would come down on you even harder. They believe he has been too soft."

"We welcome the fight," Ayman said tersely.

"For to win one hundred victories in one hundred battles is not the acme of skill. To subdue the enemy without fighting is the acme of skill," Aziz quietly recited from memory.

"Sun Tzu, the ancient Chinese warrior. I was warned you would eventually quote him," Ayman said with resignation. He wanted to help Aziz, but knew it was not possible. "I am sorry, my friend. The council's decision is final."

"So be it," Aziz said with seething anger. "You choose to follow the path of fools. I can't help you; but I no longer consider you a friend. When my plan comes to fruition you will bow before me with humility, and regret the decision you make today." Aziz turned away from the window and quickly made his exit just as more explosions rocked the city. He had preparations to make.

Louisville, KY
May 5, 1973

Eddie Lauren's body revolted, refusing to accept the 3:15 a.m. time that was being thrust upon it. With a steaming cup of coffee in his right hand, his ever-present note pad in his left, and a pencil behind his ear he made his way down the long line of stables along the backside of Churchill Downs. Fresh out of college, Eddie was working his first Derby for the local paper. A local kid, he grew up sneaking into the track to catch glimpses of the three-year-old thoroughbreds that made the one-and-a-quarter mile Kentucky Derby their launching pad to stardom. The owners, trainers, and stable hands would not be up and about for another forty-five minutes and he wanted to be the first one on the scene. He had a story to tell, one he was convinced would put him on the map. It was a story he thought was being lost in the shuffle as the discussion of whether Secretariat could live up to the hype continued to be the only thing the experts wanted to discuss. Earlier in the year, thirty-two investors had forked over a whopping $6,080,000 to syndicate Secretariat. Two weeks ago his amazing string of ten consecutive wins came to an end in the Wood Memorial. There were now a lot of nervous men in town for the race wondering if their sure fire investment of $190,000 was about to become worthless overnight.

While he found the story intriguing, Eddie was onto something that he thought could have a tremendous impact on horse racing over the next twenty years. The entry of Desert Sheik, owned by Aman Kazim, a Middle-Eastern playboy who owned several casinos in Las Vegas, appeared to be the first Arab trained horse that posed a threat to win the Derby. Once the horse was entered in the Derby, Eddie began investigating the horse's pedigree and how it competed in Europe. It was impressive, and he felt certain the media was ignoring the horse because it was not coming to the Derby through the usual channels. The local paper would be hitting the city's front porches in a few hours, and

Eddie had picked the horse to win the Derby in an upset. He talked to Aman yesterday during a small media event at the stables and told him of his impending prediction. He also requested a one-on-one interview and a chance to see the horse put through its morning routine. Eddie was convinced it would make for a great story if the horse pulled the upset.

"Yes, yes I would be honored, Mr. Lauren." Eddie replayed the eager man's response in his mind. Aman had jumped at the proposal. He had been desperately trying for the last ten years to make it big in thoroughbred racing in the States, and while he had won some smaller races, this was his first chance at winning a major race. Aman had agreed to meet him at the stable at 3:30 a.m. to give Eddie the one-on-one interview. Eddie sipped his coffee, continuing to try to adjust to the abnormal hour as he strode by the locked stables. Even the horses were not awake yet. His feet shuffled along, stepping on scattered pieces of hay, as he made his way to the barn at the end of the row. Desert Sheik's stable was separated from the others by another one hundred feet. This provided the extra privacy its owner preferred. Eddie squinted his eyes as he looked up, noticing a small glow coming from the stable. *Aman must be an early riser.*

"Damn it," he muttered to himself. His drowsy mind suddenly remembered some additional questions to ask, and he furiously scribbled some last-second notes onto his legal pad. His adrenaline began to overcome the chilly morning air as he realized this could be the beginning of big things if his upset pick could somehow pull it off. As he approached the stable, a groan in an unknown language emanated from the open stall. Eddie froze, surprised by the noise. It sounded like a grunt of frustration. He crept forward, using the barn to shield his approach. The cold, hard ground crunched under his feet, and he stopped fifteen feet away from the half-open stable door.

He continued his cautious approach until he stood face-to-face with the swinging barn door. The grunts were accompanied by a punching sound that he could not decipher. The noise reminded him of the sound a seasoned boxer makes as he pounds his gloved fists into a training bag. Brushing back his shaggy brown hair, he cautiously brought his head to the edge of the barn door and peered into the open stall. The horrific carnage jolted his system, and he heaved involuntarily.

Eddie stared, fixated on the unimaginable scene before him. He closed his eyes, hoping the early morning hour had thrown off his senses, but he reopened them to the same gruesome sight. A horse, which he could no longer recognize but assumed to be Desert Sheik, was lying on a small pile of hay. There were hundreds of cuts slashed haphazardly over its body, and the horse's blood enveloped the floor of the stable in a sea of crimson. The blank slates of the horse's eyes registered no feeling or movement, leaving no doubt that it was already dead. The killer had a vice grip on his machete, and he quickly jolted his head around at the sound of Eddie's vomiting. Eddie froze in fear as he eyed the perpetrator; the killer's coal black eyes registered no feeling of remorse. Eddie instantly recognized him as one of the young stable hands that Aman employed to watch over his prized possession. He thought the kid could not have been older than seventeen. *What could possibly make him do this?* His mind raced as he tried to shake loose of his fears and decide what to do.

"What's going on here?" Eddie asked meekly. The stable hand began marching menacingly toward him, and Eddie backpedaled quickly. He did not see or hear the short, stocky figure approaching from behind. The powerful hand gripped his shoulder, causing him to shudder. He dropped his legal pad in panic, but before he could let out a cry for help a familiar voice whispered in his ear.

"Eddie, my friend, be quiet," Aman's voice was firm, yet soothing. They both turned their attention back to the boy, whose wild rage instantly melted into abject fear as Aman shot him a piercing stare. Aman let loose with a torrent of words in Arabic. The tone of the boy's response was clearly sarcastic, but he dropped the machete without any prodding and walked out the back entrance of the barn. His sagging shoulders registered defeat. Eddie stared at Aman, not sure what to say, he stated the obvious, "Christ, you scared the hell out of me!" It was not an attempt at a joke.

        "Eddie, my dear friend you must speak of this to no one. It would ruin me," he said. Aman's commanding voice clearly would not take no for an answer.

PART I

THE BAIT

Chapter 1
Early December, 2004

      Forty-two year-old Zachariah Hardin locked onto the silhouetted figure striding across the raised platform. The strobe lights intersecting the darkness only served to enhance her statuesque figure. Even his bodyguards struggled to focus on their job instead of the magnificent dark-haired beauty standing before them in high heels and a nurse's outfit that could only be appropriate in the gentleman's clubs of Las Vegas. It was Friday night and the main room was crammed with ogling men of every age and background, each one drinking six-dollar beers without a second thought. Zachariah could be mistaken for the average businessman who just left work to meet some friends and have some fun. He was dressed in a dark blue Brooks Brothers double-breasted suit with light pin stripes that, in this particular setting, glowed in the dark. He would have looked slightly ridiculous were it not for the cold stare on his olive-colored face.

      His mentor had told him not to frequent this club anymore, but he simply did not care. It would not be long before their roles would be reserved. He knew his mentor was nothing without him. Besides, Zach was on the far side of the stage, surrounded by ten bodyguards that formed a "U" shape around him. He was perfectly safe. The only gap in their human wall allowed him to view the stage unimpeded. No one could get near him. The rest of the patrons could only guess at which rich man had a quarter of the room to himself; forcing the rest of them to sit closer together than they would prefer.

Zachariah downed the last of his vodka tonic, and motioned to the waitress standing just outside his phalanx of guards to bring him another. He squinted as the lights of the stage dimmed and the first deep chords of a rap song blared out of hidden speakers. He had no use for rap music; it was just another wasteful indulgence created by the American public. The music reminded him of his deceased wife. She had despised it, and he remembered how she donated large sums of her inheritance to organizations dedicated to doing things like putting warning labels on music. Zachariah thought it was a monumental waste of time.

She was working with one of those organizations when the doctors first found the cancer in her brain last year. It had already metastasized into an advanced stage. Zachariah could not believe his luck. His mentor had been formulating a way to eliminate her when divine intervention took care of the problem for them. Zachariah was convinced it was a sign that their mission was blessed.

Folding his arms across his chest, he tossed his memories into the shadows and returned his focus to the stage. He stared, mesmerized as the stripper began slowly moving with the rhythm. He had never seen this girl in the club before. He watched intently, barely noticing his bodyguard sit his third vodka tonic down on the tiny table. Zachariah unconsciously brushed his hands across his slicked back hair, making sure it was in its proper place. There was just a hint of gray around the edges that he would have preferred to dye but his handlers refused to let him. They told him it helped him appear scholarly and thoughtful to the public.

He refocused as the woman yanked an unseen bobby pin, sending a glimmering cascade of raven black hair down past her shoulders. She stepped confidently along the edge of the stage, enticing the hushed crowd closer with a smile that every man pretended was for him alone. She slowly worked the crowd, smiling seductively while the closest patrons to her all reached robotically for their wallets in hopes of attracting her undivided attention for a few short seconds. She purposely stepped onto a vent situated at the front of the stage floor. A fan inside the vent sent a burst of air upwards, pushing up her ivory skirt for a few seconds and teasing the crowd with a glimmer of black lingerie gripping tanned thighs. She finally made her way to his side of the stage and stopped, her hands moving down her legs, caressing them.

Zachariah casually sipped his drink, and a cocky smile expanded over the top of his glass. The nightclub had some new flesh for him. He was glad. He was getting tired of the regulars. He found their efforts lacking to say the least. The bronzed beauty on stage gave him a once over, appearing to size him up, and then proceeded back to the middle of the stage without so much as a smirk for him.

"Excellent. A feisty one at last," he chuckled quietly to himself. Normally the dancers came right up to him and ignored the rest of the patrons. She was challenging him, and making him work for his reward. He watched her intently, her perfectly formed backside now staring at him as she continued to match the intensity of the music with more glimpses of flesh. For the second time in a few minutes, Zachariah motioned for his personal waitress to come over. He eyed his bodyguards, motioning for them to let her through. She leaned over to take his order, and he spoke into her ear, "Send the girl on stage over to see me when she's done," he commanded.

"Anything else, sir?" Her lips were right up against his ear, but she had to yell to be heard over the music.

"Yes, another vodka, please. By the way, what's her name? I didn't catch the introduction," he asked as he pointed at the dancer.

"Her stage name is Marilyn, sir. She just started a few weeks ago. I don't know her real name yet, but I can find out if you like," the waitress replied.

"Not necessary, just get me my drink," he said as he smacked her gently on her rump and sent her on her way. Marilyn. *What a stage name*, he laughed to himself. He found the irony of the situation almost too perfect. Whoever she was, she was truly audacious, and he assumed she would be an incredible lay.

One of his bodyguards pointed to his Rolex watch and Zachariah acknowledged the gesture. It was later than he realized. The Secret Service may be his bodyguards but they were ruining all his fun tonight. He would only have time to talk with the new girl tonight. President-Elect Zachariah Hardin waited for the dancer to finish before getting up from the table. He would at least get her phone number tonight, he thought. Zachariah already had a meeting planned with his mentor to discuss the upcoming inauguration. It would be one of a truly historic nature if things went according to plan.

Chapter 2
December 31, 2004, 11:03 P.M.

Allan Gray did not feel like the most powerful man in the world as he sat slouched behind his desk in the Oval Office. He stared at his telephone, waiting for it to ring. "I hope this will be some good news," he muttered as he sipped a glass of water.

The New Year's Eve party was muted, thanks to his defeat at the ballot box. This would be his last New Year's Eve in the White House, so he finally acquiesced to his nagging wife and allowed a full-blown party to be thrown. He was no longer one for the late night celebrations. His time as governor of California had forced him to attend more late night parties than he cared to remember.

Allan felt like he was at a wake more than a party, and in a sense it was true, except in this case he was being forced to attend his own funeral. Most of the guests were old friends or the few Washington politicians who remained loyal to him as his political fortunes changed for the worse. One of the men had even been up for re-election, and instead of turning his back on the President had continued in his unwavering support. His loyalty to President Gray ended up costing him his senate re-election bid. Allan made a mental note to make sure the Senator from Florida obtained an easy consulting job somewhere that paid him entirely too much. Loyalty in this town was a rare commodity and it had to be rewarded.

Allan now had one more problem he was working on though; one that only a few others in his government were aware of, and this one had the potential to be a true political firestorm. He had agreed to the operation only because if it were true, it had the potential to rock the very foundation the Executive Branch was built upon. He expressed his misgivings to CIA Director Malcolm Ray, but the Director had been very persuasive. In the end, Allan agreed to the operation. Besides, his own political career was already dead, and he could not be killed twice.

A few minutes earlier his Secret Service agent had pulled him away from a few people at the party seeking last minute pardons for friends. The agent whispered in Allan's ear that he would be receiving a call from the CIA Director shortly. Allan politely excused himself from the party, apologizing for the interruption, and promised to return after tying up a few loose ends.

The quiet vibration of the phone interrupted his random musings. He grabbed it before the first ring could even be completed.

"She has disappeared. We can't find her. It appears she may be dead," the baritone voice of CIA Director Malcolm Ray could not hide its dejection. "I'll contact you again later."

The line went dead before President Gray could issue a demand or ask a question. He hung up the phone, and stared at it for a few seconds before standing up, and grabbing his dinner jacket. "Maybe I'll have a drink," he contemplated briefly. It all appeared to be over now anyway. He strode out of the room, a look of dejection permeating throughout his normal jovial persona. He patted his Secret Service agent on the shoulder, and gave him a nod of appreciation. "That was it Jamal. Let's get back to the party. I think I'll have a drink," President Gray said with an even tone.

"Yes sir," Jamal Mahmoud, the head of his Secret Service detail said with authority. He held the door open for his Commander in Chief.

The President stepped across the threshold of the Oval Office and headed back to his party. The only consolation he took out of all this was that if the press discovered their investigation, at least there would not be enough time for them to impeach him. He knew his days were numbered when barely avoiding impeachment seemed like a victory.

Chapter 3
Thursday, 10:43 P.M., Pacific Time, January 2, 2005

From a distance Alex thought it looked like an oasis of sin, glowing in the desert night. Southwest flight 3112 descended through the thin layer of clouds without a shudder of turbulence, and approached the glimmering lights of Las Vegas. The pilot gave out his cursory final instructions to the crew and passengers to prepare for landing. The four-hour journey was coming to an end, soon to be replaced with a few days of drinking, gambling, and every other vice imaginable.

Alex Bryce's anticipation rose higher as the plane slowly lowered, and he reached his arm across the aisle to nudge his drowsy friend awake. He gleefully pointing out the green glow of the MGM Grand Casino & Hotel like a child pointing at Mickey Mouse after entering Disney World for the first time. He still vividly remembered his first trip to Las Vegas seven years before. It had been during spring break in college that he first found the combination of gambling and late night carousing to be the perfect stress reliever from the toil of college and his pursuit of a double major in history and economics.

"Michael! Wake up. We're coming in," Alex said as he rubbed the palms of his hands together like he was trying to keep them warm. He knew this would be the last time he could act like an adolescent for a long time and he intended to soak in as much fun as possible over the long weekend.

"Yeah. Great, Alex. I've seen it plenty of times before," Michael said with one eye cocked open before laying his head back onto his girlfriend's shoulder.

"It even looks gaudy from up here. You promise this will be fun?" Michael's girlfriend asked. Michael and Cindy flew all the way from New York, and Alex boarded the plane at a layover in Indianapolis, where he had been working until recently. He had spent the last several hours of the flight getting acquainted with Michael's girlfriend, and so far he was impressed.

"I guarantee it. This isn't just a man's playground you know. Plenty of shopping for the ladies," Alex replied, trying his best to sound enthusiastic. Cindy seemed like a nice girl, but he was not sure how much fun they could have in Las Vegas with a girl tagging along.

"I promise I'll do my best to keep up with you boys. I know you're looking to let loose a little. When do you have to report for duty?" Cindy was having her own doubts about whether she should have come on this trip, but she was determined to be positive. Michael had insisted that she accompany him after all.

"A week from today, I report for training. I was told the training takes at least six months," Alex said, the intrusion of his new job and its inherent dangers casting a momentary shadow over his excitement.

The pilot's voice crackled as it spoke over the intercom, interrupting their conversation. The attendants began preparing for landing. The thought of his new job brought Alex out of his playful manner as he thought about the drastic change his life was about to take. A few years ago he was a happily married attorney living a normal life. Now he was divorced, and about to go to work for the Central Intelligence Agency.

"Do you know where you head to after that?" Cindy continued probing for information.

"No idea. They won't let me know until they decide

16

what they think I'm best suited for," Alex replied.

The attendant strolled down the aisle, and Alex turned his head to peer out the pressurized window at the barren landscape below. A night landing in Las Vegas always gave him the sense that he was landing on the surface of the moon, and Las Vegas was the only settlement on the planet.

Alex guessed his new job would soon give him the same alien feeling. For what seemed like the hundredth time, he questioned whether or not it was the right decision. When he told his wife he wanted to apply to the CIA, she had been less than supportive. When he actually was offered the job, she lost it. It would mean a smaller paycheck, and it had the potential to be very dangerous, depending on his assignment. He knew he had to do it though.

The attacks of 10/01/00 were his first eye opener. When an Al-Qaeda sleeper cell was dismantled in Indianapolis, the federal prosecutor in the area used Alex's firm to help on the investigative side of the case. Alex was assigned to research background information on the three defendants, and assist with the local aspects of the case. The research opened his eyes to a danger he never knew existed. When the defendants were allowed to walk on a technicality before the case even got to trial, he knew he was in the wrong line of work, and applied to the CIA the next day. The new career choice destroyed his marriage. He was just thankful they had no kids to fight over.

Alex scratched his closely cropped chestnut hair, and stretched his muscular six-foot frame as far as he could as he listened to the loud clanging of the wheels slamming into position. Three minutes later, the wheels skidded onto the concrete expanse of the darkened runway. Like most of the passengers, Alex began to prematurely unfasten his seatbelt.

"Everyone please keep your seatbelt fastened until the plane has stopped," the stern voice from the cockpit sounded unusually harsh. Alex and Michael looked at each other and laughed simultaneously.

"You ever hear a pilot sound like that?" Michael asked

17

"Nope. Must be an ex-military guy. I kind of like it though," Alex responded. As he looked around the cabin of the aircraft he could see a collective grumbling from the faces around him, but they all obeyed the orders.

The plane finally came to a stop, and after the customary welcoming by the pilots and warnings of shifting baggage, they made their way off the plane. "You better enjoy this weekend buddy. It could be your last fun for a while," Michael said as he slapped his buddy on the back.

"I plan to." Michael's comment reminded him of his final discussion with the woman who was going to be his trainer at "The Farm," the CIA's training facility in Virginia. She called him just a few days ago and warned him to be on the lookout in Vegas. She was running some "pre-training exercises" as she called them, to see how her new recruits handled adversity, and Alex was one of the lucky ones who had been chosen to possibly be put through the gauntlet.

Alex, Michael, and Cindy stepped into the terminal and were immediately greeted by the familiar "ching, ching, ching" in rapid succession as thousands of slot machines tempted the arriving and departing tourists. As they headed to collect their baggage, Alex soaked in the surroundings. Even the airport had an exciting feel to it. The familiar sights and sounds brought back memories of his last trip to Vegas. Alex, Michael, and a few other buddies had come out for Alex's bachelor party. Did that make this a divorce party?

Chapter 4
Friday, January 3, 2005, 1:57 A.M. E.T.

"Any news?" Six-foot five-inch Sean Hill said apprehensively as he stampeded through the open doorway. The sound of his voice announced his presence just before his massive figure appeared.

FBI Director Bret McMichael stubbed out another cigarette in his ashtray, pinched his beady eyes together as if he had a headache, and put his spectacles back on before motioning to his underling to take a seat. A spectacular view of the Washington D.C. skyline was visible through the massive window of his penthouse office. Sean flippantly tossed the director's perfectly tailored suit coat onto the floor and took the offered chair.

"She's vanished, Sean. Malcolm called me an hour ago. Marilyn missed her scheduled eight a.m. check-in. Our people in Vegas searched her place and the safe house. Both are empty, and appear not to have been visited by anyone." He was regretting this little CIA-FBI joint task force he secretly agreed to. It was blowing up in his face, just as he feared.

"Shit. You want me to send in the cavalry?" Sean asked a little too eagerly.

"For what? We have no proof. I'm afraid if we push this thing any further it will get leaked, and then this whole town will squash us." Bret had been in Washington D.C. for over thirty years and he had mastered the art of covering his backside.

"I will continue to have the men stake out her place and the safe house. It's been a full day and no dead bodies have turned up so she could be on the run and just unable to contact us," Sean said hopefully. He recommended Marilyn to Bret for this mission, and it took some arm bending before Bret agreed to the op. Now everything seemed to be falling apart.

"Damn it, Sean. We're all going to hang for this. Why I let you and Malcolm talk me into this crazy scheme, I'll never know," Bret spoke as much for the hidden recorders in the room as he did for Sean. He was beginning to think it might be time to completely abandon the ship and go into full cover- his-ass mode.

"We all understood the unique risks, Bret. We both agreed she would be perfect for this. Besides, there are not too many women available to us with the necessary physical and mental attributes to pull this off. The senator is a pervert, and this was the only way to get to him. We both know that."

"Well, let's hope we see her again with her head

still attached to her body, and preferably with some useful information," Bret said just before involuntarily yawning. He cursed his age. Twenty years ago he would never have felt this tired, regardless of the time. He was sixty-four years old, and there were rumblings that the incoming President wanted a fresh face for the FBI. He was many things, but fresh no longer fit his description.

"Are you going to brief the President?" Sean asked.

"Not yet. He gave us the "okay" for this operation, but neither Malcolm nor I ever gave any exact dates. I'm going to wait a few more days and see if anything new develops. Besides, I have no desire to tell him the real reason for tracking a U.S. senator until it becomes absolutely necessary."

"Makes sense to me." Sean nodded his approval.

"I'm glad you agree. Now go home and get some sleep. I will stay here in case something comes up. If I hear something, I'll call you."

"Sir?" Sean waited for permission to speak. As a former military man he was used to following orders. "Sir, maybe I should go out there and lead the search myself?" The idea had been on his mind all evening, and he finally blurted it out.

"Hell no, Sean! You stay here. Aman seems to know something is going on. We may have a leak somewhere. I'll be damned if I know where it could be, but I don't need you getting us in deeper just because you feel bad about sending her into the fray." Sean was one of his best operations men, but he could also be an oversized mother hen when it came to protecting his assets. The fact that this one was a woman made it twice as hard for him. Bret could see the worry in his eyes.

"Sean, go home. That's an order." Bret swiveled his chair back to face the Washington skyline. After he heard the footsteps of special agent Sean Hill recede into the distance, he returned his mind to the problem he faced. Was there more to the relationship between President-Elect Hardin and Aman Kazim other than son and adoptive father? He was beginning to think the consequences of finding out were not worth it. They could have their peace deal with the

Israelis and Palestinians, just so long as I keep my job," he mumbled to himself before reaching into his desk drawer for a fresh pack of cigarettes.

Chapter 5
Thursday 11:20 P.M. PT, January 2, 2005

Alex, Michael, and Cindy made their way towards the baggage claim area, completely oblivious to the woman keeping pace with them. She was stalking them from the other side of the rows of slot machines that bisected the airport terminal. She watched Alex closely. He was definitely the same man. She kept her bronzed face obscured with a baseball cap pulled down to her eyes. A ponytail of charcoal black hair stuck out the back. The baggy sweat pants hid her slender five foot seven figure, and the oversized Las Vegas t-shirt she wore looked every bit as tacky as what most of the tourists were wearing. The slot machines in the middle of the terminal kept her out of their sight. She picked up her pace, getting ten rows of machines in front of the three musketeers as she designated them in her mind, and then stole a quick look behind her. It appeared she succeeded in eluding her unwanted company for the moment.

Now in front of the trio, she began cutting across the middle of the terminal. The slot machines hid her perpendicular course towards them. She gradually slowed her pace, stopping for a moment to gather her wits. For the benefit of the people around her, she loitered in front of one of the machines while she waited for the three of them to catch up. She glanced behind her one more time. The cops still had her pursuers pulled aside for questioning. "Come on," she muttered impatiently to herself.

Alex and his friends were now only one row away. She made her move, darting into the open space of the terminal. With her eyes staring at the ground, she briskly walked out of the jungle of slot machines. The timing was perfect. She ran straight into Alex, interrupting a conversation in mid-stream.

The collision caught him completely off guard, and he fell backwards as the weight of her body knocked him off balance. Her training kept her in complete control as she allowed Alex's body to keep her from falling all the way to the floor. She extended her arm around his back, and expertly slipped a small cell phone into his pocket while holding him upright. "Alex, hold onto this. I'll contact you later. Don't tell your friends," she whispered in his ear as she disentangled herself from the collision. She issued a loud and curt apology before taking off down the terminal, giving none of them a chance to respond.

***

"What the hell was that about?" Alex said with a shocked look on his face. He barely had time to comprehend what happened before it was over. He silently cursed to himself. It sure did not take long for his "pre-training" to begin. It seemed his vacation might already be over.

"Someone is in a hurry," Cindy quipped, unable to hide a slight twinge of anger in her voice. Despite the very brief glimpse afforded them, they all recognized the exotic beauty of the woman. While the hat obscured most of the face, it could not hide the sensuous lips and tanned skin of the unknown woman.

"Hey, honey, relax. You see all types of whackos like that out here. Probably a hooker who forgot to pay her pimp or something," Michael offered.

"Or jackass, maybe she's late for a plane," Alex responded, his mind still whirling from the encounter. "After all, we're in an airport." The two exchanged smirks as they got onto the elevated monorail that would take them over to the baggage claim area.

The doors opened after a two- minute ride, and they jumped off at the other end of the airport. The terminal was lined with the usual ads trying to be the first to catch a visitor's attention. Alex noticed one for the Rosewood Grille restaurant depicting a man in a tuxedo holding a monstrous lobster like he just wrestled it from the sea himself. "I see the Rosewood is still doing alright," Alex said. He must have seen the same ad a thousand times during his trips to Las Vegas. It seemed as permanent a fixture as the prostitutes and strip clubs.

"Maybe we should give the place a try this time. It's got to be better than the buffets we get at these hotels," Michael suggested. He tended to be a picky eater, and found most of the hotel buffets rather poor in quality.

"Our hotel may be different this time. Let's give it a chance before I spend money eating that should be supporting my gambling habit." Alex hoped he was masking his nervous tension.

"What's the name of our place again?" Cindy chimed in.

"The Imperial Palace. It's in a Japanese motif; not the swankiest place on the strip, but it gives us a good central location..." Alex stopped in mid-sentence as he saw the one bag he checked on the plane making its way around the conveyer belt. He darted over to pick it up, his paranoia about having his luggage stolen kicking into high gear.

"Look's like someone is ready to gamble," Michael laughed as he said it. Five minutes later Cindy and Michael had their bags in hand as well, and they all headed to the outside of the airport. After standing in line for a few minutes they were herded into a minivan taxi and whisked off towards their hotel. They took a left onto Tropicana Avenue, heading towards Las Vegas Boulevard, better known simply as "the strip."

On their right, as they approached the corner of Tropicana Street and Las Vegas Boulevard stood the MGM Grand, currently one of the largest hotels in the world, its green lighting illuminated the night sky. Directly ahead of them stood New York, New York with it's scaled down version of the New York City skyline and Statue of Liberty facing the street for all the tourists to see. A huge roller coaster wrapped around the entire hotel, and the screams of the coaster's occupants could faintly be heard from inside the taxi as the coaster made its way through several loops.

Construction certainly appeared to still be where the real money in Vegas was Alex surmised. The last time he had been here many of the hotels including New York,

New York, Mandalay Bay, and Paris had not even broken ground yet. Turning his head to the left, Alex inched closer to his window and peered out at the Excalibur and Luxor hotels. The Excalibur was a giant castle in the King Arthur mode, and The Luxor was a gargantuan black pyramid modeled after the famous pyramids in Egypt. The sheer size and gaudiness of everything always provided you with entertainment. Alex squinted, trying to get a better look at the renovation to the front of the MGM Grand. As he pressed his face closer to the glass, his right leg brushed against the side of the door. He felt the cell phone in his pocket, and tried to decide how to play the CIA's little game. Should he be aggressive or wait to be told what to do?

He looked over at Michael and Cindy, and saw they were engrossed in their own conversation. Michael was pointing out the different hotels while attempting to dance around the questions of which strip clubs they visited when they were here for Alex's bachelor party. They seemed to be enjoying themselves. Alex was happy for his friend. 10/01/00 led directly to his being hired by the CIA, destroying his marriage. He knew he made the right choice though. If they were right for each other she would have been supportive of his decision. On the other hand, that same event brought Michael and Cindy together. Michael was a doctor in NYC at the time and Cindy was a nurse. They met during the frantic hours after the collapse of the towers as they worked together to handle the massive influx of patients flooding into the hospital. They had been inseparable ever since. Alex guessed an engagement ring could be coming at any time.

The cab turned right onto Las Vegas Boulevard., heading in the direction of their hotel. The Imperial Palace sits almost in the center of the strip, making it perfect for travelers looking to sample all the different hot spots on foot. As an added bonus, Caesars, perhaps the most well known Vegas landmark stands directly across the street from the Imperial Palace. Alex reached into his pocket and pulled out the small cell phone. In a way, he was disappointed with the monotony of the item.

He decided to stick with his first instinct, and wait

24

for the strange woman to make the first move.

He slid the cell phone back into his pocket and looked up as the taxi made a right turn into the covered portico in front of their hotel. The incident was forgotten for the moment as they pushed through the main doors of the hotel and became engulfed by the expanse of green tables, people yelling, and the constant rattle of coins cascading into tins.

"Michael, how about we show your girl how to roll the dice before calling it a night?" Alex said. The familiar sights and sounds of the casino immediately entranced him.

It took thirty-five minutes to check in, take their luggage up to their rooms, and make their way back to the casino. A feat like this could only be accomplished late at night when the weary travelers who came in on the red-eye flights checked in. This was another one of these tricks of the trade Alex learned on his previous visits; never fly in at a normal hour, or you risked standing in line for an hour for everything.

The main casino of the Imperial Palace sits at the very front of the hotel's ground floor. To get there, they had to follow the unusual course of riding the elevator to the second floor, then heading down an escalator, past a small strip of stores, and into the gaming area. At a few minutes past midnight, the casino was humming with a palpable energy, and it took two circles around the crowded gaming area before they found some space around one of the craps tables.

Cindy watched from behind as Alex and Michael both plopped two hundred dollars down on the table. The dealer silently took the money, and the croupier slid a large stack of chips back over for them to play with. They had lucked into a decent spot at one of the ends of the table. Alex glanced around him, amused by the cornucopia of different people that encircled the table. Gambling certainly did not discriminate. A heavy-set man with greasy, unkempt hair stood to their right, a Harley Davidson tattoo encircling most of his flabby forearm. To their left, a tall black man with a sculpted chest rattled the dice in his hands. Alex thought he looked like the prototypical linebacker, big but fast. The rest of the table consisted of a few couples in formal evening attire, and at the opposite end of the table, a lone obese man in a caramel colored suit. The tall black man rattled the dice one more time for good luck. Judging by the amount of chips sitting on the pass line, and the thick stack of chips in front of him he looked like he was taking the table on a winning ride. The round placeholder on the table indicated his current point to be nine, and Alex did not hesitate to try to catch the wave of luck. He dropped thirty dollars worth of chips onto the pass line.

***

Shakir adjusted the crotch of his caramel colored suit, and use his left arm to pull in another batch of his winnings. He did not care about the money he was winning. He just wanted to be relieved of this job so he could go back to his normal duties. He received the call from his superior an hour earlier, while he was staking out his usual area outside the airport terminal. His new job description was vague to say the least. The orders were simple but nonsensical. Follow any group of three people that he saw coming out of the baggage claim area as long as the group contained two men and just one woman. The sparse late night crowd at the airport made the task feasible; albeit still difficult. He knew the boss always kept plenty of watchers at the airport besides him, and they were now dispersed throughout the city, following all the threesomes they could find. He had no idea why, but he would follow the orders. He knew better than to question commands from his superiors.

It seemed strange for two guys and a girl to come to Vegas, he thought. *Could they be swingers?* The girl with them seemed attractive enough, and they all seemed pretty chummy. After a few more seconds, he refocused his attention on the table, and the black man about to roll the dice. A flick of his powerful wrist and the dice went flying across the green expanse of the table, finally coming to a rest with a five and four showing; another winning roll. A collective yell of excitement erupted from the table. The celebration caused some people walking by to stop and observe for a few seconds before continuing on their original path.

While stacking more of his winnings, Shakir gave his quarry another once-over, trying to implant their faces in his mind. An eleven followed the nine, giving everyone standing around the table another influx of free money. Shakir watched as the taller of the two men covered the board with some aggressive bets. He began to follow suit when the cell phone clipped to his belt began vibrating. He yanked it off and watched the tiny rectangle of glass as a text message popped up on the screen.

"Continue surveillance. You will be replaced asap. Don't lose them." It was not much help. He sipped his diet cola and put another minimum bet on the table. He needed to make his money last as long as possible.

Shakir wondered what could possibly be the reason he was being forced to watch these three. They seemed harmless. He tugged at his shirt. Despite the frigid temperature of the casino he was sweating profusely. Pools of sweat were visible around the armpits of his white dress shirt. The last hour of following these three had been nerve wracking. The order to trail threesomes had come from one of the boss's top security men, and it had been accompanied with threats of permanent maiming for any disobedience. He knew he was currently out of his element, and that could land him in trouble if someone did not replace him soon. He preferred his normal job. He was muscle as his superiors liked to say. If he had been Italian and lived during the heyday of the mafia, he would have been what the families referred to as a soldier. He followed orders and broke things, or people, if the situation warranted it. He was a blunt instrument of aggression to be wielded at his boss' request.

***

Looking down at his watch, Alex could not believe it was almost two a.m. The crowd around the craps table finally dispersed when the black man's run of luck ended. Now only two other players remained besides Alex and Michael. Cindy finally decided to join in the game thirty-five minutes earlier, and a string of beginners luck gave her a quick one hundred dollars and a look of disgust from her two more experienced companions. She quickly picked up her chips after her coup and cashed in the winnings. "I'm exhausted, honey. Let's go to bed before I blow my money on something else." The words were partially drowned out by a yawn from Cindy's impish mouth.

"Alright. I'm beat myself. Alex, you staying?" Michael asked.

"Yeah, I think I'll hang around a little longer," Alex replied. "See if the luck holds. Remember to wake me up early. We can show Cindy the strip in all its glory." A sly smile crept across his face despite his best efforts to suppress it. It appeared quite obvious to him that Cindy was ready for bed, but not actual sleep.

"No problem, bud. See you in the morning." Michael pretended to ignore his friend's look. He could feel his girlfriend's eyes boring into the back of his head. Taking her hand, they headed in for the night. Alex quickly turned his attention back to the table and selected two of the six dice the dealer offered him. The dealer was miffed at the game being held up for a few seconds, and Alex apologized immediately. He understood the importance of a smooth, flowing game.

The rattling of dice in his hands brought back fond memories of when he first learned the intricacies of the game of craps. It had been during spring break of his junior year in college. It had been his first trip to Vegas, and he just turned twenty-one the month before. A long night of drinking at a nightclub for the young twenty's crowd in Vegas ended in a failure to pick up any women. Unable to find a cab, he walked back to his hotel in a drunken haze. His friends, including, Michael had given up a long time ago and gone to bed, but Alex was stubborn. He never felt as tired in his life as when he pushed through the casino doors after two hours of walking.

"Eleven is a winner." The monotone voice of the dealer brought Alex out of his happy excursion down memory lane. It looked like it could be a very profitable weekend as the dealer dropped fifty more dollars worth of chips in front of him.

"Same dice, please," Alex said sternly, not wanting to jinx the streak of luck he was having. He promised himself he would go to bed as soon as he crapped out. The

28

jet lag was catching up with him as the excitement of the arrival began to wear off. *Besides, I've got all tomorrow, Saturday, and Sunday to continue this.* Grabbing the offered dice, he rattled them in his fist and sent them hurtling across the table. The dice showed a total of three. Alex kept his promise to himself, accepted the loss, picked up his winnings, and headed off to bed. He did not notice the obese man in the brown suit hurriedly cashing in his own stack of chips for larger denominations.

Chapter 6

The door's dead bolt lock silently slid into its housing, and the two men peered inside the tiny office before entering. The small, darkened room was a mess. Rows of miniature televisions lined every available space on the walls, and boxes of VHS tapes were scattered across the floor. They were at the airport, underneath it to be more precise, thanks to triple the usual fee. They left the night watchman standing outside in the cool desert air, nervously chain smoking cigarettes, and counting the wad of hundred dollar bills they gave him. It was just after three a.m., and they were in a hurry to complete their self-appointed task. The two men, both with grim looks on their faces, each grabbed a box, and began flipping through the tapes.

"Somebody hit it big," Gregor commented as he glanced at one of the television screens showing various parts of the airport. The slot machines in the airport, like any other gaming area in Las Vegas, were constantly under surveillance. The lady on the screen appeared to be in her mid-fifties, and while there was no sound coming from the television, both men could clearly see the steady stream of coins cascading out of the bin and onto the floor. The lady was in hysterics, not quite sure what to do as strangers began to stop and gawk as if they were looking at the aftermath of a wreck on the freeway.

Paying three thousand dollars to get in tonight was exorbitant, but they had no choice in the matter. They rarely made an unannounced appearance, but when they did, they knew the greedy prick would really stick it to their pocketbooks.

At least it's not my money, Solomon told himself. Aman had told him to do whatever was necessary, and he was obeying those orders. When Aman called him to complain that a girl had seduced Zachariah and made off with a private cell phone, Solomon thought it sounded comical. He stopped laughing when Aman went into a tirade, and had Solomon put the entire network on alert. The specific orders were that nothing else mattered until she was apprehended with the cell phone.

"That little bitch has no idea what she has gotten herself into," Aman had seethed to Solomon before slamming down the phone. Solomon's network of watchers picked up her trail within minutes of being given the order. Solomon took personal control of the operation and followed her to the airport. Nabbing her there seemed like it was going to be easy, until she suddenly vanished through the security checkpoint with the rest of the departing travelers. He thought she made a fatal mistake when she hopped out of the cab and ran into the airport. He now realized it was a premeditated move. Solomon hurriedly purchased a ticket, and rushed through the security checkpoint after her. He left his weapon with one of his men outside the airport.

She played the cat and mouse game surprisingly well. She weaved through the crowds, disappearing for seconds at a time as she darted around, behind, and through the sea of heads coming and going from Sin City. It was impossible to tell if she discarded the stolen cell phone in a trash can or handed it off to an unknown accomplice. He caught sight of her just as she bumped into a group of three people, but he was too far away to get a good look at the trio. That was when two airport security guards grabbed him from behind, slammed him into a wall, and began harassing him. She had spotted his surveillance. The questions the cops bombarded him with implied that she told them that he was an ex-boyfriend that was stalking her. Solomon was impressed with her quick thinking. He found it difficult to believe she was just the stripper Aman claimed her to be. After twenty minutes of trying to finagle his way past the security guards he finally used a stern warning followed by a good old-fashioned bribe. He found the stick followed by the carrot to be a more productive way of getting what he wanted. Once he dropped the name of his boss, the cops gladly accepted the bribe and let him go. As soon as he was freed, he phoned his men outside and gave instructions to trail any group of three people that consisted of two guys and one girl. The descriptions he was able to provide were vague at best, but it was at least better than nothing.

"Got it! This is what we need," Solomon said, the sigh of relief in his voice quickly repressed by professionalism. The Frenchman was slowing losing his accent, and his English almost sounded like he was a native speaker. It was Solomon's linguistic skills that first brought him to the attention of the French SDECE; the French security service that eventually morphed into the DGSE in 1982. He had a short career in the French army, during which time he mastered Russian, English, and German. His linguistic ability combined with his average height and skinny build, made him the ideal intelligence officer. He was quick- witted and capable of easily vanishing into a crowd. Both skills proved useful during his time on the African continent as he helped the Nigerians in their failed attempt to wrestle control of their oil-rich Biafra region away from the British and Americans.

After the debacle in Africa, he was moved back to France by his superiors to work counter-intelligence. He spent much of the 1970s and 1980s tracking spies on French soil. In 1986 he was moved into the Operations Division, orchestrating clandestine operations against allies and enemies of the French government in countries all over Europe and the Middle East. The end of the Cold War changed his superiors' thinking, and many in the DGSE who were previously lauded by the politicians, soon came under close scrutiny for their shady dealings with the dictators and despots of the world. Solomon decided it was time to vanish before his past caught up with him and made him another nameless body in a back alley of any of one of the numerous countries in which he operated illegally.

He had been preparing for the day of his escape for years. There were large sums of money sitting in bank accounts in Grand Cayman and Rio de Janeiro. When another DGSE agent named Jacque Mille disappeared into South America amidst heavy suspicion of selling radar secrets to drug lords, Solomon was finally given his opportunity. He was sent to track down the defector and bring him back. Instead, he used the opportunity to vanish into the mountains of South America. Ironically, he wished he was back in the steaming jungles of South America now. They were dangerous and wild, but the lawless mountains provided easy remedies for dealing with traitor and whores.

"This is the tape for the hour we chased her," Solomon said as he grabbed the tape. "Let's have a look at it. I was in ...Terminal One, right?"

"Yes, put it in," Gregor replied. "The kid was jittery about us showing up. Let's make this as quick as possible. We don't want any surprises." Originally from East Berlin, Gregor enlisted in the army at the age of eighteen. His clandestine potential was noticed by a member of the Stasi, East Germany's security service that collected thousands of bits of information on everyone in East Germany during the height of the Cold War. When the Berlin Wall collapsed, so did Gregor's unflappable faith in Communism, and his love for East Germany turned into a seething hatred. All the leaders of the promised revolution disappeared, telling the West whatever it wanted to know and collecting large sums of money for doing it. Solomon used every moment available to him to poke fun at the tall German for actually believing that Communism was a viable form of government.

Arab oil billionaires who paid top dollar for the best bodyguards available on the open market eventually recruited Gregor. Despite the exceptional income, Gregor did not like living in a region as unstable as the Middle East, and he quickly accepted a job offer from Aman. Solomon continued to remind Gregor that he got his job only because of Solomon's recommendation. It was just one of many areas of difficulty that caused friction between the two former Cold Warriors.

Solomon shoved the tape into the closest VCR. He could not believe that the airport had not upgraded their surveillance equipment to a newer format. He pushed "play" and a full view of Terminal One appeared on one of the numerous televisions. The time showed as 10:07 p.m. at the bottom of the television. Solomon fast-forwarded through the first portion, watching in silence as crowds of people flew threw the airport in the hyperactive motion that could only be provided by holding down the fast forward button. He keenly observed the clock in the corner, searching for the correct time. Gregor peered over his shoulder like a fifth grader trying to cheat on a test, and followed the speeding clock as well.

"This should be about the correct time," Solomon spoke softly. Both men stared intently at the screen, looking for the woman. She finally came into view for the first time. The camera doing the filming was located behind her, and they watched her hustling through the crowd. She disappeared into the bathroom once before coming back into view. She appeared to make several circles around the same area as if she was searching for something or someone.

"There's one possible drop," Solomon said. "We need someone to search that bathroom immediately. Check all the toilets," Solomon commanded Gregor, who nodded silently.

This same sequence of events continued for twenty minutes with the different cameras throughout the terminal. She would disappear off the screen and another camera would pick her up a few minutes later. Solomon finally saw his own figure come into the picture. He allowed himself a small smirk of pride. He moved methodically and patiently in the video. The performance was pleasing, even to his critical eye. Finally he stopped the film at the point when he almost caught up with her. He closely studied her collision with the three strangers, and decided it could have easily been avoided. He pushed "pause" on the VCR and stared intently at the surveillance video. It was not much help in identifying the three people.

"Worthless. This tape is worthless. Can you see their faces Gregor? I certainly can't," he asked in a frustrated tone.

"Nothing," Gregor replied. "They all have their backs to the camera."

Solomon once again made a mental note of their appearance as best he could tell. Perhaps he could find some better shots of them somewhere else in the tape.

"That cell phone could be anywhere, but my bet is these three," Solomon concluded. "They're the only group she actually collided with. All the other contacts were simply brush ups," he added, now even more convinced she was an agent. FBI? DEA? He would have to check with Aman when he returned. Aman possessed several great resources inside the government. He never divulged how he obtained the information, but Solomon had some hunches.

"I think you're paranoid. Look at her erratic movements," Gregor quickly disagreed. "She's scared shitless and doesn't know what to do. Are you sure it wasn't just pure luck that she was able to escape? She could be sitting in some motel room on the strip getting high, and debating whether or not to flush that phone down the toilet. Worst case she could be a society slut or gossip columnist looking for a breakthrough story," Gregor said in a staccato voice. Although Solomon did not say it out loud, Gregor could tell he was debating whether she could be some type of government agent.

"No, Gregor." Solomon pointed at the footage and began to explain. "Her skittishness and jerky movements. It looks like she went up and down this same terminal five or six times. Why?" He answered his own question. "Because she knew exactly what she was doing," Solomon nearly shouted. "This was planned. She had to have purchased a ticket beforehand to get to the departure area. This can only mean that was her intention. She was going to catch a plane, and we would have never caught her! Instead, we caught up to her quicker than she anticipated, so she was forced to dump the merchandise," Solomon finished and waited for a response. After a few seconds of silence, he turned to see Gregor's sharp-edged face and closely cropped salt and pepper hair still staring at the small television in front of them.

"Yes, I have to admit you could be right," Gregor finally spoke. "Still, we should keep all options on the table. If you're correct, then the real problem we have are those three people," Gregor said as he pointed at the frozen image on the monitor. "Are they someone she just chose in a panic to dump it off on, or are they friends?" The German's analytical mind contemplated the options. "If they are friends that makes things much more difficult. Nevertheless, we know our job. Find her. Kill her. It's that simple," Gregor concluded calmly.

"I hope so," Solomon replied. "Let us go. This tape is going as well." Solomon hit the "eject" button and gently placed the tape inside his sport coat. He hoped that after reviewing it again, he would be able to find a better shot of the three mystery people. Things would be much easier if they could narrow their search. As they stood up to leave the night watchman suddenly came back in unannounced, startling them both.

"That's it, boys. Time's up. Now get out of here before you get me fired," the watchman said sternly, his trembling hands revealing the false bravado of his voice.

"With pleasure," Solomon said with a smile. "Thanks for the time again, Jimmy. Here's another grand for your trouble." Solomon reached into his pocket for a wad of bills and pressed them tightly into Jimmy's hand. "We're taking a tape. Use a blank one in its place, and erase this night from your memory completely," Solomon said in a relieved tone. He was ready to leave.

"I don't even know what day it is fellas," the watchman responded, his eyes lighting up at the additional cash. Solomon knew what he would do with it. It would be blown at one of the brothels on the outskirts of town; one of the brothels that Aman had a secret ownership stake in.

Chapter 7

The private elevator silently glided upwards until it reached the penthouse suite of the Desert Dust Inn. The "ding" of the elevator announced that it had reached Aman's floor. He set aside the papers he had been scanning for the President-Elect. Aman watched Solomon burst out of the elevator and rush across the long expanse of lavender-colored carpet. *The man is moving much too quickly for such an early morning hour.* He turned and maneuvered the blinds so that they blocked part of the early morning desert sun beginning to stream into the office. He ignored the magnificent view of Caesars and the rest of the Las Vegas strip just a few blocks away from his hotel. At twenty after six in the morning, it was one of the few times during the day when traffic was sparse. Anyone on the road was typically returning from an all night drinking marathon, or up early to hit the golf course before the blistering Las Vegas sun hit its full stride.

At a shade over five feet five inches, and weighing two hundred fifty pounds Aman Kazim was a large man in pure size, if not height. His hair was jet black and it was one of the few parts of his body that seemed unaffected by his seventy plus years of hard living. He preferred spectacles to contacts since they did not irritate his eyes, and his face was a small oval that looked out of place on his large frame. He said a silent prayer that Solomon was bringing him good news. Bad news had the potential to destroy the empire that surrounded him. Losing his wealth was not his concern, it was losing what the money was so close to finally bringing him that made him nervous. My father would be so proud, he thought, as he reminisced about the beginning of his journey. Lately he had found himself to be much more sentimental than he ever imagined possible as he flashed back to his early days.

Born during the 1920s, Aman spent his formative years running through the streets of Cairo with his friends. His mother was Jordanian and his father Egyptian. They escaped to the United States just before the Nazis began their march across Europe and North Africa in 1941. His father secured a job working in a factory that mass-produced tanks for the war effort, and he was killed when he was crushed by a tank in a freak accident at the plant. The death of his father was a shock to Aman, and made him shut down emotionally. With many of the nation's youth off fighting the war, Aman was able to gain admittance to a small college in New York City, where he later graduated with honors. He quickly followed up his accounting degree with an MBA.

The end of Aman's schooling brought along with it another strange and traumatizing event. His mother was killed in a mugging attempt gone wrong. The cops could not solve the case, and Aman grew more frustrated and depressed by the day. The war was wrapping up, and he was now an orphaned immigrant. As far as he was concerned, his adopted country had killed his parents. His life had been stripped from him before he was ever given a chance. He contemplated returning to Egypt. There seemed no place for him in America.

Aman recalled the frustration he felt during those times as he stared at the tattered photo of his long deceased parents sitting in a gold encrusted frame on his desk. He raised his eyes from the photo as Solomon came to a stop in front of his desk. He looked up at the Frenchman. The realization that his father's legacy now depended on the help of the French made him squirm with fear. He adjusted the tight fitting polo shirt as best he could and grabbed for the whiskey and water sitting on the left of his desk. He took a long pull and stared at his head of security with tired, bloodshot eyes.

"Please tell me you have some good news," Aman stated gruffly. He sat the drink down a little too roughly and precious whiskey sloshed onto the shiny desk.

"Nothing of the sort boss," Solomon replied. He never liked mincing words unless he was plying his tradecraft in the pursuit of a member of the opposite sex. It was one of the reasons Aman kept him around. Solomon got straight to the point, and as a man whose time was precious,

37

Aman greatly appreciated it.

"Let's hear it," Aman beckoned. He gestured like the conductor of an orchestra, giving his approval for Solomon to continue.

"Sir, we could have a serious problem on our hands. I have been viewing the surveillance tape taken by airport security for the past hour. I can't tell what she did with the cell phone you're after. We tailed her to the airport, so I know that was the first public place she was in. She was able to get through the security checkpoint at the airport though. I got in myself, but it took some time. She had a lot of opportunities to do something with it."

"Could the idiot whore have just stuck it in someone's bag?" Aman asked.

"It's possible, but if she is what I think she is, she would have held onto it. My concern is how she handled herself at the airport and managed to escape. The film footage I saw suggests she was not some hooker high on drugs. It looked more like a very methodical and very professional escape given her circumstances. There are very few places in this city she could have gone to escape your reach. We have informants all over this city. But she went to the one place that allowed her to buy some time. I believe she intended to jump on a plane. We thwarted that by sheer luck. It will be hard to find her before its too late. What's on that cell phone that's so important anyway? If I knew, it may be able to help me in my search. It could give us some clue where she is heading perhaps."

"Don't worry about that. When I think you need to know, I'll tell you." Aman wagged his finger at his employee to express his disapproval. "It's your job to find her and bring her back here!" Aman suddenly brought his fist hurtling downward. It pounded into the desk, and he let out an animal growl that was part frustration and part pain as more of his drink spilled. "This can't be happening." Aman forced himself to relax. "What do you think she is?" He was afraid he knew the answer, but he wanted to hear an explanation from Solomon. This was the kind of thing his head of security was paid an exorbitant amount of money for after all.

"Sir, she went straight to the airport and right through security. She had every intention to hop on a plane and get out of this city. I stopped her from hopping a flight because I was close enough to her where I would have known what flight she was on. We would have stopped the plane and pulled her off, or met her at her final destination. When she realized a flight was not an option she went to plan B; a diversionary tactic to fool us." Solomon paused briefly to try and gauge Aman's reaction before he continued. "There is one group of three people she came into contact with. They are either her friends, or a way to throw us off guard. She must be some sort of spy or government agent of some sort. Either that or a very good undercover reporter. You could help me narrow that down. Who would want to set up, Zachariah?"

"Half this country would," Aman fired back. "He has more than his share of enemies. Don't worry about that though. Can we catch her?"

"Possibly," Solomon replied, clear hesitation in his voice. "No matter how good she is our organization here is huge. I have the city on lockdown and every available man working on it. I pulled the surveillance photos of her coming into the hotel for your party, and had copies dispersed to all our people. I also have a few other potential leads I am looking into."

"Good," Aman said. "And Solomon, it's *my* organization. Not ours. Just remember that." Aman had grown to depend on his head of security, but never hesitated to remind his subordinate of his authority. "What does Gregor think? Is he of the same opinion as you?" Aman hired them both because he liked a second opinion to satisfy his highly paranoid personality.

"Gregor thinks I'm a little paranoid but that is coming from someone who can't come to grips with the fact that a woman got the better of him." Although Solomon tolerated working with his partner, he also took advantage of his opportunities to dress Gregor down for his flaws as a spy and bodyguard. "He's a chauvinist, just like all the Germans. He still refuses to believe what his father did as an SS man with Himmler was wrong."

Aman chuckled at the childish jab. His two heads of security would never trust each other, and this was the way he preferred it. Europeans had long memories that were easily exploited. Solomon still looked at Gregor as a Nazi barbarian, and Gregor had more than once hinted at the weakness of the French; a country that relied on the U.S. and Britain to do its dirty work. They could be overly critical of each other, but both were professionals who were the best at their business. Their different backgrounds and nationalities kept them leery of each other without hampering their ability to do the job properly. Aman found this got him excellent intelligence while minimizing the off chance that they would ever plot against him.

"Where do we go from here?" Aman asked as he downed the rest of his drink and reached for the half-full decanter in the cabinet behind him to pour another.

"I have everything in motion, sir," Solomon quickly responded. "Spotters are out all over the city. I have tracked down where she lives. At least I have the address she gave to her employer at the club where she danced. She hasn't been back there, and I would be shocked if she showed up. I have somebody there though, just in case. You may have to use some of those favors you have saved up over the years."

Aman put the decanter of whiskey away and turned around so they were face to face again. "What is that supposed to mean?" He asked in a hostile tone. "Am I going to have to start digging under Hoover Dam to hide some bodies?"

"I hope not, but it's a possibility." Solomon had no desire to start killing people, but he knew it was going to be necessary. He had been in this business too long, and his instincts told him that the only way to stop this from reaching the wrong hands would be liquidation.

"Okay, you have free reign to do whatever you see fit, but no deaths except for the girl unless absolutely necessary," Aman said emphatically. "I will pay whatever it takes to keep this under wraps. I can't afford anymore screw-ups." He then made a mental note to check with his senator friend in Washington D.C. Perhaps he had heard some rumors.

"Also, if you get me out of this unscathed you will get a 250k bonus in your numbered account. I'm going to make some calls. Use up some of those favors. I'm going to catch a few hours of sleep before my round of golf with Zachariah. Call me as soon as you hear anything new," Aman finished, and motioned for his employee to leave.

With Solomon gone he wheeled around his leather chair to face the early morning rays of sunshine that were filtering through the partially closed blinds. Unnerved, he turned around to face the opulent suite of offices. The cavernous room yawned back at him. "I did not come this far to have my destiny stolen from me," he muttered to himself. His mind drifted back once more to those lonely days in 1945 when he began his first steps towards a seemingly impossible goal.

***

It had been a few weeks after his mother's death. He was at her tiny apartment in the Bronx, cleaning it out as best he could when a middle-aged man who appeared to be an Egyptian appeared in the open doorway. He was tall and slim, and although there was no hair on his head, his face was covered with a coarse black beard that was just beginning to show a few specks of grey. The stranger introduced himself only as Hussan, and he said he had something important to discuss with him. Aman remembered acting like a petulant child and yelling at the man to get out. The man was insistent, and when he said it was in regards to Aman's father, he reluctantly agreed to accompany Hussan to a small mosque.

While sipping hot tea and sitting on cushions on the floor of the basement, the news shared with Aman changed his life forever. He remembered sitting in rapture as Hussan first told his own biography. He described how he had escaped the German assaults in Egypt, and was granted asylum in the United States in exchange for providing the U.S. government with information regarding the Nazi stampede across North Africa. Hussan also described how he and Aman's father became close friends and business partners throughout the 1930s, and worked to free Egypt from the tyranny of British rule. Aman's father managed to escape before the war started. Hussan explained that he and his father eventually became members of a small cadre of men working to restore the Caliphate. For too long now their people and their religion had been hijacked and used by the Western governments.

Aman remembered Hussan venting about how their forefathers were betrayed at the peace conference after World War I. Their lands were carved up like pieces of pie and divvied out to the glutinous victors who did as they pleased. They were nothing but pawns to be moved so the West could conquer their lands, and keep their people enslaved. It must change.

The first step was to learn about their enemy up close. The European countries were the junior members of the peacemakers of World War I. He remembered Hussan's voice choking with emotion as the man said, "In order to see the true face of our adversary, we sent your father to America."

Aman would never forget the look of steely determination on Hussan's face. It immediately endeared him to the cause before he even fully understood what he was getting himself into. A true Muslim Caliphate had not enjoyed real global power for hundreds of years. The Caliphate reached its pinnacle only years after the death of Mohammad, and its power was slowly drained until it no longer existed. The Caliphate's fate followed the same downward spiral as the Muslims themselves.

Aman remembered the man's cracking voice as he continued his pleas. "Your father did much for our cause and …" Hussan had hesitated as he struggled to find the words.

"What?" Aman remembered spitting out the word with a mixture of anger and disbelief. He could still remember Hussan's hesitation, followed by the man's body shaking violently.

"He was about to ask you to begin working with us when he was murdered. That was why he moved you and your family to America. He was not running from the war, but embracing it. Burrowing himself in the den of the enemy. Studying their true strengths and vulnerabilities. He realized the truth; the truth that killing Jews was pointless, regardless of how good it made some of our countrymen feel. Hitler learned this the hard way. To truly bring the Muslim faith back to prominence, the entire animal of the West would have to be slaughtered, not just the Jewish parasite invading it."

**

It was over sixty years later and Aman still marveled at the forbearance of his father and Hussan. If organizations like Arafat's Fatah movement would have adhered to similar principles, then the world could have been a different place. It was just as well, Aman thought to himself. The glory was his for the taking, and now was the time to seize it.

Chapter 8

Alex's eyes popped open, interrupting what was quickly becoming a horrific nightmare. Sweat beaded on his forehead as he swung his legs over the side of the bed and turned down the thermostat. The wall-mounted air conditioner kicked to life. He slowly got out of bed. The late night dinner he treated himself to with his winnings had finally caught up with him, and he groped in the dark towards the bathroom. After five minutes on the toilet, he felt human again. He stared into the mirror, closely scrutinizing the beginning of a beard. He had dreamed that his ex-wife was the unknown woman who dropped the cell phone in his pocket, and that she was actually a spy who was going to be his boss at the CIA. She was taking him to work attached to a leash when he woke up in a cold sweat.

The nightmare reminded him of his strange encounter at the airport. He grabbed the blue jeans sitting across the chair and felt inside the pocket until he found the cell phone.. He forgot about it after all the excitement in the casino. He pulled the phone out and gave it a close examination. It did not appear to be anything out of the ordinary. He scrolled through the numbers and names saved in it, but saw nothing that caught his attention. If they are looking to jump-start my learning curve, this was certainly a novel approach, he silently admitted to himself.

The question that plagued him though was how to handle it? If this was a test, what should he do about it? His instincts still told him to be patient. The woman would have to appear again and point him in the right direction. He just needed the first signal to get the ball rolling.

Thirty minutes later, and feeling much better after a scalding shower followed by an ice cold rinsing, he lounged on his bed reading a biography of Winston Churchill. A few pages into it he set the book down, unable to concentrate. He continued to work through the different scenarios the unknown woman could potentially try. "Just let her come to me," he said aloud to himself. A familiar voice in the hallway interrupted him.

"Hey, you awake in there?" The knock on the door brought Alex out of his haze, and he stuffed the cell phone into his pocket before letting Michael into the room.

"You feeling all right? You didn't get trashed after we left did you?" Michael asked.

"No, I stuck around for another hour though. Luck held up, and I got a bite to eat before going to bed. Been paying for it."

"No kidding! I noticed the foul smell as soon as I stepped through the door," Michael responded with a laugh. "That's sweet that you made some more money. Lunch is on you then. How much did you clear?"

"I haven't counted it all yet, but I think it's over three hundred," Alex replied as he pointed towards the wad of crumpled bills sitting on the table. Alex always found their adolescent banter amusing. The fact that they were both professionals did not prevent them from falling back into the same immature patterns from college as soon as they got to together.

"I know where you are heading tonight. Which strip club you gonna blow those winnings at?"

Alex gave his friend a wry smile. "I'll decide that later," he replied. "What's on tap for today?"

"How about breakfast?" Michael suggested. "Cindy is taking a shower. She will be at least an hour. We can eat and do a little more blackjack until she's ready. Then we can check out the new hotels on the strip. Sound good?"

"Sure. Let me grab a few things first," Alex said as he stepped into the bathroom.

Ten minutes later they were devouring a plate of scrambled eggs, bacon, and toast from the hotel buffet. Between bites, Alex noticed a large man sitting several tables away. The man was methodically nibbling on fruit and cereal. The haggard look on his face, and the crumbled clothes he wore suggested his long night had turned into an early morning. He did not notice the caramel colored suit coat hanging over the empty chair opposite the man.

Chapter 9

Zachariah Hardin untucked his lime green golf shirt and let it fall over his waist as he paced back and forth across the floor of the penthouse suite of the Desert Dust Inn. They were going to be late for their tee time. Zachariah glanced at his watch and fiddled with his khaki pants. He cursed the stripper for her boldness and his adoptive father for his tardiness in successive breaths. The annoying part of it was that he knew Aman was right. He pushed his luck too far, and it finally caught up with him. He was the President-Elect of the United States and would officially take the oath of office in less than a month. He should be more careful. The more dangerous half of his personality still thought he deserved to have some fun. He spent more than ten years of his life married to a woman he absolutely despised just so he could keep up the proper appearances. Was he not entitled to a good lay now that she was dead and the election was over? He knew what Aman's response would be; he would tell him the mission should always come first.

He thought Aman was being overly cautious. There

was nothing that could stop them now. Their plan was in its final stage, and they had succeeding in sneaking their Trojan horse into the city walls. The thought of their plan unraveling now was horrifying, but the death of his wife had already confirmed their destiny as far as he was concerned. Still, he vowed to be more cautious and stick to the girls with whom he was familiar. One of his friends from the Senate had suggested a platinum blonde call girl who was especially good at her job. He would ring her up as soon as he got back to the capitol city.

He glanced at his Secret Service agents who were standing vigil by the elevator. Their robotic movements and lifeless stares gave him a chill, as if they could read his soul. He turned around so he did not have to face them and stared at the Las Vegas landscape. The selection of this city as the base of operations for Aman's empire was either the ultimate irony or a brilliant stroke of luck. The city was the perfect representation for the decadence of the West. Aman always refused to divulge how he got his start here. All Zachariah knew was that his adoptive father had lived here almost since the city's infancy, and his influence and power grew along with the burgeoning strip of casinos in the desert.

The first hotel to be constructed in Vegas, the Flamingo, opened in 1947 thanks to Bugsy Siegel and his financial backbone Frank Costello. The idea of the "city of sin" originated with Meyer Lansky, who ran the books for Costello. In 1938 Lansky worked for Lucky Luciano in New York, and he traveled to Cuba at the behest of his boss to meet with Cuban dictator Fulgencio Batista. They came to an agreement that Lansky would take over control of all the casinos in Havana from the military, which was inefficient at running a business. Lansky turned Havana upside-down as the excitement of his casinos attracted American film stars and numerous other upper crust individuals looking for a good time in an exotic locale. This experience served Lansky well when he and Bugsy Siegel decided to open up a casino in the barren desert of Las Vegas. Nevada legalized gambling in 1931, but no one tapped the potential of this golden opportunity until the mob stepped in.

Zachariah knew that Aman entered this

environment soon thereafter with funds given to him by friends in Cairo. He did not know where the money came from, but he guessed it came from hordes of Nazi gold. Aman's benefactors in Cairo all made their fortunes selling information during the crazy and dangerous days of World War II. Whether that information was true or not did not matter.

By the 1950s Las Vegas was the place where the rich and famous went to party. The fact that the city was controlled by gangsters gave it a hint of danger that everyone seemed to relish. Zachariah remembered Aman telling him the story of his early days in Las Vegas. Aman purchased a hotel called the Desert Dust Inn from one of the first Italian mobsters to try and give up his life of crime. From there, Aman made numerous connections around town while keeping a low profile. Some of the other casino owners tried to quietly inquire about partnerships, but they were politely rebuffed. When some mobsters mistook Aman's quiet demeanor for weakness and tried to move in on his expanding empire they quickly discovered that Aman was not someone they wanted to mess with. Zachariah could understand and sympathize with their mistake. He tested his adoptive father at the very beginning of their relationship as well and paid a steep price. He learned not to cross his father unless he was prepared to deal with an angry hornet's nest of a man.

Aman learned the workings of the mob in Vegas, and by the early 1960s he was a well-known figure who worked both sides of the city. All the important "friends" in town knew him, but did not interfere with his business. They had their hands in enough crimes, and wanted no part of the rumors that were floating around regarding his burgeoning empire. The values of the Desert Dust Inn, and the two other smaller casinos he took over soared along with the rest of the prime real estate in Las Vegas. With the massive amount of income being generated by his small cluster of casinos, Aman officially became a major player in Nevada politics by 1960. He began to cultivate relationships with the appropriate people in preparation for an entry into national politics. Zachariah knew those greased hands were the

47

catalyst that helped launch his own political career. He picked up the photos of Aman's parents and studied their proud faces. They reminded him of his first mentor; Aziz A'zami. Aziz must be almost ninety years old now, Zachariah realized as he did the math in his head. He longed to see the old man one more time before he passed on.

The noise of the elevator caught his attention. The doors slid back, and the portly figure of Aman motioned for him. Zachariah hurried towards his mentor. "It's about fucking time," Zachariah said with authority as they crowded into the elevator with the two Secret Service agents. "Let's go. We can't keep the bigwigs waiting." They descended to the basement of the hotel in silence where an armored limousine was waiting to whisk them off to the golf course to make their tee time.

Chapter 10

"You okay, man?" Michael asked as he adjusted his glasses and stirred his second mug of coffee. The waitress had just removed their empty plates and they were relaxing for a few minutes before heading to the casino.

"Yeah, just still wound up from last night," Alex explained. "You know how I get when I win, always afraid I'm going to lose it right back." Alex sipped his orange juice. He never could adjust to the horrible taste of coffee, and he preferred starting the day with something that was actually healthy instead of an artificial caffeine high that lasted fifteen minutes.

"You're about to become a spook, for crying out loud. You need to relax some if you want to keep the world safe."

"I know. I tell myself the same thing. Eventually I'll learn," Alex responded as he shook his head.

"Don't take me too seriously. I would imagine a little paranoia in a job like that is a good thing. Keeps you one step ahead and keeps your name out of the newspaper," Michael said with a nervous smile. Alex knew his friend was trying to be positive, but he also knew his new job scared his friend. Michael saw the devastation of the Twin Towers up close and personal, and he understood the immense evil that perpetrated the heinous acts.

He still thinks I'm a little nuts for wanting to go toe-to-toe with them, Alex thought to himself before replying. "Don't worry. I'll be careful. That case I worked on opened my eyes though. You have no idea what these types are capable of." Alex downed the last of his orange juice. "Forget about it. We have three days of fun ahead of us. We can talk about the other side of life later. Let's go gamble," Alex said as he tossed his napkin onto the table and stood up to leave.

The early morning was a dead time for the casino, and Alex and Michael quickly found two seats at a blackjack table near the front entrance of the hotel. The night owls had just gone to sleep a few hours ago, and the casino would not pick up until the early afternoon gamblers came in. They sat down at a five-dollar minimum table with a lady who looked to be about sixty years old. The two large stacks of chips in front of her looked impressive, but her stoic face gave no hint as to whether she was winning or losing. Alex slipped his six-foot frame into the middle chair at the table, and Michael took the seat to his left.

"Damn, it's cold in here," Alex said quietly. The frigid air of the casino was a jolt to his system this early in the morning. Still, he knew the cargo shorts he was wearing were a necessity if they planned on walking outside in the desert heat. Looking at his watch, he saw that Cindy was not due to meet them for another twenty minutes. He palmed a fifty-dollar bill onto the table, figuring that should be more than enough to occupy his time until she arrived.

After fifteen minutes of playing, Alex's good fortune still stood intact and he gave his friend a look of confidence just before the dealer busted again, making his hand of thirteen a winner. The dealer placed another thirty dollars worth of chips in front of him. Years of playing blackjack had taught him to ignore his hunches and follow the percentages no matter what he tried to talk himself into. It did not always pay off. It was gambling after all, however he found that if you randomly made decisions, your odds grew progressively worse. A quick accounting of his stack showed that he was ahead another ninety dollars since they sat down at the table. The weekend seemed destined to be a profitable one.

A waitress dressed in a skimpy version of a Japanese kimono brought him out of his contemplation as she sat a Diet Coke in front of him. He took a sip and looked up from the table to hand her a five-dollar tip when he caught the familiar face. Sitting at a blackjack table to their left was the same short, stocky man who was at their craps table the night before. The man sat at the far end of his table, and he had a perfect view of Alex's table. He studied the stranger for a few seconds before turning his attention back to his game. He was the same man sitting near them eating breakfast, Alex suddenly realized.

Could it be coincidence? He admitted it could, but now that he had seen him three times in less than twelve hours, his first guess was that the fat man was somehow connected with the woman. Alex stole a glance at him again, keeping his gaze on the man until the set of tired eyes came up from the table, locking with Alex's for a brief moment. They quickly returned their focus to the hand being dealt. Did the eyes turn away a little too quickly? There was something odd about the way he looked, but Alex could not place what it was. As the dealer finishing shuffling the deck of cards Alex eyed the man one more time, implanting his image in his mind. His short height was given away by his feet, which were dangling in mid-air as he sat at the table. The man's obese physique, along with his glistening hair reminded Alex of the stereotypical gangster character. The man had the beginnings of a five o'clock shadow on his face, and the bags under his eyes betrayed a lack of sleep. Alex involuntarily shivered as he realized what was so odd about him. The stranger was wearing the same suit as the night before.

"Hey boys, how's it going?" Cindy snuck up, slapping them each on the back with one hand. The dealer

50

immediately turned up a natural twenty-one and swept everyone's money off the table. Alex wondered if she was bad luck.

"Ready, Alex? I think that last hand may be a hint to get out of here," Michael suggested.

"That's fine, let's go." They both cashed their small chips in for larger denominations, and Alex downed the last of his drink before flipping the dealer a ten-dollar tip for his services. A few seconds later they pushed through the front doors of the hotel, and stepped out into the desert heat, heading towards the South end of Las Vegas Blvd. It only took a couple more minutes before the drastic rise in temperature began creating sweat beads on the men's foreheads. Alex's mind raced with the thought of the man at the other table. He admitted it still could be a coincidence. The man could easily have a gambling problem. There was no shortage of those here after all.

The crowd on the sidewalk already was large as the weekend was officially under way. They headed south down Las Vegas Boulevard at a brisk pace. Alex turned around to see if they were being followed. The morning sun obstructed his vision, and he squinted as he tried to spot the large man. Unable to see anything he turned his attention back to his friends.

Chapter 11

"Yeah?" Aman's gravely voice at the other end of the cell phone sounded agitated.

"It's me." Despite his boss's constant assurances, Solomon did not like using the phone given to him. Aman insisted numerous times that they were encrypted; a small gift from a friend in Washington. Aman swore the phones could not be detected, tapped, or bugged in any fashion. Solomon still thought it best to keep his conversation short, to the point, and as cryptic as possible.

"Oh, how's our situation?" Aman did not expect a call so soon. The blaring of his phone had caused him to slice a drive out of bounds and into the rock strewn desert surrounding the fairway. His mind quickly diverted roads, and he motioned to Zach to go back to the cart.

"The woman has been spotted several times this morning. She slipped away though. I told you that you should have let me hire my own guys." Solomon warned Aman several times about his lax security personnel, but he was always rebuffed. He still questioned what most of the "protection" was really for. They were lousy at surveillance and none of them were proficient fighters. Solomon thought there was a strong possibility that they were secretly being trained for some sort of suicide mission in the States or somewhere abroad. He was constantly keeping his eyes and ears open for any strange behavior patterns from them. If he came across any solid evidence he could always take it to the U.S. government and bargain with them.

"Enough. They do their jobs honorably," Aman said in a rather annoyed voice. "They come from poor families in Cairo. They would never get a chance to work here and get a good education were it not for this opportunity." Aman paused briefly before getting back to the business at hand. "What do you have? I'm assuming you didn't call me to vent."

"I thought you wanted to be kept in the loop. Also, we've found one of the groups we're looking for. Do you want me to handle it personally?" Solomon asked.

"Yes. I want you to handle any problems personally if it becomes necessary. I don't want anyone else knowing the extent of our little problem."

Solomon closed the cell phone and locked his private office at the Desert Dust Inn. He had to get over to the New York, New York hotel as quickly as possible.

***

Aman pounded his thousand-dollar driver into the ground in frustration before tossing it in Zach's general direction to pick up. He decided to walk up to the area where his ball disappeared. It would give him a chance to blow off some steam. The President-Elect's overactive sex drive was the one thing Aman blamed himself for. In his weaker moments he wished he gave Zachariah a few more opportunities to have fun when he was younger, but deep down he knew that the strict discipline he imposed on his protégé was an absolute necessity. They would not have reached this point were it not for their laser like focus on their goal. At least they now had the Secret Service to help keep his sexual forays hidden.

He yanked off his glove and motioned to Zach to drive the cart. Maybe he was being too hard on his adoptive son. After all, the former Senator from Nevada already did the hard part, getting himself elected the President of the United States. He certainly could put on a show for the cameras, and when it came down to it that was what the media really wanted; a good story to sell to the public.

Zach's interesting story became irresistible once his wife died tragically. It also inoculated him from much of the mudslinging that occurred during the primary battle. It did not prevent him however, from continuing to use his own scorched earth policy to get the nomination. The main election proved an easier victory. The sitting President saddled himself with an unpopular war and this combined with his bunker mentality allowed Zachariah to win the election with relative ease.

The past year had gone remarkably smoothly up until this point. Now he had an unfolding problem that was beyond even the best political manipulation. It needed to be solved quickly and permanently, or Zachariah would become the fastest lame duck president in history; and that would be the best-case scenario. Aman would never allow this to happen. He had come too far to have things fall apart now. He did not like the idea of ordering murders, but his top intelligence officer was telling him it may be an absolute necessity. Despite his initial misgivings, he trusted Solomon's vast experience. The idea that Solomon was pursuing his own agenda was far-fetched and ridiculous, and Aman knew it was only a product of his own fear and paranoia. Solomon would be a complete fool to botch a job like this. He would have nothing to gain from it. No intelligence agency or individual could afford the salary that he was paying the former member of the French DGSE.

Aman watched as Zachariah drove the golf cart into the middle of the fairway a hundred yards in front of him and stopped and stepped out. Zach yanked a fairway driver out of his bag, sauntered up to his ball, and blasted a drive that screamed towards the flag until it skidded to a stop just a few yards short of the green. The President-Elect was causing him enough trouble with his blatant womanizing, and now he was taking his money on the golf course.

"Nice shot, you son-of-a bitch. You know you shot out of turn!" Aman motioned for the corporate CEOs in the other cart to head towards their shots. When Aman drew closer to Zachariah, he whispered quietly to him, "Solomon is working a lead. Hopefully he will end this quickly."

"Sorry. I'll be more careful from here on out. I've learned my lesson," Zachariah said contritely.

"Good." Aman headed towards the rocky desert to find his ball.

Chapter 12

"I would love to know who the hell came up with that idea," Michael commented as he, Alex, and Cindy watched the massive roller coaster that surrounded the New York, New York hotel go through a series of loops and corkscrews.

"Only in Vegas, Michael. I've got to give the people here credit. The coaster was definitely an original idea." Alex continued to scan the crowds since they left the hotel, but so far the man from the casino still did not appear to be following them.

"Let's take a look guys. It could be fun," Cindy suggested.

"That's fine. We haven't been in it yet. Maybe check out their tables to," Michael responded.

"Alex?" Cindy asked.

"No complaints here. Let's get a move on." Alex led the way down the crowded sidewalks.

***

Shakir glanced at his watch before looking up in disgust. The three people he had been tracking were nowhere to be seen, and after a desperate five-minute search, he knew he would not find them except by blind luck. Making up his mind he decided to head north towards downtown Vegas, hoping to spot them along the way. After a meticulous thirty-minute vigil, he found himself at the Stardust Hotel. They were nowhere to be found so he walked back to the middle of the strip. He stopped in front of Caesar's Palace and doubled over, his chest heaving in exhaustion as his suit clung to him from a combination of sweat and the previous days filth. He watched a group of tourists riding the long, covered moving sidewalk into the heart of Caesar's, hoping to get lucky and reacquire his lost targets. Solomon would not be pleased if he phoned in that he lost them.

His eyes involuntarily fluttered, and he realized he was in desperate need of some sleep. He grabbed his phone and began punching in the number for Gregor. Like a child going to the more pliable parent, he knew Gregor would be more sympathetic. Several minutes of complaining worked, and Gregor promised to get someone to replace him within the hour.

***

Solomon cursed to himself as he battled his way through the throng of people in the New York, New York casino. He slid his cell phone back onto his belt clip. The news from Gregor that one of the groups under surveillance disappeared did nothing to help his already foul mood. At least he caught up with this group. He replaced one of Aman's men twenty minutes earlier, and he was now tracking one of the threesomes from the airport, or at least two-thirds of one. It was a couple in their early forties who were bickering. The other man traveling with them had returned to his own room to retrieve some more spending money. The thug Solomon just replaced did do one good thing; he pick-pocketed the man earlier in the day, and now

55

Solomon knew his target's name. The wallet also contained one of the flat plastic keys that all large hotels on the strip used for their rooms.

The target's name was Dan Stevens, and his driver's license stated that he lived in Florida. The rest of the wallet revealed nothing significant, only a few credit cards and twenty-six dollars in cash. Along with the cash were receipts from the casino ATM machines showing that he already had withdrawn two hundred dollars on four different occasions. It was obvious he was either a poor gambler or in the middle of a string of horrendous luck. Considering he just arrived in Vegas the night before, Solomon guessed the former. He kept his distance as he saw the man's lady friend stop and disappear into the restroom.

Taking advantage of the opportunity, he placed a call to his men and gave quick instructions for them to find out which room Mr. Stevens was occupying. Mr. Steven's significant other re-appeared from the bathroom just as Solomon pushed the "end" button on his phone. The couple continued their trek through the casino. They caught an escalator up to a second level gaming area where numerous video games kept children busy.

The second floor also housed the entrance to the roller coaster. Solomon politely excused himself as he gently pushed his way through the crowded escalator. The couple stepped off at the second floor. Now only a few feet behind them, he began to visualize possible scenarios. Solomon's years in the intelligence business could be noticed by no one. He looked like any other Las Vegas tourist, his eyes giving off the outward appearance of being awestruck by the gaudiness around him, hiding the analytical mind that was whirling away. The couple stopped again, and he meandered over to the railing, pretending to watch the action in the casino below. They were still fighting. He strained to hear them over the sounds of the casino.

"I can't believe you lost your wallet. First you get drunk and gamble away a thousand dollars and now you lose your wallet with the hotel key and all your credit cards!" She glared at him while jamming her ATM card into the machine to withdraw some money.

"I swear it had to have been stolen." The husband's face showed a mixture of exasperation and embarrassment.

"Yeah, honey. Whatever. Well, let's forget about it for now. I have my debit card and one credit card, so that should be enough to get us through the next couple of days. Come on. We're going to do something I want to for a change."

"Mary, I don't think getting on that roller coaster is the best thing I can do for myself right now. I haven't gotten all of those drinks from last night out of my system."

"Stop whining. It's your own fault you can't control your drinking. Besides, this will be fun and it will be the first time you get something in return for your money." The comment was accompanied by a smile. "You won't even notice the headache as soon as we head down that first big hill." She took him by the hand as if he were an uncooperative child, dragging him towards the ticket line.

Solomon dialed the appropriate number on his cellular phone while continuing to follow them. His idea to get someone from his team working on the roller coaster full time looked like it was going to pay off. He thought at the time he was probably being overly cautious, and would never have to use it for a job. His intuition was paying off now, and he was pleased that his paranoid tendencies had not been swallowed by the easy living of the past few years. The cozy American lifestyle could quickly eat away at your discipline if you were not careful.

The line rang once before being answered with a curt, "Here, sir."

"Augustine, I need to use the coaster for a job. I'll be sitting in the seat behind the subject to make sure everything goes smoothly. Follow our normal procedures." Augustine was one of the few men Solomon trusted to do a job properly. The young man was lured away from another casino owner, and was not part of Aman's little party of Middle Eastern malcontents. Solomon made one more quick call to one of the women in the organization before slipping the phone back into his pocket. He immediately purchased two tickets and sidestepped some teenagers debating whether or not they should ride. He slipped in behind Dan

57

Stevens and his wife just as they stepped into the long line for the roller coaster.

Now that he was in behind them he relaxed a little, but his paranoid nature would not let him rest. He began to look for the woman he had called and he made two more calls before she finally appeared after twenty long minutes.

"Darling! I'm over here," Solomon shouted as he waved his arms in the air. As soon as she was close enough he grabbed her by the arm. "Just stay close to me and be quiet, I just need you to stand here and look pretty," he whispered in her ear. Everything was now in place.

Two of Aman's employees who were also security guards for the hotel were already in place at street level, ready to be the first ones on the scene. They would confirm the deaths, quarantine the area, and discreetly confiscate any cell phones belonging to the deceased. An operation out in the open was very risk but Solomon was willing to chance it. If it could be pulled off properly, it would look like a freak accident to the public, and a freak accident focused attention on things like the hotel's safety measures. Solomon's companion was a showgirl. She was not particularly bright and did not ask questions. Her only concern was how much they paid her. This made her easy to control. She was also physically exquisite, with lustrous blonde hair and long legs that attracted admiring looks from many of the men, and glares from most of the women. She fit perfectly into Solomon's plan. No one around them would remember his face because of the attention drawn to her. Solomon turned his own attention back to his quarry. He could tell the argument was over, and the man was now beginning to focus on his fear of the roller coaster.

Their conversation betrayed nothing that sounded as though they may have possession of anything that did not belong to them. He knew his people should be turning their hotel room upside down at this very moment. They were now approaching the front of the line. One of the attendants ushered them into a maze of railings like a traffic cop monitoring an intersection. The attendant opened the gate for two people at a time to walk up to the solitary railings that stood next to the tracks of the roller coaster. The seating for the front rows filled up first, and Solomon watched as the Stevens' took a spot near the back. Solomon put his arm around his girl in a show of affection as the attendant opened the gate and motioned them towards their choice of seats. Walking towards the back, Solomon and his girl made a minor commotion as they pretended to bicker over what seats to occupy before finally settling on the two spots directly behind the Stevens'.

Glancing across to the other side of the tracks, Solomon made brief eye contact with Augustine. His hotel employee's uniform shirt was untucked and hanging out on the left side, signaling that everything was safe to continue. The far away noise of the roller coaster began to grow louder, causing Solomon to tense up. The rumbling of the coaster announced its arrival a few seconds before it came roaring into view. The slowing of the ride was met with the typical shouts of "Wahoo!" and "Hell yeah!" It slowed to a halt, and the bars that held everyone in their seats simultaneously clicked and rose up so the passengers could disembark, and make their way towards the exit that would funnel them back into the casino.

Solomon let his lady friend slide in first, taking the left seat for himself. He brushed his shaggy black hair away from his pale forehead. Each car could hold a total of four people, and Dan Stevens and his wife sat down directly in front of them. The U-shaped metal bars lowered simultaneously to lock everyone in their seats. The attendants moved quickly up the cars, giving the metal bars the obligatory pull to show any scared riders that they were securely locked in place.

Dan Stevens refused to give up. "I'm not lying, honey. I have to throw up." Solomon was beginning to sympathize with the angry woman. The man sounded like a spoiled child.

"Shut up Dan! Jesus Christ. If you would not drink so damn much..." The movement of the coaster stopped the beginning of another argument. "It's about time. If you throw up just lean the other way," she said in as callous a manner as she could.

The roller coaster picked up momentum and moved out of the station and into the golden Las Vegas day. It exited on the side of the hotel and circled around to the backside before making a final pause at the base of a huge hill. The gears of the track took hold, slowly pulling the coaster towards the top of the hotel and the Las Vegas skyline. Solomon never had any reason to ride the coaster before, and as approached the top he found the view quite impressive. Approaching the precipice, it appeared they were at eye level with all the tallest hotels around them. He quickly returned to the business at hand, digging into his pocket for his phone. Solomon listened as Dan Stevens softly whimpered to himself.

A chorus of hands went up in the air together as the roller coaster began climbing over the top of the hill. The first screams from the passengers quickly followed suit. Solomon found himself involuntarily gripping the handrail as the coaster crested the hill and hurtled downwards at breakneck speed. The force of the long fall pushed him into the back of his seat. He felt like his stomach was trying to escape out of his throat when the coaster finally hit bottom and began ascending again. Gathering himself after the initial shock, he looked below. They had now made its way to the other side of the hotel, and he could see the main entrance to the MGM Grand Hotel on the other side of Las Vegas Boulevard. The coaster maintained a steady pace as it raced across a few small hills.

They were now at the front of the hotel, and Solomon could see the gawking bystanders below stopping to watch them as they made a sharp turn around the model of the Statue of Liberty. He flipped open his phone. His man inside would be watching everything on the hotel security monitor but he wanted to make sure it would be timed perfectly. The man had strict orders not to act until he received the proper instructions.

The roller coaster was now near its original starting point. Solomon gripped the phone a little harder than necessary as they went around a sharp left-hand curve. The coaster picked up a new head of steam as it approached the first loop of the ride. Solomon held his finger calmly over the proper button. He slowly counted the seconds as the coaster picked up speed, racing downward towards the loop. *Now.* He pressed the button as they headed into the loop. The single ring of the phone sent Augustine into action, and he flipped the appropriate switch. For a brief moment nothing happened, and Solomon glanced at his phone as the giant centipede entered the loop. He relaxed as he heard the loud "click" from the seats in front of him and the bolts holding the U-shaped bars slid back into their housing.

The Stevens' both had firm grips on their U-shaped handlebars when they heard the noise of the supports coming off. They exchanged a quizzical look that instantly turned to fear as they reached the apex of the loop and the bars slid forward, pulling their arms away from their bodies. They both let out hysterical screams, their bodies pulled out of their seats by gravity's now sinister force. They fell several stories before crashing into the sidewalk below. The roller coaster lurched to a stop as soon as it came out of the loop. Solomon strained to peer below him. The two broken bodies lay lifeless on the concrete expanse below.

Chapter 13

"Alex, what the hell is going on?" Michael slapped him on the shoulder. He and Cindy had just exited one of the stores on the Strip selling cheap and tacky Las Vegas themed clothing. They both had bags in their hand.

"Two people fell out of the roller coaster when it went through the loop." Alex motioned skyward and noticed for the first time that it had stopped on the tracks after coming out of the loop.

"What?" Michael stared dumbfounded at the stopped coaster, trying to roughly calculate how far they had fallen. They both turned to Cindy who had a stricken look on her face.

"Easy, honey. Relax. I guess we won't be riding the roller coaster after all." The poor timing of the remark did nothing to relieve the tension.

"Amen." It was the most appropriate response Alex could think of. Their vacation was getting stranger by the minute.

"Honey, let's go check out the MGM. I'll show you around," Michael said. He recognized the pale look on her face, and decided it would probably be best to get her away from the scene. "Alex, do you want to head on over with us?"

"Go on ahead. I think I'll head on over to the Luxor and gamble a little. How about we meet there for lunch in ninety minutes?"

"Sounds good to me." Michael gripped Cindy's hand and pulled her towards the giant lion's head of the MGM Hotel's entrance.

Alex fought his way around the gathering crowd and headed towards the Luxor. He was craving some air conditioning and a cold beer. He did not notice the lithe woman following him from a safe distance.

***

White House, Washington D.C., 8:00 A.M.

President Allan Gray furiously made his way through the short stack of papers in front of him, scribbling his signature at the places his doting secretary had marked for him with large arrows stuck to the side of the paper. His head still ached from the New Years Eve Party a few nights earlier. He fumbled in one of his drawers until he found the aspirin he wanted and swallowed them dry. This was the price he paid, he told himself, for getting a little drunk after not touching the stuff for over twenty years. The good news was that he had no desire for another drink at the current moment.

He always wanted to know how he would handle it if he decided to drink again. He was never dubbed an official alcoholic; he had quit of his own volition many years before due to the strain it was causing in his personal and professional life. Giving it up had helped his energy level tremendously, and he credited his dry lifestyle with getting him elected governor of California twice. His cautious stewardship of one of the largest economies in the world served as a springboard to the highest office in the land. His time in the Presidency, however, was not panning out quite as well. He casually flipped the papers aside and hit the intercom button on the desk.

"Yes, sir?" Jamal Mahmoud, the current head of his Secret Service detail, immediately answered the call.

"Is my wife ready to go? I want to get this over with as quickly as possible." The President had to meet with another sports team for a brief photo op. He had lost track of which team it was this time, and he really did not care anyway. The secret investigation he allowed the CIA Director to put together was currently his only concern, and it appeared to have fallen apart. He was still holding out hope for some bit of good news. Allan Gray was arguably the most powerful man in the world, but he felt helpless at the moment.

"I just called upstairs, Sir. They told me she was on her way down now. Should I send her in when she gets here?" Jamal asked.

"Yes please," President Gray replied. "Oh, and I guess congratulations are in order for you, Jamal. I understand they will allow you to remain on to continue to lead the security detail for President-Elect Hardin. You've earned it, son. You've definitely put in your time." He liked his new agent. He took over less than a year ago after the previous agent suffered a mental breakdown. Due to the high stress level of the job, they normally rotated the head of the security detail with the inauguration of a new president. However, Jamal had received his appointment just months earlier, so he was given special permission to continue in that position with the incoming administration.

"Thank you, sir. I appreciate the vote of confidence," Jamal replied in an even tone. "Also, sir, the CIA Director's office called a few minutes ago to cancel his appointment with you. Would you like to schedule someone else to fill the time slot?"

"No, don't worry about it, Jamal. Things are starting to wind down a little quicker than I anticipated," the President responded dejectedly before pressing the "end" button on the intercom.

***

Washington D.C. FBI Headquarters 9:33 A.M.

The mixture of cigarettes and coffee were finally jolting his mind awake. Bret McMichael sat behind his desk, staring blankly at the couch that also served as his bed last night. He barely slept, whether it was due to the cramped couch or his nerves, he could not be sure. He stared at the phone, willing it to ring, but nothing happened. He wanted to make a more informed decision before deciding whether or not he should cut his losses and distance himself from this little political storm that was gathering strength on the banks of the Potomac. If the storm turned into a hurricane, he wanted to be sure to be out of town when it made landfall.

Sean would be in any moment now, and if his people did not check in soon, then he may have to let Sean go to Cairo. Malcolm was already pushing for it but Bret knew when to be non-committal. As a Beltway-lifer he learned a long time ago that the best reply to a request was often silence. You rarely got in trouble in this town for doing nothing. It was when you over-reached that someone always broke your exposed hands. The soon-to-be ex-president learned this the hard way.

His intercom button buzzed loudly. "Yes? Send him in," Bret said to his young sentinel of a secretary who monitored all the comings and goings of his office. The door flung open and Sean Hill drug himself through the threshold looking just as tired as Bret felt.

"Judging by the fact that you're already smoking, I'm assuming we don't have anymore news?"

"No, but the newspapers sure can't get enough of our newly-elected President. They are ready to have the inauguration right now instead of waiting," Bret said as he motioned at the newspaper sitting on his expansive desk.

"As long as there is nothing in the paper about the current POTUS and our little operation I'm happy." As a former Secret Service agent, Sean still used the acronym for the president out of habit.

"Bret, we're going to have to make some kind of move soon. At least give President Gray some more information so he can make a better decision." Sean desperately wanted to keep the operation going. The fact that Marilyn vanished could only mean she was onto something.

"Not yet, Sean. We have already had this discussion. Just be patient. Trying to force something will only make matters worse." Bret crossed his knees and listened in disgust as they cracked, his body once again reminding him that it was wearing down. The ring of the phone interrupted their conservation.

"Director McMichael speaking," Bret answered the phone with a cheerful smile. He may be exhausted, but he still loved flaunting his title. Sean watched his body language as he talked on the phone. A few grunts and affirmatives and he put the phone back on its cradle.

"A little good news. Malcolm said she left a signal at the airport. Apparently she's okay. At least for the moment."

"How does he know?" Sean asked.

"No idea. Malcolm never gives up any secrets. That's why he doesn't have any friends in this town." The CIA Director was a constant thorn in his side. He could not remember the last time a man with so much influence never used the power of the perfectly placed leak to get what he wanted. The man had spent too much time in the field.

"She's alive for now then. What's our next step?" Sean asked expectantly.

Brett made a snap decision. He decided to relent to Malcolm's wish and pack Sean off to Egypt just as the CIA Director had been begging him to do ever since Marilyn came back from Cairo a few months ago. If Sean got caught doing something illegal there, he could just place the blame on the CIA Director. After all, Bret had his tape-recorded request sitting in his safe. It could be brought out if things

65

continued as Bret thought they would; and on the off chance Sean succeeded, he could take the credit for the gutsy decision.

"I want you on the next plane to Egypt, Sean. Follow up on her research. Malcolm and I can keep track of things here in the States. I'll have a plane ready for you in two hours. I'll call Malcolm and tell him you're heading out."

"Yes, sir," Sean said in an excited tone.

Bret watched the display with annoyance. It was clear to him that Sean was becoming too attached to his partner. She was certainly beautiful, but everyone had a job to do, regardless of any perceived feelings they may have about agents in the field. Bret could not help but laugh a little at the irony of the situation. He was concerned that feelings were keeping Sean from properly doing his work, while he was not worried about Marilyn in the least. Maybe women were the stronger sex. He stubbed out his cigarette and decided to take a shower. He needed to look decent for his upcoming meeting with the CIA Director. He wanted to look his best as he lied to the man's face.

Chapter 14

"You feeling alright, honey?" Michael asked as he dropped his hotel key card onto the desk along with his wallet, which was a little lighter after running into his first string of bad luck.

"Sure am. I'll be out in a minute," she called out from the bathroom in a mischievous voice. The playful tone suggested to Michael that the day's events were being forgotten already. He eyed his suitcase and tried to decide if now would be an appropriate time to break out the engagement ring stashed inside it.

"I'm trying on what I bought while you two were throwing away your money. Want to see?" Cindy called out.

Michael was about to say no when he glanced at the bed and noticed the empty Victoria's Secret bag. It looked like Las Vegas fever had caught up with his girlfriend.

"I'm up for a little fashion show. I'll just lie on the bed here and judge..." a knock on the door interrupted him. "I'll call you in thirty minutes, Alex," he called out, not wanting to break the sexual tension that was creeping into the room.

"Hotel security, can we have a minute, sir?" It was not a question, despite the phrasing. Exasperated, Michael got up from the bed. "Stay in the bathroom honey. I'll be one minute. Someone's at the door." Michael opened the door a crack, trying to see who was there. Did he forget to give them a credit card last night?

"Sir, we have a small problem." The very slight accent sounded almost European. Michael was not surprised. Las Vegas attracted its employees from all over the world.

"What can I do for you..." Before he could finish the sentence the door exploded in his face. He went sprawling back into the hotel room, blood spurting from his broken nose. He watched as a slim man with a fair complexion, dressed in slacks, a blue button down dress shirt, and corduroy sports jacket stepped into the room. Michael's eyes scanned down to the man's right hand, and noticed the gun for the first time. He froze in horror. His last thought was of Cindy in the next room.

***

Solomon closed and locked the door by feel, never taking his eyes off his target. The look of fear on the smashed face of his prey's eyes told him this was going to be easy. He leveled the silenced FN Herstal 5.7mm and gave the trigger one delicate pull. The single action pistol sent one perfectly placed bullet through the heart, ending the man's life before he could muster any pleas. Solomon strode cautiously over to the bathroom door, pushing it open to reveal a petite redhead in black lingerie. Her freckled skin turned ashen at the sight of the stranger, and she groped for a towel. She did not scream like he expected her to. She just stood transfixed on the weapon pointed her way. He decided to try a long shot.

"Where is it? The package the woman gave you? Give it to me and I will let you live." The quizzical look on her face told Solomon's trained eye she did not know what he was talking about, and he quickly emptied one shot into her chest. Her half naked body slumped to the cold tile floor, her arms pulling toiletries on the sink crashing down all around her. He holstered the Belgian made weapon. It took fifteen seconds to finish them both off. He immediately went through the woman's purse, emptying the cash and credit cards before doing the same to the man's wallet. His gloved hands expertly searched both bodies. He then proceeded to meticulously go through the entire room.

Solomon's luck had finally changed for the better an hour earlier when Shakir had a stroke of luck, and reacquired the threesome he had lost as they were leaving the MGM. Solomon still was milling around the area at the time so he took it upon himself to assist. They followed the trio back to the Imperial Palace. Solomon instructed Shakir to deal with the single male, and Solomon would take the more complicated job of dealing with two targets.

His ten-minute search of the room turned up nothing of interest, and he quickly accepted the fact that he probably just killed two completely innocent people. His phone vibrated. Shakir had instructions to text him to inform Solomon of which floor he was on. The fat Arab was two floors below. Solomon dashed out of the room, shutting the door behind him. The stairs would be quicker than the elevator. He sprinted down the hallway, hoping the boss's minion did not screw things up before he could get there.

***

Alex opened the door of his room, and smiled as he saw that the maids had already cleaned up his mess from the previous evening. He made a mental note to leave a nice tip for them since he was sure the bathroom had not been fun to clean. He dropped his wallet on the table, and headed straight to the toilet to relieve himself. The weekend was certainly off to an exciting start. Two people falling off a roller coaster and plunging to their deaths did not relax the tension he was already feeling thanks to his mysterious encounter the previous evening.

He glanced at his ever-expanding wallet again as he washed his hands. His string of good fortune had continued unabated at the Luxor. He was beginning to feel invincible every time he sat down to gamble. He immediately scolded himself for the thought. The moment one starts to think one cannot lose was normally when lady luck yanked their chair out from under them and beat them over the head with it. A quick nap was in order right now though to re-energize for the evening. He started to crawl into bed when he realized that he did not close the entry door to the room all the way. He slid off the bed to take care of it.

Alex placed the palm of his hand against the door and started to give it a shove. As he did so, he felt a slight pressure pushing back. The door would not budge, as if someone was trying to open it from the other end. He peered around the crack in the door and caught a glimpse of a large man in dress slacks and an open collared shirt leaning against the door. It was the same man he had seen several times in the casino.

The man hesitated, surprised at being caught in the act. "Uh, hotel security, sir." The voice did not convey authority. He sounded unsure, as though he were trying to remember a script he had been rehearsing. The thought of the cell phone and the strange woman flashed across Alex's mind. Was this part of the test that he had been nervously waiting for?

"Is there a problem?" Alex asked. The man's only response was to take a step back, and then crash his portly body against the door with all the force he could muster. The impact sent Alex flying back into the room, his body sprawled across the floor at the foot of the queen size bed. His mind raced, trying to come up with a plan of action. Was he supposed to fight back? His shoulder throbbed from the blow, but nothing appeared to be broken. He tried desperately to regain his normal breathing pattern as the man stepped inside the room, using his meaty paw to slam the door.

"Am I supposed to fight back, buddy? You have to tell me what the plan is." The man answered by reaching into his sport coat and pulling out a gun. Alex lunged for the dresser to the left of him, reaching for a bottle of cologne to toss at the man. He hurled it at his attacker, but the man's gun already was poised for the kill, its single black eye looking at him with no emotion. Suddenly, there was a loud explosion as a gun went off, the noise echoing in the hallway. Alex stared dumbfounded as the intruder stopped in his tracks and looked down at his chest, which now had a black stain in the middle of his white shirt. The shot did not come from the fat man's weapon. Another shot erupted and the man's knees buckled, his pistol falling harmlessly on the carpet and landing just a few feet from Alex. The bulky carcass of the man crashed to the floor. Instinct told him to grab the dead man's gun. His confusion now turned to fear. The man was certainly dead. Two rapidly increasing dark spots enveloped the large man's back as his twitching body lay face down on the hotel floor. Standing in the threshold of the open doorway, already holstering her weapon was the beautiful woman from the airport.

"Alex, grab your wallet and the cell phone I gave you. We're leaving right now," she demanded in a tone that was very calm considering the situation.

"Who the hell are you, and what the ..." Alex got cut off in mid-sentence.

"No time to talk. We need to get out of here or we'll both be dead. More men are on the way. Grab the phone or I'll shoot you as well." The shocking comment and serious look on her face stunned him into motion, and he rushed for the bathroom sink to get it. She grabbed it from his hand and they raced down the hallway to the staircase.

"What about the elevator?" Alex blurted out as they ran.

"No way. This is faster. Besides he may have men controlling it. Not sure."

The metal door leading to the stairwell closed behind them. Alex glanced back, peering through the small glass square at the top of it. A few people had poked their heads out of their rooms, trying to ascertain the source of the noise. Alex watched as another man exited the stairwell at the opposite end of the floor with his gun raised. The man purposefully made his way down the hallway as the curious hotel guests went into self-preservation mode and slammed their doors shut.

"What are you doing? Get down here now!" The woman demanded from the flight of stairs below him.

"Someone came out of the other stairwell. He has a gun."

"No shit. I told you they were coming. The valet will not hold my car much longer. You have two seconds before I put a bullet in your head." They dashed down the stairs without another word. Alex followed the woman like a dog being led around on a noose by its owner. There did not seem to be any other options. They raced through the casino, drawing annoying looks from gamblers, and loud reprimands from the pit bosses who barked at them to slow down. It was still quiet in the casino. The evening crowd was still a few hours from arriving.

As they approached the front entrance of the hotel he suddenly realized he may be an accomplice to murder. He could see a hotel employee holding open the door to an SUV. The young man was staring at them with a look of annoyance. Alex's only hope was that this was part of the game. The woman pushed through the revolving door at a rapid pace, causing the doors to hit an elderly couple who were moving slowly on the other side of the circle. They toppled to the floor as Alex and the woman emerged from the interior of the casino out on to the front portico of the hotel.

She stuffed a wad of money into the valet's hand and apologized for being late. With no one else to trust, he followed her lead as they climbed into a silver Toyota 4Runner that was idling at the front of the line of vehicles. She floored the gas, and the bulky vehicle shot out onto Las Vegas Boulevard, causing a limousine to slam on its brakes to avoid hitting them. Alex did not know where they were going and did not care. He just desperately wanted some answers.

"I need to know what's going on here if I'm going to pass your test." The woman shot him a look of fiery intensity with her eyes that told him to remain silent. Alex

71

immediately thought of the dead man in the hotel room and shut his mouth.

Chapter 15

Aman stretched his portly figure across the massive purple couch, trying his best to make himself comfortable. The man just would not shut up. He held the phone away from his ear so he could clearly hear the sound of the East Coast accent, while not having to actually listen to the words. The man Zach chose to be his attorney general continued to read through a long list of things he wanted to do and people he wanted working for him. Attorney General designate Samuel Rodenbeck was a typical Northeastern personality who expected to get what he wanted as soon as it was asked for. He was currently rattling off a string of abuses that the previous administration committed, and how he intended to rectify them.

A top graduate of an Ivy League law school, which one Aman had purposely forgotten, Samuel liked to claim he had spent his entire life fighting for the rights of the poor who had turned to crime because society rejected them. Now he was determined to reestablish the principles of the Warren Court of the 1950s and 1960s that had helped to bring fairness back to the judicial system. Those rights were slowly eroding over the last twenty years, but Samuel was sure he would be the one to put a stop to it. After five minutes of polite listening, Aman assured him that Zach was still in agreement with him, and Aman promised to talk with Zach regarding the additional appointments. Aman hung up the phone in disgust before the man could start in on another cause-celebre.

After more than thirty years in the country he still did not understand the American thought process, especially among some of those in Zach's own party. It seemed to Aman to border on suicide. They loved to play nice with the criminal element of their society, as if this would convince the criminal to change his ways. The freedom they claimed to love did nothing but provide a haven for every subversive and decadent behavior a person could dream of. He smiled, knowing that Zach would soon be in a position to create monumental change. It would be the type of change that would create enough devastation so the rest of the world would finally be forced to sit up and take notice.

Aman dropped the list of candidates he had been reading through with Mr. Rodenback, and stared through the window at the sunset splashing shadows across the cityscape of Las Vegas. With the end so near, he found himself thinking back to the beginning of their hunt once again. They had come so far since then. When his handlers first told him about their idea, he had been distraught. Now, like all their other directives, it had proven to be inspired.

It was 1962, and Aman had been managing the casino for only a few years. The profits he was bringing in then were already huge, and he was eager to immediately begin wreaking havoc, either in America or the Middle East. He looked back at their patience with awe. His forbearers knew they would most likely not live to see their work come to fruition, but they persisted with their plan.

***

1962

Aman stood in his open-air owner's box, gazing out over the most famous racetrack in the world. Churchill Downs in Louisville, Kentucky was filled with a sea of people, and he was soaking in the perfect spring day that the Derby was famous for. The thermostat read sixty-eight degrees, but the cool breeze blowing across the track brought a crisp chill to the first Saturday in May.

If my horse can perform in the scorching heat of Egypt, then he should fly around this track. Aman originally started his stables at the behest of his superiors just three years ago. He had no idea why they wanted him to do it, but he had learned to do as he was told, and his questions would eventually be answered. He now had a few race-worthy thoroughbreds, and this was his first visit to Churchill Downs. The first jewel of horse racing's Triple Crown, and the premier horse race in the world was the Kentucky Derby, and he was under orders to attend. His stable of horses was based in Cairo, and one of his horses would be running in a smaller race that went off before the Derby. His handlers told him they would make contact with him at the appropriate time. His palms were sweaty with the anticipation of the meeting.

Horse racing, Aman later learned, provided the perfect cover for his partners in Egypt to enter the country with little or no supervision. They received only cursory glances from customs, and it was a simple matter for them to bring in the annual funds that Aman used to keep his organization in Las Vegas growing. Aman still remembered the excitement he felt that day as he waited for a member of the Brotherhood to meet him in his owners' box.

Most of the other owners lingered around their stables in order to inspect their horses, but Aman was given strict orders to stay away from the stable. His superiors told him the trainer they used was a fanatic, and desperately wanted to win some races in the United States. The trainer needed space to work, and Aman was to provide him with it. He felt out of his element around the stables and paddock area anyway, so he was content to stay in his private box in the grandstands, watching the day unfold through his binoculars. He was studying the latest odds for the next race when a young man in dirty overalls appeared out of the double doors just below him. The man whispered furtively to the green-jacketed employee guarding the entrance and pointed in Aman's general direction. The employee gave the young man permission to continue, and the boy bounded up the steps towards him. Aman noticed that the boy's face was layered with a thin film of dirt.

"Aman, they need to see you in the stables," the boy said through pants of exhaustion. Aman immediately stood up, eager to meet with one of his superiors for the first time in years.

"Tell him I'm on my way. Julie?" He turned to the leggy blonde showgirl who accompanied him on the trip from Las Vegas. She worked at the Flamingo Hotel, and was a gift from one of his mobster acquaintances. "Go bet the number six horse for me in the next race. Put one hundred to win. Take the rest and play with it as you please." He peeled off three hundred dollars in twenty-dollar bills. She snatched up the small stack of money and quickly vanished. Aman handed the young man a small tip and told him he would be there shortly. He stood up, and brushed some stray peanut shells and food crumbs off his suit. He glanced down at his mid-section in disgust. His solid physique was showing the first sign of turning soft.

Twenty minutes later, he stepped out of the breezy spring day and into the tiny, dark stable the managers of the track had allotted him. The sinewy, gaunt figure of the trainer was tenderly brushing the stallion's charcoal hair. The man ignored Aman. Several dirty young men hurried about the stall hanging saddles, feeding the horse, and tossing hay around the small space. The trainer stood at the eye of the storm, and did not seem to notice the flurry of activity going on around him. Taking a hint from the trainer, Aman stepped back into the sunshine to give everyone more room to move.

Five minutes later the last boy left and the trainer ushered Aman back inside, closing the barn door behind him. Streams of sunlight shined through the tiny cracks of the wood structure, throwing rays of light across the horse, and the trainers face. The strong smell of manure permeated the small space, and the trainer cracked a window to help filter the air.

"How is our horse coming along?" Aman asked.

"Good. Praise Allah. He will win if he is not fatigued from the long journey. This is the first time he has traveled overseas for a race. We have more pressing issues to deal with though." The trainer spoke in a voice that left no doubt that he was the superior, and Aman the lackey.

"Welcome to America. It's always an honor to speak with a member of the Brotherhood. How are you, Aziz?" Aman took a cigar out of his sport coat, struck a match, lit the cigar, and exhaled the smoke with gusto. The strong scent of Cuban tobacco helped to neutralize the offending smells of the horse.

"I see you have a good memory. I am Aziz A'zami." The trainer moved around his horse and embraced Aman with a strength that did not look possible from his small frame.

"What have you brought for me?" Aman learned from Hussan that it was best to always come straight to the point with the members of the Brotherhood. They possessed a single-minded focus that made them economical in their movements and conversations. They were true believers; each one of them using every second of their life in utter devotion to the cause. It was an insult to waste their time.

"Gold to help keep empire running. It came with horse. It is already loaded to train for trip to Las Vegas," Aziz said in broken English. Aman knew he was still learning the language, and he appeared to be picking it up quickly.

"It is truly an honor to meet you, Aziz," Aman said graciously. "Hussan was in awe of you. After he told me the story of your life, I dedicated myself to the cause and yourself." Aman bowed reverently as he recalled the incredible story of Aziz; a skinny, short, man of forty years who had already accomplished more for Islam than all the current leaders of the Middle East combined. He remembered Hussan's dictations almost word for word. Aziz's father had worked in the underground resistance in 1919. The movement had tried to return Egypt to self-rule after Great Britain and the West failed to live up to their promises after World War I and the peace treaty of Paris.

Aziz followed in his father's footsteps, and by the 1930s he had developed two passions; horse racing and a free Egypt. He credited his love for horses to King Farouk of Egypt, who adored thoroughbreds and maintained a large stable on the outskirts of Cairo. Aziz's father was one of the more senior diplomats, and he took his son to the stables often. In 1935 Aziz traveled with his father to England. They were part of a delegation fighting for Egyptian sovereignty. Aziz would relax by spending weekends at the track. Here he learned the intricacies and minute details of creating a champion steed, and the first seeds of his double life began to be planted.

In 1936 a peace treaty was finally agreed upon, and Egypt appeared to have finally achieved its long sought freedom. Aziz began to consider starting his own stable when they returned to Egypt. He had the knowledge and the connections to be incredibly successful. The dream of Egyptian autonomy did not last long though, and his life changed forever with the outbreak of World War II. The war effectively ended the treaty. Britain needed Egypt as a staging ground to turn back the Nazi tide led by Erwin Rommel that was sweeping across the North African desert.

The war taught Aziz, who was then in his mid-twenties, one very important lesson that his father and his compatriots never figured out during their years of negotiations with the British. The West would never give up its imperial lust until the proper amount of blood was spilled. A signed piece of paper was worthless, something that could be ignored. However, if enough of their sons returned home in wooden boxes, that could alter their plans. Aziz became a full-fledged Egyptian nationalist, determined to rid his country of Western influences for good. He used his father's contacts in the government to put him in touch with a Nazi spy network in Cairo. He began actively working against the British war machine. Working for the Germans also meant he was assisting in the destruction of the Jews, so his employment would serve a dual purpose.

He infiltrated the British camps that circled the city, providing his German masters with as much first hand intelligence as he could get his hands on. After the first two years of the war, he became one of Nazi Germany's most important agents in the North African arena, and the German military sent an Abwehr agent to personally assist Aziz. He had contacts all throughout Cairo but his funds were drying up quickly. The Germans had not been expecting such a load of information, so they snuck the Abwehr agent into Cairo along with a horde of Nazi gold on a stolen Allied boat typically used for humanitarian purposes. The millions of dollars in gold were exactly what Aziz was waiting for, a gift from the heavens so he could begin his true calling. The Abwehr agent disappeared; Aziz put a knife in his back one night and deposited the body in the Nile before vanishing into the throng of different cultures inhabiting war torn Cairo so he could wait until the struggle concluded.

The Nazi advance was eventually destroyed as Allied ships intercepted Rommel's supplies traveling across the Mediterranean Sea. This, combined with the Fuhrer's rash decision-making, ended the siege of Egypt. The Germans retreated back to the European front to try to prevent their homeland from being run over by the increasing juggernaut of the Allied Forces. Aziz spent the last few months of the war dashing from safe house to safe house trying to stay one step ahead of the small fraternity of German spies determined to recover the millions of dollars in gold they entrusted him with. At the same time, Aziz managed to avoid the British as well. There were enemies around every corner, and Aziz relied on a small group of his father's most trusted contacts to stay alive.

In 1945, with the war finally over, Aziz emerged from hiding and began orchestrating his plan. With his finances in order he returned to the Al-Zahraa horse farm, twenty kilometers from Cairo in Kafr Gamos, where his father's agents had stashed the gold in cellars underneath the horses' stables. He began training horses for King Farouk, who owned the Al-Zahraa farm. At nights he had meetings with his father's trusted confidants who had kept him alive during the latter stages of the war. They were patient, slowly accumulating power until the timing was right to strike. To show their solidarity to their new cause, they had KK in Arabic, which was short for Caliphate Creation, burned into their inner thighs. A new fraternity was quietly taking shape. He just needed someone with more influence to join their Brotherhood.

Aziz foresaw the coming battle long before other groups in the Middle East. World War II opened his eyes to the raw power the United States possessed. It had gone from a country wallowing in misery in the late 1930s to a powerhouse overrunning Nazi Germany in just a few short years. Yes, the Russians assisted by softening the underbelly of Germany, but most of the major powers had considered the U.S. too weak and divided to even enter the war, much less be a deciding factor. In just a few short years the

American war machine overtook the Germans and Russians in conventional forces, and beat the Germans in the race to develop the atom bomb.

Aziz understood that the return of Islam as the predominant force in the world would never be accomplished by an Arab despot wielding power from his small enclave in Cairo. The destruction of Britain, while pleasing to him in principle, would also mean nothing. Only by bringing the United States to its knees could Islam begin its ascent back to greatness. Aziz closely studied Sun Tzu, the classic Chinese war strategist from 500 B.C. who wrote what could best be described as a field manual to victory. It would later become known as the Art of War, and Aziz studied it as fervently as his Koran. "Know *the enemy and know yourself; in a hundred battles you will never be in peril.*" Aziz's father gave the book to him when Aziz first began to show his Arab nationalist tendencies. It was meant to temper him, and make him think before he acted. After WWII Aziz now understood what his father had in mind, and why at the outset of the war, he sent Aman's father to live in the United States.

The small cadre of conspirators began covertly laying the foundation inside the Egyptian government that would be necessary once they found the proper warriors. It was at this time that Aman first met Hussan in his mother's apartment in New York, and began his long journey towards what he hoped would be immortality.

Aman now watched as his benefactor and friend looked him in the eye and spoke with a fiery passion about their latest plan. "Today is the beginning of the end for America, Aman. The plan will take years, but we must be patience. Your task begin soon," Aziz said.

"Tell me what to do, and I'll do it." Aman could not hide his anticipation as he listened to Aziz. What attack on the West were they going to have him direct? Would his fledgling empire in Las Vegas launch a wave of jihadist attacks?

"We have found two boys with strong potential. We need you to begin making necessary contacts to make their entry into the U.S. smooth and hidden." Aziz's voice remained low and conspiratorial. "You have great insight to America and your empire in Las Vegas is vast. Once we get someone inside it your job will be to teach boy and make sure he fit in. We secure the rest of his training before we bring him over to you. You need be ready in five years. You will burrow him deep in American society until one day he will be so far inside the enemies' gates, so deeply ingrained in their culture that no one suspect, and then he will strike for us. He will be like cancer that invaded the American body. Nothing will be able to stop him from spreading. Timing need be perfect. We get one chance. Understand?" Aziz asked.

Aman's shoulders slumped, and he let out an exasperated sigh. He nodded his understanding. He trusted his handlers implicitly, and Aziz certainly appeared to believe in this plan, but Aman had been hoping for something quicker. Can this actually work? Raise a boy to infiltrate America? But to what end? How much damage could he inflict? Aman thought the racial strife currently engulfing America was something that could be better used to their advantage. If they assassinated one of the American Negro Civil Rights leaders, it could lead to rioting in the streets. This seemed like the perfect solution to him. If that happened even the charisma of their President would not be able to keep the county from tearing itself apart. All that was needed was a light to start the fire, and he could provide it. *If they would only give me the go ahead I will make it happen.*

"You believe this can work?" Aman asked in disbelief.

"Have faith, Aman. We know what we doing. Cairo is our home. America is yours for the moment. The boys we selected are young, but perfect. In time they be ready, and so will you. We will be in touch." Aziz motioned for Aman to leave.

"Honestly, Aziz. This country is full of strife right now. Racial riots. It can be exploited with ease. I have the means to strike a blow," Aman blurted out his skepticism.

Aziz became angry for the first time. "You have been in this country twenty years and you already think like them. Short term only. It will never work," Aziz then switched to Arabic. "Patience. Remember Sun Tzu? *It is because of disposition that a victorious general is able to make his people fight with the effect of pent-up waters which, suddenly released, plunge into a bottomless abyss.* Remember him. Our waters are not yet pent up. When the dam is full and the waters ready, then and only then, we will plunge the U.S. into that abyss. Until then, patience!"

Chapter 16
Present Day, Las Vegas

Solomon stood in the hotel room, staring at the massive girth of the dead body sprawled across the floor. He locked the door to prevent any curious hotel guests from interrupting him. He estimated he could stay two to three minutes before hotel security, and eventually the cops both arrived on the scene. He assumed one of the other guests was currently calling the front desk in a panic. When he heard the shots as he sprinted down the stairs he feared the worst. He knew his man had a silenced weapon, and a loud gunshot could only mean that someone else was there. He performed a quick search of the room that yielded nothing. There was no more he could do, so he grabbed Shakir's wallet from his pants and headed out. The longer it took the police to identify the body, the better off Solomon would be.

At least he knew he could stop killing people, he thought as he jogged across the hallway and down the stairs. A quick phone call would allow him to find out the name of the person that the hotel room was listed under. Reaching the bottom of the stairs, Solomon purposefully pushed through the emergency exit door that set off the fire alarms. He wanted to create as much confusion as possible.

He stepped gingerly into the concrete jungle of the alleyway, cautiously stepping over a homeless drunk who was sitting in his own urine. He had a flash of inspiration and tossed Shakir's wallet onto the sleeping man's stomach. Solomon glanced towards the street where a hooker in a tight black mini-skirt and fishnet stockings stood with her back to him, attempting to sell her goods to the steady stream of humanity strolling the sidewalks. The smell of marijuana was heavy in the enclosed air of the alley. The alarm continued its merciless clanging as he walked purposefully down the alley, past the surprised hooker, and then crossed Las Vegas Boulevard and waltzed into the Desert Dust Inn. He needed to talk to the boss immediately. As he walked into the freezing air of the casino he dialed Gregor's cell phone to update him on the situation.

***

The Toyota 4Runner cruised down the freeway at seventy-five miles per hour, heading northwest on the I-95 highway that ran along the Arizona-California-Nevada border. It would eventually lead to Reno, "the biggest little city in the world," as the local government liked to call it. Alex glanced back at the diminishing landscape of Las Vegas. The sun was beginning to lose its strength, and in less than an hour it would be nightfall. It had been twenty minutes since they left Las Vegas, and the woman had yet to say a word. She just concentrated on the road, constantly checking her mirrors, presumably watching for anyone who might be trailing them.

"You want to talk now? I've been watching. I don't think anyone is following us. I need to know what I've gotten myself into," Alex said. The silence was beginning to eat away at him.

"Not now, Alex. Give me an hour to get further away from Vegas. Then we can talk. By the way, I'll be the one to decide when we are in the clear. Just because you were accepted in to the CIA doesn't mean you know jack shit about surveillance. Leave that to me," the woman said with an edge to her voice. At least he could assume she was a CIA agent. How else would she know he had just been hired?

"Can you at least tell me where we're going Ms..?" he asked. Alex still did not know her name.

"You can call me Marilyn. We're going to Reno. It's about seven hours away. Now shut up and give me an hour of silence. Take a nap if you can. I can't guarantee you'll be getting much sleep any time soon."

Alex decided it would be best to obey, so he propped his head up against the glass of the passenger side window, closed his eyes, and wondered how he was going to explain his disappearance to Michael.

***

Aman was back at his desk after a long day on the golf course with the President-Elect. Zachariah Hardin was on the floor below, and Aman had dictated strict instructions to the Secret Service to not allow any women into the room, regardless of what Zach told them to do. His male cravings were causing enough problems. The one positive aspect about Aman's current situation was that, at the moment, he had more control over the Secret Service agents than Zach. As Zach's main confidant, adoptive father, and campaign manager, he still wielded the power over safety issues. The President-Elect was on the verge of limitless power, but technically remained powerless for at least the next few weeks. For now, Aman could tell the agents what to do without worrying about being overruled. The cell phone on his hand-crafted oak desk came to life. Only Solomon and Gregor had the number.

"Yes?" Aman said hastily.

"I'm on the first floor. I'm coming up," Solomon replied.

"You have news?"

"Of a sort. If anyone else is with you, send them away." The phone went dead in Aman's ear. Solomon was his usually chatty self. Hopefully he would have good news to share.

"Where's the horn dog?" The American slang sounded strange when combined with Solomon's slight accent. He looked at the haggard figure of Aman, slumped in his chair. A day of golf and the old man looked exhausted. Solomon wished he would get a little exercise once in a while. If the boss died he was not sure he would be able to keep his job. He knew Aman was merely a front man for someone, and any decisions after he was dead would probably come from somewhere in the Middle East.

"Zach is in a suite below us. I've given the agents strict orders not to allow any women in the room."

"Good. I don't want to have to track down any more incriminating photos. The last twenty four hours have not been enjoyable."

"What do you have for me?" Aman ignored the quip about the photos. He never told Solomon exactly what the stripper had photographed with her cell phone; only that it needed to be recovered.

Solomon gave him the run down of what happened while Aman was at the golf course. He ended with the incident across the street at the Imperial Palace. Aman listened intently, it was not exactly the news he wanted to hear, but things were improving somewhat.

"At least there will be no more deaths besides the girl and her accomplice. The press is already crawling all over this city looking for any trouble they can find. They may love Zach now, but they're fickle. It wouldn't take much for the jackals to turn on him if those photos ended up in the wrong hands. What's our next move then?"

"I called Gregor and gave him instructions, as well as a description of this Alex Bryce that the room was registered under. We need to run this guy's name by your sources. See if he is a government agent. I would assume he is the lady's partner. I have as many people as we can spare watching the hotels and airport, but I would bet they have already left the city."

"You still have not solved the problem yet." Aman did not hide his annoyance. If they were already out of the city, the chances of catching them without drawing attention to themselves grew exceedingly more difficult.

"They can't get out at Vegas's airport. I have men crawling all over that place. I called Gregor right before I told you I was coming up. He has already checked things out at the Imperial Palace and found out that a man and a woman matching our quarry were seen sprinting out of the hotel and into an SUV.

"Where do you think they are heading?"

"Reno most likely. That's the closest airport. And your organization is not as strong there. I'm going to charter your plane to Reno and see if I can find them myself. Gregor is putting out some calls to the few men you keep in Reno to advise them of the situation and what to watch for. He'll also have a license plate number for their car as soon as they let him in to view the security cameras of the Palace's valet area. One good thing about Las Vegas, cameras are everywhere."

"Fine. Now get out of here. I'll call our flight boys and make sure they have the plane ready for you." Aman's pudgy right hand grabbed the phone on his desk while his left motioned for Solomon to leave. He poured himself a drink after making a call to the airport crew. He would update Zach on the situation after finishing his drink. If Solomon recovered the phone, he would have to consider having him permanently dealt with. He hated the idea of doing it, but he could not risk Solomon seeing what the woman stole. It would be the ultimate blackmail tool.

***

Somewhere Between Reno and Las Vegas

Alex stared straight ahead at the never-ending expanse of concrete freeway lit up by the SUV's headlights and continued trying to wrap his mind around what was happening to him. He was unable to obey the woman's earlier command to sleep. Looking down, he noticed for the first time that he still had a vice grip on the pistol he picked up off the hotel floor at the woman's request. He loosened his grip and his body uncoiled, finally releasing some of the tension from the last few hours.

"I was beginning to think that you would never give it up. I thought I would have to use the jaws of life to get that gun out of your hand," the woman said with a smirk.

Alex thought the joke sounded more like a critique than an attempt at humor. "I hope you are a better spy than you are a comedian." He shot her a look of disgust, and noticed for the first time that she had cut her hair. He mentally scolded himself for not noticing it immediately.

The slight alteration made a huge difference in her appearance.

"I am," was her only reply. "We appear to be clear. I don't believe anyone is following us. That could be very good or very bad news," she said matter-of-factly.

"What are you talking about? I thought this was some sort of training." Alex still held out a faint hope that the blood spilled back in his hotel room was fake, and this was all a charade.

"The man you saw in the hallway outside your hotel room, was he about five foot eight, pale skin, with shaggy black hair; weighing, say, 185 pounds give or take?"

"Yes, that's probably a good description."

"That's Solomon. He's good. He picked you up outside the MGM, and followed you back to your hotel."

"And what about you?" Alex asked with trepidation.

"I've been keeping tabs on you ever since I dropped the phone on you in the airport. I've been your guardian angel."

"Are you telling me this is not a training exercise?" Alex was now desperate for a concrete answer.

"It's not a training exercise. You were my secret safety valve. Your trip out here coincided perfectly with a secret op I'm running."

Alex sucked in air. His thoughts turned back to his two friends. "If this is real then they probably saw me with my friends." He stared out the window at the shadow of the desert, too afraid to admit the obvious.

"They are surely dead. I'm sorry. I know this sounds cold, but you're going to have to try to forget about them for the moment. There will be time for grieving later, assuming you live." She was quiet for a few seconds before continuing. "I know all about your background, Alex. The case you worked on in Indianapolis could be helpful in your new job. That is assuming we get out of this alive," she said with a resolute tone.

"Okay," he whispered meekly, accepting his fate. He was numb from the realization of his friends' probable murder. "Aren't you going to tell me what is so important about that phone?" He gestured towards the pocket he saw her put it in.

"Not now. When you need to know something, I'll tell you. For now, let's just say that what is in this cell phone could cause our President-Elect a lot of bad publicity. It could end his term before it has even begun, if it's what I think it is."

"That doesn't exactly give me a whole lot to go by. For all I know, you could be lying and be some sort of rogue agent," Alex replied. He was beginning to wonder if he should try to escape now. But what could he do? He glanced at the pistol he dropped on the floor.

"If I thought you believed that, you'd already be dead. If something happens to me and you somehow survive just try and reach Sean Hill at the FBI. Tell him you are reporting in for Marilyn, and I guarantee he will take your call, no questions asked." She stole a glance at him to see if he was taking her seriously. "Also, don't even think about trying to grab the gun and get away either." She waved a disapproving finger in his direction, and he cringed at her ability to read him so easily.

"Why can't we just stop off at the nearest pay phone and call this friend of yours. This whole thing seems like a lot of unnecessary work to me. Driving all over Nevada. Why can't they just swoop in and get us?" It seemed simple as far as Alex was concerned.

She gripped the steering wheel with annoyance. "My investigation involves Zachariah Hardin. The President-Elect or someone close to him may have an informant somewhere in the U.S. government. I've been digging into Mr. Hardin's past, and someone does not seem to like it. Trying to call in will probably get us killed. I tried to email the picture using the phone, but the piece of shit isn't working. It's probably safest for me to deliver it by hand. Besides the picture is just one piece of the puzzle. I need some additional information before we take it to the next level."

Alex suddenly thought of something. "I thought you said you worked for the CIA? But this Sean Hill works for the FBI? Since when do you run joint operations? I know you're both very protective of your respective turfs and I know that by law, the CIA is not supposed to run operations on American soil," he continued to think out loud.

She nodded her approval, and a smile of satisfaction spread across her face, softening her jaw line for a brief moment. "Good to see you are paying close attention. This was a one of a kind operation. Special permission was granted. I'll tell you a few basics about the operation because I need you to trust me," she said cautiously. Alex's behavior was one other unknown now added to the mix, and she knew his attitude could be the difference between survival and death. "I can fully understand why you might think it would be safer for you to abandon me, considering you have already seen me kill someone. But you won't last long without me. What do you think? Can I count on you to behave?"

Alex bit his nails and looked down at the floor of the vehicle. "I don't think I have any other option at the moment. It appears you saved my life though," he replied hesitantly.

"Not a ringing endorsement, but I'll take it." She decided to try and encourage her new partner by getting him thinking. "Now, tell me what you know about Zachariah Hardin. Every detail you can recall from his life story that you've heard."

Feeling like a college student being called out in front of the class, Alex began reciting everything he could remember about Zachariah Hardin. "Let's see. He's forty-four, Senator from Nevada. He's the first naturalized citizen to be elected president. His wife died about a year ago from cancer. I think this was either his third or fourth term as senator. Is that the kind of info you had in mind?

"That's fine, but tell me about his childhood. Do you remember anything about it?" She continued prodding him.

"Sure. I must have heard it a hundred times. The press loves to talk about it. He was orphaned in Cairo before being adopted by Aman when he was a teenager, and brought to the U.S. He was raised in Vegas."

"What about his real parents?" She interrupted him

again.

"His father was Egyptian. Mother was European. Was she from Spain?"

"She was French. How did his real parents die?"

Alex hesitated for a moment. He read it somewhere but could not pull the information out of the recesses of his mind. "They died early I think. I know he says he barely remembers them.

"They supposedly died during the Six-Day War of 1967," she answered for him.

"You don't believe it?" Alex could not hide his surprise.

"I'm skeptical, by nature. Just leave it at that. Continue please. He was brought back to Las Vegas. What happened from there?"

"Everyone knows that. He does great in high school. Earns a scholarship to Yale. Becomes class president. Undergrad was in political science. Then he gets a master's in international relations and heads back to Nevada and becomes a congressman, then senator, and now the ultimate prize. Is that it?"

"Yeah, the classic rags to riches story. Do you remember who led the charge to amend the constitution in the mid-nineties?" She asked as her eyes continued to roam back and forth among the road ahead, her rear view mirror, and Alex.

"Mr. Hardin did," Alex responded. He remembered the time period because he had just started law school and got married. The world seemed much safer to him then. The peace dividend of the 1990s brought along by the collapse of the Soviet Union lulled him into thinking the world was changed for the better. He thought about the arguments of the time when Zachariah Hardin first began extolling the virtues of amending the constitution. *After all, were they not a country of immigrants? Was not everyone, or at least their ancestors from a different land? The time for change had come, and they needed to stop the lingering discrimination that prevented foreign-born citizens from becoming President.* He had no problem with the argument, and still thought it made sense. He remembered those days as a rare

89

time for the nation to come together. Both political parties believed they could benefit from the change, so it was pushed through the Congress. The citizens followed suit, and a rare amendment to the constitution was agreed upon in 1995, and quickly ratified by the states.

"You got it. He also made a vow to not run for President for at least twenty years in order to prove that he would not take advantage of the new law *he* helped to push through. Remember that?"

"Oh, yeah. He claimed he didn't want to run this soon, but he was drafted by other members of his party who pushed him into it. He certainly has an ego, but there is nothing illegal about that. Where are you going with this?" Alex asked.

She hesitated before answering. "Okay, here's the problem. It's the FBI's job to investigate everyone who runs for public office in Washington. I consider it to be one of their more important jobs. Most people who run for office in D.C. are after one thing, and that's power. However, if they have too many skeletons in their closets, they are easily twisted and used by their enemies. For a congressman, that may not be a big deal. They're all corrupt anyway." She left no room for debate on the subject. "So what if one of them gets some money added onto a bill that can be sent back to their hometown, and wasted on some bridge or historical monument. Right?"

She looked at Alex who nodded in agreement. Then she continued, "But what if it's a congressman or senator sitting on a powerful committee like the Armed Forces or Intelligence Committee? Those individuals often have access to some of the same information the president has, and they normally have bigger mouths. Every senator, whether they admit it or not, wants to be president, and they all think they can do it better than whomever the current office holder is. So they show off their knowledge to someone they shouldn't, and before you know it, someone overseas is dead because of their big mouth."

"You don't trust him to keep certain things private regarding CIA activities?" Alex asked.

"No, I don't. But that's only part of it. Let's just say I am uneasy with the prospect of him becoming Commander in Chief."

"Why?" he asked. She was still dancing around the question, and it was becoming tiresome.

"The problem with Mr. Hardin is that it has been nearly impossible to find out anything about his childhood in Egypt. When they pushed through the amendment, no one thought about how difficult it would be to do background checks on candidates like him. A lot of these countries have not kept very good records of deaths, births, and things of that nature. The FBI likes to employ a full cavity search when they look into the backgrounds of candidates. With Hardin, they were hitting a dead end. He was not brought to the States until he was a teenager. We know nothing about his parents or childhood in Cairo. That's where I was brought into the picture due to my..." She tried to decide how to word her next statement. "Due to my previous experience with Cairo. With Mr. Hardin, it's not what I know, but what I don't know that scares me."

Alex stared at the snow that was beginning to filter down from the mountains in the distance. The western scenery was beginning the rapid change that it was known for. He never realized the FBI did background checks, but it made sense. The question now was who was after her, and now him? Whoever they were, they were willing to kill, and that meant they were in the big leagues. Staring out the window into the final moments of daylight, the silhouette of the mountain range was splashed with the rays of the setting sun, giving the final seconds of daylight a religious feeling. The glorious sight soon vanished, and his mind mirrored the blackness around him. His thoughts turned back to his friends. Could they possibly be alive? He knew it was next to impossible. He said a silent prayer for their souls before closing his eyes once more in a vain attempt at sleep.

Chapter 17

The two Secret Service agents standing guard motioned Aman through with only a cursory wave. He was the only person who could see the President-Elect without being meticulously searched. Aman gave them both a fake smile before slamming the door shut, leaving them to guard the entryway to the hotel suite. Aman knew they called him the Teflon Arab-Don, in honor of John Gotti, behind his back because he managed to avoid being arrested when Las Vegas was purged of the mob during the 1960s and 1970s. The FBI came up empty during its investigations of the only Arab casino owner. He used that fact on a regular basis whenever someone hinted that he might not be a legitimate businessman.

Aman found Zach sprawled out on a dark leather sofa, watching the news. Aman felt a twinge of jealously looking at his forty-two year old adoptive son, at the zenith of power, and about to accomplish all the goals his predecessors had set out so many years before. Zachariah was still wearing his golf outfit, and did not appear to have taken a shower. He immediately sat up as Aman came into the hotel suite.

"Any news, boss?" He had been Aman's student and adoptive son for so long he still could not shake the tendency of speaking to Aman as a protégé, instead of as a man about to become the leader of the free world.

"Solomon found the woman, but she has escaped with an accomplice of some sort. The good news is no more killings. Solomon is trying to tie up the loose ends now. Let's just leave it at that. Have you been going over your little speech you have to give tomorrow?"

"Yes, but Aman, can we keep the meet and greet to a minimum? I'm exhausted. Between the last few months of campaigning, putting together a transition team, and choosing members of the Cabinet, I am beat. I need some rest."

"I know, but we have to keep the media honeymoon going as long as possible. The only way we do that is letting them have access to you. We can't have them snooping around now that we are this close. Besides, in a few weeks it will all be over, and we won't have to worry about what anyone thinks anymore."

"Yes, but I'm tired of this charade. It has gone on for far too long, and we are so close." Zach stood up. The exhausted figure that was lying on the couch just seconds earlier was now animated. "I'm ready to finally unleash our presence on the world. The name Bin Laden will be a mere footnote when I'm done," he said as he pounded the coffee table to finalize his point.

"Keep your voice down you fool. What if you slip up when one of those agents is in the room? We both know damn well they despise us. I don't trust them. I will feel much safer when we get back to Washington and you are protected by Jamal."

Aman was testy and nervous, and the mention of Bin Laden caused a vein of tension to appear on his forehead. Bin Laden was a fool. He was charismatic, but like so many of his type he was too impatient, and eager to strike at the West anyway he could. The day of 10/1/00 was etched in Aman's memory. Bin Laden's little assault almost ruined their chances at reaching the point they were now at. Aman had been petrified that after the attacks someone would start investigating backgrounds, and lock up Arabs the way the Japanese were rounded up after Pearl Harbor.

He was grateful for the short attention span of the Americans. No one even called to interview him about the attack. During the early months after the attacks Zach played his part as senator perfectly. He supported the strike in Afghanistan that was launched by the outgoing president, but quickly denounced the invasion of Iraq ordered by President Gray a few years later. It was a bold move at the time because most of his own party voted in favor of the assault. Zachariah understood the hatred between the Sunnis and the Shias, and knew that a bloody war was a high probability. When the blood began to spill soon thereafter it helped to turn his political fortunes golden. Zach appeared

93

tough when voting to eradicate the Taliban, and thoughtful as he denounced the Iraq War.

Zach chuckled, bringing Aman out of his reverie. "My own mentor, have you not learned to understand the American psyche after all these years? Yes, those men outside probably despise us, and they may not trust us, but their distrust for us is overtaken by their love for this wretched country. They revere the presidency even if they despise the office holder. I've beaten President Gray fair and square as they would say, and while they don't like it, they would never screw with that system. Their love for their country overrides everything else." He paused. "It will be their last mistake."

Chapter 18

The tiny, family-owned restaurant in the swanky Washington D.C. neighborhood of Georgetown was empty except for FBI Director Bret McMichael. The restaurant was situated between Glover Park and Wisconsin Avenue, only a few blocks from the vice-president's residence. It was tucked into a corner between two small one-way streets. The fact that he had never been here before told him how serious things were becoming. Bret's two bodyguards occupied the only other available table. The rest of the tables had chairs flipped upside down, resting on top of them. The sign on the front door of the café read "closed for fumigation." Bret thought the sign might hurt business, though he doubted the CIA Director was concerned about the profitability of his little safe house.

Their meeting scheduled for earlier in the day had been cancelled, and he received a cryptic call an hour ago to meet here for a discussion. He presumed Malcolm preferred meeting near his alma mater, which was not far away, but he was distressed that he had never heard of this place before. He thought he knew the locations of all Malcolm's safe houses. He made a mental note to castigate the people who were supposed to keep track of these places for him. Malcolm was crafty. Bret had to give him credit for that. The man had not been in the field for more than ten years, yet he still was operationally sound.

He just hoped Malcolm would have some new information that would make his decision a little easier. They were in uncharted territory, jointly investigating the President-Elect of the United States, and they were swapping field agents in the same manner George Steinbrenner swapped free agents for Bret's beloved Yankees. The number of laws they bent, or outright broke, was staggering, and he was desperately searching for a way out of his predicament. He fidgeted in his chair, sipped his water, and glanced around the room nervously. Where was that son of a bitch? He glanced at his watch. Malcolm loved to make you wait.

The two black Chevrolet Suburbans appeared from a side street just as Bret turned off his cell phone. They pulled up to the front of the café and three bodyguards jumped out of the first car, the CIA Director squeezed in the middle of them like a Hollywood star trying to avoid being photographed by the paparazzi. Two of the three remained at the outside entrance while the last one escorted Malcolm Ray into the café. One of the vehicles disappeared. Bret watched with amusement. He knew it would be heading around to the back entrance to make sure no trouble originated there. The CIA Director sat down and waved his guard away, indicating for him to go chat with Bret's men on the other end of the eatery.

"I've never been to this place before," Bret said in greeting. He did not try to hide his annoyance with Malcolm's tardiness.

"It's an old college hang out of mine. The owner and I go way back," Malcolm Ray responded. Bret smirked at the comment, assuming this meant Malcolm owned the place.

"Mind if I smoke?" Bret asked. "It's been a long day."

"Be my guest." Normally Malcolm would not allow it here, but he wanted Bret to be as relaxed as possible. He preferred his friends and his adversaries, of which Bret could often be both, to be cooperative, and the best way to achieve that was to allow the man his vice. Malcolm detested cigarettes, he tried them along with alcohol in college, and had sworn off both ever since. Washington D.C. was a weak city, and by allowing his opponents to indulge their bad habits he discovered they would normally make some small mistake, and provide him with a piece of information they should not have let slip. Malcolm eased his five foot ten frame into the chair directly across from the FBI Director. Malcolm's only addiction was the hour-long workout sessions he put his body through every day at his personal gym at CIA headquarters. It was another habit he formed in college. He found his mind worked best when his body was operating at peak capacity. Everyone else in Washington seemed to think their top form included two double shots of bourbon, and a couple of smokes. He would never allow them to think otherwise.

Bret studied Malcolm's face to try and gauge his mood, but found the normal blank slate. They were complete opposites; Bret came from a blue-collar family in New York, while Malcolm grew up in the gangland areas of Los Angeles. "Sean got in touch with me earlier today. He's currently en route to Cairo. I understand your man finally came through for us." Bret attempted to needle the CIA Director. Malcolm ignored the comment, his cool demeanor always present.

"Colin is about as good as they come. That is why he's stationed in Cairo. I would say a twenty-hour turnaround is pretty good for government work. The only thing this city can get done in that time is order up a prostitute." Malcolm used to respect Bret's bulldog attitude. It was a throwback to the original G-man era of the FBI, and it was the reason he thought he could get Bret to go along with their operation.

It appeared that Bret's years in the Washington bureaucracy had taken their toll though, and he was having deep regrets about involving the FBI director. The current situation was a land mine waiting to blow up in their faces. Right now he was not sure what would be worse, their little investigation being discovered by the press, or their fears actually turning out to be true. Each option had a set of problems about which Malcolm was deeply concerned.

"Yes, I know. I appreciate the assistance." Bret did not like owing Malcolm Ray any favors, but the CIA's man in Cairo possessed a lot of helpful contacts.

"Any more news on my lady?" Malcolm asked, referring to Marilyn. He had not been given any information regarding her time in Vegas since Bret called him to inform him that she vanished. He was tired of being the last person to know, but it had been the only way to convince the FBI Director to agree to the operation.

"No. I'm beginning to fear the worst. No body has turned up yet though. I guess you can call that good news."

Malcolm nodded in silence. The comment was not worthy of a response. The flippant answer told him that Bret did not take the operation seriously. Malcolm began to wonder if Bret might be looking for a way out. A way out in Washington normally entailed using someone else's political carcass to shield you as you vanished from the room.

"If Mr. Hill picks up any useful information in Cairo I will need to know immediately. Understood?" Malcolm said with a slightly menacing tone.

"Of course. We're in this together, Malcolm."

"I just want to make sure you're not getting cold feet, Bret. I had a senator asking me some uncomfortable questions a few days ago. It made me think that perhaps someone was leaking information. I don't want this investigation blowing up in our collective faces," Malcolm said with disdain. He made sure his glare left no doubt that he was losing faith in Bret. "Those pricks in Congress are constantly looking for ways to curtail my supposed power." Malcolm's honeymoon with Congress after 10/1/00 only lasted a year before they were at his throat again. It had been just three years since the attacks, and the Beltway was already focusing more on his supposed abuses of power instead of the crazed terrorists who were still running free. Malcolm found it laughable that the CIA was so despised by much of Congress. At least they hated him until something terrible happened, and then the very same people would criticize him for not having the wherewithal to stop the attack.

One thing he learned quickly about Congress is that they always try to make what should be a simple problem as confusing as possible. Their latest issue with Malcolm and the Agency was the harsh interrogations he was utilizing. Congress spent two months after the attacks in New York lambasting him for not being tough enough. Now he was being told terrorist fanatics that broke every rule the civilized world ever made should be tried in open court like they were car thieves.

The Al-Qaeda types were either going to slit your throat, or die trying, there was no middle ground to stand on. He still remembered when he lost his first man in Afghanistan during the war against the Taliban. His man was killed during a prison uprising. A group of Al-Qaeda and Taliban prisoners had started a riot, and then tried to escape. They eventually became trapped in a basement with a stash of weapons, refusing to surrender.

The Afghan commander in the area sent in a humanitarian group to try to coerce them to surrender. The group was fired upon. Then they sent in the local mullahs to try to talk sense in to them. Once again failure. Then the Afghan commander got pissed off and he poured gasoline into the basement, setting it on fire, and burning some of them alive. The holdouts still refused to surrender. Only after a full day of pumping freezing water into the basement did they finally capitulate. How was he going to get this type of person to start talking without roughing him up a little? Malcolm knew the answer, and he would continue to enjoy breaking every foolish rule Congress tried to impose on him.

"I understand. Can I go now?" Bret asked. Malcolm motioned for him to leave, and a minute later he had the café to himself. He looked around at the politically themed decorations covering the walls. He hated to use this place for a meeting, but a substantive phone conversation with Bret was out of the question. He could not come back here for a long time. Espionage was a dangerous game, and the only way to win was to keep your choices, and the rules you played by, to a minimum. Events rarely played out as planned, but sometimes those surprises could become an advantage if you recognized your opportunity quickly. That time had come for Malcolm.

First he would retrieve the recordings from the previous evening. This particular café was one of the best ideas he ever had. It was right by Embassy Row, and there were all sorts of diplomats who stopped into the quiet little café for a "private meeting" that normally ended up on the desk of the CIA Director within a few days. It had been Malcolm's own idea; an idea he stole from one of his contacts when he was working undercover in the heart of Africa.

Chapter 19

Alex's eyes shot open. He took in his surroundings as his mind scrambled to remember the events of the past few hours. He surveyed the room; it had three wood paneled walls that gave it the feel of a rustic cabin. The strange woman who was responsible for his current predicament was seated next to the sliding glass door, overlooking a royal blue, tranquil Lake Tahoe and the snow capped mountains enclosing it on all sides. In another time he could see this being an enjoyable moment. Unfortunately, there was someone who wanted both of them dead creeping closer to them with each passing hour.

They drove through South Lake Tahoe and the Heavenly Village last night. The little town at the bottom of the mountain was like a village from Old Europe, only instead of serving the local townspeople, it catered to tourists. At this time of year those tourists consisted of thousands of skiers and snowboarders who crowded into the surrounding lodges and hotels to ski at the numerous resorts that straddled the California-Nevada border. Alex and his companion were now less than an hour from the Reno airport. Their journey across the western border of Nevada had transpired without a hitch until they approached to within a few miles of South Lake Tahoe. It was there that the night turned bloody. They had stopped for gas in the early morning hours, and the woman spotted someone tailing them.

A lone man huddled in a sedan was watching the gas station from an empty motel parking lot across the street. The woman had been right. Alex remembered her warning him that there were probably vehicles camped out near gas stations all along their route, waiting for the inevitable fill of the gas tank. She then gave Alex a quick summary of her plan to try to fool them. Their pursuers would be expecting her to rush to Reno as quickly as possible, but she decided on a more risky course of action. She would take the initiative and become the aggressor.

"Alex, we've got our first problem so keep quiet and do nothing unless I tell you." He remembered the stern voice giving him the orders. Pulling out onto the two-lane mountain road, she glanced in her mirror as the other vehicle's lights came to life, and pulled out onto the road at a casual pace. She suddenly floored the gas, and after twenty minutes of dangerous driving on the dark mountain road she decided she had created enough distance between her car and the stalker's vehicle. On the outskirts of the small town, she spotted a secluded lodge sitting along the lakefront. She wrenched the steering wheel to the left, pulling the bulky SUV into the lodge's parking lot that was hidden from the street by massive pine trees that seemed to be the size of redwoods. She hurried inside, instructing Alex to remain in the vehicle.

It was easy to secure a room at the late hour. The New Year's crowds had vacated the mountain a few days earlier. The building housed eight comfortable condos, of which only five were occupied. Marilyn explained to the manager that her new husband had come down with a virus, and they needed rest before they could drive the rest of the way to the Reno airport.

Alex remembered her yanking open the passenger door, pulling him out, and quietly instructing him to lean against her. She explained their cover story briefly as the manager's figure appeared from the dimly lit front office. He motioned them to follow, and led them around the west side to the back of the lodge. He unlocked the sliding glass door and ushered them in. The old manager graciously made his exit, informing his guests that he would be going to bed. She immediately pulled the curtains, blocking the moonlight that was reflecting off the lake.

***

"Alex, sit in the corner there. Keep that gun out and ready. I'll be back in a few seconds. I'll knock four times, otherwise fire away and start screaming for the FBI if I die. I think I saw our friends' lights coming down the road." She disappeared out the glass door, her shadow heading the opposite direction from which they had made their way to the room.

Marilyn peeked around the corner of the building. The man had arrived. His car sat right behind hers, blocking her into the parking space. It was almost five a.m., and the first glimpse of the western day was beginning to creep out from the darkness, providing her with some additional sight. She silently cursed to herself. The man found them quicker than she expected. She hoped he would have spent more time checking the other lodges they passed. Her silenced pistol touched her leg, the weapon providing some comfort as the fingers of her right hand loosely held the gun, ready to spring into action at a moment's notice.

She cautiously made her way along the front of the building, stepping gingerly to avoid slipping on the numerous patches of ice that dotted the walkway. She was grateful for the small windows and lack of lighting along the front of the building. As she approached the corner of the darkened office once again, she stopped and listened. Hearing nothing, she slowly peered around the corner and saw her stalker. His back was to her, and he was doing the same thing she was; hunting his target. She brought her left hand up to assist with the grip on her weapon. She saw his hand reach for the cell phone attached to his belt, but then he stopped.

Having apparently changed his mind, he vanished around the back of the lodge. She dashed down the side of the building after him, approaching the entrance to her room. The man was an amateur. She recognized him from the party a few nights earlier. She stuck her head around the corner, and watched as he fiddled with the door, seeing if it would open. His hands were trembling from either nerves or the cold and the idiot was not even wearing gloves. *He must be trying to bag us himself and get some extra money out of it.* Marilyn leveled her silenced Sig P225 pistol, and stepped away from the side of the building, revealing herself to the familiar face from a few nights before.

She preferred the Swiss pistol because it could be carried without having any safety devices to worry about turning off. She stepped into the stalker's line of view. Her movements were graceful and smooth. Her left eye squinted as she fluidly lined up the front sight of her pistol between the two rear sights and fired one perfectly placed shot into the man's shoulder. He dropped his weapon on to the cold concrete. Before he could react, she lowered the target sights and blew out his kneecap with another bullet. He fell to the ground. She dashed over to the man. Just as he started to scream in pain, she kicked him across the face, silencing him into a groggy, semi-conscious state. She picked up the empty shell casings off the ground, grabbed the man's weapon, and knocked on the door four times.

Alex opened the door, scared, but not surprised as she dragged the man's limp body over the threshold as if it was a wild animal she had just slaughtered and brought home for dinner. He found the situation fairly emasculating even though he knew he should not. She was clearly a professional.

"Is he dead?" Alex asked. He stared at the man dressed in black skiwear lying spread eagled on the thick bearskin rug in front of the fireplace. He half-laughed at the ridiculous sight in front of him.

"No, but keep that gun trained on him for a second." She stuck her head outside and listened. No one else seemed to be disturbed, and no new lights had been turned on. She shut the door, locked it, and closed the blinds for the second time in the last hour. "Let me find something to tie him up with, and then I'll wake him to see if he is willing to answer some questions."

"What about his wounds?" Alex asked.

"Get some towels and wrap them up. We don't want to get blood on these nice hardwood floors."

Alex grabbed some towels from the bathroom, and wrapped the man's knee and shoulder as best he could. Marilyn bound his hands together with one of the bed sheets, grabbed a chair, and began gently slapping him across the face until his eyes began to flutter, signaling his return from dreamland.

"There you go," she said sarcastically, as if praising a child. "Can you hear me?" The man groggily nodded an affirmative. "Good, can you talk?"

"Yes." The word was barely audible.

"Excellent, because if you want to live, you'll answer all my questions. Now, we can do this quickly or slowly. I normally prefer the slow way, but my guess would be that you will not." The clear threat was relayed without the slightest rise in her seductive voice. Alex stood and watched from the corner of the room, out of sight of the helpless man.

"Did you call in our position before getting here?" She ran the barrel of the silenced weapon across his face, letting the tip of the weapon hover over his mouth. He shook his head in the negative.

"Use it or lose it. I want to hear your voice. I barely heard you before," she said as she moved the weapon away from his face.

"No," he said in accented English.

"That's better. I've seen you before. What's your name?" The man hesitated and the barrel of the pistol came to a rest so that it was pointed at the man's one good knee. "If you want to be able to walk again you better start cooperating. I don't have much patience, and there is a big lake out there with plenty of fish waiting for a meal." She made a casual gesture toward the glass doors, and the serene lake beyond them.

"Hussein Kmal," he blurted out as he squirmed. Beads of sweat were already starting to form on his forehead.

"Thank you, Hussein. You remember me, don't you? We met a few nights ago when I was with your boss's friend. I seem to remember you were supposed to be handing out drinks, but instead you spent the majority of the night staring at my cleavage." As she talked she grabbed a chair with one hand, placing it over his stomach so he was pinned to the ground. She sat down with her stomach facing the back of the chair. She tipped the chair forward, balancing it on two legs, and leaned closer to his face so he could have another view of her chest. "I don't think Allah would approve of your gawking."

When he remained silent she continued. "I know you don't approve. You can admit it. I know you are a good Muslim. It's an admirable trait. I watched you during the party while your friends were pounding shots. You just sat quietly and watched all night. They probably all got laid that night. What about you?"

"You are nothing but a filthy whore used by a politician," he spat out the words.

"Well, that I may be. But I'm an infidel, so what can you expect. You are a strong man of Allah who has only been in the States for a few years, and you are already blinded by the decadence of America."

"Fuck you. I have been true to my faith for years."

"Then why spend time in America, the worst of the worst? How long have you been here now?"

"Six years. I hate it all the time."

"Why are you in Tahoe?" Marilyn asked. She needed to get back on track. He hesitated, so she brought her pistol to bear on him again. He quickly started stammering.

"The boss send me here few days ago along with friends to relax. The boss has small mosque in the mountains. I go. Pray all day."

Without warning, she pistol-whipped him across the face. "Stop stalling and answer my question!"

104

"We get call at mosque to head out and stay near gas stations. Boss's man tell us to watch for silver SUV with you and a man. He offer us much money if we kill you." He spoke in a rapid manner to avoid being struck again.

"Kill me or capture me?" Marilyn asked. She wanted to be sure.

"He said whichever is easiest."

"Why does he want me dead?"

"I don't know. He just told us what to do and we obey."

"What do you do in Aman's organization?"

"Nothing. I provide security at his hotel. I'm a student. My father send me here to study."

"Where are you from?"

"Cairo."

"What else were you brought over to do?" She asked as she continued to gently rock the chair, moving it in unison with the pistol twirling around her finger.

"Nothing. Just study."

"I find that hard to believe. I've never trusted Aman. The kids he recruits, like you, always seem to vanish after they are done with their schooling. Are they still in the U.S. hiding out, or do they head back to Cairo to plan a bombing?" She decided it was time to push some buttons to see if she could get him mad.

"Aman is no help to the cause of Muslims. He has done nothing his entire life but make dollars and be involved with American politics. The man is an apostate. He is like the Saudi rulers. I would still be in Cairo if not for my father. He forced me to come." His eyes fluttered and his head moved from side to side, trying to avoid the constant blaze of her stare.

"I find it interesting that you equate bombings with helping the cause of Muslims. Enough of the lies, Hussein. What's your boss up to? Why is he after me? All I did was sleep with his son. That doesn't warrant a death sentence. At least not in my country." She watched as Hussein gritted his teeth, his cheekbones protruding as if he was steeling himself for a beating he knew was inevitable. She knew it was a sign he was hiding something of consequence.

105

"I swear..." He tried to finish, but was cut off.

"No more. What's your boss up to? This is your last chance." She leveled the gun at his chest.

***

Hussein looked up at the infidel woman pinning him to the floor with her chair. The pain from his wounds was beginning to ratchet upwards due to his prone position on the floor. He now regretted not calling in his position when he had the opportunity. He thought he could take her. Now he realized it was probably the last mistake he would ever make. He would die for the cause. It was something he did not think was possible when his father first told him he was being sent to the United States.

Hussein knew his father financed some of the martyrs in the Middle East, but he had always been kept on the periphery, never allowed to participate for fear of making him a target of their enemies. He was raised in Egypt the first twenty years of his life, and subjected to the regimen of prayer six times a day. The strict adherence to his religion instilled in him a respect for his father. It also created in him a strong desire to do more for the cause of Islam. Before he could have his moment though, his father packed him off to the U.S. to stay with Aman and go to school in America. It also kept him as far away as possible from the action.

Until a few days ago, he thought Aman was just another Muslim selling his soul to the American political system. Then he received the phone call from Aman that changed his life. Aman was not a traitor, but a man who spent his entire life hiding in America. He was now ready to strike the ultimate blow against the West, and return the Muslim Caliphate to power.

"Are you going to answer my question or do you want me to put a hole in your head?" The woman asked him.

"I only answer to Allah. You will soon see him," Hussein said with conviction as he lurched forward, attempting to grab the gun out of the woman's hand. She brought the butt of the gun crashing onto his head, and then fired one round into his heart, bringing the conversation to an abrupt end.

***

Now sitting up in bed after the long night, Alex was simply glad to be alive. Hussein's body, which had been strewn on the floor when he fell asleep was now gone. He assumed it was at the bottom of the lake. His sleep deprived mind made the events of the previous hours seem like a bad dream, and for now he thought that would be a good way to keep things.

"You feel better?" Marilyn turned away from the window to face him, her ever-present gun tucked into her sculpted waistline.

"Yeah, I still don't know why we've been waiting around here for the last several hours. We should have headed straight to the airport. You are gonna get us killed." He had thrown a child-like temper tantrum after she killed Hussein last night, and was still perplexed that they had not moved from their current location.

"Shut up and trust me. If you want to shower, you have ten minutes. Then we're out of here." She had not told him that part of the reason she was lingering at the lodge was because she had left a special indicator in Las Vegas, which once discovered, would tell Malcolm where she was heading. She just hoped he would discover it in time.

Alex jumped out of bed. "How long have I been asleep?"

"Only a couple hours. It's 9:30. I've already talked with the manager and thanked him for his hospitality."

Alex hurried into the bathroom. As his head cleared, the danger of the situation ignited his adrenaline. He felt like he had lived a lifetime in the last twenty-four hours, and he could only guess what would be next. Looking down, he noticed that his gun was still in his hand. He slept with it under his pillow, and never relinquished his grip. The small piece of weaponry offered the slimmest bit of solace and protection in a new and dangerous world. *Am I really up to this way of life?* It was a question he hoped to live long enough to answer.

Chapter 20

Solomon sat in the Reno airport, sipping a poor imitation of French blended coffee sold at the airport café. He studied the local newspaper spread across the small table. He sat with his back to the wall so that anyone passing through the security area before proceeding to their flight would have to walk into his line of sight. Solomon was beginning to feel like a vagabond. His crumpled pants, and dress shirt clung to his body, but at least he was outside the stuffy cabin of the airplane. He arrived at the airport on Aman's private jet last night, and parked in the private hangar they rented with a few other wealthy patrons. He spent the first hour making phone calls, and setting up his dragnet to catch the woman who was causing them so much trouble.

His problem was that none of Aman's men knew anything about surveillance. They were either exchange students or muscle men, used to guarding the boss and his friends; or in the case of the students, doing whatever menial task Aman needed completed. Solomon never expected to run a full surveillance operation, and frankly, never thought it would be necessary.

He studied the sparse crowd as they hurried by. His targets still had not shown their faces. Taking another sip of coffee, he continued to ponder the situation, which was getting worse each passing hour. Solomon's analytical mind was beginning to assess the possibilities. He now wondered if Aman was divulging the full story to him. Several peculiarities continued to eat away at him. The fact that the woman had still not appeared at the airport validated his first instinct from early Friday morning at the Vegas airport. She was more than just a stripper. Otherwise they would have arrived at the airport last night, and already been caught by his men. If she was not a stripper looking for a score, then she was not digging for money or attention. This meant she was targeting him for another reason. The big question was "why?"

Aman called late last night and informed him that whoever the woman was, she was not an FBI employee. The database check and his contacts in Washington D.C. turned up no one at the FBI who resembled her. This new piece of evidence only served to muddy the already murky waters. Solomon immediately threw out the possibility of the National Security Agency or the Drug Enforcement Agency. The NSA would just spy with a satellite, and the DEA surely had no reason to come after Aman. After all, he never dealt in narcotics.

If she worked for the CIA she would be breaking every law in the book by operating inside the United States. Assuming for a moment she was CIA and was taking this monumental risk, Solomon could only assume that Aman was either withholding information from him or telling an outright lie. Even the spy agencies possess their share of risk adverse bureaucrats, and Solomon found it hard to believe that they would run an operation like this merely to obtain photos of the new President-Elect in a compromising sexual situation.

There were many less risky ways to obtain sound blackmail intel. Surely old J. Edgar Hoover had bequeathed some of his secret techniques to his followers, Solomon thought sarcastically. He could not find a reason why they would run the risk, unless the reward was worth the consequences. Getting caught in such an illegal operation would be devastating for all involved.

The other nagging concern for Solomon were the photos themselves. If they were *just* photos, why not involve the Secret Service in the hunt? There were plenty of agents in town. One order by Zach, and they would put the full force of the government behind the search. He suggested the idea to Aman, who immediately brushed it off with a few poor excuses about not wanting to bother them with Zach's personal issues. Solomon found the argument unconvincing, but did not pursue the matter. Whatever was going on, Aman was trying to keep it low-key. It could be simply vanity, and an attempt to avoid bad publicity at the start of an administration, but Solomon guessed it was something more sinister. If Aman found it necessary to lie to him, then

109

Solomon knew he would be seen as expendable at the end of the crisis. He went through the options before him, and formulated a plan of action for how to stay alive when, and if, he got his hands on this woman and her stolen treasure.

Chapter 21

Sean Hill stepped off the government plane, and into the stifling heat of the Egyptian desert. It was hotter than the worst summer day in Washington D.C., and he could not imagine ever being permanently posted to this region of the world. The local CIA station chief had a limousine waiting for him on the runway. As he assumed, the CIA officer chose to retain a low profile and did not meet him at the airport. Sean bounded down the stairs of the plane, and was immediately ushered into the air-conditioned comfort of the limousine waiting for him on the tarmac. He squeezed his large body into the back seat, his privileged status as a government official preventing his suitcase from having to pass through the routine check that all other visitors were normally subjected to.

The bulletproof limo exited the airport and headed towards the embassy with two Ford Explorers guarding the front and rear of the vehicle. Sean wiped the sweat off his brow, and stared absent-mindedly out the window. The vehicle merged onto the Sari Salah Salim Highway, heading southwest towards the American embassy. He received a brief email from Bret just before they touched down. There was still no word from Marilyn. The inauguration was only a few weeks away, and even if he found what he came to look for, it may be too late. Sean found it easier to think of her as her code name instead of her real name. Thinking of her as Marilyn helped him concentrate on the mission instead of dwelling on their friendship that had blossomed over the last several months. The sounds of blaring horns mixed with screams and yells caused him to look up and survey the highway in front of him.

"What's going on up there?" He asked the driver. The window separating the front and back of the limo was rolled down so they could communicate freely.

"Looks like a big accident, sir." The driver gently tapped the brake, and began to slow the speed of the limo. They were approaching a line of parked cars less than a mile in front of them. The highway was quickly becoming a parking lot. There were crowds of people hopping out of vehicles, gesturing wildly at each other, and at the other vehicles stopped in front of them.

Without warning the SUV on guard duty in front of him darted quickly to the right. It swerved off the freeway just before becoming trapped in the snarl of traffic up ahead. Sean's driver followed suit. He yanked the steering wheel too hard, and the vehicle shuddered before regaining its balance.

"Hope this guy knows where he's going," Sean muttered. He sat back in his seat as they exited the highway and merged onto Galam Al-Murur Street. He turned his attention to the road in front of him. It was quickly narrowing, and he stiffened as he watched the bustle of the local markets they were driving past. A mass of humanity was going about their daily lives, darting around the limousine with baskets full of goods to be sold or bartered. The limo's pace slowed to a crawl, and the close proximity of the crowds made Sean nervous. He was in a prime area to be attacked if some fanatic happened to be nearby. He flicked off the safety of his pistol just to be safe.

Five minutes later the street finally began to widen. The convoy of three vehicles increased their speed slightly. Sean watched the crowds, most of whom were gawking at his limousine, trying to see the important person that was surely inside. They were now on the outskirts of medieval Cairo, one of the oldest parts of the city. Sean stared in awe at the massive structure of the northern gate of Bab al-Futuh just in front and to the left of them. He thought it bore a resemblance to an ancient castle of a Scottish laird.

The driver suddenly pounded on the wheel in frustration, and Sean turned his attention back to the poor excuse for a road. There was another accident blocking the road in front of them. The vehicle in the lead turned left onto Al-Muiz Lidin Allah Street, heading towards the castle-like structure at which Sean was just staring. The driver of the lead vehicle made a mistake, and Sean instantly recognized the error. The dusty road was used more as a thoroughfare for market goers than as a street for cars. A hodgepodge of handcarts and donkeys blocked their path. The lead driver laid on his horn to try to scatter the crowd. It only served to anger them and make them more obstinate. The narrow road ran right through the massive gate of the castle, opening up on the other side. The construction reminded Sean of a tunnel built into a mountain.

Sean's driver braked to avoid getting too close to the lead security car as it did its best to part the sea of traffic. Suddenly, from somewhere inside the massive stone structure, Sean thought he heard what sounded like a revving motorcycle engine. The lead SUV finally scattered the crowd and entered the tunnel that ran through the middle of the medieval castle, heading in the direction of the revving noise. Dust flew up as tires from the three vehicles grinded into the dirt, obscuring the view. Sean thought the revving noise was growing louder. He peered into the darkness of the tunnel trying to locate the source of the noise.

Finally, he spotted it. A single light in the darkness bolted towards the lead car. Before he could finish his thought a massive explosion jolted his body. The Ford Explorer directly in front of him was a smoldering flame of twisted wreckage. The handlebars of a motorcycle were jammed into the shattered windshield. The limousine driver froze, staring at the entrance of the tunnel, unsure of his next step. Sean quickly turned around, and saw another motorcycle racing towards his vehicle. His driver hit the gas and roared into the tunnel in an attempt to escape. The hasty decision had them trapped inside with the wreckage of the lead vehicle partially blocking the exit. Sean thought there was just enough space between the wreckage and the wall of the tunnel to squeeze by.

"Floor it!" Sean yelled. They would need some momentum if they were going to blast past the flaming hulk. As the limousine shot forward it clipped the side of the burning wreckage, causing the smell of burning gas and charred flesh to engulf the interior of the vehicle. Sean gagged as he tried to yell at his driver. The limousine moved slightly, but not enough for them to fit through the narrow opening between the wreckage and the wall. The driver's side of the vehicle scraped against the wreckage, while the passenger side screeched as it rubbed against the side of the castle, shearing off metal like it was the dead skin of a snake. The sound of metal on metal was like fingers down a chalkboard.

"That was a bad idea," Sean said to himself. He knew they must free themselves quickly to avoid becoming an easy target. Sean turned his head around in time to see the second motorcycle approaching dangerously close to the rear security vehicle.

The timing of the attacks was slightly off, and the driver of the rear vehicle was given a few precious seconds to prepare. He swung the SUV into reverse, causing the motorcycle to clip the corner of the rear bumper instead of ramming directly into him. The corner of the vehicle erupted in flames, but it was not as spectacular as the first attack thanks to the driver's quick thinking. Sean watched as both the driver and passenger flung their doors open, rolling out in controlled spins before coming to a stop in an upright position. They were both on one knee and had their weapons drawn. There were four loud "pops" as one of the men fired into the burning figure that still clung to the motorcycle.

The suicide bomber's hands had been tied to the handlebars to prevent him from falling off his guided missile. If the dead suicide bomber had anymore explosives strapped to his chest he would not be able to set them off without the assistance of a beating heart. The two guards immediately began circling the area with their weapons, searching for another target. They stealthily walked forward with their backs to the entrance of the tunnel, using it like a third defender.

The screeching of metal continued as Sean's driver revved the engine, trying to escape the trap. Another motorcycle engine could be heard roaring from somewhere. "How many of these assholes are there?" Sean yelled as he popped the sunroof of the limousine open, and stood up so that his large torso was now outside of the vehicle. The motorcycle came into view amidst the wisps of the smoke from the wrecked vehicle. It was approximately fifty yards in front of him.

He steadied his Model 22 Glock pistol and fired off a forty caliber round at the oncoming figure. The figure was hidden by a hood and hunched over the handlebars, trying to minimize the target area at which Sean could shoot at. Just as Sean pulled the trigger the limo jerked forward, the driver still trying desperately to free the vehicle. The shot went wide and the empty shell from the fired round clattered across the roof of the vehicle before vanishing over the side.

Sean pounded on the roof of the car, "Take your foot off the fucking gas so I can shoot!" The driver eased up for a moment. The motorcycle was now only yards away. He had time for one more shot. Sean squinted through the smoke, methodically lined up the sights on his pistol, and fired several rounds in succession at the front tire. The wheel exploded from the direct hit and the suicide bomber was thrown into the air from the force of the explosion. As soon as the assailant thudded to the dirty ground Sean unleashed five more rounds into the man's chest, thumbed the release to empty the spent magazine, and slammed a new one into the butt of the pistol.

"Sir, are you okay?" The agents from the rear security car were cautiously approaching the back of the limousine while continuing to scan the area for potential targets. Sean turned around and spotted another hooded terrorist lying face down just a few feet behind his vehicle, blood oozing from a massive head wound.

"Yeah, I'm fine. Where did he come from?" Sean gestured to the dead body.

"Other side of the wreckage. He was the only one without a set of wheels."

"Thanks, let's get out of here. There could be more coming." Sean crawled out of the sunroof, and jumped onto the ground. "Driver! Floor it now so we can get out of here."

The limousine rocked back and forth, but was still unable to free itself. After a quick examination they discovered the back of the limo was entangled with the burning vehicle beside it. The three men lifted the rear of the vehicle just enough to free it from the wreckage before jumping across the trunk, and crawling down the open hole of the sunroof. They fell into the backseat, crashing to the floor of the limousine in an awkward tangle of arms and legs. The vehicle roared forward once again, finally tearing itself free and racing off towards the safety of the embassy.

"So much for keeping a low profile," Sean muttered in annoyance from the bottom of the human pile.

***

The "Deputy Chief of Cultural Affairs", otherwise known as the local CIA officer, had a tiny office unbecoming of his fake title. The office was in a private area in the back of the embassy, and it was protected by an extra set of Marine guards. The spit polished shoes of the guards could be heard clattering in unison on the tile floor outside the office Sean was sitting in. The guards were clearly on edge due to the attack on Sean's convoy. He sipped a bottle of Evian water and fidgeted in his chair. He was anxious for the CIA officer sitting across from him to finish up his phone call. The TV perched high and behind the CIA man was tuned to CNN.

The officer finally put the phone back on its cradle and sighed deeply to express his frustration. Colin Archer had been a field agent in the Middle East for twelve years, and the numerous contacts he nurtured in the area made him an invaluable asset to the Agency. Most of his contacts could only guess for whom he worked, and they were all kept off the agency's payroll and placated through special accounts he kept. He provided the agency with valuable intelligence, and he kept his informants to himself. This allowed the information flow to continue as long as he was around to pass it along. It also kept the desk jockeys' boxes full of useful intelligence. They knew however, that it would be cut

115

off if something happened to him. Colin controlled his own destiny, and this system provided him with extra job security. In a wild city like Cairo, Sean thought, the man was probably right to hedge his bets.

Sean Hill stared at the man across the desk. He could see why Colin was assigned to this region in the first place. His spectacles and goatee gave him the look of an aloof college professor, but he had a penetrating stare reminiscent of the imams who ran the mosques. A bad case of male pattern baldness had eradicated most of the black hair. His natural tan and underwhelming stature made it easy for Colin to blend in to the local population.

"You are certainly causing quite a ruckus already. Welcome to Cairo." Colin grabbed the remote control off his desk, put the television on mute, and propped his feet onto his desk in a casual manner.

"This is not what I needed," Sean replied. "We were trying to keep this low key but someone knew I was coming."

"Well, I can assure you there were no leaks on my end."

"We tried to keep knowledge of my trip on a need-to-know basis. Either we had some bad luck and just happened to run into the wrong people, or they were alerted to my arrival. It seemed like a coordinated attack, so I will assume the latter." Sean continued to watch the muted television for anything of interest. "Any news from our local friends?"

"No, they're still giving me the run around," Colin responded. "They are going to twist some arms, and probably get us what we need. It's going to cost me though. It will be a while before I can ask for any more favors." Colin preferred being the person owed the favor, but he had been told to fully accommodate Sean. The days of bickering and hiding sources between the FBI and CIA were supposed to be over.

"Thanks. I'm assuming you have been briefed on what I'm here for?" Sean hesitated, even though he knew Colin assisted Marilyn just a few months before.

"Yeah, I'm sure it was a sanitized version, but the Director himself called me earlier, and gave me strict instructions to cooperate fully. I can understand the concern, but you're taking a huge risk. You do realize that, don't you?" Colin did not like the odds of success of their investigation.

"Yes, we went over it several times. They still haven't come up with anything concrete. My boss has expressed some misgivings about going any further. We're playing a hunch. Let's just leave it at that," Sean said.

"Well, we only have a few days," Colin said in a distressed tone. "I took the liberty of putting out some calls regarding Aman as well. I can tell you if Aman is mixed up with any unsavory characters, he has hidden it exceptionally well. I've been in this region for twelve years and have heard it all, but his name rarely comes up. No one around here seemed to know who he was until his newfound fame as campaign manager, and foster dad of the President-Elect. I can tell you this city is all abuzz that relations with the U.S. will improve. They think Aman's Muslim heritage will have a lot of influence on the new President. Everyone around here thinks they have a fair arbiter for the Palestinian-Israeli conflict."

"We searched Aman's background long and hard, and he appears to be clean. He has been on the periphery of some players in the local terrorist trade around here, but you can say that of almost anyone who possesses money and influence in the Middle East. Have you seen anything around here that could tie him to Al-Qaeda?" Sean asked. He knew all the major players of Al-Qaeda were in the Pakistan-Afghan areas, but anything was possible.

"No. He won't have anything to do with them. Aman has visited this region a few times. He started coming to Cairo during the 1980s. During the 1990s he actually made some speeches preaching against Al-Qaeda. He has sworn off that form of violence on several different occasions."

"What about any other groups like the PLO, or the Al-Asqa Martyr Brigades. Does he have any friends there?" Sean continued to probe.

117

"Nothing. And trust me, I've looked into all of them. He has donated money to some local charities that are known to funnel money to some of these groups, but that appears to be the extent of it. Those charities help bring orphaned kids over to the States to get a good education. Besides, every company in this region has some indirect tie to what we would consider a terrorist group. I do have one guy who provides me with useful intel sometimes. Older guy. He was once part of the Muslim Brotherhood when it first started. He disagreed with the militant approach they took during the 1950s, and broke with them. He was a big proponent of trying to bring the Muslim Caliphate back. Anyway, I meet with him every few weeks. He had seen a picture of Aman with the President-Elect in the local newspapers. He claims he met him once years ago. He seemed quite proud of him, which is the reaction I have noticed in others around these parts. But he seemed almost impatient with Aman, as if he had been waiting for this moment for years. Maybe I'm reading too much into his reaction, but I just got the impression he was not telling me the full story. I took Marilyn to meet with him, as well, but he wasn't much help. He seemed to be stonewalling. I think he's beginning to regret dealing with me. He has been keeping a low profile over the last few months."

Sean was intrigued. "Marilyn mentioned him in her report. What exactly is the Caliphate? I know I've heard the term somewhere before."

"You probably have heard Bin Laden call for one. He likes to throw out the term during his pronouncements. Anyway, the Caliphate was, for several hundred years the symbol of a unified Muslim people. The Caliphate dates all the way back to the death of the Prophet Mohammad in the 600s. He is considered the successor, for lack of a better word, of the prophet. The Caliphate was abolished by the Western powers after the destruction of the Ottoman Empire at the end of World War I."

"When the Ottoman Empire was carved into today's countries you mean," Sean interjected.

"Exactly. You have to understand; most Muslims identify themselves by their religious sect, not by what

118

country they are from. There has been a lot of in-house fighting between the Sunnis and Shias over the years. Hell, most of their countries were randomly carved out of the sand by our European allies. For roughly thirteen centuries the Caliphate was the supreme Muslim ruler, and for much of that time Islam dominated their Christian counterparts in Europe."

"So the Brotherhood of the Caliphate wants one ruler for all Muslims?" Sean asked.

"Yes, although the Caliphate is as much a religious leader as anything else. The splitting of the Ottoman Empire helped us out by creating a lot of rivalries within the Muslim community, all vying for different goals. The generation of today has grown up with the PLO, Hamas, and Hezbollah, each one of them pushing for all sorts of things from the destruction of Israel and their occupation of the Holy Land, to America's occupation of Saudi Arabia, along with a long list of other real and perceived grievances. With so many factions, the hope of a Caliphate has died out except in the older generation who remember the world wars and the failed peace treaties that followed."

The brief history lesson started the wheels turning in Sean's mind. "A single Muslim state would be extremely powerful. If the Ottoman Empire had survived World War I, we would have had a hell of a time controlling the region." Sean picked up on the subtleties of the situation quickly. His intuition was one of the qualities that made him particularly good at his job.

"That's a fair assessment," Colin said with a contemplative nod. "Imagine World War II with the Ottoman Empire working with Germany, and then think if the Ottoman Empire had come under the control of one of these hardcore fundamentalist types. I doubt there would be any Jews left in the world today. Like I said before, there were just too many varying opinions and religious sects to deal with though. By the 1940s Saudi Arabia already signed their first deal with Standard Oil, and Egypt was working hand-in-hand with the Soviets by the 50s. They couldn't even get the Muslim leaders to choose sides in the Cold War, much less the Arab street."

"Well, it's an interesting history lesson if nothing else. Not sure if it will be useful for me or not," Sean said as he glanced at the numerous clocks behind Colin's desk. "I need to shower and call the boss."

"I'll have a guard show you where everything is." They both rose simultaneously, and shook hands. "As soon as you get settled in we can start our search. Aziz will be hard to find though. He seems to have gone to ground during the last few weeks," Colin said.

"I figured as much. Take me to all his normal places starting tomorrow morning. I also got a few ideas from Marilyn regarding where to locate him."

Chapter 22
White House – Oval Office

The outgoing President gazed out onto the West Lawn of the White House as he waited for the FBI and CIA directors to arrive with the latest information. He could see the workers dismantling the massive Christmas tree. All the power this small room vested to its occupant could do nothing to stem the mounting frustration and weakness he felt as his term as President rapidly approached its conclusion. The holder of the most powerful and sought after job in the world typically did not wait for anyone, but Allan Gray was already a lame duck, two months removed from being voted out of office after only one term. The vein just below the last remnants of his graying temple of hair bulged with anger as he replayed his numerous mistakes over the past few months. The expensive tumbler of bourbon in his hand did nothing to soothe his temper. He yanked his tie down, ignoring his normal protocol, and for what seemed like the hundredth time, tried to come to grips with his predicament.

Allan Gray considered himself a true patriot, a man who came from a broken family, no money, and yet lived the American dream by ascending to the Presidency. He was about to return to those humble roots. He still believed in his heart that he fulfilled his promises, but the voters rejected him, stabbing him in the back, he thought, in a rare moment of self-pity, after traveling a long and difficult road together. The truth was much more complicated, and he knew it.

The attacks of 10/01/00 occurred right in the heart of his campaign for the Presidency. The outgoing President responded quickly to the attack, invading the sanctuary of Al-Qaeda in Afghanistan. He left office with soaring approval numbers after pulling off the ultimate curtain call. The Vice-President normally would have been in a prime position to easily win the election. With the economy flourishing, all he needed to do was run a cautious campaign and promise to continue the same economic policies. The strategy worked perfectly until the attacks devastated New York and Washington D.C. that sunny October day.

Allan had received his party's nomination by default. Most of the other major players wanted nothing to do with an incumbent party with a sixty percent approval rating. As the Governor of California, Allan had a huge advantage against his primary opponents that he leveraged to the hilt. He welcomed the fight for the highest office in the land and threw himself full throttle into the primaries, and once he secured the nomination, the general election.

Allan was forced to take an aggressive approach in order to have a chance at winning the general election. He talked tough on foreign policy and warned the American people that the last few years were a mirage, and that the country always had to be ready to defend itself from external enemies. The rhetoric fell on a deaf public, and the electorate considered him to be a loose cannon until after the attacks. He then looked like a sage, and the media was forced to take notice.

He rode this new wave of support to a stunning victory, vowing to ignore party lines and continue to take the fight to the terrorists in Afghanistan and beyond. The normal two-month honeymoon enjoyed by a new president stretched for a little over a year, and he soon finished the task his predecessor started in Afghanistan. The country now possessed a fledgling democracy. With victory in hand,

Allan Gray turned the military's focus to another rogue state, Iraq, and its brutal dictator. He warned the American citizenry numerous times to expect casualties, perhaps many thousands. He was convinced that in the long run, any American deaths would save ten times that number from the iron grip of a man who had already shown a propensity for gassing his own people when they stepped out of line.

Allan made one crucial mistake however, that he now felt had cost him the election. Instead of immediately launching the invasion against Iraq, he tried the diplomatic route through the United Nations, even though he knew it was a doomed enterprise. He knew that there were already eight years of sanctions that the U.N. systematically ignored. Instead of punishing the dictator, these sanctions were used by many U.N. members as a way to enrich themselves with black market Iraqi oil and all sorts of other government contracts that were thrown into the maze of bureaucracy. Once inside the black hole of the United Nations, the contracts were fixed to the bureaucrats liking, until they came out on the other end of the pipeline. A lump of coal turned into the proverbial diamond, Allan thought in disgust.

What he first thought would look like a gracious effort by him to give the U.N. one more chance only allowed Saddam to better prepare, and the "peace nuts" to rally throughout the world. Of course, he admitted to himself, he knew the war would have to be waged once he moved the army into place. He also knew Saddam would never give in to their demands. He was convinced that once he called the U.N.'s bluff, then they would grudgingly have to enforce their own sanctions.

Allan now realized he had thought too highly of the United Nations. The Iraqi leader routinely massacred thousands of his own people by gassing them with chemical weapons, and paid rewards to families of Palestinian suicide bombers for murdering Israeli civilians. If this was not enough, the Iraqi leader butchered hundreds of thousands of Muslims by starting a war with Iran.

Allan had simply never thought the horrid deeds of the "Butcher of Baghdad" would be lost amidst the shouts of "No blood for oil." He belted back another swig of bourbon at the thought and laughed sardonically at the infantile slogan. If all he wanted was oil, all he had to do was allow the sanctions to be lifted, and the oil could start flowing. He knew this was one of the real reasons so many at the U.N. opposed him. Most of the countries that complained the loudest already had oil deals signed with the dictator, and they were just waiting for the shackles of the sanctions to be lifted so they could start importing their booty.

By the time he gave final authorization for the invasion, it had already become a media event. The military mounted a lightning-quick strike that conquered the country in a matter of months, but upon their approach into the capital, Saddam's forces resisted and a bloody battle for control of Baghdad ensued. Several thousand U.S. soldiers died in the bloodbath. The aftermath of the war also proved to be difficult. When no chemical, biological, or nuclear weapons were found, the united front Allan put together after his election quickly began to crumble.

Compounding the problem was the bitterness still festering between the majority Shia population and the Sunnis who dominated the country for thirty years. Iraq soon became ravaged by two smaller wars; a sectarian conflict between the Sunni and Shia, and the counter-insurgency against the Western armies. Added to this volatile mix was a group of foreign invaders answering the call to jihad. While the foreign jihadists could not defeat the U.S. militarily on a battlefield, the mounting deaths from IEDs began to wear down public support of the war.

Allan stared into the brown liquid of his glass and contemplated his mistakes. He now believed his major strategic blunder had been his mad dash to the capital. In their haste to end the war, the army moved at a breakneck pace to encircle Baghdad. Instead of actively seeking a fight, the U.S. military only engaged the Iraqi army units that were directly in their path. Once they chose to flee, the army let them go, and continued to streak towards the capital instead of taking the time to round them up. This allowed thousands of regular soldiers and Saddam Feddeyan guards to melt into the civilian population, where they would later wage a brutal war of attrition against the occupying army.

123

The opposition party pounced on the apprehension of the populace and demanded that Allan chart a new course of action. The plight of the Iraqis was not worth American lives anymore, the opposition argued. After all, we already conquered Saddam, therefore the Iraqis should be left to their own devices. They demanded an immediate pullout. Allan found the argument ridiculous and did not attempt to counterattack, thinking the idea would never gain any traction. By the time he realized his error and began to use the bully pulpit of his Presidency, it was too late to repair the damage. Allan believed that true freedom, no matter how difficult, was the only way to solve the deep problems in the Middle East. After all, it took the U.S. over ten years and thousands of deaths before it devised a workable system of its own. Times were different now though, and the population no longer had the attention span to see difficult fights through to their conclusion.

He continued to reserve the majority of his frustration for the media. A sarcastic grimace spread across his face as he thought about the media's utter hypocrisy. Reporters loved to shout the horrors of the world to the nation every evening on the news. The media would constantly whine about all the different populations being brutalized across the globe and ask, why were we not more engaged?

Yet, whenever the U.S. ventured into a volatile situation like Iraq the same people would accuse him of imperialism at the earliest opportunity. They only wanted to help other brutalized populations while U.S. citizens and soldiers were guaranteed safety and protection from all these same horrors. As soon as U.S. citizens or military members died, as when the bodies of U.S. soldiers were dragged through the dusty streets of Khartoum in the early 1990s, the media would clamor that it was no longer worth the effort. The same people who claimed to be the champions of the downtrodden apparently thought the freedom of other people was only important if it could be done without sacrificing American lives.

After he lost the election fifty-five percent to forty five percent, and took a bloodbath in the Electoral College, it took Allan a few days to accept his defeat. Shortly thereafter, the CIA Director approached him with a piece of unnerving information and a concern that Allan frankly found hard to believe at first. The thought that the Senator from Nevada could have a forged background raised all sorts of questions. Who were the individuals that helped arrange the potential lies about the Senator's past and why? The Senator was perhaps lying about his background at a time when fanatical Muslims like Bin Laden were calling for the destruction of the United States.

The thought of a worst-case scenario regarding the Senator's background caused Alan to approve the covert operation the CIA Director proposed. He was determined to defend his country to the last day. It was not politically correct, but he no longer cared. He was already finished politically so the media could cause him no further harm. He set his drink down and tried to compose himself. The rehashing of his failures over the last several years did nothing to help his foul mood. The intercom on his desk interrupted his silent self-loathing.

"Yes?" He asked in an annoyed tone.

"Your guests are here, Mr. President," said the chipper voice of his always-friendly secretary.

"Send them in," he responded coldly. Allan immediately felt bad for snapping at her. She was an angel, and he would miss her greatly.

Bret McMichael and Malcolm Ray were ushered into the Oval Office. The door behind them closed with the help of an unknown pair of hands. They had no assistants tagging along, and Allan did not have any advisors in the room; even his always-present Chief of Staff would not supervise. Their meeting had been purposefully planned to be completely off the record.

It was early Sunday morning, the best time of the week to meet with the President and avoid media coverage. The major media networks were busy parsing through all the week's news and interviewing whichever bigwig from the Senate or House of Representatives they could find to come into their studio. The Sunday talk show circuit was the time for the political players to shine, rebut the President, and if

125

they were lucky, make a name for themselves with some quick wit. The fact that Allan Gray was a lame duck only served as chum in the water. Most of the major senators and congressmen's staff spent the previous week cashing in favors in an attempt to be on the air and get some face time in front of the nation before the President-Elect rode back into town on his white horse.

Ignoring the normal formalities, an upset Malcolm Ray immediately started in with the President. "Mr. President, I really prefer this discussion be held somewhere else."

The President raised his hand in a hushing motion, setting his drink on the desk at the same time. "Relax, Malcolm. I turned off the tape recorders myself. I want this kept quiet just as much as you."

"Sir, I don't question your desire for secrecy, but there are still plenty of other rooms in this building with no recording devices." Malcolm looked at the drink sitting on the table with disapproval. Approaching the age of fifty, Malcolm was one of the younger directors of the CIA, and he looked at the President almost like an older brother. Malcolm Ray was the first black director of the CIA. Allan's predecessor appointed him to his current position, and after the change of administrations in January 2001 Malcolm was fully prepared to be thrown under the bus as the sacrificial lamb of the intelligence community.

The fact that he was not fired, but instead allowed to turn his agency loose for the first time in decades instilled in him a great loyalty to Allan Gray, and he placed more trust in him than any other politician in this town. He just hoped the drink was not a sign that the man was cracking under the pressure of the past few months. Malcolm spent a lifetime studying his fellow man very carefully, and was normally able to pick up on the small signs that would foretell future problems. He had saved the CIA a lot of grief over the last few years by yanking a few operatives out of potentially disastrous situations by recognizing the warning signs.

"Relax, Malcolm. This is my first and last one of the day. I know it's a little early, but it's the only time I can do it and not get lectured by my wife or one of my staff."

126

Malcolm took the President at his word and dropped the issue. Allan Gray was many things that people in this town did not like, and one of those things was that he was a straight shooter and rarely minced words. He liked to burrow to the heart of the matter and deal quickly with the problem. This meeting would be no exception.

"So, how is our investigation going? Any more news from your people in the field?" The President asked.

"Yes, sir," Bret McMichael spoke his first words of the meeting.

"Let's have it. I want the full story now," Allan demanded impatiently. "No more bull shitting around. We are weeks from the inauguration so there is no longer a need to protect me." Both directors had only given Allan sporadic details over the last few months in order to try and inoculate him from any fallout when and if it were to occur.

Bret started to explain, "Mr. President, as we told you a few months ago, we did send someone out to Las Vegas to try and get close to Zach and see if they could find out anything. That person's code name is Marilyn."

The President's eyebrows arched and his body stiffened in his chair. "So you did send a woman after him? I thought you were lying to me when you told me that!" He could not believe they were trying a simple game plan like dangling a woman as bait in front of him. As a senator, Zach had garnered a reputation around town. Washington D.C. could be like a college campus when it came to the rumor mill, and while he preferred not to hear the gossip, someone was always passing information on to him in an attempt to win favor. "You just tried to hand him a beautiful woman and see if he would take the bait?"

"More or less, sir." Bret replied.

"I'm to assume this was an attractive F.B.I. agent? We all know the Senator's rumored tastes."

"She definitely meets his qualifications. But there was no one in the FBI who could even attempt to pull off this little stunt, so we took Malcolm's advice," Bret replied like an older brother blaming a broken heirloom on his younger sibling.

"What the hell are you saying, Bret?"

127

"Malcolm did more than just provide advice and consent. Marilyn is a CIA asset, sir." Bret dropped the bombshell, and then waited for the reaming that would certainly follow.

The President watched the two of them closely as his mind whirled with all the problems this news created. The CIA was typically prohibited from operating on American soil. If there was one thing that launched Congress on to their high horse, it was domestic spying. Any other time, this piece of information would have led to a firing somewhere down the line, but he told them at the beginning to pull no punches. If they were willing to risk their careers for this operation, he only thought it fair to make sure they understood they had his full support.

"I'm assuming you felt this was your best option?" President Gray asked.

"Absolutely, Mr. President," Malcolm interjected.

"Now I know why you didn't inform me of your plans. Neither of you would be around very long if this leaked out."

"Sir, I suggested this to Bret, and after examining all our options we both agreed it would be our best shot." Malcolm continued his defense of the operation.

"Fuck, Malcolm! I realize my career is coming to an end, but you don't have to come with me. Who is she?" The President rarely cursed, and the word came out of his mouth like an eight-year-old just discovering it for the first time.

"One of our best field operatives, sir. She was stationed in the Middle East for the last few years. She was recalled to American soil specifically for this mission. Her father was an American diplomat in Egypt. He met her mother while overseas. She was born in Egypt and spent the first part of her life there until she came back to the U.S. with her father when she was sixteen."

"Came back with her father? He didn't marry her mother?" President Gray could be very old-fashioned about certain things.

"They were married, but when she was fourteen her mother was caught in the middle of an attack by the Muslim

128

Brotherhood. They assaulted some tourists near Luxor. Her mother was taken hostage with some of the tourists. She was assisting with tour guides to the pyramids and other attractions in the area. As far as the Muslim Brotherhood was concerned her mother was even worse of a traitor to Islam than the tourists. She was one of the first ones to be killed during the hostage standoff. A few years after that, Marilyn's father was assassinated when he returned to Cairo."

"Jesus Christ!" The President found himself swearing. "I think I can see where this leads to."

"Mr. President, she didn't join the CIA simply for revenge. The attack opened her eyes to some of the horrors in this world. It certainly was a motivational tool for her as she went through college. Our talent spotters picked up on her when she was nineteen. She was the ideal candidate: American, mixed ancestry, spoke Arabic fluently, and grew up in the Middle East. We officially employed her right after she graduated, and she has since been involved in some of our most sensitive and successful operations run in that part of the world. She thinks on her feet better than any of our male operatives, and she has been able to spend the last several years in Egypt, Palestine, Syria, and Saudi Arabia undetected. That area is probably the most chauvinistic area in the world, and most of the men over there don't even think twice about a woman being a danger to them." Malcolm finished. He would not go into any more details. She was too valuable an asset.

The President caught one phrase that intrigued him, "What did you mean by 'officially employed by the CIA,' Malcolm?"

"She returned to Egypt one summer with her father. Let's just say we gave her a little assignment to see how she handled it, and she exceeded everyone's expectations. Let's drop the subject on her background now if you don't mind, sir. The less you know about her the safer you'll be." A tiny smile appeared on Malcolm's face. He rarely got to brag about his agents, it was one of the curses of the job. He reveled in the ability to tell the Commander in Chief something he did not know.

"Fine, let's deal with the current situation then, since it appears she is presiding over her first possible screw up here," President Gray said. His patience was evaporating with all the innuendo and lack of straight answers he was getting from his two directors. He turned back to Bret again. "So how did you get dragged into this, Bret?"

"Malcolm came to me with some information Marilyn had gleaned while in Cairo, concerning the Senator's benefactor in Las Vegas. It was sketchy, to say the least. Aman has been on our radar for years, mainly because he was such a unique factor in the Las Vegas mob scene. Other than that, he really didn't seem to be any trouble. He looked to be your typical Americanized Arab, swimming in a pool of gambling money that his casinos poured in over the years. He's probably the only Arab billionaire in the world who has not made his fortune off oil reserves. Apparently his only ties to Egypt were an occasional speech each year to an organization that helps him choose the kids who get to come over to the U.S. to study. Anyway, while she was in Cairo she learned that Aman was probably a member of the Brotherhood of the Caliphate."

Malcolm cut in again to provide some more background. "The Brotherhood was formed around or a little after WWII, sir. The CIA didn't even become aware of its existence until the 1960s. By then it appeared to be dying out anyway, and to be honest, sir, compared to all the other groups in that area, these guys were really calm. We never heard of any attacks done in their name, and we thought all their members were deceased until Marilyn came across them a few years ago. She happened to catch a speech in Cairo by Aman in the late 1990s, and the Senator from Nevada was in the country as well on a photo op with some other senators promoting free elections throughout the world. She followed them to a restaurant where they ended up meeting with Aman and an old man who afterwards took them to some government buildings, apparently for some kind of tour. It all appeared to be on the up and up so she forgot about the encounter until early last year. She received a call from Sean Hill, one of Bret's men, who was in the

130

process of doing his background checks on the presidential candidates. He was having problems tracking down information on Zach's childhood in Egypt. They were short of men in Cairo, and Marilyn was in a lull at the time so we loaned her to Sean. She was on foreign soil anyway so we didn't think it would be a problem."

Allan stared at both of them with a perplexed look, trying to soak in all the background information, and decipher what was going on. "Please don't tell me Zach is some sort of terrorist."

"No, sir, but she discovered one piece of disturbing information regarding Aman and the older man. We couldn't get the necessary proof we were looking for though, and since we were becoming so short on time, I came to Bret with a suggestion."

"I had my reservations to say the least, sir, but the stakes were just too high, so I agreed to let her come back to the U.S. and lay the trap. Since Sean did the background work on Zach I paired him together with Marilyn and let them plan the operation. She was the field agent, and he ran everything from here in Washington. Once it looked like the operation had gone sour, I sent him to Egypt as a last resort to follow up on her work. Sir, I have warned both you and Malcolm about the dangers of this operation. I think it may be time to pull the plug. Sean will certainly hit a dead end in Egypt, and if we go any further without absolute proof we could all be in jail." Bret hoped President Gray was lying, and that the tape recorders were picking up his mea culpa.

Allan released a sigh of frustration and then his temper began to creep back to the surface. "Why the hell didn't you send someone else out to Egypt as soon as you pulled her into the U.S.? Now we're down to the wire here, boys. This is no time to jack around."

"Mr. President, you've already pointed out how sensitive this little operation is and that our balls would be hung from the Washington monument if it got leaked! We were and are still concerned that there is a leak somewhere. We just found out Sean's convoy was attacked as soon as he set foot in the country. As dangerous as Zach may or may not be, we had to play this one close to the vest. Once Bret

131

sent Sean out there we did alert an officer in Cairo, but that was the extent of it." Malcolm vigorously defended his position. The President was dead wrong on this one. Nothing was more important here than secrecy. If this became public it would be just the ammunition certain members of Congress could use to de-claw the CIA for years to come.

Allan nervously moved a stack of paper around on his desk in a haphazard manner. He stared at the bright yellow carpet with a distant look. He was not sure if Malcolm was correct. This was truly a unique situation; an outgoing President who approves the investigation of the man who defeated him in an election. It would not set a good precedent, that was true, but he still believed the risk that this man possibly posed made it worth his while. "So you still haven't told me where she is guys." Allan's eyes darted back and forth between them, waiting for an answer.

"The good news is it appears she discovered something in Vegas because she warned us off with a signal at the airport. None of the safe houses she set up appear to have been messed with, and Zach is still holed up in a hotel room at Aman's casino with the Secret Service watching over him. We've had no contact with her though so I believe she is probably dead," Bret said, giving him the worst case scenario. He hoped it would push him towards a decision to stop the investigation.

Malcolm jumped in immediately to protest. "I have to disagree with his assessment, sir. I think she has escaped. I called Aman to ask if I could fly out there and give Zach a personal briefing on some national security issues. Aman declined. He claimed they were dealing with some of Zach's personal problems and it would have to wait. Aman said he would call me back. He sounded like he was in a panic so something is going on out there that is not to his liking," the CIA Director retorted.

"When is Sean going to be checking back in?" The President realized he would not be getting any more information for the moment.

"Any time, Mr. President. As soon as we hear from him we will provide you with an update," Bret finished.

"Fine, I know you both have plenty to do, but keep me in the loop. Now get out of here and try not to be photographed as you are leaving." The President was already out of his chair, and ushering them to the exit. He placed a hand on the shoulder of each man to show his full support for both of them. After they left President Gray stood by the window and looked out at the small crowd of tourists admiring the White House Christmas decorations that sat on the open field, just beyond the gates of the South Lawn. His shoulders slumped, and he wondered once again if he was saving the country he loved or assisting in its destruction.

Chapter 23
NEVADA

Gregor closed his cell phone and allowed himself the slightest moment to gloat before returning to his German roots, which consisted of a taciturn stare. The extra precautions he put in place with his people in Reno were paying dividends. The call he had just made to Solomon to give him the news was the most enjoyable thing he had done in weeks. He loved one-upping the Frenchman, and he was already looking forward to their next meeting with Aman so he could rub it in his face. He knew they would have to finish the job first. He glanced at the clock on the dashboard and pressed on the gas. The black BMW X-5's engine responded immediately and the vehicle quickly gathered momentum, despite the increasing volume of snow that was beginning to fall on Route 395 between Las Vegas and South Lake Tahoe. He needed to get there by nightfall.

It had been less than forty-eight hours, and they finally found the woman and her companion. The call came in from one of his watchmen. Gregor never trusted Aman's Arab posse, as he thought of them. Aman only employed a handful of surveillance people on staff so Gregor had been forced to be creative. A few years prior he helped a private investigator in Reno out of jam. The man's gambling problem landed him in trouble with the wrong crowd. Gregor made the problem disappear, and the man had been on the payroll ever since. The only condition was that if he started wagering again Gregor would hand him over to his former creditors.

It proved to be one of his most inspired moves. The man was incredible at tracking people. He spent several years in Vietnam roaming the jungles for Viet Cong, and now spent his time skiing the mountains around Reno and Lake Tahoe and doing special jobs when called upon by Gregor. Gregor promised him double the usual fee if he succeeded, and left open the opportunity for more. His job description was simple. He was ordered to follow Aman's watchers. Several hours later the private investigator was tracking Hussein.

The trail ended late the night before at a small inn on the outskirts of South Lake Tahoe. Hussein entered the inn in the middle of the night, and the next morning a man and a woman took off in his car. The private investigator made a quick decision, and cautiously trailed them back to the small ski town at the base of the mountain. He snapped several photos, and watched them pay for a room at a cheap motel nestled between the large casinos and the lake.

Gregor now admitted that Solomon's first thoughts about the woman were definitely correct. She was undoubtedly some type of federal agent, probably FBI. There was no way that a normal person would double-back as she was doing. It was a clever ploy; an excellent way to throw off one's stalkers, and it would have been a success were it not for the private investigator Gregor used as a safety valve. As long as they stayed at the motel for another hour or so they would have her. Solomon would call Aman with an update, then begin to make his way through Carson City and into the ski town via Highway 50 south, which ran down the mountains and along the lake. Gregor and his men planned to travel up from Highway 50 north and trap her.

The electronic chirp of the GPS device attached to the windshield alerted him that the exit that would put him onto Highway 50 was quickly approaching. He had a head start on Solomon, and the competitor in him had every intention of taking out their targets without waiting for the Frenchman. He knew it was irresponsible, but the two professionals in the back seat silently cleaning their Heckler & Koch 23 handguns gave him a quiet confidence. It would be three against two, and he had the element of surprise with him. He saw no reason to wait for Solomon. A fourth person rushing into a small motel room would do nothing but make things more confusing, in addition to providing more bunched together targets for the woman if they happened to walk into a trap.

Gregor made a right onto Highway 50 North. As he drove along the two-lane road he could feel the 4-wheel drive kick in, gripping the road through the thin layer of snow. Traffic was sparse. Most of the vacationers were already inside the casinos, and the locals were hunkering down to prepare for the small blizzard the weather forecasts had been predicting. The snow trucks were omni-present, already driving up and down the highway and plowing the snow away as fast as they could. Gregor began a mission briefing with his companions. They discussed different scenarios, and established parameters for the pending assault. They nodded in silence as they lovingly prepared their weapons for what they hoped would be a quick outing.

***

Alex sat in the old, tweed chair and practiced the quick firing motions Marilyn had been going over with him the last few hours. It was a good way to kill time. The thin walls and cheap carpet of the motel room provided no warmth from the blizzard that was beginning to form outside their window. Alex was dressed in full winter regalia, minus a winter coat they had just purchased which was lay crumpled at his feet. Despite the woman's assurances he still felt uneasy sitting in a hotel room when an unknown number of people were looking to kill them. Every survival instinct he ever had was keeping the adrenaline flowing through his body, so he passed the time by working the small pistol, trying to adjust to the feel of it. He had never held a weapon before, and frankly never had the desire to.

Interviewing for the CIA came not out of bloodlust or revenge, but out of frustration. The terrorist cell uncovered in Indianapolis had been a jolt to his system, and when his law firm was tasked with assisting the federal prosecution he jumped at the opportunity to be on the research team. The months of planning and learning about the enemy they were facing opened his eyes even more than 10/1/00 did, but what really scared the shit out of him was the way the terrorists could manipulate the court system.

When they were let go because some of the evidence against them was collected off a battlefield in Afghanistan in an inappropriate manner, he knew he was in the wrong line of work. The judge in the case evidently expected the military to properly document evidence while dodging bullets. Alex knew the courts were not meant to handle them. Rather, the courts were set up to deal with common criminals; the kind who abused the free society they lived in by circumventing the law to accomplish their own personal goals. These homicidal maniacs were in a different league altogether. They used the free society to try and destroy the very same people that created those freedoms. These types saw it as a life-and-death war with the United States. There was no U.N. resolution that could ever placate them. The only way to engage them in this struggle was to join the battle, and for Alex that meant applying to the CIA. His year of working on the trial with the federal prosecutors pushed his name to the top of the list, and he eagerly accepted the job when offered.

Alex stopped practicing with his weapon and looked at his gorgeous companion who was standing at the window, peering through the shades into the evening that was now upon them. She was dressed in black from head to toe, and her hair was tied up in a ponytail.

"I thought spies stayed in ritzy hotels. This place is a dump," Alex said. He was tired of the silence.

"You've seen too many movies. How does the gun feel?" She was now accustomed to his childish attempts at humor and just ignored them. Everyone dealt with fear in his or her own way, and she recognized his defense mechanism. It could be a problem later in his career if he lived long enough, she thought. People who cannot keep their mouths shut typically do not last long in this type of business.

136

"I think I have the basics, but I still will not be much good in a real fight," he replied. His lack of self-confidence was apparent.

"A little fear is a good thing. I would rather have you unsure of yourself than arrogant. If something happens just stay low to the ground and blast away at whomever you see. You need to make yourself as small a target as possible. This will make it more difficult for them to kill you, and easier for me to avoid shooting you." Her eyes stayed focused on the parking lot, scanning for any sign of trouble. She would go check the bedroom window in another ten minutes. She did not tell him, but she also had her new get away vehicle picked out. She had been watching a group of college kids unpack their Land Rover for the last twenty minutes. Their room was two doors down, and she studied them closely while they unloaded their snowboards and endless amount of coolers, no doubt full of beer for some evening festivities. The Land Rover had California tags on it. Their demeanor told her they were typical spoiled kids, probably up for the weekend from either Sacramento or San Francisco to take in a little fun on their parents' dime before heading back to college.

It had been easy to get what she wanted. She had waltzed up to them and asked a few questions about where to find the most intense spots on the ski slopes. Their hormones overtook all of their other senses, and she filched the keys to the vehicle from the driver's pocket. The Land Rover was just what she would need. A luxury 4-wheel drive vehicle was the norm in this part of the country, and it would not stand out amidst all the other wealthy show pieces that vacationers drove around. By the time they woke up from their hangovers tomorrow morning she would be done with it and on an airplane. The vehicle would be found in the Reno airport with no damage other than a few extra miles put on it.

She originally planned to stay the night, but she no longer considered it a smart play. She knew she was lucky to run into one of Aman's amateurs. She could only push her luck so far. Solomon could easily figure out her plan, and if they were taking precautions the man she killed could have been followed. She cursed herself for not thinking of it earlier. Her gambit bought her some time, but that was all. She would just have to wait a few hours longer for her frat-boy neighbors to pass out, and then they would get out of here. As long as Solomon's men did not show up in the next four to five hours she thought she could escape unscathed. She reached down and touched the cell phone in her pocket, confirming it was still there.

Snapping Zachariah's photo had proven even easier than she thought. Getting back with it alive would be a different matter. There were too many unknown variables to do anything but hand deliver the phone and its contents. She could not risk it falling into anyone else's hands. Zach had been easy to seduce. The weeks she spent studying his personality and reading about his antics gave her all the weaponry she needed. She was just his type, and all she had to do was play hard to get for ten minutes at the strip club, and he would not leave her alone. He was so used to pillaging at will that the slightest push back from a prospective conquest drove him crazy with lust. She led him around by the balls for a few weeks until she finagled an invitation to one of Aman's famous parties at the top of his hotel.

She treaded carefully that particular night. One misstep and she was certain Zachariah would bring down his Secret Service agents on her. The evening quickly went sour when the Secret Service agents confiscated all the belongings from her purse before the party, including her cell phone. She improvised by stealing one from someone else, only to discover later it was barely functional and the photo she took with it was marginal thanks to the dim lighting. The good news was that Zach got so ticked when she took the picture that he tossed her out. She would have slept with him if necessary, but she shuddered at the thought of it.

Alex interrupted her silent mission briefing. "How do you feel after you kill someone?" He asked.

"Why do you want to know?" The question caught her off guard.

"I spent the better part of a year studying these fanatics during the trial preparation. They all seem to have almost a blind, robotic belief that what they are doing is right. It scared the shit out of me; the callousness. I asked myself how a human being could get to that point. It's what made me apply for the CIA. I felt it was the only way to really do something about it," Alex said as he placed the gun on the armrest and stared at her.

"I've seen the type all my life. They're indoctrinated almost from birth. Most do not know any other way. Still, they all chose their path freely. Most of the leaders have Western educations so I have no qualms about killing their type. If the roles were reversed they would not hesitate to slit my throat and rape me, probably in that order."

"You never answered my question."

Her back was turned to him while she continued to keep her vigilant watch on the ice covered parking lot.

"It's not something I enjoy by any means, but what I did was necessary. That is how I justify it. By killing, I have also saved a life." She let the obvious inference hang in the air along with the ice shards just outside the window.

"You seemed like you enjoyed humiliating the guy in the cabin. I was surprised; it actually bothered me a little. When you hear about this crap from a distance it's easy to forget that real people are involved."

"The only real people for those types are the true believers. There is a sick little part of me that enjoyed the act I put on, but that is all it was. Guys like Hussein have perverted their religion to such a point that anyone else is not worthy of anything but their utter contempt. When I have one in my control it drives them crazy. Every moment I spend dominating them drives them crazy. They would rather die than be subjected to a woman in that way. They surrender information quite rapidly to me so they can die sooner. It's what makes me good at what I do, but if I ever truly enjoy it I will have become just like them. I can promise you that will never happen."

Alex fell silent, not sure what he should say. The last two days now seemed like two years ago. He looked around at his surroundings, and realized that he was tired of spending time in hotel rooms. The last several had all ended with dead bodies in them. His mind returned to Michael and Cindy for the first time in several hours. The guilt over his friends' almost certain death was slowly beginning to pile up. He had become so focused on his own survival that he almost completely forgot that they were massacred just a short time earlier. He hoped he would get the opportunity to apologize to their families.

"You're going to have to stop thinking about your friends. At least for now." Marilyn read his silence perfectly.

Alex glared at the slim curve of her back, "Is that how you deal with death? Just forget about them?"

"There is nothing you can do that will bring them back. I know it's harsh, but you can grieve later. I would prefer you try to focus on the task at hand for now. The hardest part of this line of work is learning to separate yourself from your emotions. Try to channel your anger into the moment. Otherwise, you may not get an opportunity for vengeance."

"What is the task at hand? I could use some more information."

"Sorry, that's not for me to decide. But we are leaving tonight. I've arranged for some transportation and we will be out of here by midnight at the latest. I need you to do something for me though. I need a few hours of sleep. If I don't get it, I'll get us killed. I already have made one stupid error and I can't afford another one." Marilyn moved to the window by the front door and pulled the shade to the side, showing him the room a few doors down where the college boys were staying.

"There are a few college guys in that room, drinking it up and having a good time. As soon as the lights go out wake me up and we'll get out of here. I have the keys to their car. If the lights are not out by eleven wake me up. That will give me a couple hours of sleep, which should suffice. If you think we have unwelcome guests, just yell. I'm a light sleeper." She closed the shades and disappeared into the small bedroom.

Alex took in his surroundings; the small TV in front of him, the tiny kitchenette off to his right, and the love sofa all yawned back at him. What should have been typical surroundings seemed alien to him. He had never felt so alone in his life. He tightly gripped his pistol. He was beginning to understand why soldiers felt comfort with the care of their weapon. It was the only element in battle one has complete control over.

CIA Headquarters, Langley, Virginia

Malcolm Ray set the phone back in its cradle and propped his legs up on his desk in a relaxed fashion. The phone call from the FBI Director had been the second good piece of news in the last twenty-four hours. First, one of his "cleaners" had found Marilyn's sign at the airport indicating her escape route. Now this. It seemed the head of Zach's Secret Service detail, Vince James, had called his boss in Washington D.C. to let him know that Zach had a small scuffle with a woman two nights earlier. The woman appeared to be a stripper. Zach had told them to forget about it, that he knew her, and it was no cause for alarm. Vince had felt it best to report it just in case the woman eventually tried to extort him for money. This sort of thing had been an ongoing problem over the years.

Malcolm smiled to himself. Politicians liked to press the flesh in more ways than one, and their inflated opinions of themselves often convinced them that they could avoid any problem with some smooth talking. They felt they were invulnerable, and there were plenty of women at the fundraisers or campaign stops willing to jump into bed with the power brokers of the country. While most of the women were party loyalists to whomever they were sleeping with, there were always a few who were simply looking for cash or fifteen minutes of fame.

Malcolm studied the notes he had jotted down during his conversation with Bret. Vince was convinced the woman was a stripper. She ran out of the party later that night in a fit of rage. Vince did not want the President-Elect to start off his term defending himself from rape accusations.

141

He relayed his concerns to his boss in D.C., who in turn called Bret to apprise him of Vince's concerns. Since the FBI handled federal kidnapping and extortion cases, they wanted Bret to know the basics in case the woman suddenly appeared in the press a few weeks later claiming she was raped or even pregnant.

Malcolm could only guess how the Secret Service would react if they knew the stripper was actually a CIA agent. It would not be pretty. She was good at her job though. Her performance was so convincing that she had Zach's security detail concerned about what she may do. It was the statement about her being from Reno that brought a smile to his face. He knew how she operated in the field. Every piece of information she offered to the adversary meant something. This little nugget matched with the special sign she had planted for him at the Las Vegas airport. He grabbed the phone and dialed the number from memory.

"Lance here, what can I do for you, sir?" His personal pilot's southern accent always gave Malcolm the impression that he was in a jovial mood.

"Have the plane ready to go in one hour. I'll be there as soon as possible."

"Okay. The destination, sir?" The ex-Navy pilot asked.

"Reno, Nevada. Don't call ahead though. We can alert air traffic control once we are approaching. I need to keep this quiet. I don't want anyone in Reno to know I'm coming in," Malcolm told him.

"Yes, sir. I just want to warn you they will be pissed. A night landing with no forewarning tends to make people nervous," his personal pilot replied. Intrigued by the sudden request, Lance tried to guess what the problem could be. His years in the Navy taught him to not ask questions on certain matters. Ignorance was normally bliss when it came to requests from his boss.

"It can't be helped. I'll deal with them myself. You just get the plane ready to go. I want a skeleton crew, Lance. No one on the flight unless they are absolutely necessary to our safety. Understood?"

"Loud and clear, sir." The line clicked off, Lance had a lot to arrange in a short amount of time.

Malcolm grabbed his cell phone and sport coat and strode out of his office in a controlled rush. The bodyguards standing in the waiting room just outside his office scurried to catch up with their boss.

Chapter 24
Lake Tahoe, Nevada

Gregor made a left hand turn off of Highway 50 and onto the dead-end street. He immediately doused the lights of his BMW X-5. The two-lane stretch of road sloped downward for approximately a half-mile before ending in a thicket of trees, with the edges of Lake Tahoe just beyond. The small strip of road was lined on both sides with cheap motels that catered to the skier or snowboarder on a budget. They were a few blocks away from the casino hotels including Harveys, Caesars, and Harrahs which dominated Highway 50 on the lakeside. The mountainside of the road consisted of a long strip mall constructed entirely out of cedar wood.

Gregor eased off the brake, and let the vehicle's momentum carry him down the small incline. The private investigator who tracked the two people here told Gregor they were staying at the Blue Lake Resort, which should be two more blocks up and on the right side of the street. The night was unusually bright due to the large snowfall that continued unabated. It would soon be unsafe to drive unless one had 4-wheel drive or chains on one's tires. A few seconds later the mammoth sign for the Blue Lake Resort came into view. A giant St. Bernard with a barrel around its neck announced that there were vacancies.

"Get your gear ready. This is the place." Gregor issued the instructions as he whipped the vehicle over to the side of the road. The plan was for his two men to enter from the front, and Gregor would approach from the backside.

The motel sat perpendicular to the road, and from their parking spot he could see all the way down the backside of the cheap resort. Each room on the first floor had its own small deck on the back, providing the perfect entry point for him. He counted the sliding glass doors on the back of the building. According to the private investigator, hers should be the seventh one down the row. He yanked the black ski mask over his head, tucked the gun into his waistband, and casually stepped out onto the dark street.

"Everything looks as advertised, boys. Head around front. Set your watches and begin exactly when we discussed. Then let's get this offending lady and get out of here,"Gregor said. They both nodded affirmatives, got out of the car, and made their way to the parking lot at the front of the motel. They were dressed in flannel shirts and jeans. The untucked shirts hid the Heckler & Koch 23 pistols. The safeties on the weapons were turned off. The mission was officially hot.

***

William Gardner Johnson IV was intoxicated. He did not realize it until he tried to stand up for the first time since they started playing their drinking games forty-five minutes earlier. He nearly fell flat on his face before making it to the bathroom to relieve himself. I am going to have to stop if I plan on getting up at eight to hit the slopes, he realized as his glazed eyes stared at the bathroom mirror. He felt like he was going to throw up. The half-liter of Gray Goose vodka he opened an hour earlier was already empty. One of his buddies had suggested a bonehead drinking game where they roll the dice and then drink the difference in shots. The game obviously did not last long. The sweat forming on his temple told him he was losing the struggle.

"Hey, Prince William! You okay in there?" Jeff yelled out his nickname because he knew it would aggravate his friend. The question was more an attempt to have fun at his expense as opposed to being concerned for his welfare.

"Fuck you, Jeff. I'll be out in a second," he yelled back. The taunting helped strengthen his resolve.

"Good. You still need to go next door and put the moves on our hot neighbor like you said you were going to,"

Jeff continued the ribbing of his college roommate, enjoying every second of it. A few hours earlier a woman they all agreed was incredibly hot, even if she was about thirty years old, had come out of the room next door to ask questions about the local ski resort. William had been the lucky recipient of the question and answer session. He may have been the lightweight of the group when it came to drinking, but all his friends were envious of his numerous successes with the ladies. This case seemed to be no different, and they were all convinced that the dark-haired woman had been flirting with him. Now, after an hour of drinking to heighten everyone's arrogance they all were able to convince William that she was willing and ready for him, and all he needed to do was to go next door and make a move on her.

He would show them he was still the ladies' magnet of their group. Spraying a few ounces of his favorite cologne over carefully chosen parts of his physique, he stepped out of the bathroom feeling much better. His friends let out a collective yell of encouragement; pounding their drinks on the coffee table they had moved to the middle of the room.

"Alright, fellas. It's time to show you what a real man is made of. Watch me work my magic." William possessed the typical cockiness of a twenty-one-year-old from a wealthy upbringing in Northern California. As he tried to sidestep around the coffee table his foot caught the leg of the bed, sending him crashing to the floor. His friends broke out in laughter as he dusted himself off and flipped them the bird. He sheepishly made his way out the door into the crisp night air, and turned to his friends one last time.

"Don't worry, boys. I'll still be ready to go tomorrow. I'll make sure she does all the heavy lifting." With a wink he slammed the door and left his friends to debate whether or not he would succeed.

William gripped the handrails and cautiously walked down the short flight of stairs. The thin layer of snow made them extremely slick, and even in his drunken haze he knew he could easily break his leg if he was not careful. His inebriated mind began fighting off the alcohol, trying to come up with something witty to say. After a couple of seconds he came up with an idea. He stood there shaking, unsure if it was the cold weather or nerves. He crossed the short distance over the parking lot and began climbing the stairs that led to the woman's door. There was a man in blue jeans and a flannel shirt standing in the small hallway. Was he beaten to the punch? He breathed a sigh of relief when the stranger reached into his pocket and began fiddling with the door opposite the woman's. William climbed the short flight of steps.

"Whaz up?" William's words were slurred as they spilled out of his mouth. The man ignored him. For a brief second he considered heading back to his room, but the thought of his friends harassing his manhood forced him to take the plunge. He rapped on the door several times, the cheap hinges moving more than they should have. Glancing into the parking lot, William noticed another man standing at the bottom of the stairs. He did not recall seeing him there before. He never got the opportunity to try out his improvised play for the lady.

***

The banging of the door shook Alex out of his relaxed state. He sat up straight in his chair. His right hand immediately grasped for the Smith & Wesson 3913 he had been practicing with for the last few hours. His arms trembling, he raised the gun and aimed it at the door.

"We have company," he blurted out, not sure what else to say.

"Hello? I'm sorry, I think I have the wrong room," William replied from the other side of the door. The man's voice inside the room confirmed he would be going home empty-handed. He started to turn around when a muscular arm wrapped around his neck, and what felt like a metal rod was jammed into his back. He started to speak, but his body convulsed in agony as a bullet ripped through his back and into his lungs from point blank rage. He went from agonizing pain to the numbness of death within a split second. Gregor's man held onto the limp body to use as a shield and gave the door a resounding kick, his black belt skills barely being tested by the poorly maintained door.

Marilyn was sleeping lightly in her hiding place inside the over-sized closet when the sliding glass door crashed to the floor in a thousand tiny shards. She immediately stood on one knee with her pistol ready. A silhouette of a man appeared, and she watched through the crack in the closet doors as gloved hands repeatedly pulled the trigger of a silenced pistol, unloading a hale of bullets into the group of pillows she had carefully placed underneath the sheets to resemble a human. It was an old, but effective trick. The would-be killer hesitated for a moment, and then stepped into the room. Marilyn sprung her trap. She focused her silenced Sig Sauer P229 and pressed the trigger, unleashing two bullets into the man's chest.

"Ahhh!" She recognized the voice of Gregor, one of Aman's security detail, as he yelped in pain.

His cry of pain told her he was not wearing body armor so she fired five more shots at the easier target of his chest. He crashed to the floor, landing on the shattered remains of the glass door he had just demolished. She walked quickly out of the closet and over to his writhing body. The silenced barrel of the weapon found his head, and she squeezed the trigger one more time, ending the German's already faltering life. The empty shell casing from her gun fell onto the dead man's body before rolling onto the floor. Her gun was unmarked and could never be traced so she left all her shell casings where they were.   In the living room area Alex fell to one knee and positioned himself behind the frayed chair, providing as small as target as possible. The large man stepped through the threshold, using the dead body of William Johnson IV to shield most of his muscular frame. The massive picture window to Alex's right shattered simultaneously. A man in a ski mask appeared in the open space with his gun raised.

Alex wasted no time. The man in the window was only ten feet away and had to be dealt with first. Alex pulled the trigger as hard as he could. The weapon fired, and the loud explosion reverberated in the small room, shocking his eardrums. The discharge of the pistol was surprisingly strong, and he was disorientated from the noise. Alex panicked, his hands weaving back and forth from the force of the bullets exploding out of the barrel. The intruder rushed at him in a flurry of motion. Alex fired off the rest of the bullets in the chamber, finally catching the intruder in the chest with a lucky shot right before his gun began clicking harmlessly. The intruder lay motionless on the ground in front of him.

The man in the door way rushed forward, seizing the opportunity. He had strict orders to try to keep this one alive. The intruder dropped his human shield to the ground, and lunged towards him. Alex desperately flung the weapon towards his attacker, who batted it harmlessly to the floor. Alex then reached for the 1970s era table lamp and stood straight up, preparing to swing it like a baseball bat. Exposing himself was an error as the attacker caught the lamp with his left hand, and pistol-whipped Alex with his weapon, sending him sprawling to the floor, just barely conscious.

"Gregor?" he called out cautiously. There was no sound coming from the bedroom.

Marilyn, gripping her pistol in the classic two-handed fashion, appeared from the far corner of the room. The hooded intruder noticed her a split second too late. His weapon flashed upward, but she was already squeezing her trigger. Her first shot caught him in the stomach, and he doubled over as the searing pain enveloped him. His gun fell to the floor, and she hurried over to where he collapsed on the floor, firing off one more round, execution style, into his forehead. No witnesses, she thought to herself.

Alex groaned in pain. She ran her hands over his body and found no bullet wounds. She helped him to his feet, and they stepped over the broken door lying on the floor and walked out into the snowstorm. They had to get out quickly before the police arrived. They stumbled across the parking lot. Alex was draped over her shoulder and moaning in agony. She unlocked the Range Rover, opened the back door, and maneuvered him into the back seat. He was just conscious enough to provide a miniscule amount of assistance.

"Try to get some sleep. You'll feel better in an hour." Marilyn hopped in the front and gunned the engine, leaving the lights off until they were out onto Highway 50. She then flicked on the lights, and swung a sharp left onto the main road, passing the casinos on her way out. She threw on a baseball cap that was lying on the front seat. It helped to hide her profile, and provided additional warmth. The temperature was in the upper twenties, and with the gas tank only half full, she refrained from turning on the heat in order to conserve fuel. She needed to be sure she would have enough for the forty-five minute trip to the Reno airport. She just hoped there would be someone there to pick them up. Otherwise, they would have to try and board a commercial flight, and considering the way they both looked, she knew that could raise all sorts of questions from the authorities.

The tires of the Range Rover lost their grip on the mountain road for a second, bringing her out of her thoughts. She flicked on the 4-wheel drive and the tires reasserted themselves, biting through the snow to grip the road beneath. They were ascending a steep incline, and she cautiously moved the steering wheel, carefully maneuvering the bend in the road. To her left, the lake shimmered in the midnight sky. Up ahead she saw a two-lane tunnel dug into the side of the mountain. Enormous pine trees, buried twenty feet in the snow followed her on the right side of the road. The next twenty minutes of the drive would be the most dangerous. The steep mountain, dropping temperature, and continually falling snow would be very hazardous to navigate. One slip of the tires and they would be off the side of the mountain or plowing head first into a snowdrift or pine tree.

Headlights appeared from the tunnel, and she could see another vehicle coming the opposite way down the road. The bright beams seemed to be staring right through her. The silhouetted vehicle accelerated out of the tunnel, traveling much too fast for the conditions. Marilyn tapped the brakes, and eased the Range Rover closer to the mountain. The last thing she needed was to be involved in a head-on collision with some idiot. The small truck passed her at fifty miles per hour, traveling downhill towards the ski town from which they had just come. The headlights of the Range Rover revealed the driver of the oncoming vehicle as

149

it passed, and she gripped the steering wheel in a moment of fear. She only had a split second look, but she was sure it had been the agitated face of Solomon. As she approached the entrance to the tunnel she carefully watched her rearview mirror. Solomon was continuing on his opposite path. After five more minutes and no sign of headlights in her mirror, she relaxed again. Alex was already stirring in the backseat. He was tougher than she thought. She figured he would not move again until they arrived at the airport.

***

Solomon knew there was trouble when he saw the flashing police lights as he turned onto the side street. He cursed Gregor. He told the idiot to wait for him so they could mount the operation, but the German's desire to one-up Solomon must have overcome his common sense. He backed up the truck and parked on the street. He approached the parking lot of the cheap motel. A small crowd had already gathered outside, trying to see what all the fuss was about. Solomon meandered up to a group that was being told to back off by two agitated police offers. Solomon fabricated a story to a few people around him about how he heard some commotion from the casino a few blocks away.

He studied the four young men with stunned stares on their faces standing next to a hole where a window used to be. Snow was pelting their faces as they listened to another police officer ask them questions. After fifteen minutes of chatting with some of the other bystanders he determined there were definitely three dead men inside the motel. The ambulance in the parking lot sat waiting to take the bodies away. He heard a few of the other people in the motel say they heard shots, and one saw a Range Rover speed quickly out of the parking lot shortly after the episode. They could not be sure, but they thought the driver was a woman. Solomon flashed back to the vehicle heading the opposite way on Highway 50. He was sure it was a Range Rover. He remembered wondering what the fool was doing on the road, and the short glimpse he caught with his headlights confirmed a young teenager wearing a ball cap. Now he realized what he missed. It was not a young kid, but a female face inside the cap. Solomon glanced at his watch.

By now she would be very close to the relative safety of the Reno airport.

He silently congratulated her and accepted his own fate. Her escape was no longer a concern for him. He now had a scapegoat in Gregor who could no longer defend himself, and he wanted nothing to do with this woman right now. She was cornered and dangerous, and he was not ready to continue risking his life for Aman unless the payoff was going to be increased dramatically. He headed back up the road to where he left the truck. He would head back to Reno at his own pace, which would include a stop at the local bordello. Once he arrived back in Vegas he would give Aman an ultimatum. If he was not willing to accept it, then it would be time to make a visit to the Bank of Grand Cayman and disappear for a few months.

***

Aman closed his cell phone and stared at the President-Elect with a look of annoyance. "You are your own worst enemy sometimes. The problem will not go away. She has escaped again. Solomon will be back here in a few hours to provide more details." They were sitting at an opulent desk in Zach's suite, going over Cabinet selections and policy strategies when Solomon called. It was past midnight, and both were exhausted and ready to finish up.

"Sorry," was the only reply Zach could muster.

"You're causing us serious problems. Solomon claims she must be a government agent. That is certainly not good, but it does provide us with an option. It's time to have our friend in D.C. call our favorite reporter and pass along a very interesting piece of information. Let's see how long this little investigation can last when the media get their hands on it."

"I don't like it, Aman. This is one area where we don't need the press. If some over-eager jackass starts digging he may find something." Zach was becoming nervous for the first time as he realized she was not a stripper after all. "We need to call that strip club where she works. Find out how she got the job and where she came from," Zach said. Now that she was an adversary and not a conquest Zach began to focus on what needed to be done to stop her.

"I'll have someone look into it as well but I think Solomon already has. Don't worry about the press. It will be a targeted leak. If they are continuing to launch an investigation we can use their little political vendetta against them. Our man in D.C. has a reporter who is very sympathetic to us. We just need the story in the press. It will put some heat on whoever is looking into your affairs. Maybe it will make them think twice before putting their ass on the line.

"You're sure this is a good idea? I still don't like it," the President-Elect said.

"It will work. I'll ask our senator to call some hearings if things look like they may get out of hand. Enough for tonight though. Let's get some sleep." Aman tossed the stack of papers he was holding onto Zach's lap before walking out of the room.

"When are we heading back to D.C.?" Zach called out to him.

"Tomorrow afternoon. We'll have to finish our work there. The rest of the team headed back yesterday to work on your inauguration speech and start contacting some of the local players we'll need on board. The campaign volunteers can clean up this place tomorrow. We can't stay here any longer. Plus, it will look better if you are in D.C. when this story breaks, and not in this morally bankrupt city. Perception is reality in politics." Aman stepped into the elevator and disappeared. Zach would put up a fight on some things, but one area where he trusted Aman implicitly was dealing with how things played out in the public sphere. His ability to read the mood of the nation and capitalize on it was uncanny.

***

The snowstorm finally subsided as Marilyn and Alex left the outskirts of Carson City on their way towards the Reno airport. Each passing minute Marilyn became a little more confident that she was going to live through this ordeal. For the first time she began to contemplate long term strategies instead of simply focusing on her next move. Highway 395 North was completely deserted as they pulled off at the exit for the Reno airport and she stared intently in her rearview mirror, looking for any sign that she was being followed. She made an intentional wrong turn on Plumb Lane, heading towards the downtown area of Reno before doubling back to S.Virginia Street and into the airport.

A large open field surrounded the Reno airport. She could see a few airplanes; their lights flashing on the tarmac as she approached the parking lot. At the moment she was more concerned about the Range Rover being recognized by the police than seeing Solomon or his minions. She was sure a stolen vehicle report had been called in by now, but the blizzard would have kept most patrol cars off the road. Luckily, the storm stayed strong until they reached the outskirts of Reno. She was eager to get rid of the stolen vehicle, so she floored the gas, propelling the vehicle into the covered, long-term parking area.

Alex's bruised face was going to attract some attention in the airport, but it could not be helped. He was sleeping soundly in the backseat. She had woken him as they drove through Carson City, and told him the quick story she had formulated about their vehicle sliding off the road. She would tell anyone that asked that Alex smacked his head on the dashboard. She finally parked the SUV, left the keys in the ignition, and shook Alex awake. She grabbed one of the bags the college kids had left inside the vehicle to help them blend in as they walked into the terminal. Two passengers with no luggage could raise some questions she preferred not to answer. The automatic doors slid open, and they crossed the threshold from the chilly night air into the cozy confines of the terminal. They simultaneously looked at each other, the pleasant surprise of still being alive evident on both their faces.

PART II
THE HUNT

Chapter 25

Marilyn felt like a sadistic mother as she closed the door, leaving Alex sound asleep in the CIA Director's private bedroom. He protested, saying he felt fine and wanted to be a part of the discussion, but she slipped a tiny dose of the necessary concoction into his glass of water and now he was in a deep slumber. They entered the Reno airport an hour earlier and were about to make an attempt to buy two tickets when she glanced at a bank of slot machines in the terminal and saw Malcolm Ray casually dropping quarters into an Indiana Jones themed game that was blaring the famous theme song through hidden speakers.

He smiled at her, showing his perfect set of teeth, while his bodyguard stood at attention, nervously surveying the empty airport for any signs of trouble. The fact that he only had one bodyguard with him told Marilyn that he had probably snuck out here without telling anyone. The man was breaking every rule of safety ever written, and inviting disaster for a public figure with plenty of enemies.

It was almost two in the morning, and the airport was a veritable ghost town. Malcolm nodded to his bodyguard when they saw Marilyn, and they intercepted her before she bought a ticket for a commercial flight. She knew Malcolm would be shocked to see a stranger with her. Alex looked like he had been through the ringer. His face was badly bruised, and his eyes had the look of a hunted animal that was about to give in to his stalker if he did not quickly find sanctuary. Marilyn was not sure what to expect when she entered the terminal, and seeing Malcolm waiting for her at a slot machine was as good as she could have hoped for.

Now that they were safely in the air aboard his private Gulfstream G500 jet she allowed her heightened senses to relax a notch. She felt a little remorse for lying to Alex and giving him a sedative to knock him out, but it was truly a necessity. She needed to have a private discussion with Malcolm. They were passing over Missouri now, and were still a few hours away from their final destination, a CIA safe house buried in the woods of Virginia. Once at the safe house they would decide what to do with Alex. She knew they would have to let him in on some of the situation. Another person on the trail might even be helpful. The extreme sensitivity of the mission had forced them to keep the group to a bare minimum, and because of his bad luck, Alex already knew way too much for his own good.

The cynic in her told her they would be better off if Alex had been killed, but despite the problems it would clear up she knew the thought was not something to be proud of. The previous few months spent undercover had been extremely taxing, and she felt almost like she was becoming what she despised. Alex was already about to join the CIA, and now he was going to be given a chance for the quickest promotion in the history of the agency. She reminded herself that his background and his knowledge gleaned from the trial he worked could potentially prove useful.

"He's asleep. Where's your bodyguard?" Marilyn said as she walked into the main cabin of the jet, and sat down in a plush, leather chair embroidered with the CIA logo. Everything else in the cabin was stenciled with the same initials. She found it ostentatious, but that was the way the bigwigs of government traveled. One could not do anything without being reminded for whom you were doing it for. The chair swiveled, and she swung it around like a child trying to entertain herself. The playfulness only lasted a brief moment. The short time to relish her escape was over.

"In the cockpit. He's a trained pilot and he's serving as the co-pilot for our little unscheduled jaunt. I needed to keep my staff on this flight to a bare minimum. Anna, you will have to forgive me, but we will have to pour

our own drinks tonight. Care for some vodka?" Malcolm offered her a crystal container filled with the clear liquid. "It's top of the line," he added as he sipped his Perrier.

It was the first time she had heard her real name in months, and it took her a few seconds to respond. "You never were much of a connoisseur, were you, Malcolm?" She laughed and let him pour her a glass. The biting alcohol would be the perfect elixir after the last few days. She took a long pull and let the fiery liquid roll down her throat. She felt perfectly relaxed for the first time in months.

"Don't get too comfortable. We've still got some work to do," Malcolm said. He could see her tension melting away. The rigid lines of stress relaxed into the features of a gorgeous woman who just happened to be a spy.

"I know, but I've been in the field for a few months now. Cut me some slack. How is everything in Washington?"

"Not good. I think Bret is getting cold feet. He was convinced you were dead, and I think he has been slowly laying the groundwork so he can bail on us at the right moment. I did not tell him I was heading out here after you." Malcolm looked out the tiny window into the black midwestern sky.

"That doesn't surprise me. I never trusted him." She made eye contact with Malcolm. His face gave nothing away, but she knew he desperately wanted to ask the question.

"Did you get it?" He finally asked. She reached into her pants and seemed to go through several layers of clothing before pulling out a cell phone and placing it on the table between them.

"The photo is in there. The camera on that phone sucks. We will need to do some tinkering, but the tattoo was there. I was right," she stated flatly as she downed the last of her drink and held out the tumbler for another one.

"I knew you could do it. Let's put this in a safe place." He snatched it up and walked over to the onboard safe to put it away for the duration of the journey. "I just hope Sean has been able to pick up your trail in Egypt," he said as turned the dials, waiting for the clicking sound of the safe opening.

"Bret sent him out to Egypt?" She did not think he would risk an international incident if he thought the operation was already shot.

"Yes. I was surprised, as well. I think he's just covering his ass. He wants the mission to fail, but does not want to be blamed when everything collapses. I set Sean up with Colin in Cairo. Hopefully we'll have a message from one of them when we get back." Malcolm locked the safe and sat back down.

"Let's hope so. We still could be in over our heads. If Aman gets desperate he may try to sick the press on us if he thinks he can get away with it," she responded.

"I know. So the guy in there sleeping? Who is he?" Malcolm was running down the mental checklist of questions he had been accumulating since they took off.

"He was part of the next class coming in to the Farm. Remember how you insisted on me training the next batch of recruits coming in? Just before this assignment was dropped on me? Well, he was going to be one of them. I was going through the list of my trainees just before we put together the final phase of this operation. I came across his name. I already thought he would be a good recruit due to his background working on the Indianapolis sleeper cell case." Anna stopped to sip her drink.

Malcolm crossed his legs in a relaxed manner and waited patiently for her to continue. "He noted on his application that he would be in Vegas just before the training was scheduled to begin so before I gave the list to the trainer who was going to take my place, I gave Alex a call. First, I confirmed he would be in Vegas. Then I told him we might give him a little test while he was there, and that he should be ready. A warm up so he could hit the ground running when he got to his actual training with the CIA," Anna said. She diminutively sipped her second glass of vodka as she waited for the angry response that was sure to follow.

"You planned on using a completely green agent for this mission?" Malcolm looked at her incredulously.

"Come on, Malcolm. I never actually believed I would have to use him. I just wanted something to fall back on if the shit hit the fan. I was trying to be creative. Hell, I was basically trying to avoid Aman's network and the Secret Service at the same time. I was looking for something that no one else knew about other than me. It was crazy and stupid yes, but in the end it may have saved my life. If no one else knew about him other than me, then I knew it could not be leaked. It was something I could use as a safety valve if everything fell apart. And trust me, It nearly did." Her almond eyes pierced him.

He tilted his water bottle towards the ceiling of the jet and took a long drink from it so as to avoid her angry stare. "I'm sorry. It's just a crazy story. Not exactly something we would suggest to the trainees, huh?" He chuckled, and re-crossed his legs. Every time he thought she could not surprise him she came up with something new. "Anyway, try to get some sleep, Anna. I want you fresh when we get to the safe house. Have you slept at all over the last few days?"

"A few hours." She stretched out on the couch against the side of the plane and was soundly sleeping within a minute. Malcolm covered her with a blanket.

Chapter 26

Solomon stalked into the chaos of Aman's penthouse suite and scanned the room for his boss. The room was abuzz with the constant chatter of campaign volunteers mingled with full time employees all talking on cell phones, shuffling paper, and moving about as they boxed things up. The month of planning in Las Vegas for the incoming administration was abruptly coming to an end. The campaign manager wanted everyone back in Washington D.C. within the next few days. Why they were leaving a week early, no one knew, but the typical rumors were circulating. The employee gossip continued as they put together reams of policy papers, suggestions for the few remaining cabinet posts, and everything from the first executive orders he would be signing to potential judges to fill vacancies that were upcoming in the courts.

Solomon ignored the young college students who seemed to constantly be cutting across his path. He meticulously searched the suite, peering into every room as he looked for Aman. The constant noise was irritating. These kids are all a bunch of idiots, he thought to himself. They were all foolish idealists, and young enough to believe that the administration they had fought to get elected was going to change the world. If he were not so annoyed with his boss at the current moment he would have laughed at their naivety. In six months most of them would either be fired or quietly told their services were no longer needed.

He was about to dial his cell phone and curse Aman when the old Egyptian appeared from the cavernous closet just off the master bedroom. He acknowledged Solomon with a brief glance while he handed a stack of ruffled papers to a girl who could not have been older than nineteen, whispering instructions to her and sending her on her way. He motioned for Solomon to follow him into the closet, closing and locking the door behind them. It was a closet in name only. Over a thousand square feet, it was larger than many of the homes that were sprouting up around the city of Las Vegas every few days like the weed that you can never quite kill. Empty boxes were strewn around the floor, and a few expensive suits were still on hangers scattered throughout several different areas of the closet. Sensing Solomon's unease, Aman spoke first.

"The room is soundproof. Nothing to worry about. All of them are too focused on the next great President heading to the White House anyways," he said as he dismissively motioned to the door and the volunteers behind it.

Solomon's icy stare centered on Aman, "I've been told not to worry about other things that happened recently. It nearly got me killed. I hope you have a good reason why I should not kill you right now."

"I think we are past the point in our relationship, Solomon, where we need to make childish threats to one another. The specter of death doesn't scare me. Besides, if you kill me Zach will soon have every resource in the world at his disposal to hunt you down. You would never get a chance to enjoy that little retirement pension you have been squirreling away for yourself in the Cayman Islands." Aman watched the muted reaction. Solomon hid his emotions well. This was the first time Aman acknowledged that he was aware of his offshore accounts stashed in the Cayman Islands abroad.

Solomon ignored the comment and made a mental note to move the money again as soon as he had the opportunity. "Enough with the games, Aman. I need to know what I've gotten myself into. This is clearly more than just one of Zach's little trysts. I'm not aware of too many strippers who could kill a former member of the German Stasi and two professional killers. If you want this job finished I'm going to need the full story along with some additional assurances. This was supposed to be a simple job of catching some whore on the run, not tracking down what is clearly some type of covert agent," Solomon finished.

"You suspected this from the beginning, Solomon. I don't know why you act surprised when your original assessment is proven true. I went by what Zach told me. Clearly he has been duped. I warned him to stop hanging around the strip clubs in this city, but he refused to listen to me. Any guesses on who she's working for?" Aman asked. Although he already had the choices narrowed, he wanted to hear what Solomon's first reaction would be.

"Don't give me that shit, Aman. I have no doubt you have a good idea who it is. And if you want this job finished you are going to tell me." Solomon was tired of fooling around, and he was not going to get into a political war. He had intentionally avoided dealing with Zach over past last few years unless he had to.

Aman's shoulders hunched, and he stared at the floor of the closest as he told Solomon the half-truth he devised earlier in the day. "It appears Zach is still under the careful watch of the current administration. The FBI came to

160

us a few months earlier and performed some standard interviews. This is normal practice. All prospective presidential candidates have background checks performed. It's just common sense. I was told that the investigation was wrapped up though. It appears President Gray has taken it upon himself to continue with his own personal vendetta, I mean investigation," he said with a half smirk as he raised his head to make eye contact with Solomon.

"Why would they do that?" Solomon eyed him skeptically. "Did they find something during the original background check that made them nervous?"

"Of course not. Zach is a model citizen, aside from his inability to keep his pants on in front of the ladies. But that is common. I don't know too many politicians who don't have that problem. Even the little goofy ones can get it on demand. Besides, you have seen the current Gestapo we have running this country. They have invaded a country, pillaged it, and are now leaving it to rot. President Gray understands one way: war. We have provided an alternative. That is why Zach was elected. He will bring real peace to that war-ravaged region. His mixed blood will allow him to be the first honest broker, and will help the Palestinians get their state and the Jews keep theirs, assuming they agree to work within our framework."

"Why would Gray want to destroy such a noble venture?" Solomon asked with a hint of sarcasm.

"Mr. Gray is trying to ruin Zach's reputation before he even takes the oath. Zach is not even Muslim. He's a Christian with family ties to the Muslim community, and he is the first real threat to the war machine of this country. That is why Mr. Gray's spy must be caught. She will no doubt try to get her pictures published somewhere. We have shown this country a better way. Zach just needs the opportunity." Aman's whole body stiffened as he finished his impassioned speech. There was enough truth sprinkled throughout the falsehoods to make his passion honest.

Solomon listened intently. It made some sense. He did not care as long as Aman agreed to pay his new fee. "Now I understand why you did not want to involve the Secret Service just yet. If the wrong person found out about the woman Mr. Gray himself could become aware of the situation," Solomon added.

"Exactly." Aman grinned, knowing the Frenchmen would take the bait. "So, will you go to Washington D.C. and finish the job?" Aman asked.

Solomon's face remained stoic. He was hoping for the offer, but he did not want to seem too eager. "Two million dollars is the fee. Apparently you know the account number to deposit it in."

"Half now, and the rest once you complete the task," Aman responded.

"Of course. But where do I begin? I need a starting point if I'm going to catch her."

"I have learned one thing. It appears she may be an employee of the CIA. When you were on your way back here I called one of our low-level informants in Reno. He has a minor job at the airport. It appears an unscheduled flight from D.C. arrived in Reno in the early morning hours. I had him throw around some money to the air traffic controllers. It turns out it was a CIA plane. And not just any plane; one of the director's planes. An unscheduled flight to Reno in the middle of the night by either the CIA Director or someone close to him? I do not have to be in the spy business to solve this little mystery," Aman said.

"I take it you are not planning on keeping this informant around after this?" Solomon laughed.

"Who knows? We certainly have enough dirt on him to keep him in line. That is the beauty of running a business in this state. Everyone is either up to their eyeballs in debt because of their gambling addiction or they cannot keep their hands off the whores. And then the really easy ones to control have both addictions."

"Can you have Zach arrange a meeting with the CIA Director? He may be able to find out the name of the woman. That would certainly make my task easier," Solomon asked.

"I'm working on obtaining more information. I will leave it at that. As soon as I have something useful I will pass it on to you. We were planning on sending over some of Zach's closest advisors to CIA and FBI this week

162

anyway. Let them get the lay of the land and introduce themselves to some of the men they will be working with on a regular basis. Zach did not make any friends with either the FBI or CIA during the campaign. It is time to pretend to mend some fences, and hopefully gather some useful information for you at the same time."

"Good. I will get to D.C. my own way. I will contact you once I am there and let you know how you can reach me."

"Agreed. You know which phone to use." Aman opened the closet door and motioned for Solomon to follow him out. If all goes as planned I will never see you again, Aman thought. "May I wish you good luck." Aman offered his hand to the Frenchman in grudging respect. He knew Solomon's skills had made his own job much simpler over the last several years.

"Never seeing you again will still be too soon," Solomon replied, reading Aman's thoughts. He had no desire to be in this man's control any longer. He questioned whether he should take this final job, but the money was too much to resist. He would finish the task and disappear into the Caribbean. Maybe he would even return to France. He had enough information about the incoming President of the United States to be useful to his former bosses at the DGSE.

Chapter 27
Washington D.C.

Sarah Steele strode confidently into Brown's restaurant at 920 15St NW, jostling her way past a small line of people begging the hostess for a table. The Washington D.C. landmark served up Southern style food on white tablecloths. The gold tables and gold walls gave it the sophisticated feel that was necessary to keep the D.C. clientele happy. The early evening crowd included the typical movers and shakers of both political parties who routinely filed in each night to be wined and dined by the latest lobbying group vying for their attention.

The hostess immediately recognized Sarah and motioned for her to follow. Ms. Steele brushed past the line of people, ignoring the angry looks as the hostess navigated between packed tables until coming to a stop in the corner next to the bar. Sitting alone at the corner table was the old man who had urgently asked to meet her here. Heads looked up from various tables and then quickly diverted their eyes back to their martinis before Ms. Steele, a head reporter for the Post, could acknowledge their presence. Sarah Steele was by no means what most men would consider a particularly attractive woman. She was short, plump and Ivy League educated. This was a bad combination for a town full of Ivy League educated politicians who all thought they were the saviors of the country, and thus entitled to ignore nosy reporters.

The crowd turned their attention away from her because she was one of the most aggressive reporters in town, and one that did not take any bullshit. Educated at Yale, she was a tried and true New England liberal who believed her party was selling itself out to its moderate wing. Both sides of the political aisle feared and respected her at the same time. Unlike most reporters in town she did not try to slip her beliefs into her articles. She bludgeoned the reader with them, and the reader knew what they were in for when they read her column.

Her opposition enjoyed talking to her more than her own party because they knew they were going to disagree, and were happy to get a piece published showing them fighting the media about which they constantly whined. It was those in her own party who actually feared her the most. She did not write "puff pieces," and had no problem calling out politicians on issues where they would prefer to take a "nuanced" approach. The man she was meeting tonight was going to provide her with some useful information about the outgoing administration. It was already two months after the election, but she was still riding a wave of excitement after Allan Gray was voted out of office. Another term and she was convinced the whole world would be engulfed in a war.

Now there was a chance for real peace, and if she could put the final nail in Mr. Gray's administration she would be happy to oblige.

"Cosmopolitan," she commanded to the approaching waitress. They were in the back corner of the restaurant, and her dinner companion was hidden by the shadows. "Why are we sitting all the way back here? I want these vultures to know I'm in their midst."

"Be quiet, Sarah. If it was up to me we would not even be meeting," Yohan Rosenbaum's velvet voice spoke in a hushed tone. Always the polite gentleman, he could never tell anyone to shut up. The Jewish senator from New York eyed the reporter over his horn-rimmed glasses. He was not much taller than Sarah, and the crumpled conservative blue suit he wore was now wrinkled from a long day of work. Tired and ready to go home, he wanted this to be short and sweet so he could get some sleep. In his early days in the Senate eight thirty in the evening would have been the beginning of a long night. Now five years away from turning eighty he just wanted to go home to the wife who still loved him, despite the numerous times he had been unfaithful to her.

She never gave up on the marriage, and he rewarded her by not straying during the last fifteen years. Whether he was just tired of getting laid or felt guilty about it, he was not sure, but it brought them closer together, and for that he was truly grateful. Hell, compared to most of the people in this town he felt like a saint, but he knew he was only fooling himself. He sipped his dirty martini and watched as the waitress quickly reappeared and set Sarah's cosmopolitan on the table. She ordered one of the few vegetarian dishes on the menu, while he opted for the gumbo. The waitress disappeared amongst the growing crowd. Sarah immediately started the meeting, her short temper not wasting any time in rearing its ugly head.

"Thanks for sitting so close to the bar." She tipped her glass in a sarcastic manner. "I understand you have some new stuff for me. It better be good. I already got him out of office." She took a careful taste of her drink and put it down approvingly.

Yohan's wrinkled face broke into a delicate smile. "Why does every reporter in this city think they are the most influential one?"

"Because I am," she shot back.

"The press always complain about how egotistical and cocky we are over on the Hill, and then I have to sit here and listen to this." Yohan was always amused by her antics. This was not the first time he had been asked to pass on information to her, and he always found the encounters enlightening.

"Hey, I'm just keeping up with the Jones's, honey," Sarah replied. She adjusted her glasses and glanced back towards the rest of the tables. She did not like having her back to all the other powerful patrons. "Can we change seats?" She asked in a suddenly submissive tone.

"No. Don't worry. This won't take long. I need to head home as soon as we eat." Yohan knew she was uncomfortable, and he preferred to keep her that way.

"Let's have it then. You're the one who called me out here at the last second."

"Yes, yes. Do you think you could get it published tomorrow?" Yohan asked.

"I will have to get it to my editor quickly, but at the current rate this conversation is going I would say no. Of course, it's also going to have to be worthy information for a rush printing job."

"What would you think if the current administration had launched an investigation into the background of Zachariah Hardin, and that investigation was still continuing as we speak?" Yohan knew her answer, but wanted to get her worked up first.

Sarah eyed him suspiciously. "I wouldn't be surprised in the least. That ass has done nothing but crap on the Constitution ever since he came into office. He has used a national tragedy as an excuse to trample as many rights as possible. He's done nothing but piss off every country that used to be our friend, and don't even get me started on Iraq." She stopped, realizing the immature ranting for what it was. "But, for me to go to press with such an extreme accusation you better have some proof." She took another diminutive sip of her cosmo, and straightened out the crumpled napkin underneath it. She gingerly sprinkled some salt on the napkin, an old trick she picked up from her Ivy League days that prevented it from sticking to the glass.

"I can't give you a name, but my source tells me that someone very close to the President overheard a discussion between the FBI Director and the President. They are obviously trying to keep the investigation quiet. Apparently only a handful of people know about it."

"When you say someone close to the President, who are you talking about? A cabinet member? Secretary? Wife?" She watched him carefully. There are certain things you can just toss into the paper, then watch how everyone reacts. This was not one of them. The journalist in her told her she needed more information, and she knew she had to be careful. She could smell blood in the water, but she had no plans to jump in blindly and find the pool already drained. A false accusation such as this could end her career prematurely, and right when things were taking a turn for the better.

"I was not told," Yohan admitted.

"That's all? Come on, Yohan. If I go to press with this and Mr. Gray sends his Gestapo after me, are you going to bail me out? I doubt it."

Yohan frowned at the comment. He lost several family members in Nazi Germany, and did not take kindly to flippant jokes.

"Sorry, I shouldn't have said that," Sarah replied sincerely. "But I'm going to need something else."

"Apology accepted. My own people are not free from mistakes. That is why I'm here. This incoming President will be the first ever to have a real opportunity to forge a lasting peace. That is why you must trust me. He must remain anonymous. I can tell you he was in the room for the conversation. The person who told me to pass it on would not lie about this."

She followed his eyes, trying to discern if this could somehow be a trap   "Why give me this story?"

"Now you suddenly have modesty? Give me a break, Sarah. I'm getting old, but not naïve. Everyone in this

167

restaurant probably knows you, or at least your reputation. They may not like you, but they respect you. You're not a phony, and you have a very large readership. Some in this town will curse you for dancing on a man's political grave, but it will generate a buzz. Besides, it is true. I've seen the proof myself." The last sentence was a lie, and he fidgeted slightly in his chair when he said it. However, he was told to do whatever it took to make sure she bit on the idea. The information was true, but like so many other things in this world, what was left out was just as important as what he told her.

The waitress appeared with two steaming plates of food before hustling off to get two more drinks. Sarah ate in silence while he fed her the basics about the investigation. Her mind raced, thinking of potential pitfalls, but the same thought continued to come back to her every time. She could play an instrumental part in changing an area of the world that appeared beyond help. It was an opportunity to not just be famous in her own lifetime, but for many years to come. The romanticism of the concept proved too much, even for a cynic like Sarah.

"Alright, Yohan. I'll run it by my editor." After fifteen more minutes she set her fork down and pushed the empty plate to the side. She gulped the last of her drink, dabbed her mouth with her napkin, and abruptly stood up to leave.

His scrawny arm reached out with surprising quickness and grabbed her wrist. "Remember, no names, including mine. You mention no one by name except the current President and his FBI Director. If my source does not like your column he can make life very uncomfortable for you."

The veiled threat caught her off guard. She was normally not talked to in this manner. For the first time in years Sarah Steele felt flustered and a little intimidated as she gathered up her jacket and purse.

"Fine, but you're buying dinner. If this is wrong though, you're going to give me names or I'll blame the whole thing on you," she said. With that, the thirty-eight-year-old reporter dashed out of the restaurant. The cold night

168

air jolted her senses, and she quickly slung her coat on for warmth before reaching into her purse in search of her cell phone. How reporters got by before cell phones she could not fathom. She punched the speed dial for her editor and got no answer. He was probably out running. He was an exercise freak. She left a message that she was on the way to his townhouse. She waved her arm, looking for one of the ever-present taxis that roamed the city. Her composure returned as the taxi pulled up to the curb. The threat from Yohan certainly caught her by surprise, but now she realized that his threat was a good sign. If his source was willing to make such a volatile accusation then it must be true. There was too much downside for them to take the risk considering that the election was over, and President Gray would be forced out within a few weeks anyway. It made no sense to want this information out in the open unless it was the truth. She barked the address to the Eastern European cab driver and settled into the back seat, snuggling up against the door in a wasted attempt to remain warm. The thought of a Pulitzer crept into her mind as the taxi circled around 15th Street and drove away into the chilly night.

Chapter 28

Alex Bryce stood on the deck and stared down out at the river rushing by one hundred feet below him. The cabin they were staying in sat on a precipice overlooking an unknown river. The sheer rock wall below the cabin provided a natural defensive barrier against any attackers. He did not know where they were. No one had volunteered that information as of yet, but they were definitely no longer in Lake Tahoe. The lack of snow was the first sign and the density of the air told his lungs he was no longer at the six thousand foot altitude of Lake Tahoe. When they boarded the CIA's plane he was still in a state of shock from the pistol whipping he received. However, seeing the Director of the CIA at the Reno airport did erase any doubts he had regarding the seriousness of the situation they currently faced.

A crisp morning breeze ruffled the flannel pajamas provided to him by his host. He knew he would only be able to tolerate the frigid air a few more minutes before he would have to step inside the cozy confines of the cabin. Their hideout was obscured by a thick forest of trees that kept it hidden from view. He had no idea how long he had slept, and there was nothing in the cabin to provide any information as to what day it was. His only notion of time came from a clock on the wall telling him it was morning. Marilyn must be asleep in another room, he thought. She left a note beside his bed instructing him to make himself at home when he woke up. The note was signed "Anna," which Alex guessed must be her real name.

He gripped the railing of the deck and peered downward a final time, soaking in the scenery of the rushing river. He was anxious for her to wake up and fill him in on what this was all about. He was annoyed that they lied to him, then gave him some sort of sedative on the plane, but he realized they probably did not have any other choice. His mind turned once again to his murdered friends and how their families would react once they received the news. *What if they think I killed them?* For the first time he realized he may be a fugitive from the law. His best friend murdered, and another dead body in his own hotel room in Las Vegas. It did not look good from an outsider's point of view. He made a mental note to ask Anna when she woke up. The cold air was now doing more harm than good, and he stepped in through the sliding glass doors, anxious to pour a cup of coffee from the machine that had just stopped percolating. He would have preferred something else to drink, but it was all he could find.

"Pour me a cup if you don't mind," Anna said as she appeared in the doorway of the kitchen.

Alex looked up front the kitchen table, caught off guard by her voice. "Sure. Sorry didn't hear you there," he stammered. "You always move around that quietly?"

"Helps keep me alive. Pour me a cup. I'll be back in a sec." A few minutes later she reappeared and sat across from him at the table. The rusty metal table looked like it belonged in a kitchen from the 1950s, and it rattled as they both tried to get comfortable. Alex kept his head down while he sipped the steaming brew, letting the heat of the liquid envelope his face.

"How do you feel?" she asked. Her eyes bore into him, looking for any signs of frustration. She saw none.

"Okay. A little groggy, I guess. How long have I been out?"

"Just a day. It's Tuesday morning." She gestured to the clock perched atop the wood paneled wall of the kitchen, indicating it was almost nine a.m.

"Where are we? If you don't mind my asking." Alex sat up and looked straight at her. Her jet-black hair was disheveled, but her face looked just as good as before. He thought make up would be a detriment to her looks. It would only serve to hide her natural beauty.

"Somewhere in Virginia. I've been told that's all I can say right now." She looked at him, waiting for the response.

"Close to D.C.?" He continued prying for information.

"A few hours away. I apologize for sneaking that pill into your drink, but I figured you wouldn't voluntarily take it. We also needed some time to decide what to do with you. You were pretty high strung when we got on the plane, and people that aren't used to killing normally don't react too well when they first do the deed." She gripped her unruly hair and put it into a ponytail so it would be out of the way.

The vision of the man coming through the window forced its way back into Alex's mind. He remembered firing off several shots, and not being sure if any of them had even hit the mark. Now he knew. "Well, I'm still here so I'll take that as a good sign."

"It is. But you and I are going to have to lay low for a few weeks. Besides, you can actually be of some use to me now. We have a lot of research to do to see if my escapades

171

in Nevada were actually worth it. Malcolm is back in D.C. He couldn't afford to be gone any longer than a day. If he doesn't show up at certain functions people will start asking questions, and right now he needs to keep a low profile." Anna stood up and looked out the bulletproof glass doors that provided the spectacular view of the river.

"What kind of research can we do in this place?" Alex motioned towards the rustic confines that appeared to surround them. The kitchen floor was sub-flooring with no vinyl or tile, and the carpet in his bedroom and the hallway was as old as the cabin.

"Don't worry about that. This house belongs to the Agency, and we've plenty of computers here to access any information we need. We can even tap into Desist if necessary," Anna said, referring to the counterterrorist computer system the CIA shared with the FBI and a host of other government agencies. "Everything is hidden behind all the locked doors you probably tried to open while I was asleep. This is not just some hideaway for fugitives."

"What about your prize you brought back from Vegas? Do I finally get to find out what the hell it is?" Alex asked.

She nodded in the affirmative. "Later. Let me take a shower, and then we'll head upstairs. I scanned it into the computer. It's possible you may actually be of some assistance. The trial of the terrorist cell in Indianapolis you worked on certainly was a good background for you. That was why you were hired in the first place." She turned around to face him. "Anyway, give me an hour to refresh myself, and then we'll get to work." Anna sat her empty mug down and walked down the short hallway, not waiting for a reply.

Alex heard the bathroom door shut, and he stared blankly into the front sitting room of the cabin. He was not sure if he should be relieved that he was finally going to get some real answers or petrified that he was about to be brought into something that seemed to be growing more dangerous by the second.

Chapter 29
Washington D.C., White House

Allan Gray slammed the newspaper against his desk, and punched the code for his secretary for the third time in thirty minutes. "Is Bret here yet?" His anger and frustration boiled to the surface. His always-cheerful secretary repeated her negative reply, and he disconnected the line before she could say anything else. His eyes scanned the article again. He could no longer bring himself to touch the paper. It was radioactive waste as far as he was concerned. The headline was his worst nightmare come true.

Gray illegally investigates President-Elect Hardin; the headline blared to the world. The article was short and to the point, accusing him of continuing to delve into the background of Mr. Hardin after the FBI had already given him a clean bill of political health. The article stated that President Gray was on a political witch-hunt, and out to weaken the new administration before it even had a chance to hit the ground running. When he awoke this morning the Post was the last paper he skimmed through. None of the others mentioned anything about it, so it was obvious that Ms. Steele had landed herself a nice little scoop. President Gray stole another look at his watch. Bret was late for their daily meeting. The FBI Director had called him to let him know that he saw the article, and wanted to do some digging before coming in.

He was a full two hours late now. President Gray stared at the bottom drawer of his desk, and considered turning his morning coffee into an Irish drink. His common sense overcame the temptation. It would only prove all his enemies right, he told himself. He picked up a transcript of a speech he was scheduled to give later that day, and tried to make some minor adjustments, but his mind continued to stray back to the article. Had he been betrayed? Was either Bret or Malcolm after his political hide for some reason he did not know? Their investigation was known by such a short list of people he could not imagine any other way this could have leaked out into the open. Should he even meet with the FBI Director?

Allan felt like he was assisting in the digging of his own political grave at the current moment. In a wild flash of paranoia he imagined Bret showing up with a group of G-men to charge him with some federal crime. God knows, he probably had committed quite a few over the last several months, all at the behest of the FBI Director, of course. The beep of his intercom interrupted his frustrated thought process. It was his secretary. Bret McMichael was in the sitting area waiting for permission to come in.

"Sorry, Mr. President," Bret said as he barged into the room.

He looked as haggard and out of sync as himself which made the President feel slightly better. Bret took a seat on the small sofa without asking permission.

"Coffee?" Alan queried.

"Thank you, sir." Bret looked up sheepishly as he realized the President meant for him to get it himself. He walked over to the small table, and poured some into the Presidential china. Bret's calloused hands held the steaming brew gingerly. The time had arrived for him to formally distance himself from this mess.

After taking a few sips Bret continued. "There was very little real information in that article, sir. I warned you it would be difficult to keep this thing quiet. I think if you give this a few days it may go away. With nothing to corroborate her story she could be in a world of trouble." *At least until I pass on something to her.* The article helped Bret because it gave him the excuse he needed to try to shut the operation down. The problem was that first impressions were difficult to erase from the public's mind, and even worse; the article mentioned the FBI. He would have to find a way to let Ms. Steele know that it was a CIA agent investigating Mr. Hardin.

"The only problem here is that it's true! The fact that she went ahead and published it only means her source must be really high up." Allan Gray's eyes bore into "his" FBI Director, making the accusation without actually saying anything. There were only a select few who could have

174

leaked the information, and Allan knew he was staring at one of them.

Bret squirmed in his chair, his hands fumbling with some papers sitting beside him. He knew this did not look good to the President. "Sir, I can assure you we're on the same side here. I'm certainly not her source," Bret spoke up. His voice was defiant, but not pleading.

"Well, she is getting her info somewhere. Any ideas? This puts me up against a wall. We have been deluged with calls from the press, and you know how anal Randy can be." Allan said, referring to his ultra-cautious press secretary who never answered a question with a straight answer. "He's going to want to be told what to say before going out there today. Otherwise he'll get creamed."

"Sir, with all due respect, I don't think this is the time to worry about spin. I could care less if he gets torn to shreds out there. We have more important problems to deal with. You need to call off the dogs. Tell Malcolm to stop. I'll recall Sean from Cairo, and we can blame it on an overly zealous agent." The irony that he was going into "spin" mode himself was lost on Bret.

Allan stared him down, his frustration now at its zenith. "God damn it, Bret! I don't care about how it plays in the press other than I don't want it interfering with whatever is left of this pathetic excuse for an investigation! What about Malcolm? How come I haven't heard from him on this yet?" He tried to call him earlier, but all he was told was that Director Ray was unavailable.

Allan needed to find out if there was news regarding the whereabouts of the woman. Bret seemed eager to give up, and the President was beginning to think that Malcolm might be correct. Bret seemed to be looking for the right moment to bail. Allan knew he was in a bind when he was relying on the head spook to give it to him straight. This was turning into the political equivalent of a sixteen-car pile up on the freeway, and the entire nation would soon be slowing down to gawk at him.

"I've been trying to reach him. Still no luck. But back to the possibility of a leak, sir. I can't help but think there may be a bug planted somewhere. I don't know if it's

175

here, in my office or at the CIA, but that is the only thing that makes sense to me. There are just too few people who know about this, and I would bet my life that they wouldn't divulge anything."

"Our offices are swept everyday for bugs. You know that better than I do. That is as implausible as a leaker," Allan said with a disbelieving look.

"I know, but I can't think of anything else." Bret was truly concerned about how the news got leaked to the press. He was glad to see it, but someone beat him to it, and he needed to find out who had the contacts to unearth such sensitive information.

Allan stood up and motioned for Bret to leave. Bret swept his belongings into his briefcase and was ushered out the side door by the President. After seeing him out Allan stretched his tall frame and pushed his hands against his lower back to stretch. He was very much looking forward to exercising more when he left office. When he was elected he was a sixty-six year old with the physical conditioning of a man twenty years younger. Now he felt like a seventy-year old with the aches and pains of someone in a nursing home.

The stoic face of a Secret Service agent appeared in the same doorway a second later, his chiseled features displaying no emotion. Allan Gray looked at his favorite agent and laughed. "I hope you're having a better week than I am, Jamal." Jamal acknowledged his boss with a nod and a smile.

"Call my wife for me and tell her I'll meet her in an hour. I want her to look over this speech I have to give. She is better at this fluff stuff than I am."

"Yes sir. Don't forget about your videoconference with General Thomas as well sir. That is in twenty minutes."

"Yes, yes. Give my wife a call first though. Then we will head down to the control center. I need to do a few things here first. I will need a few moments to myself." He motioned for Jamal to close the door. The Secret Service agent pulled the curved door shut, leaving the President alone with his thoughts.

Slumping in his high backed wooden chair his mind turned back to Bret's warnings. A bug would make more theoretical sense than someone leaking information, but he just did not see how it was possible. The security team took too many precautions for someone to pull off a stunt like that. Plus, the person would have to have the highest clearance to get access to any of the areas where they even discussed the operation. That left only a handful of potential culprits. In addition to the difficulty in placing a device, the bug would also have to be removed, or the team of sweepers who constantly inspected every room would catch it.

An awful thought crossed his mind for the first time, and he looked at the closed door and hypothesized that perhaps Jamal, or another Secret Service agent planted the bug. What about the team that swept the offices? Perhaps one of them was the culprit. The list of possibilities suddenly appeared much greater, and the threat less benign the more he contemplated it. He thought about Jamal once again. Was it possible? A man in the Secret Service for over ten years with an impeccable career and unblemished record? Jamal worked hard all his life, rising through the military ranks, Special Forces, and eventually to the Secret Service. He had done more for the United States than every self-centered politician in the city of D.C., and Allan knew it. He felt ashamed at the thought and tried desperately to distance himself from it.

Their chance for a successful operation was rapidly closing though, and he vowed to keep an open mind to all possibilities. No one could be fully trusted at this point. He made a mental note to call Bret and have him pull the files of all the Cabinet members and Secret Service agents who were assigned to the White House detail. The backgrounds of the president's closest confidantes and guardians were checked every year for any personal problems that could lead to them being blackmailed by a foreign enemy. One more search of the files appeared to be a good idea right now. Pulling on his charcoal gray suit coat he walked out of the Oval Office, making his way towards the living quarters of the White House. Jamal fell in silently behind him, followed closely by the Military Attaché carrying the latest nuclear weapons codes.

Allan gestured to his Chief of Staff who was sitting in his office, the phone stuck to his ear and a look of extreme irritation on his face. The voice on the other end of the phone was yelling so loud that the President could hear it in the hallway. He could not tell who it was, but the tone was clearly aggressive. The Chief of Staff motioned to his watch, informing the President that he was running behind.

"I have one thing to take care of upstairs, Barry, and I'll be right back," Allan said, and then took off without waiting for a reply. The White House no longer felt like the secure environment it should have been, and for the first time he felt entrapped by it instead of empowered. All the people closest to him could be his biggest problem, and not the great asset he thought they were. He wondered if this was how Nixon's paranoid mind first started operating.

Chapter 30

Alex sat in the living room of the cabin, reading the printout of the article Anna pulled off the Internet for the second time. She had received a phone call earlier that clearly upset her, and then appeared from her room a few moments afterwards, handing him the article and requesting he read it carefully. He was now officially on the payroll, and he poured over every word looking for some sort of clue. The headline along with Anna's reaction left no doubt that things were heating up sooner than anticipated.

Gray illegally investigates President-Elect Hardin, blared the headline of the Post. Alex continued reading. *For the last three months President Allan Gray has been using the Federal Bureau of Investigation to investigate the personal affairs of the incoming President. All potential presidential candidates are vetted by special agents of the FBI, but a source close to the President has stated that President Gray, who lost his re-election bid on November 2nd, has been conducting an illegal investigation since being*

defeated at the polls. The source stated that, in addition to
an illegal probe into President-Elect Hardin's past in his
home state of Nevada, President Gray also sent a special
agent of the FBI to Egypt to look into the history of Mr.
Hardin's family. The source also confirmed that the agent
caused a minor diplomatic crisis with their badgering of
Egyptian government officials. This led to the U.S. embassy
in Cairo receiving a formal complaint from the Egyptian
government. The special agent was then forced to leave the
country.

President-Elect Hardin's adoptive father and
guardian Aman Kazim raised him since Mr. Hardin arrived
in the U.S. in 1974. According to the source, Mr. Hardin
has no surviving family members. It appears President Gray
attempted to prove the incoming President's family has ties
to terrorist organizations operating out of Cairo. President
Gray's office has refused to comment on the allegations."

Alex finished the article and looked out the large
picture window of the living room. The gravel driveway
leading to the cabin was surrounded by a dense forest of
pines, oaks, and other foliage that allowed only the bare
minimum of light to hit the front of the cabin. The shadows
of the huge trees created the appearance of late evening
instead of mid-morning. It was the exact opposite of the
view from the deck, where sunlight streamed in, magnified
by the reflection off the river. For the first time he noticed
the thickness of the window. It was certainly bullet proof,
and served as a reminder that the cabin probably held many
hidden secrets.

"The window can take just about anything except a
direct hit from an RPG. No small arms fire can take it down
though." Anna strode into his line of vision, dressed in dark
jeans and a black mock turtleneck.

"This article can't be good news for us," Alex
replied as he nervously rapped the paper against the small
end table. Judging by the hundreds of cuts and scrapes in the
table he figured it must be as old as the original cabin.

"Good assumption."

"Is there any truth to it?" Alex asked.

"Yes, but of course everything has been turned on its head. Being in D.C. is like Alice in Wonderland. Everything is backwards. It does give me a good launching point for where we need to begin though."

Alex leaned forward in his chair, anticipating the curtains about to be lifted. "Yeah?"

"The agent in the article? The one who got kicked out of Egypt?" Anna asked the rhetorical question. She waited for a sarcastic reply from Alex, and when it did not come she continued. He appeared to be slowly learning. "That was me. As I told you before, the FBI was investigating Zach as part of the routine background checks done on all presidential candidates. Since he didn't come to the U.S. until he was fifteen, and due to my knowledge of Cairo, the job fell to me to do a little checking up on his background there."

Alex listened in rapt silence. Anna Starks stood with her back towards him. She stared out the large window, her eyes soaking in the dense forest surrounding the cabin, as her mind returned to that time period a few months earlier when she had spent several weeks in Cairo hunting for a past that did not seem to exist.

***

She arrived back in Cairo in early October, just a few weeks after receiving her instructions from Malcolm. It was just a month before candidate Hardin became President-Elect Hardin. A heat wave was stifling the smog-filled Cairo air when her flight touched down in the ancient city. The long drive from the airport on the northeast end to downtown Cairo, where the American Embassy and Egyptian government buildings were located, proved worse than normal. Anna had spent a large chunk of her childhood in Egypt so she was accustomed to the traffic. Her father was an American diplomat and her mother an Egyptian from a wealthy family. Her mother was disowned when she told her family she intended to marry the American.

When Anna Starks was first told this story as a young child it laid the groundwork for her distaste for the strict interpretation of Islam that her grandparents adopted, and that was growing in popularity throughout the 1980s and

1990s. She could not understand why her grandparents wanted nothing to do with her family. Her mother loved her father, and that should have been all that mattered as far as she was concerned.

She sat silently behind the wheel of her tiny car. She had already turned down a more reliable vehicle numerous times. The small car was the way to blend in. Whether it was donkeys in the early 1900s, or the present-day mass of compact cars, the city always overflowed with different modes of transportation. The one sure way to stand out was to be a woman driving an expensive car. She checked her battered mirrors and saw nothing of concern. She was not being followed. She maneuvered the French-made vehicle cautiously. There was only one rule on the highways into the city, and that was that anything goes. One did not avoid accidents in Cairo by obeying stoplights, merging correctly, or coming to a complete stop, but by closely watching for the winks and nods from other drivers. It resembled driving by feel instead of sight, and Anna was extremely careful whenever she got behind the wheel. A dusty baseball cap disguised her feminine face. There were few women drivers on the road, and she knew the occupants of the compact European imports darting by her were still uneasy with a woman right beside them in the traffic jam.

At over one hundred and seventy-five square miles Cairo is approximately half the size of New York City. However, it contains double the number of residents compared to the Big Apple. Anna was sure every one of them was driving on the freeway today as she shifted gears and slammed on her brakes, bringing her dust covered Peugeot to a sudden stop on the Sari-Salim Freeway. After fifty-five minutes of start and stop movement she finally managed to turn off the freeway and onto Abd Al-Aziz street. She began making her way towards downtown Cairo and her appointment at the U.S. Embassy. She had an early afternoon meeting scheduled with the American ambassador, a man whom her superiors had warned her about.

A career diplomat, the ambassador was a man who made a living kissing up to his superiors and never rocking the boat. This strategy was a sure fire way to have a long,

181

successful career in U.S. diplomatic circles, and he was content to live the easy life, using his government pension as play money. Anna knew he married into wealth, and that he requested a placement in Cairo for one reason. His wife wanted to spend four years exploring the culture, and the ambassador knew better than to upset the person holding the purse springs.

She made a right-hand turn onto Al-bustan Street and passed the Tahir Square. In the heart of downtown Cairo, the area around her was once swampland, but Khedive Ismail transformed it into the Paris-on-the Nile in the late 1800s. There were beautiful gardens, wide streets lined with trees, and even an opera house which provided the distinctly European feel he was trying to replicate in the North African city. A mass of tourists flooded the streets, and once again her journey came to a crawl. Ten frustrating minutes later she was past her final obstacle and pulling up to the heavily guarded compound of the American Embassy. She was technically on American soil once again.

The whopping five minutes the Ambassador took out of his day to meet with her turned out to be more of a lecture than a meeting. He preferred to spend the time making sure she understood she was not to cause a scene by upsetting any Egyptian officials.

"We're already on unsure footing around here thanks to President Gray and his unbridled use of the military," the Ambassador vented. "I'm doing my best to repair our strained relations. I'm expecting you to be on your best behavior."

"Of course, Mr. Ambassador. Were you able to get me an appointment at the proper government ministry?" Anna pretended to take his lecture seriously.

"Yes. Your appointment is for ten a.m. tomorrow. Please be sure to keep your inquiry quick. You may view birth records and any other pertinent information on the presidential candidate, but that is it," he said like an instructor dealing with a particularly difficult student.

She stood silently while he lectured. Her relaxed features showed no signs of anger, but her eyes bore into him as she imagined the humor she would find in taking him

182

to some of the areas of Cairo she knew well. Her stoic reaction, however, did not betray her thought. Anna continued to play the meek woman, "Don't worry, Mr. Ambassador. I won't be a problem." A curt goodbye and she was out the door to catch a cab to her hotel. She had plenty of work to do, none of which she had any intention of informing the feckless bureaucrat of, before meeting with the Egyptian officials in the morning.

After signing some routine paperwork for the State Department she exited the building and stepped out of the gated safety of the American Embassy. Suitcase in hand, she walked like a rich child leaving the safety of the parent's mansion. A block away a crazed sheik wandered aimlessly through the congestion of vehicles, shouting about the end of the world and pending triumph of Islam. A green string was wrapped around his finger. He was dragging a dusty American flag along the ground behind him. A few drivers shouted words of encouragement while several bystanders turned away from the spectacle. They were clearly ashamed, but unwilling to launch a protest, feeling it was not worth the problems it would surely cause.

Anna motioned to a Marine guard that she needed a ride. She decided to leave her car in the embassy parking lot for now. The guards standing on each side of the gated entrance raised their hands simultaneously. A taxi broke free from the congestion a block away, and rolled up to the front of the embassy. Five minutes later the taxi dropped her off a few blocks short of the Nile Hilton. Constructed in 1959, the Hilton was the first five-star hotel built in Cairo, and to this day it continues to draw a mass of visitors. In its heyday it served as the temporary residence of icons such as Frank Sinatra.

Now, however, it served a less glamorous role as a launching pad for thousands of European and American tourists who came to tour the ancient city. After depositing her small amount of luggage in her room, Anna made her way back to the hotel lobby, passing through its courtyard coffee shop where many of Cairo's upper class enjoyed mingling and discussing the day's events. She stepped out into the sweltering heat of the midday sun and walked the short distance to the world-renowned Egyptian Museum, which sat conveniently next door to her hotel. The meeting with her contact was still an hour away, but she wanted to arrive early to check out the museum's design and look for escape options if something happened to go awry.

Anna had never dealt with Colin Archer before. She was told he had been in Cairo for ten plus years, and while she did not doubt his skills at gathering intelligence, he was still someone to avoid unless absolutely necessary. He could be under the watchful eye of any one of the numerous terrorist organizations that operated out of Cairo, and after such a long time in the same place she figured there was a strong chance that complacency had set in on his part. One can only stay on high alert for a certain period of time, no matter how dangerous the area. By now someone had surely fingered him as more than just a government bureaucrat.

Anna stepped out of the oppressive heat and into the pleasant chill of the museum. The crowd waiting to get in was sparse, and after a few minutes she was shuffled through the poor excuse for security and passed through the grand rotunda that led into the museum. She meandered around the large central court of the first floor, taking in her surroundings as she made note of emergency exits and potential problem areas. The museum was not very large by American standards, and the entire first floor was an open court encircled by large sculptures from different Egyptian periods. She made her way down the outskirts of the open corridor, pretending to soak in the chronicles of early Egyptian history that surrounded the central court. She passed a limestone statue of King Djoser from the 27th century b.c., one of the oldest pieces in the museum. It had been discovered in 1924 next to the Step Pyramid in Saqqara.

The Old Kingdom galleries led into the Middle Kingdom galleries, and on to the New Kingdom of the eighteenth century dynasties. She nonchalantly watched her fellow tourists, keeping an eye out for Colin, or anything that may appear out of place in the high-ceiled main gallery. Twenty minutes later and placated for the moment, she ascended the southeast staircase to the upper floor where she could view the entry point of the building from a safe distance.

Exactly forty minutes later, and on time to a tee, Colin Archer meandered into view at the front of the building. His eyes roamed the room as if he were a gawking tourist. He was, in fact, checking to make sure no one had followed him. He caught sight of Anna eyeing him from the top floor, and they exchanged fleeting looks. After fifteen minutes of following the same path she had taken, they stood on the railing of the second floor together, peering out at a small group of American tourists huddled around the glass case in the center of the gallery below them.

"How was your trip?" Colin asked as they both continued watching the activity on the floor below.

"Long. Thanks for showing up on time," Anna said in a clipped and business-like manner.

"My pleasure. You look even more gorgeous in person than in the photographs Sean sent me. You were easy to spot."

"I'm not sleeping with you, so no compliments. I have a job to do, and I understand you can be of some assistance." She made sure her annoyance was obvious. She did not like playing games. "Besides, I don't like paunchy, bald guys."

Colin squirmed uneasily. Sean Hill warned him that she could be abrasive. That was putting it mildly, he now realized. "Sorry, just trying to break the ice. I understand you're trying to do a little background check on the potential president. I can tell you right now the FBI asked me to look into it a few months earlier. I got a call when they starting doing workups on all the serious candidates in January. I couldn't find anything useful though. As far as I can tell, all his family that lived here died some years back."

"Well, we will see if I can do better. We have people working over some Egyptian government types. I should be able to view some records tomorrow if everything goes smoothly," she said in a confident manner.

"They got you in already? Mr. Hill must have some pull in Cairo. The politicians around here make our guys back home look like models of efficiency. You do realize you probably won't find anything?" Colin said.

"I don't have high hopes. That is why I'm talking to you. I understand you have some contacts that you think may be useful?" With the bad cop routine now over, Anna could get down to business.

"Follow me," Colin said. Without waiting for her he made his way to the top of the staircase and bought two tickets for them to get into the Royal Mummy Room on the second floor. Anna pulled her ball cap further down on her head and walked briskly to catch up with him. She did not like being led around by the nose.

They walked in silence past the eleven embalmed royals whose final resting place was now the darkened room of a museum. The bony remains of Seti I and his son Ramses II lay in silent repose in the Royal Mummy Room as the two American agents made their way through the deserted space.

"What are we doing in here?" Anna asked.

"This part of the museum is the safest place to speak. The walls are specially designed to keep out moisture, and any other element that could hasten the demise of our predecessors." He motioned to the encased bodies, keeping his voice hushed. "There are plenty of cameras, but no way to get any listening devices in here. It's an ideal place for a meeting. Being an American inside a museum for tourists helps, as well. One of the few places in Cairo where we don't stand out."

Anna looked at him with grudging respect. "Good to see you thought things through. Now what do you have in mind? I have a few things to take care of back at the hotel. I'm assuming you have the meeting with your contact set up today?"

"He'll meet us at 3:30. After mid-day prayers are completed he will be home and we can stop by his apartment. He lives in Islamic Cairo so you will have to dress appropriately," Colin said.

"I figured as much. Should I cover myself?" Anna knew the area from her childhood. Islamic Cairo was the heart of the original city, and many of the narrow alleys that

186

made up the area were still reminiscent of medieval quarters. The area was home to ultra serious religious movements. Many of the hardcore terrorist groups that attracted so many of the poor had a huge presence in the area. Women were looked at with anything between mild disdain and outright hostility, and in order to avoid attention needed to dress modestly. Anna knew that because she resembled a local, it would be best to hide her features in order to avoid any unwanted confrontations. The excessive clothing also provided plenty of room to hide weapons on her body.

"Yes. Dress modestly, and like a local. Meet me on the second floor of your hotel. Room 200. I keep the room as an extra safety valve. It's got all types of little odds and ends that come in handy sometimes. Meet me there at 3:00." Colin disappeared through the same doorway they entered. Anna lingered for a few moments, taking in the splendor of the Tutankhamen galleries. After five more minutes she left to prepare for her meeting with Colin's unknown contact.

The narrow alleyway could not have been more than ten feet wide. Colin and Anna walked quickly across the stone floor at Khan al-Khalili, the expansive bazaar deep inside Islamic Cairo. Their footsteps echoed off the hard surfaces all around them. The buildings on each side shot up at a steep angle, obscuring any chance of viewing the many domes and minarets that dotted this area of the city. They stepped aside as a teenager flew furiously past them on his bicycle. The alley was much too small for any other modes of transportation.

Anna observed Colin through the slit of her burkha. His tanned features and weather beaten face allowed him to blend into the crowd that filled the tiny streets around them. The late afternoon meant there were still tourists walking about, mixing with the locals. They were looking to bargain with the stream of merchants lingering around, inside, and through the entryways and windows of the buildings. Shouts and curses echoed back and forth, the noise amplified by the proximity of the buildings. Colin played the part of a dominant husband as he maneuvered Anna by the arm through the bustling marketplace.

They finally came to a stop in front of one of the few doors that was closed. It made the building appear deserted when compared to the raucous marketplace around it. A quick rap of the heavy door brought no reaction. Anna fidgeted, glancing through the eye slits of her disguise at the fortress of buildings enclosing them. The alleyway came to a dead end a few hundred yards away. She felt trapped. Anna put her right hand inside the burkha and let it rest near her pistol so she could act quickly if it became necessary. The door finally creaked open, and a youthful eye appeared in the crack of the door, fluttering back and forth between them. The sound of heavy bolts could be heard being pulled back, and the massive door was slowly pulled open.

The young man could not have been more than twenty years old, and the Kalashnikov rifle that his fingers were wrapped around seemed too heavy for his rail thin body. The boyish face possessed a steely look that radiated inner strength, and his eyes silently acknowledged Colin. The boy continued pulling the door until the opening was just wide enough to let them inside. He then threw his full weight into it, slamming it shut as if he was trying to keep a medieval plague from entering the dark and dingy abode.

He motioned them into a tiny room to the right and shut the door behind them. The room was covered wall to wall with a magnificently embroidered rug. Luxurious pillows dotted the center of the floor. After a few seconds, Anna's eyes finally adjusted to the darkness, and she noticed the frail old man standing in the darkened corner of the room. He limped into the light and sat down on some pillows on the floor. The pillows barely seemed to move under the weight of his bony frame. He made the young boy look muscular by comparison. Despite his frailty, his posture was ramrod straight, suggesting the old bones were stronger than they appeared. The sight of him sitting cross-legged on the floor reminded Anna of a Buddhist monk silently praying.

"Aziz?" Colin spoke the words quietly and with the respect a grandson shows his grandfather. The old man was dressed in a dirt-stained robe and sat in silence. He watched them for a few seconds through his thick bifocals before

188

motioning his head towards the pillows in the center of the floor. They took a seat and Colin pointed his finger at Anna, gesturing that she could remove the hood that obscured most of her face.

The building did not have air conditioning, and the cramped quarters quickly escalated the temperature in the room so that it felt like a sauna. The old man watched her perspiring face, seeming to study every detail while they sat in silence. The door re-opened and the young boy appeared again, this time sans rifle, and with a dirty tray and three cups of steaming tea on top of it. After passing out the glasses the boy disappeared, and they heard the definitive sound of a lock being activated. They would not be disturbed again.

"Thank you for seeing us on such short notice, Aziz. I realize that your time is precious during this time of year. My government is not always as courteous as I would like, and they give me these diplomatic jobs at the last second." Colin waited while the old man tasted his drink. A wagging of the crooked fingers told him to continue. "My government has sent over a representative to do a standard background check on Zachariah Hardin," Colin said.

"Of course, Aman's adoptive son. He raise him since he was a boy. Allah bless him and his patience." The old man's voice was soft and kind. Anna thought she would have loved to have him for a grandfather. His velvet voice welcomed them into his world. "Such tragic luck for the poor boy. He was orphan at a young age. Aman always had good heart. I was not surprised when I hear that he take a young man under his wing." Aziz sat his cup of tea down, and pushed the glasses that were starting to slide off his nose back against his face.

Anna prepared her notes before beginning, "Thank you for taking the time to talk with me. As Colin said, we know you are busy, but this won't take long. I just have some questions regarding Zach's time here in Cairo." Anna pulled out a small pad and pencil from underneath her robes.

"Yes, yes. I am happy to assist. I must admit before we start that I am biased. I hope Zachariah becomes your

next President. He will be best hope this area have in years."
Aziz smiled paternally at her.

"I appreciate your honesty, sir. Now if we can get started. How long have you known Aman?"

The old man pondered the question for a few seconds, his eyes staring at the ceiling. He seemed to be counting the years to himself. "I would say since 1940s. I met him when he was a young man. His father and I prayed at the same mosque. His father was becoming disenchanted with our government and he decided to move to America when war broke out."

"He brought Aman with him to America then?"

"Yes. He was frustrated with Cairo. He worried Cairo would be overrun by the Nazis. He also thought Aman would have a better education in the United States." "Did you see Aman or his father after they moved to America? Or have any contact with them after that?"

He hung his head in sadness. "I never see his father again. He was murdered soon after they went to America. I did not see Aman for years after that. He came back to visit his family right after he adopted Zachariah. I think he took him in because Zach reminded him of himself. Both lost their fathers at an early age to senseless violence."

"When did he adopt Zach? I can't quite recall." Anna asked.

"Sometime in early 1970s, I think."

"Why didn't they stay in Cairo?" She asked as she continued making notations.

"I do not know. He came to see me. He tried to visit many of his father's old friends to pay us respects. I tried to talk him into stay here, but Aman was blinded by American dream." He paused for a few moments and thought about whether he should continue. After another sip of tea he started again. "I like Americans. They seem to be truly caring people, even if they do not follow the one true path. But they are naïve. The crime waves that run through your country," Aziz said in a disapproving tone. "I tried to convince him not to go back, but Aman had tasted success, and money was too much for him to resist. I still do not understand how he lives in your country for so long. I pray to Allah for his soul everyday."

"Has he come back to visit since then?"

"Not to see me. He came back before to make a speech and donation to our mosque here. The one his father prayed at. It is his own way of keeping touch with his roots. Forgive my bad English. I do not spoke it often."

"You are doing fine." A little too good, she thought to herself. Why would this man even bother to learn English? "Yes, I've read about his donations. He is generous." Her head focused on her notepad as she asked the next question. "What about the rumors that many of the men who came to hear Aman speak were members of the Muslim Brotherhood, and some of the other more fanatical groups around this area?"

Aziz glared at her. He sat in silence until her eyes came up from her notepad and made contact with his. "I do not appreciate that comment, my lady." The voice turned cold and condescending for the first time in their conversation. "You cannot walk up this alley without meeting someone who has some affiliation with any one of the groups your government refers to as terrorist. I will not condone some of Brotherhood's acts over the years, but they also have helped many of the less fortunate in this city who are left to rot by their government. If Aman give money to them over the years I will not blame him. Many of them in Old Cairo are friends of mine, and we have helped each other during good times and bad times. The young man who let you in has been graciously assisting me for three years, ever since I re-injured my leg. He runs errands for some of the Brotherhood. Does that make him a terrorist?" The lecture gave way to calm.

"I'm sorry if I offended you. I'm simply passing on some of the information I've heard."

"That is alright. I get defensive when it comes to the people of Cairo. They are like my own children."

"When was the last time Aman came back to Cairo?"

"I am not sure. Ten years ago at least. I went to see him. I was afraid it would be my last chance. He has spent the last decade engaged in your American political system. But I do not hold it against him. I just hope I live long to see Zachariah get elected to your presidency. That will truly be great day. He will be the closest to a fair mediator our Palestinian friends have had. Zachariah is a Christian. His Catholic mother raised him until she died, but his father was a believer. The terrorists, as you call them, think he is an apostate, and that he is Muslim since his father was. He has Islam in his blood, which is good enough for me. Did you know his father was a believer?"

"Yes, I did come across that in my research. I was hoping to find some of his relatives. Maybe someone who could shed some light on Zach's family history. Are you aware of any family members who are still alive?"

"No. I believe they have all left this world," Aziz responded.

"Aman never mentioned Zach having any other relatives alive? No one at all? It's like his entire family just disappeared," Anna replied. She was glad to be probing a useful line of questioning.

Aziz shifted on his pillow, attempting to find a more comfortable position. "Aman never mention it to me. I heard rumors that Zachariah's father was a soldier, but Aman never told me, and I never asked. Aman always was good at protecting the boy's privacy."

"When Aman came back to Cairo the last time, did Zach come with him then? Maybe use his influence to help Aman with donations from benefactors in the States?"

"No, no. Of course not. From what I can remember, he was by then already a member of your U.S. government. How do you say, a congress man?" The two words came out awkwardly.

"You mean a senator," Anna corrected him.

"Yes, yes. Thank you. A senator. And one with a lot of power from what I hear."

"That is true. He was popular enough to push through a new law that allowed him to run for the presidency." She continued to try to piece together the puzzle.

"I was not aware. I try not to follow your American politics. I find it tedious. You seem upset with him, my dear," he replied. Aziz picked up on the hint of disdain in her voice.

"It was quite convenient for him. Pushing through a law that benefits him soon thereafter."

Aziz shook his head from side to side. "I am sorry, but I do not understand Americans. What is the point of power if you do not use it for your own benefit? That is honesty in its highest form. From what I see of Americans they like to pretend they help others, when really they just want to improve their own power. They have taught this skill to many of our leaders in Cairo I am afraid. Why not be honest? He helped push through this law, and he used it. Everyone knows this too. Let your people be the judge? Would you not agree?" Aziz smiled softly, quite pleased with himself.

Anna let it go. "I see your point. Just a few more questions, and I'll leave you in peace. By the way, how did you first hurt your leg?" Her eyes studied him carefully, watching and waiting for the response.

Aziz eyed her curiously. "Just an injury that has come back to haunt me in my old age. I fell off my horse."

"You look too big to be a jockey."

"Not a rider. I trained horses back in my young days. Before he was deposed the King had me train his best stallions. I have not done it in years. Unfortunately, the injury is constant reminder. It came from a stubborn animal; one I was convinced if I tame him he would be one of the greatest. His speed was amazing. It was matched only by his determination not to be broken." A smile reappeared on his face as he talked about his youth.

Anna jotted the information onto her scratch pad and made a mental note, as well. "Sorry to get you off track. Back to Zach. I've heard rumors that he has an uncle who may still be alive. Zach's wife, before her tragic death, apparently had mentioned that his uncle still lived in Cairo, and was a real religious zealot. He was supposedly not happy with Zach's Christian upbringing, or the fact that Aman took him to the U.S. after adopting him."

193

"I have heard the rumors, but I can assure you they are not true. They were started by someone jealous of his success. Many people in this city are looking to hold onto anything that will give them the appearance of importance. His wife was spoiled American who liked gossip. Nothing more."

"Well, that is good to know. That's one less rumor I will have to continue researching. Thank you for your time. I truly appreciate it." Anna and Colin both stood up, and then assisted the old man off his spot on the floor.

"You are welcome. I hope I have been of assistance. It is always good to feel needed. At my age, there are not too many people who want to hear me speak."

The conversation ended with a traditional American handshake, and the young bodyguard appeared once again to usher them out. The alleyway continued to teem with life. Tourists mixed with locals were now milling about everywhere, and the afternoon bartering sessions were in full swing. Anna was anxious to get back to the hotel and review her notes. The conversation seemed innocent, but a few points were gnawing at her analytical mind. The old man was probably of no use to her, but there was one thing he said that piqued her interest. His pride had let it slip, and she did not miss it. If he was telling the truth and actually trained horses for the King, then he had to have some connections somewhere. It was not much, but it was something to look into.

Chapter 31

Colin slammed on the brakes. Anna put her hands up against the dashboard to stop her forward momentum. It appeared Colin thought part of blending in with the locals was driving erratically. Traffic was at a standstill so she took the opportunity to ask him some questions about Aziz.

"How did you meet Aziz? Did he approach you?"

194

"No, he didn't. I sought him out after seeing him around town at some of the political gatherings. That was one of my first jobs when I originally got assigned here; check out the local scene. The good and the bad. I took my time and tried to see if there was anyone willing to give me information. Most of the major players in this area show up at the big events to try to make a name for themselves or their organization."

"Let me guess, your superiors told you they wanted a feel for the Arab street?" She watched as he nodded an affirmative. Then she continued, "That's their favorite phrase, mainly because it can mean anything they want it to mean."

"Won't argue with you there. Anyway, it took me a few months of seeing Aziz around before I approached him. I think it was around one of the last times Aman was in town. I spent some time debating the pros and cons of different societies with Aziz. Nothing serious. He lived in Old Cairo, so I thought he would be the perfect person to send me stuff on some of the more dangerous organizations in the area. A lot of them operated on his turf."

"Did he agree to help you out immediately?" Anna asked with a surprised look. She waited while Colin pressed the gas pedal. Traffic was moving again.

"No. It took a few more meetings and debates. Don't get too many people around here willing to talk if they suspect you're an American. I think he's just an old man who likes attention. He gives me something useful every now and then, but not much. I think he just enjoys my company, so I've kept up the contact. I've noticed one thing though."

"What's that?"

"The few times I met him inside Islamic Cairo I noticed that he sure was treated with some reverence. He may keep a low profile, but even other guys his age steer clear of him. I asked him why." Colin made a quick left. They were almost back to the hotel.

"And the reason?" Anna asked.

"He says they're scared of him because he knew King Faisal. I checked around, and it seems when the King

195

was deposed after WWII anyone with close connections to him was rounded up and made to disappear if you catch my drift. But Aziz is still around. The King's personal horse trainer survived. Some of the locals are convinced he has friends high up in the government, as well as some pretty good blackmail information on someone. Otherwise, they claimed, he would have been dead a long time ago."

"Did you ask Aziz if any of it was true?" Anna was intrigued.

"He laughed them off. Said they were all superstitious crazies." He pulled up to the front of the hotel to drop her off.

"Thanks for the lift. I'll call you tomorrow after my morning session at the ministry," Anna said as she stepped out of the car.

"Sounds good." Colin floored the gas pedal. The boxy French Renault burst into the street, leaving behind a cursing bellhop.

Anna walked up several flights of stairs until she reached her floor. She always avoided elevators if at all possible. They were death traps. She cautiously opened the door that led into the hallway. Her room was just three doors down, and she could see the door was slightly open. A stream of light escaped into the poorly lit hallway. She yanked out her gun and waited patiently. Five minutes later a young man came out, took several furtive glances down the hallway, closed the door to the room, and walked briskly towards the elevator. Anna dashed back down the stairs she had just come up. It seemed that someone in town was interested in her.

She reached the ground floor and remained in the stairwell until the young man came out of the elevator. He immediately headed to a pay phone on the other side of the lobby. As he whispered furtively into the mouthpiece she studied him carefully, memorizing his features. He was in his early-twenties, perhaps even younger, but his budding mustache was deceiving from a distance. It was more peach fuzz than real hair. The traditional robes he was wearing suggested he was more studious and religious than most boys his age. He looked out of place in the cosmopolitan

196

lobby of the hotel, like a character in a play stepping out of rehearsals for a quick break.

Anna smirked as she realized he was at most ten years younger than herself. Despite this fact she still thought of him as a boy. He turned away from her to watch the entrance of the hotel, and she used the opportunity to move out of the stairwell, and walk towards the enclave of the restroom. She was too far away to make out any of the conversation, but he was clearly agitated and talking quickly. After a few more seconds he put the phone down, glanced around, and scurried out the front door of the hotel. His flowing robes almost catching in the revolving door. She walked briskly after him.

The sidewalk outside was full of tourists sprinkled with a few locals coming out to enjoy the cool evening. She picked her way through the crowd on the sidewalk and headed in the same direction she had taken to go to the museum earlier in the day. She could see the flowing robes of the young man two hundred feet ahead of her. His jittery movements continued to scream that something was not right in his world. Without warning he sprinted across the street, causing a few cars to slam on their brakes and the drivers to hurl insults at him. He ignored them, continuing on his mission. Without looking back to see if he was being followed, he jumped into a taxi idling quietly on a side street.

Anna waived at another cab that was approaching the hotel. The taxi slowed, but the driver flashed a disapproving look, indicating she should go back to the hotel and wait in line for his services. She stepped into the road anyway, forcing him to slam on the brakes to avoid hitting her. She quickly slid into the backseat and barked instructions. His protest stopped short as a wad of American dollars was tossed into his lap. A promise of more to come caused him to forget her cutting in line. He spun the rickety taxi around blindly, causing several vehicles to grind to a screeching halt while the cab driver waived a hand of apology. The taxi tore back up Muh Bassiunit Street and headed east. Anna's Arabic, more importantly her ability to speak like a native Cairene, was impeccable, and she fired

197

off a quick story about a friend's cheating husband, caught with an American no less. The driver reacted as she hoped he would. He pressed the gas pedal further down, trying to coax as much power as he could out of the circa 1975 taxi.

The poorly maintained roads were clogged with a mix of people getting off work, going out to dinner, or heading for late afternoon prayers at their mosque of choice. She finally spotted her quarry a few blocks further down the road. His taxi was stopped in traffic. He was at a standstill at the corner of Muhammad Fari and Al-bustan Streets, waiting for a three-car accident to be cleared from the intersection. An overweight, irate policeman ran around the intersection, practically foaming at the mouth while screaming orders at the parties involved. It appeared none of them were happy with what the patrolman was yelling to them.

Anna relaxed; they were only five cars behind the other taxi and should be able to stay on his tail now. The cab driver turned his head to face her, and gave her a leering smile that was short a few teeth. His blotched skin, dirty face, and yellow teeth made him look much older than he probably was.

Twilight was descending upon the capital when she spotted the boy's taxi as it made a quick U-turn and pulled up along the opposite side of Samiel Barudi Street. She commanded her driver to pull off onto a side road. The taxi she was following had stopped in front of the Sultan Hassan Mosque, one of the most revered monuments in the Islamic world.

She watched as the young man was yanked out of the taxi by the driver who was holding him by the scruff of his robe, a look of annoyance on his face. The petty quarrel was unbecoming of the scenery around it. Anna watched them in silence, trying to figure out what was going on. She knew not to go any closer. This was not a place for a woman to be. She would immediately stand out.

The driver's hand gestures seemed to suggest that he wanted to be paid. The young man continued waving his hand towards the mosque where a small group of men stood by the entrance, huddled together in private conversation. A face she immediately recognized suddenly appeared. The

198

huddled group moved out of the way, showing great deference to the short, gaunt man. He wore the full beard of a pious imam, along with a large turban on his head. His white robes were flawless, and he looked amazingly similar to Osama Bin Laden except for one obvious feature. While Osama was a literal giant in the Arab world, standing six feet five inches, this man was tiny, just barely reaching five feet tall. The watchers in the counter-terrorist center of the CIA jokingly referred to him as Mini-Bin Laden, in homage to the villain of the Austin Powers movies.

Anna thought the name suited him perfectly. His real name was Quasim Zahir, and Anna had read about him many times. He was a leader of the Muslim Brotherhood, perhaps it's most feared. The Muslim Brotherhood was once one of the most radical and dangerous terrorists groups in the world. Anna knew that Quasim had been one of its guiding lights for the past fifteen years, and rumors flowed throughout Egypt that he still had connections to Ayman al-Zawahiri, the Egyptian doctor who left behind his native country in the late 1980s to follow the real Bin-Laden on a worldwide killing spree.

The cab driver immediately released his grip on the young boy and Quasim handed him payment for the boy's fare. Quasim wagged a menacing finger at the driver indicating for him to leave. The driver did not hesitate and quickly drove off in the direction from which he had arrived. Quasim appeared to reprimand the boy before they disappeared together into the cavernous interior of the fourteenth century mosque.

Anna pondered the situation a few more seconds, then quietly asked to be taken back to her hotel. Things had just become more interesting, and more dangerous. Why would Quasim have any interest in me? And more importantly, how did he know where to find me? The thoughts immediately flashed through her mind. She knew she would be paying a return visit to this mosque in the very near future. Colin would have the necessary equipment that would allow her to enter. Whatever she found inside, she knew it would have to be better than the useless paperwork the Egyptian government was going to let her peruse tomorrow.

**

Anna stared incredulously at the uneven rows of filing cabinets scattered throughout the room. There were stacks of typing paper piled randomly on top of several of the cabinets, mixed in with yellowed, parched documents that were aging prematurely due to neglect. It was worse than she even expected.

"This is it?" Anna asked the government worker who showed her into the room inside the Ministry of the Interior of the Egyptian government. Anna arrived promptly at ten a.m., and was forced to wait for nearly an hour before the man finally appeared from the back of the building.

"Yes, all the birth certificates and other information for the time period you requested are here." The government worker adjusted his tie while giving her a surly look.

"Is there any order to the files?" Anna asked.

"I'm not sure. No one ever comes in here," he said with disdain. He was determined not to provide any useful assistance.

Anna glanced around with annoyance at the thin layer of dust that covered the entire floor of the square room. She doubted there was any particular order to the files. They could not even keep their current records in order, much less information pertaining to births from forty to fifty years earlier.

"Would you mind finding out? I would appreciate it." She tried her best to be friendly.

The man jumped at the opportunity to leave and disappeared down the hall. She gave one of the filing doors a solid pull and began the official part of her investigation.

Four hours later her time had expired. Her unhelpful assistant finally re-appeared and told her what she already knew. There was no order to the files. He explained that her allotted four hours were up, and she was unceremoniously ushered into the blistering hot sun of mid-afternoon Cairo. She climbed into a taxi, ordering it back to her hotel. Colin should be there by the time she returned. They were going to formulate the specifics for their infiltration into the mosque later in the evening. She wanted a closer look at Quasim Zahir.

***

Several hours later Anna was standing in the central courtyard of the Sultan Hassan Mosque. She stared silently at the elaborate central fountain while she waited her turn to wash her hands before evening prayers. Crowds of men all dressed in traditional robes milled about the courtyard. They talked to friends in hushed tones while waiting for the imam to appear. Colin stood uncomfortably beside her. He had voiced his concerns early and often, but she ignored them at every turn. She was unrecognizable thanks to the make-up, fake beard, and additional tricks that Colin used to transform her into a man for the evening.

Colin had visited many of the mosques in the area. Many of his contacts insisted on meeting him at whichever one they usually attended. It made them feel safer, which normally led to better information. However, he tried to steer clear of the mosques during the major prayer times. All the regulars were here, and although Anna had the best disguise the U.S. taxpayer could supply, they still received stares and occasional looks of curiosity from the regulars who instantly knew when strangers were in their midst. Anna stole a look at Colin and could see that he was nervous.

They completed their faux prayers and made their way through the courtyard, passing doorways that led to the area that served as the madrassa. This was the Islamic school in the building that housed approximately five hundred students who were being schooled in one art only, the memorization of the Koran. These schools indoctrinated many of the future terrorists of the world into the perverted form of Islam known as Wahhabism. Students began flowing in and out of the doors. Anna kept her head bowed while continuing to look for the young boy or Quasim. Colin and Anna made their way to the prayer hall and stopped to kneel on the outskirts of the large open area. The inner section of the hall was reserved for the most important and most pious of the worshippers.

The large circle of men standing in front of her all kneeled and began preparing for the prayer ritual. She now had an unobstructed view of the group gathered in the center of the open-air hall. For the first time tonight she saw the short figure of Quasim holding court in the prayer hall. Until the imam appeared to announce the beginning of the prayer session Quasim would continue to dictate. The men answered him in hushed tones, some of them leaving on his orders and heading off to relay a message to another group standing by the fountain. Others disappeared into the madrassa. It was clear to her that this was *his* house of worship. All the energy in the vast space seemed to revolve around him. He was the center of the universe, and his gravitational pull dictated what the rest of the planets and moons around him did. A smile here, a frown there, and men jumped into action, eager to do his bidding. Anna kept her head bowed, while her peripheral vision continued to monitor her surroundings, looking for any piece of useful information. The crowd slowly filtered in from other parts of the mosque, filling in the open spaces around Anna and Colin with prostrate forms quietly but fervently praying to Allah.

The imam finally appeared at the front of the prayer hall, gesturing to his flock to finish their business and gather together. After ten more minutes the huge, open air of the hall was stagnating and putrid, with body upon body lined up next to each other. All available space would be utilized in order to allow as many worshipers as possible onto the marble inlaid floor of the outdoor hall. Silence fell over the crowd until the incantations from the imam began. Others followed his lead, whispering silently to themselves with their eyes squeezed shut, trying to purge themselves of their demons. It reminded Anna of a séance, and the hypnotic rhythm of the chanting helped to slow her pulse.

She continued to keep her head bowed, chanting in Arabic the prayers her mother had forced her to memorize as a child. Her voice repeated the words in perfect unison with the other men squeezed in around her on all sides. The sea of feet and arms were inches away from one another. The false beard itched, but she refused to fiddle with it. She blocked it

202

out of her mind. Her eyes fluttered half-open as she continued to watch Quasim as best she could. She never let him out of her sight as the massive open-air prayer hall filled to capacity. There was still no sign of the young man who paid Quasim a visit the previous night. Her head tilted slightly from side to side as the incantations grew louder. She used the new found energy of the crowd to her advantage, her eyes scanning the area around Quasim, searching for anything or anyone out of the ordinary.

In unison, hundreds of turban-covered heads rose up, proclaiming Allah's name. She found the ritual quite beautiful. The fact that men like Quasim used it as a cover for the slaughter of innocents infuriated her. After a few minutes the decibel level of the chanting began dropping along with the heads of the group. That was when she saw him. The gnarled face was unmistakable, and his cloak overwhelmed his skinny frame. He was kneeling in prayer, fifty feet to the left of Quasim. It was Aziz. The fact that he was here did not prove anything. Still, it was a curious coincidence considering he lived in Islamic Cairo, home of some of the oldest mosques in the city, all of which were much easier for him to travel to when compared to this one, especially given his old age and crippled leg.

An hour later, the prayers finally came to an end. The warm day was now completely erased as the cool evening blew in from the desert that surrounded Cairo. The drastic temperature changes made surviving in the desert excruciatingly difficult. You spent all day sweating profusely and nearly passing out from heat exhaustion. Then the sun sets and the temperature would drop to near freezing. The two extremes play havoc on the body, and a person can only take it for so long before it starts to drive him crazy. In order to survive it you must have grown up with it. Fortunately, Anna had done just that.

Anna and Colin knelt silently, waiting for those around them to stand first. Hundreds of bodies began to rise, and the two of them quickly followed suit. Their knees slowly and painfully locked themselves into standing positions, no easy task after an hour of kneeling and devout prayer on the hard tile floor.

"Do you see him?" Anna whispered quietly in Arabic. The nearest group of men was ten feet away. Her eyes continued to follow Aziz. He was slowly making his way through a throng of men, like a rat feeling its way through a maze. She smiled through the coarse beard when she saw him find his way over to Quasim.

"What are you talking about?" Colin asked. All he could think about was getting out of the mosque as quickly as possible. His knees were aching and he felt out of place. He now followed Anna's eyes, and they both watched as the old man embraced Quasim and exchanged kisses on the cheek with him.

"Shit," Colin muttered under his breath.

Anna continued the conversation in Arabic, "Have you ever seen him with one of the leaders of the Muslim Brotherhood before?"

"No. Never. Honestly, I'm shocked. He always frequents a mosque closer to his home. I've met a few contacts here to pass along information to them, but I've never run into him before."

The old man continued whispering in Quasim's ear. She studied his body language carefully. It was not the deference that all the others had shown Quasim for the past hour. Quasim's back stiffened and he raised himself to his maximum height, which was still much shorter than everyone else. Aziz was acting like an equal partner with one of the leaders of the Muslim Brotherhood. There were clearly no orders being issued by Quasim. They were discussing a problem, like two business partners deciding the best course of action for their venture.

The crowd of men was now sparse, and Anna and Colin could no longer linger around surreptitiously and not be noticed. Anna slid her robe back up her arm and stole a glance at her watch. Their taxi should be waiting outside for them by now. They hastily made their way to the exit. The sound of their feet echoed off the tile floor and reverberated throughout the hallway. They were careful to steer clear of the remaining crowd as they made their way to the exit. As they approached the interior of the mosque they heard the sound of scurrying feet approaching quickly from behind.

"Mr. Colin?" It was broken English, but there was nothing broken about the steel grip that grabbed Colin's left forearm. Colin turned around to face the pursuer, coming face to face with one of Aziz's friends. The old man must have spotted him as the crowd had thinned.

"Yes?" Colin did his best to remain composed and at ease. He had a perfectly good cover story for any problems. "We're done here. You can leave." Colin issued the order to Anna, and she continued heading towards the exit.

"Aziz would like a moment with you." The gruff voice would clearly not be rebuffed.

"Sure. I didn't know he was here. I didn't think he visited mosques in this part of Cairo." Colin's confident voice belied the churning in his stomach. He had been receiving and sharing information with Aziz for years. He knew he had contacts with the Muslim Brotherhood, anyone with any influence did, but this was the first time he had ever seen Aziz in a meeting of equals with one of its top men. His teeth chattered as the bodyguard lead the way back towards the open-air prayer hall. Colin told himself it was the chilly night air, but he knew otherwise. The old man was standing alone, his arms gesturing to Colin in a welcoming manner, as if he was welcoming a misguided son back into the family. Quasim was nowhere to be found.

Anna bounded down the granite steps of the mosque and climbed into the taxi. She reached inside the folds of her robe and grabbed her Sig Sauer pistol so she could yank it out from beneath her piles of clothing if it became necessary. When he did not receive any instructions the taxi driver turned to face her. She ordered him to make a quick U-turn and park on the other side of the street. This provided her a better view as she waited for Colin to come out.

The night had taken an interesting turn. It was apparent that the old man had, at the least, a close working relationship with a known terrorist. And not just some wannabe looking to get attention from his parents, Anna thought. Aziz was dealing with one of the senior leaders of the Muslim Brotherhood. How close the two were was anyone's guess, but it made her re-examine their previous conversation in a new light. She had surmised at the time that it was possible he was hiding something. If nothing else, the old man was not being completely honest with Colin, and she realized that there was a distinct possibility that Colin was the one being used for information instead of vice versa. Or Colin himself was a double agent. The thought caused a knot in her stomach.

Twenty minutes later Colin shuffled out the front entrance of the mosque with a look of annoyance plastered across his face. He plopped down beside Anna in the backseat, and they sat in an uncomfortable silence until they returned to the hotel. After washing up and doing away with their disguises they met up again in the hotel bar. They found a small table that was tucked away from the others. The corner table also provided Anna with a panoramic view of all the other tables. The crowd was sparse, and consisted mostly of tourists planning their next day's excursion.

"What did the old man have to say?" Anna spoke after the waiter sat down two Samuel Adams lagers and retreated back to the bar area. She felt fresh and relaxed after removing the makeup and beard that hid her feminine features.

Colin stared at her in annoyance. "I knew going there would only cause problems. I had to make up a lie about who you were and why I was meeting you there."

"You work for the Company. Kinda comes with the territory," she remarked with a smirk.

"Yes, but that's not the point. He didn't recognize you, of course. That little disguise is top of the line stuff. I know the guy in the Science and Technology Directorate that developed it. He's a true genius," Colin said with pride before continuing, "Still, these people run in cliques. My sources see me at the mosque when I'm not meeting them and it immediately raises questions. They don't trust me as it is. I have to feed them useful pieces of intel every now and then just so they will continue to talk. Hell, I had to convert to Islam before they would even allow me into any of the mosques. No unbelievers are supposed to set foot in them after all."

"Well, the trip was worth it. Aziz talking with Quasim definitely raises some serious questions that I would like answered. If that means I have to rattle the cage a little, so be it. What did the old man say?" Anna asked.

"Just be careful not to accidentally open that cage while you are rattling it," Colin warned her. "Anyway, Aziz wanted to know how your research was coming along. I told him I was unsure, but since you had not contacted me since yesterday I figured you had nothing of importance come up. He seemed pleased, but a little nervous."

"What about Quasim?"

"He was nowhere to be found. Aziz did say one interesting thing though. He said it was in your best interest to leave the country."

"That is curious. Did he offer any reasons?"

"He said you were wasting your time, and that whatever information the government had on Zach in its archives is useless. He was perfectly friendly, but the veiled warning was clear. He doesn't like you snooping around. Number one, you are a woman, and number two, he said it would not be good for the U.S.'s relationship with Egypt to start off by offending the home country of the next potential president. He really caught my attention with his last statement though. He claimed he will soon be a special envoy for the Egyptian government in its dealings with the U.S. A new era of working together. All the normal diplomatic crap."

"If I'm wasting my time why should he care?" Anna swirled the layer of foam at the top of her beer until it dissipated. She sipped the lager, savoring the flavor.

"Well, these guys are sensitive about their turf." Colin's eyes scanned the room. He was still on edge from the trip to the mosque. The cold beer helped to calm his nerves.

"Any idea what Quasim could be doing for the old man now?" Anna asked. "I thought the Muslim Brotherhood tried to stay away from him? I wonder what has changed recently."

"I've heard rumors from some of my informants that the Muslim Brotherhood has been trying to find any remaining remnants of men who still want a grand bargain with the West, and wipe them out. I wonder if Aziz could be in their crosshairs. Ever since Mubarak cracked down on the extremist groups after they assassinated Sadat in '81, those groups have slowly been gaining power. The fact that those groups are being suppressed and harassed by the government only makes them more appealing to the populace. Maybe Quasim wants to use Aziz as a peacemaker. If Aziz does have connections within the government he could be a useful go-between for Quasim."

"Seeing the two of them together certainly muddies the waters. I think I need to have a chat with Quasim." Anna watched as a group of exhausted tourists drug themselves through the hotel lobby. She guessed they had spent their entire day on an excursion to the pyramids. The thought dredged up the bloodied corpse of her mother from the recess of her mind. She quickly buried the painful memory of the day her mother was murdered in Luxor. Now was not the time.

Colin finished off his beer in one large gulp and stood up to leave. "If you need anything else let me know. I think it's best we stay away from each other for a few days. I doubt you are going to quit now, and I want Aziz to know I'm keeping my distance from you. I seem to be a target, so I think it best to let you do your thing. When are you scheduled to leave?"

"The ambassador wants me out in five days at the latest. But I agree with you. If I need anything I will contact you through the embassy as we discussed. I have a few other things I want to check out that are best done alone anyways."

Colin dropped some Egyptian bills on the table for his drink. "Be careful. Aziz is probably harmless, but Quasim is a different one altogether. He is hardcore. If they get the wrong impression they will cut your head off without a second thought," Colin warned. He quickly exited the hotel. Anna watched him climb into a cab as she plotted her steps for the upcoming days.

Chapter 32

Anna paused for a few moments and allowed Alex to sift through the information. They grabbed some energy bars and water to snack on while she told him about her final days in Cairo.

The days after her final conversation with Colin were spent staking out the Sultan Hassan Mosque, and meandering through Islamic Cairo near Aziz's safe house. It was a partial reliving of her childhood for Anna. Her mother grew up on the streets of Islamic Cairo. She had worked near the U.S. embassy, where she met Anna's father, fell in love, and got married. Anna vividly remembered the days of her mother taking her through the crowded alleyways and shops, bartering for goods, and teaching Anna about her family's humble beginnings.

The streets looked much the same as they did when she was a child. The blackish vapor of dust still hung over the city and its inhabitants, and the shopkeepers still tossed buckets of water onto their little sections to keep the roadways damp and the dust to a minimum. Unlike most major cities throughout the world where sidewalks and roadways were meant for travel, Cairo's sidewalks were little zones of commerce that one picked their way across. Anna made her way through the maze of people, searching for her quarry.

During the afternoons she dressed like a tourist. She needed to blend in completely to the scene around her. Anna combed the streets, pretending to search the wares being sold while keeping a silent vigil for either the old man, Quasim, or the boy messenger. A foreign woman shopping alone drew much less attention than a proper Muslim woman out and about without a male member of the family squiring her around town. Of the three for whom she was looking, she preferred to find Quasim. He had a reputation for having a short fuse, and she figured a woman interrogating him would throw him off the deep end quickly and get him talking. Aziz was too frail. He could easily die if she put his body under too much pressure. Finding Quasim, however, could be difficult. She knew her best chance of seeing him would be near the mosque. She doubted the religious zealot would miss his prayer times. Her goal was to watch him for a few days and figure out his pattern. Then she would devise a plan to snatch him for a few hours.

She also continued to be on the lookout for the young teenager she caught watching her at the hotel. He appeared to be an errand boy, and although she was sure he was probably not a full-fledged member of the Muslim Brotherhood, she assumed he delivered messages for the members throughout town. He would be difficult to force to talk. The children of Cairo age early because many of them spend their adolescence laboring in stuffy and cramped workshops. The city contained over 300,000 child laborers, and this young man's job as a delivery boy meant he likely was paid enough money, and shown enough respect, that he was not forced to work in the squalid conditions in which so many of his friends found themselves trapped. This fact alone meant he would be loyal. If she spotted him she planned to follow him as long as possible. She hoped he might lead her to a senior leader of the Muslim Brotherhood who could shed some light on the old man and his activities.

After a few days of making her way through some of the most densely populated urban areas in the world, she became frustrated. They all seemed to be hunkered down. No one had appeared, and she could only hope the old man was not too frightened by their original inquiry.

She decided to watch the Sultan Hassan Mosque from a coffeehouse, or as the locals called it, a qahwa. It was the only institution more common in the city than the countless mosques whose pirouettes dominated the city's skylines. There were several coffeehouses that surrounded the Sultan Hassan Mosque, and they provided her the perfect place to sit and clandestinely watch the comings and goings of the faithful. Each coffeehouse serviced different patrons. The one closest to the mosque held court for many of the men after their prayers were completed. This one, she determined, provided the best vantage point, but she also stood out the most. There were very few women who entered this particular qahwa, and when they did, they were always fully covered.

The other two coffee houses sat at opposite ends of the street and served a mix of locals and tourists. She rotated her appearance at these, sometimes going with the traditional robes and other times dressed like one of the thousands of tourists who flooded the city. A miniature pair of binoculars provided her a better glimpse of the mosque if she saw something that caught her eye.

She spent seven straight days using her mornings and evenings hanging out at the coffee shops, and the daytime hunting the dark alleys of Islamic Cairo. She was beginning to think they had all vanished into the mass of humanity that was the city of Cairo. No one even made an appearance to pray. The ambassador also began to get on her case. He had already left her two messages at her hotel asking when her investigation would be complete, and to please contact him as soon as she was done so he could inform his friends within the Cairo government. She knew if she did not have new information within a few days diplomatic niceties would come into play, and the ambassador would try to force her out of the country. She knew he was afraid of upsetting his relationship with the government of Egypt. It might prevent him from being invited to some of the lavish extravaganzas the government officials liked to throw. She knew they were not up to par with the orgies of pleasure the Saudis hosted with their oil winnings, but they were still opulent by Western standards.

She despised the ambassador, mainly because he was the complete antithesis of her father, who had fulfilled his diplomatic duties the old fashioned way. Her father understood the local culture and treated Cairo as a second home, instead of using it as a free vacation courtesy of Uncle Sam. Her father came to love the city of Cairo and even found his bride here. Unfortunately, her mother's family was not as open-minded to the svelte, light-skinned American who appeared at their door one day to ask for their daughter's hand in marriage.

Her search remained monotonous, until the eighth day finally provided a breakthrough. The Pharaoh's Coffee

House was quiet for the first twenty minutes of her vigil. She motioned to the waiter to bring her another mug. She crossed her legs, setting the copy of USA Today down on the small wrought iron table. It was early morning, and there were only a few other patrons scattered throughout the outdoor seating area. Her lightweight-jogging suit advertised her as a tourist, the standard patron of this particular establishment.

She glanced down the street at the Sultan Hussein Mosque, her sunglasses dimming the morning sunshine that burst over the city. A few stooped old men in flowing robes were making their way up the steps of the mosque. Raising her binoculars for a look she saw that none of them were who she wanted. She started to lower the binoculars when a spry young man burst into her circular views of the front of the mosque. The boy sprinted up the stairs past the old men, not giving them a second look. She immediately recognized him as the same boy who searched her hotel room.

She watched intently through the lenses, wanting to be sure that it was indeed the same person. By the time he disappeared into the monstrous doors of the mosque she was positive. She quickly settled her tab, doused the last of her coffee down her throat, and stashed the binoculars into her purse. Making her way onto the sidewalk, she slowed her pace substantially, stopping every so often to look around at the shops and buildings as if she was lost and trying to figure out what she wanted to do. A few steps forward, a casual turn backwards, gazing through the glass of a tacky gift shop meant to ensnare the foolish Western tourist, and then she continued on her way.

After twenty minutes of the routine she finally crossed the three blocks, and approached the front of the mosque. The lanky teenager emerged from the mosque on cue, and for once something was unfolding as she had planned. He bounded down the marble stairs, taking them two at a time, and ran across the empty street towards a row of parked cars. Anna casually raised her arm in the pre-arranged gesture, letting her taxi driver know it was time to fire up the engine.

The boy passed in front of the cab, which was parked near the intersection. An old pickup truck sat opposite the taxi. The passenger door of the truck swung open and a gesturing hand appeared, beckoning the young man to get in. The truck pulled out into the barren street and headed north. She hurried into her cab and issued curt instructions to follow the battered, mud covered pickup. She tossed a wad of money into the front seat and issued stern orders not to lose the vehicle if he wanted more.

A short ride across the dust covered streets and they were soon in front of the Khan al-Khalili, the expansive bazaar that is the pulse of Islamic Cairo. She whispered instructions for the driver to slow down. The old pickup truck stopped fifty yards in front of them, and the boy jumped out and headed into the alleyway, which was just beginning to teem with life. The shopkeepers were scattered across the area, setting up their goods in the hopes of attracting as many customers as possible.

The aroma of spices filtered through the air, but could not overpower the smell of strong Egyptian coffee that wafted out from the coffee shops surrounding the bazaar. The boy was walking at a quick pace through the early morning marketplace, ignoring the pleasantries that a few of the shopkeepers shouted his way. Anna kept her distance which allowed her to keep an eye on him without running the risk of being seen. Her senses watched and listened for any signs that she was under surveillance, but nothing struck her as suspicious.

They were passing through one of the areas of Islamic Cairo that tourists frequented. The tourists came looking for local bargains, but often ended up with "priceless antiques" that just rolled out of a factory a few weeks earlier. The best deals a tourist could find were literally right under their feet. Thick Persian rugs covered most of the alleyways. The rugs were laid out by the storeowners who begged and pleaded for people to walk across them. The constant pounding on the rugs actually enlivened the dyes, giving them a more vivid color.

Surrounding the open-air marketplace was a much darker side of the area. Behind the storefronts most people lived by medieval standards. The sewers never functioned properly, and anyone with any real money moved out years earlier. The area was in a perpetual state of poverty. The Muslim Brotherhood was the primary group that helped to fill the economic void for the local residents. Anna knew this and accepted it. After Anwar Sadat's assassination in 1981 many of Egypt's most violent groups were rounded up and summarily thrown into prison. They languished there for years, many of them beaten and tortured until they could take it no longer. Eventually they either died or ratted out other members. Ayman al-Zawahiri was one of these men who were tossed into jail at that time. He would become one of the leaders of Islamic Jihad, a group whose only goal was to overthrow the Egyptian government. Some in the Muslim Brotherhood, tired of executions and beatings, decided to enter the political process.

The Muslim Brotherhood and Islamic Jihad went their separate ways by the mid-1980s. Zawahiri's group eventually merged with Bin Laden, creating the multinational terrorist organization whose main objective was to strike the United States. The Brotherhood continued operating strictly as a local group. Anna looked around at their handy work. The Muslim Brotherhood received enough funding from outside donors to sprinkle money throughout small enclaves like this area. It provided the locals just enough on which to get by, but the funds were small enough to keep the population weak and complacent.

At the same time, the Brotherhood blamed the people's plight on the autocratic government- which was partially true-and preached to the people that the only way to escape their situation would be a return to strict Islamist rule. The plan was slow and methodical, but after twenty years it was finally bearing fruit. The Muslim Brotherhood ran Islamic Cairo the way a mafia family runs the Bronx; with an iron fist, and answering to no one. If absolutely necessary, a dead body was used to keep the locals in line.

Twenty yards in front of her the boy slowed his pace, ducking off the main thoroughfare and into one of the tiny alleys that intersected this part of town. It was an area the tourists did not venture. The smell of human waste and breakfast cooking wafted through the enclave, creating a disgusting concoction. The boy continued plowing ahead, single-mindedly determined to get to his destination on time. The alley was empty so she backed off, not wanting to alert him to her presence. Whenever he stopped or slowed down she stepped behind the clothes put out to dry that were draped between the buildings just above her head.

The boy made one more right-hand turn, disappearing around a bend. Anna crept up to the corner and cautiously poked her head around the building. The boy walked into a dead end. The smell here was even more pungent than the area through which they just passed. He stood at an empty doorway, waiting for someone. An average sized man in his mid-twenties with curly black hair and a coarse black beard appeared. He flashed an AK-47 from underneath his robe in a show of power. The boy was clearly used to the show of force and did not seem intimidated in the least. He handed the older man a piece of paper and waited while the man vanished into the building.

A few minutes later Quasim's short figure appeared in the doorway, a broad smile on his face. He angrily growled an instruction to the bodyguard who headed down the alley in a sprint. Anna quickly ducked inside the closest doorway, escaping just in time as the bodyguard dashed past her previous lookout point. She heard him cursing in Arabic to himself. He was being ordered back to the Sultan Hussein Mosque. A few seconds later the messenger boy appeared again, sprinting past her tiny hideout, looking to fulfill the next errand Quasim gave him. It was time to make a move.

Chapter 33

Anna ran quickly to the entrance and peered through the open window. The dirty hovel yawned back at her. It showed no signs of being an important hideout for a supposed terrorist group. The interior of the room was just as poorly maintained as the cracking brick façade of the exterior. She stepped inside, closing the door behind her.

The floor was mostly dirt, with only a few lone pieces of tile lying erratically over it. There were four, weather-beaten, dirty prayer rugs in each corner of the room. A small table surrounded by two rickety old wooden chairs sat in the middle of the room. A half-eaten meal of fuul, small brown beans soaked during the night and then boiled, sat on the table, along with a few pieces of colorful fruit. Fuul was the everyman's dish of the people of Cairo, and often eaten for breakfast and lunch. She closed the wooden clapboards to cover the window, and made her way towards the back of the building with her pistol raised. Her slim figure made no sound as it stepped across the dirt floor. Her ears perked, listening for any noises.

Incantations echoed from one of the other rooms, and she realized Quasim was praying. He had most likely been interrupted by the boy's visit, and was now finishing his religious task. She was about to go get him when the voice stopped and footsteps announced he was heading in her direction. Taking four steps backward to the center of the room she stood and waited. He stepped through the threshold.

"Sabah il khayr," (Good morning). She broke the silence with her perfect Arabic. She continued in his native language. "Drop the gun," Anna ordered. If Quasim was startled, he did not show it. "Just drop it down those baggy pants of yours and let it hit the floor. I'm sure it won't break. It's a short trip to the floor." Anna immediately took command of the situation with the insult. He obeyed, and the Russian made 7.62mm Tokarev pistol dropped onto the dirty floor, throwing up a small cloud of dust.

"You should consider cleaning this place more often. It's not very hospitable for guests. Sit," Anna ordered, and gestured towards the chair with its back to the window.

He gave her an icy stare before obeying. She guessed his mind was racing through his list of enemies and trying to figure out who she could be. A rope appeared from her pocket, and she expertly bound his hands and feet to the chair. She used the second chair as a barricade, jamming it into the entrance of the building.

"You have anyone else coming to see you?" Anna asked. Quasim continued his silence. His head was bowed. He stared at the floor, refusing to acknowledge her. She knew he had probably been tortured by some of the Egyptian governments' finest. No one was better at administering torture than the Arabs. There was an excellent chance he had been thrown in prison along with hundreds of others after the assassination of Sadat. If that were the case, he would be next to impossible to break.

Anna quickly surveyed the other rooms of the small apartment and found nothing more than a few prayer rugs and an array of assault weapons, pistols, and rifles in a haphazard pile on the floor. The apartment probably served as a small weapons depot for Quasim. The entrance she just barricaded appeared to be the only way into the apartment. She strode back into the room with a strut of confidence. She did not know how much time she had so she knew she must ramp up her style. She walked directly over to Quasim, whose eyes were closed in prayer, and unleashed a punch across his face that did not seem possible given her figure. Quasim toppled onto the floor, unable to keep his balance because his appendages were all tied to the chair.

"We can either do this the easy way or the hard way, Quasim. You give me the information I need up front, and you can remain a man. Otherwise, I'll be sure to hand you over to my friends in the Saudi government. I know they are after you for the little excursions you've been running into their country. They don't appreciate you meddling with their affairs." She hoped the statement would put him on notice that she knew who she was dealing with.

She propped him back up, this time delivering a knee to the groin. It was the biggest advantage she possessed over men, and she never failed to use it if necessary. He winced in pain, his chest heaving as he tried to come to grips with the situation. A small smile creased his lips.

"Fine. You don't want to talk. I'll get right to the point then. What is Aziz A'zami's position in the Muslim Brotherhood?" Anna asked.

Quasim raised his head for the first time and stared at her quizzically. Her upper torso coiled for another strike, but Quasim finally spoke.

"You are mistaken. He's not a member. He disagrees with our use of violence. Tells us we should not be killing our fellow Muslims."

"I've been watching you for over a week. Either myself or an associate of mine has seen you meet with him on several occasions." She embellished her success, trying to make him think she was an omnipotent observer. "If you're going to lie, this will get painful." Anna traced her weapon up and down his legs in a menacing manner. She then leaned over him and let the swell of her breasts lightly brush against him in a teasing manner. Sex mixed with the fear of death. One of the most basic human needs converging with one of the most primordial fears were powerful weapons to use on a prisoner. They played havoc with the mind.

"I'm not lying. I know him. I don't deny it, but he is not a member of my organization," Quasim answered hastily.

"That's not what I hear on the street, Quasim."

"Someone has given you bad information then. He was, or I guess he still is, a member of the Brotherhood of the Caliphate." Quasim looked at her with a renewed look of confidence as he realized the interrogation was not about his activities.

Anna paced the room, gathering her thoughts. "You're talking about the other offshoot of Sayyid's group? Quasim, they have not existed for years." She smacked him across the face. "You're going to have to do better."

"No, it is true. There are a few who are still alive. Not many. Just a bunch of crazy old men whose time has past. Sayyid cursed them from his jail cell for choosing the path of non-violence."

Sayyid Qutb, Anna knew, was the spiritual godfather of the Islamic fundamentalist movement. He held a well paying job in the Ministry of Education in the Egyptian government in 1948, and was also a semi-famous writer in the country. His criticisms of the Egyptian government brought him unwanted attention from King

218

Farouk. Sayyid was on the verge of being arrested when his friends arranged for him to visit the United States to study abroad. He spent several months in the U.S., where he witnessed the decadence and corruption of the West for the first time. He stayed in New York City and watched the Americans indulge their every desire. The brand new skyscrapers shooting to the sky, alcoholic bums in the alleys, and pimps on the street corners stunned his senses and his virtues. He was appalled by the melting pot of nationalities in the city: Russians, Germans, Jews, Poles, Chinese laborers, all fighting over their piece of the pie.

Against this backdrop, Sayyid believed he had a choice. He could both fall prey to the same desires and abandon his principals, or he could take a stand for Islam. He had already been leaning towards a strict interpretation of Islamic law when he arrived in the United States. Now his decision was final.

He returned to his native country eight months later, convinced that America was the number one enemy of Islam. When he arrived in Cairo he found that many in the city were leaning towards his own way of thinking. Sayyid and his friends co-founded the Muslim Brothers, and began acting as a de facto government, funding hospitals, factories, and schools. The Muslim Brothers began quietly fomenting a revolution, which finally came to fruition in 1952. That year they assisted in a military coup that brought a young army colonel named Gamal Abdul Nasser to power.

The Muslim Brothers lust for power quickly caused fissures in the group. Nasser formed a secular government, as opposed to the Islamist theocracy that many of the Brothers had planned. This led to an internal struggle during which most of the members of the Muslim Brothers formed what would eventually become known as the Muslim Brotherhood. Sayyid followed this path. He was eventually tossed into jail by Nasser, released for a short period of time, and then picked up again on trumped charges. He was put to death by hanging after he refused Nasser's offer of release. The government refused to hand over his body for burial. By then, his writings, many of which were smuggled out of his jail cell, served as a rallying point for thousands of disgruntled Muslims.

In addition to the Muslim Brotherhood, two other factions emerged from the splitting of Sayyid's organization. One of these factions surrendered its overt revolution, and went to work for Nasser's government, hoping to change it from the inside. The final group, a handful of his closest advisors, formed the least known, and as far as Anna knew the least influential of the offshoot organizations. They called themselves the Brotherhood of the Caliphate, and their ultimate goal was the return to power of one ruler over all the lands of Islam.

She took a piece of bread off the table and chewed slowly before asking another question. "What other members are still alive?" She did not want to admit that the old man was the first confirmed member she knew of. The movement had been obscure, and from what the CIA knew, it appeared to have died out soon after it began.

"None that I know by name. I've heard the old man claim that some of his friends are still around, but I have never been able to confirm it."

"You've never met any of the other surviving members?" Anna asked.

"No. He claims they are not in Egypt."

"If Aziz is just a crazy old man why do you meet with him?"

"It's part of my job. The members of the Brotherhood of the Caliphate were all very close with Sayyid, despite their differences. For the last forty years there have been strict rules about treating them with respect and doing favors for them."

"How long have you been dealing with the old man?"

"Myself? I've been doing him favors since the early 1970s."

"Right about the time you first joined the Muslim Brotherhood then?" She peered out the wooden shutters and confirmed the alley was still empty. Quasim stiffened at the comment.

"Yes, Quasim," she said as she approached him from behind. "I know all about you. Did you really think that awful story you've been using for years actually fooled anyone? We know all about how you got your start." She watched the beads of sweat appear on his forehead. He was clearly anxious.
"He has friends somewhere high up. I know that. He passes on some useful information to me when he feels like we need to know something." He quickly offered the additional information.
"How do you even know he is really a member of the Brotherhood of Caliphate? They were almost like ghosts as far as I can tell. This is the first time I have been told a member's name."
"Years ago...one of my bosses...he refused one of Aziz's requests. He ended up with his head chopped off. Aziz has been a cripple for years, so someone had to do it for him."
"You didn't answer my question. How do you even know he is really a member of this group? I doubt the Muslim Brotherhood simply does favors for any old man that comes in off the street and asks."
Quasim continued his game of playing hard to get. She started towards him again, ready to cause more pain. "Wait," he pleaded. "The members of the Brotherhood of the Caliphate have one distinguishing feature so they can be recognized. They have a tattoo on their inner thigh. There are two letters on the thigh. Two Arabic symbols in green. It means Caliphate Creation. When I first became one of the leaders of the Muslim Brotherhood I was told that there was a select group of men for whom we had to do their bidding if they showed us the tattoo. Aziz is the only man who has made any requests of me as long as I have been overseeing this area. I heard some rumors about other Caliphate members during the late 50s and 60s requesting the kidnapping of orphans. Very strange stuff. I never asked any questions. It was no longer going on by the time I joined so it did not concern me." Quasim continued to rattle off as much information as he could recall. Aziz was nothing but a thorn in his side anyway.

"They were kidnapping kids off the streets of Cairo?" Anna knew she should not be surprised. In the late 1940s and early 1950s half of the city's kids died from a lack of basic nutrition. This made for fertile ground for kidnappings, blackmails, and other despicable acts against children.

"That is what I was told. Obviously it was before my time, so I've never been able to confirm the stories. Why they wanted to do this, I don't know. My own belief is that the few men who started this little group were all crazy, and Sayyid was just doing a final favor for some of his friends. Maybe they liked sex with young children. Why else have someone kidnapping children for you? If there was any record of the kid being alive, they would have one of Sayyid's allies within the government make the birth records disappear. Now the poor child never existed," Quasim continued in an animated tone. Maybe he could even get her to kill the old man, he thought to himself.

Anna listened intently, and for the first time realized the possibility that Zach could be one of these kidnapped children. He was approximately the same age, and she had come up empty in her search for birth records. "And they just kidnapped and killed children at the whims of these men?" Anna asked.

"They followed the orders of Sayyid, as the Muslim Brotherhood continues to honor him to this day. What are a few wretches in the streets dying compared to our ultimate quest? If we ever achieve Sayyid's dream of a truly Islamic government in Egypt, there will be no children on the streets to pick up. The ones who follow the true path will be in the madrassas, and the ones who refuse will die. It is Allah's way." The tone of his voice indicated he was not to be argued with.

The statement was typical of the Muslim Brotherhood, and Anna saw it coming. The thought process still infuriated her. She buried her emotions. There would be a better and more productive time for them to be unleashed. She had one more question she wanted to ask before she could get out of here.

"Has Aziz asked you for any favors during the last few years?"

"Yes, and some of them have been troublesome for my organization. He once requested certain members of the U.S. government be tracked when they came to Cairo. I was never told exactly who it was. He would only pass on the information to the person chosen for the job. It was presumably done to make sure they did not cause any trouble." Quasim hesitated before continuing, "I was concerned he was spying on the U.S., and if our man was caught the blame would undoubtedly fall back on us. Aziz even asked that we follow his contact in the embassy," Quasim continued spilling the information. He knew if the previous news was not enough to get her to do something about the old man, then this last piece should set her in motion.

Anna leaned against the interior wall, silently cursing Colin. "How long has this American contact been under Aziz's watch?"

"A few years now, I believe. In addition to having access to some of my best men, Aziz also has a young boy who runs errands for him."

"Is it the same boy who just left here?" Anna queried.

"Yes. The kid has been following me around even more than normal the past several months. He is the eyes and ears of the senile old man."

Anna stood silently in thought for a few seconds. The last remark Quasim made had a hint of malice and resentment in it. It appeared Quasim and the old man were rivals of a sort. She wondered for the first time if Quasim wanted her to get rid of Aziz. The Brotherhood of the Caliphate always was thought of as a peaceful movement. Maybe the old man had become aware of the next big "hit" the Muslim Brotherhood was planning, and was trying to put a stop to it. In her eagerness to acquire as much information as possible she forgot the ease with which Quasim had been speaking. She barely laid a finger on him compared to what he had probably endured earlier in his life.

The shaking of the door momentarily brought her out of her thought process. She tightened her grip around her pistol. The banging grew louder as the unknown person shook the door. She rushed to the window and flung open the wooden clapboards. It was too late. The old man's errand boy was already sprinting down the alley and disappearing around a turn. She looked at the back of her captive and made a snap decision.. She would have liked nothing more than to kill Quasim at the moment. It had been her original intention, but it was no longer feasible.

There were two different scenarios that ran through her mind. The first one was that Aziz was a harmless old man who wanted peace with the West. He certainly seemed to despise organizations like Quasim's that used violence to achieve their goals, and Quasim certainly seemed eager to throw the old man under the bus. Still, there were too many pieces that did not fit this situation.

The second scenario she considered was that Aziz was the true power broker and his secret organization had something major in the works that he did not want Quasim ruining with a useless terrorist attack. The second option would have seemed implausible to her were it not for the deference that Quasim had shown Aziz at the mosque. One of them was lying, and Anna had every intention of finding out which one of them it was.

She grudgingly decided to leave Quasim tied up. He was the known quantity in this equation, and thus would be easier to control. It was the unknown quantity that frightened her. She needed to immediately have another discussion with Aziz.

"It's your lucky day Quasim. You live for now. If I find out you've been lying to me I will return." She came up from behind him and slammed the butt of her pistol across his skull, rendering him unconscious. She was sure one of his helpers would be back soon and could untie him. She dashed into the alley, and hurried out onto a main thoroughfare to hail a taxi. Quasim's answers had opened more doors than they closed.

Chapter 34

Anna stood uncomfortably in the ambassador's office, fidgeting in her heels while waiting for his highness to make his grand entrance. She had expected the call, but at the same time had hoped to not hear from him for a few more days. After her discussion with Quasim, she spent the rest of the day searching in vain for the boy. Neither the boy nor the old man could be found, and because the enemy was trailing Colin she continued to avoid him.

She returned to her hotel for a few hours, unsure what to do with the information Quasim had provided her when the phone rang and a brusque voice announced that the ambassador insisted on seeing her immediately. The heels and short business skirt she was currently wearing were a blatant attempt to use her sexuality to soften his mood and buy her two more days. Ten minutes into her pacing, the door burst open, and the ambassador stomped into the room. He slammed the door shut, walked past her without a second glance, and took a seat at his desk. His face was controlled rage, like a red balloon about to explode in a child's hand.

"What the fuck are you trying to do? Didn't I warn you to watch your step?" The words exploded out of his mouth as if he could no longer hold them in.

"You're going to have to enlighten me, Mr. Ambassador," Anna replied in a non-threatening manner. *Great, I get the one prick politician that doesn't think with his.*

"Don't play dumb with me. I just got a call from one of my friends in the Egyptian government. They received a formal complaint today from a citizen. He claims you were harassing him. He also states you threatened violence."

Her face was a blank slate, revealing nothing. She could not believe that Quasim would turn her in. He would not want that sort of attention drawn to his activities. "Mr. Ambassador, I've done nothing of the sort. I've only met with one person outside the Egyptian government, and I can assure you no harm would come to him. He was just an elderly gentleman who a mutual friend thought may be able to assist me."

"Are you sure that is all you've been up to?" He asked in a sarcastic tone. His manicured hands fumbled with a five-by-seven manila envelope. Working the seal free, he then ripped it open in false bravado, extracted some photographs, and slammed them onto his desk.

Anna stared at the photo in disbelief. It was the body of Quasim. His head was nearly severed from his neck and he was covered in his own blood. The body was lying on a dirt floor.

"I guess you're insinuating that I had something to do with this man's death?" Anna asked in a disbelieving tone.

"Considering my source told me that someone saw you leaving the building where this body was discovered, yes, I'm curious. Plus, the fact that you have clearly disobeyed my orders regarding the parameters of your investigation makes me think that you are a diplomatic nightmare for the United States government."

Anna blocked out the insignificant peon sitting at the desk in front of her. She now realized her enemy was the old man. Aziz was setting her up. "I had nothing to do with this man's death." She was technically telling the truth.

"The Egyptian government has officially asked me to rescind your passport and have you expelled from the country. I've already agreed to the request. The paperwork has been signed and you will be escorted back to your hotel before being taken to the airport. I'm filing an official report with the FBI recommending that you be terminated," the Ambassador said with great pride in his voice.

The plane ride back to U.S. soil was excruciating. She had some tantalizing information, but nothing that would allow a formal investigation to go any further. The old man clearly had something to hide, but what that was could be anyone's guess. The key, Anna believed, was his tie to the Brotherhood of the Caliphate. Were there any surviving members besides Aziz? Could Aman, or even Zachariah, be a member of this same organization? There

226

was only one way to find out. One question tortured her the entire flight home. If Aman and his presidential candidate were members of this same group, what were they after?

Chapter 35
January 2005, Washington D.C.

Zach pulled the bathrobe tight around his body, trying to trap in the heat. The coffee sitting on the small end table was still too hot to sip, and he needed to stay warm somehow. He was on the top floor of the Hay-Adams Hotel on 16th Street. He gazed out at a majestic early morning view of the sun radiating just behind the Washington monument, throwing its beam of light onto the White House. He silently cursed the biting cold. It would be a typical January day in the nation's capital; sunny, but below freezing. He was convinced the glass doors that provided him with the magnificent scenery were also allowing the frigid January air to seep into the hotel room. He stared down at the North Lawn of the White House.

Was this how the great conquerors felt when their long sought after target finally came into view? From his vantage point he watched a Secret Service man pace up and down the roof of the White House. A tripod sat on the corner nearest to Zach, ready to support the agent's sniper rifle if some fool decided to bum rush the people's mansion. Zach soaked in the scenery. He felt like his long hunt was finally coming to a climax. He was feeling much more relaxed after time away from Aman and all his campaign minions. He let out a sigh of relaxation while pouring milk into his black coffee and swirling the mixture together with a spoon.

The voluptuous blonde had just left the hotel room an hour earlier after an evening of pleasure. Her performance met his expectations. In fact, it was the best sex he had had in months, so he had kept her around until morning instead of the usual late night send off. She left early enough to be escorted out of the hotel without a problem, but late enough for him to squeeze in a quickie.

He walked back across the thick beige carpet to stare at the White House once again and think of his young brother in arms, already inside the belly of the beast and waiting for orders. It had been far too long since they embraced. He was no longer able to keep track of the time they had been apart. Aman strictly forbade any contact between them. No meetings, letters, or phone calls were permitted. Not even the slightest acknowledgement that they knew each other existed was allowed. That would soon change. He smiled to himself, thinking of the cataclysmic change their next encounter would produce. Perhaps the White House could also be transformed into a crater of twisted metal like the Twin Towers had been? I should not get greedy, he told himself. Just stick to the plan. He closed the blinds, blocking the view of the White House. The view of his target was stirring a blood lust that had been buried for years, and he needed to simmer down.

Chapter 36

Anna turned to face Alex after finishing the narrative. He sat rigidly at attention on the couch, dissecting the pieces of information before asking his question.

"So that is how you ended up in Las Vegas, hunting down Zach? The phone you slipped into my pocket at the airport. What was on it?"

"What do you think?"

"I'm guessing a photo of Zach's inner thigh. But the key question is; does he have the symbol of the Caliphate tattooed there?"

She silently handed him the picture that was in her hand. "Here is a copy."

He took it and stared quizzically at it. He saw pale flesh mixed with black hair. Underneath the matted hair of the leg the two strange symbols in green were clearly visible.

"They are Arabic for KK. Standing for Caliphate Creation." She spoke like a professor administering a lecture.

"What do you do from here?" He handed the photo back.

"Nothing to do but sit tight and do as much investigative work as possible. After I got back from Cairo I filed a full report with the CIA Director, and my contact in the FBI. I've been told the FBI man is currently in Cairo trying to track down the old man. I just hope he finds something that we can use to either alleviate our fears or prove once and for all that Zachariah should not be allowed to take the oath of office. For now, we just have to be patient."

Alex could tell by the tone of her voice that this was going to be difficult for her.

Cairo

Sean Hill stood with his back flat against the tenement building and listened carefully for any sounds. He gave a hand signal to Colin, who was standing on the other side of the doorway just a few feet away. They were observing a strict policy of silence. Reaching into his pocket, Sean pulled out the silencer and screwed it carefully onto his Model 22 Glock pistol. Sunrise was less than an hour away, and their black outfits made them nearly invisible in the narrow confines of the darkened alley. Colin followed Sean's lead and prepared his own weapon in case the situation turned hot.

The past week had frayed both their nerves to the breaking point. The attempt on Sean's life as soon as he stepped off the plane in Cairo was bad enough. Follow this with Sean informing Colin that he had been under constant surveillance for the past few years by Aziz and they were both on edge. Colin felt like a fool. He had been played on a string from the beginning, and he knew exactly why he had not noticed the surveillance. He subconsciously believed that Aziz was just an eccentric old man trying to pretend he still had some importance in the world.

It had taken them a few days to pick up the trail from the information Anna had given them, but they eventually tracked down Aziz's errand boy, who they found near a mosque. It appeared that whenever Aziz needed to pass along information, it was through one of the thousands of mosques scattered throughout the city. It was the only tactical mistake in the unknown operation he manipulated. They tracked the boy to the alleyway in which they now stood, just off Al-Muizz li Din Allah Street. The smell of rotting food permeated the entire enclave. The errand boy had stepped outside a few minutes earlier, and was now lying on the ground at Sean's feet. He was unconscious, and bound and gagged, just in case he woke up unexpectedly.

Sean raised his hand, his fingers counting the seconds down to the assault. He then balled his hand into a fist and sprung forward with agility not typically found in such a large frame. He crashed into the door shoulder first, his silenced pistol scanning the room to look for any sign of movement. Colin followed directly behind him, crouching low to cover any potential trapdoors, and staying out of Sean's way.

A guard lay prostrate on his prayer rug, an old Russian Kalashnikov rifle lying on the floor in front of him. The bearded head jolted out of its séance at the sound of the cracking door. The arms stretched out for the rifle, but were cut short by three quick rounds from Colin's silenced Beretta. The room was barren, and they continued into the next doorway in silence. It led to a hallway that had the musty smell of ancient Cairo. Sean thought the hallway probably looked exactly the same as the day it was built, other than the photographs of numerous Muslim leaders that lined the dilapidated and crumbling walls.

The hallway was connected on each end by two more rooms. The first room was empty except for a decrepit couch that sat up against the wall, and the other room was overflowing with rusty rifles, AK-47s, and an assortment of pistols that looked like they had just as much chance of harming the carrier of the weapon as the potential victim. The entire cache of weapons appeared to be from the former Soviet Union. Sean and Colin looked at each other and exchanged confused glances. They had witnessed the old man enter the building the night before with an entourage of guards. Over the course of the night the guards slowly filed out, until only the boy and the man they just killed remained. There were no other exits. Their eyes moved to the walls and began scanning for any tiny levers that could open a door to a secret room or hidden staircase. If no such lever could be found, then they had been swindled somehow.

Ten futile minutes later, and his patience nearly exhausted, Sean was ready to assume the old man had disguised himself as a guard and vanished into the night. Colin suddenly stepped into his line of sight with a sly grin on his face. Sean followed him to the other room. The decrepit couch now sat in the center of the room. The thick layer of filth and grime covering the wall was brushed aside revealing a picture of King Farouk. Colin removed the photo from the wall and pointed at the nail that supported it. He then traced his finger down the wall a few more feet until he came to another tiny nail that was barely protruding from it. He pushed it inward and the wall folded quietly back, revealing a recessed staircase that looked much too luxurious for the dirty room. Sean gazed upwards into the blackness, a queasy feeling enveloping his stomach.

They cautiously ascended the stairs. The folding wall automatically slid back into place as soon as they were inside. Sean ascended first, using the point of his weapon to probe the pitch-black air in front of them, like a blind man using his walking stick to find his way. One arm, then another, then a leg, they crept upward, cautiously probing for the end they could not see. Finally, the tip of Sean's silenced pistol brushed against wood. He reached out his free hand, and realized the staircase ran straight into the underbelly of the second floor. Sean stopped, listening for any signs of noise from whatever, or whoever, lay on the other side of the floor above them. After a few seconds of silence he could make out the faint grunts of someone in deep thought or prayer. If it was not the old man above them, Sean realized there was a strong possibility they could be dead in the next few minutes.

He bent down to whisper to Colin. "Be ready. We're going in."

"Ok." Colin acknowledged the order, not wanting to risk any more words.

Sean gently nudged the floor above him, applying only as much pressure as he thought would be necessary to open it. The square section of the floor noiselessly swiveled upwards on well-oiled hinges, bringing a burst of light from the room above streaming into the black hole of the stairwell. Sean popped up, his bulging arms going through the opening first, his weapon sweeping the room for any potential targets.

The sheer opulence of the room was a stark contrast to the slum below them. Sean's upper body was near one of the corners of the room. The rest of the cavernous space, which appeared to run the full length of the second story, was covered with a thick, luxurious carpet, inlaid with

232

spectacular hand woven designs crisscrossing the entire area. The walls were covered in the same intricate, inlaid marble found in many of the large mosques in Cairo. It was the pinnacle of geometric decoration. Gold ceiling fans whirled above him, creating a comfortable temperature compared to the stifling heat on the first floor of the building.

On the other end of the massive room, the old man was laying on the floor with his back to them. He lay prostrate on the floor, facing the lone window that was in the wall. A niche above the window indicated the direction of Mecca. Like a giant cat eyeing his unsuspecting prey, Sean climbed out of the floor, kicking his shoes off in one swift motion as he quickly covered the two hundred feet of plush carpet in silence. Colin followed, like a cub trailing a parent. Sweat trickled down his bald head as he stepped out of the stifling heat of the stairwell.

Their stalking came to an anticlimactic ending as they came within a few feet of the old man. Sean almost laughed. The old man was snoring quietly, having fallen asleep while praying. He reached down and lightly touched Aziz's shoulder. The old man's startled eyes popped open, and he turned to look quizzically at the two men. Sean motioned for him to stand up.

Aziz stretched his scrawny figure across the plush rug, trying to shake the cobwebs loose. He quietly obeyed Sean's order.

"I would have never fallen asleep during prayer in my younger days. How embarrassing," Aziz muttered to himself before continuing. "Colin, my friend, it good to see you. It has been a while." Aziz ignored Sean, looking past him to the CIA case officer who stood behind him drying his face with a handkerchief.

"Swanky place for an old beggar like yourself, Aziz." Sean gestured at the opulence engulfing them, the business end of his pistol weaving dangerously in the air.

"I have friends who let me come here for prayers. I prefer to be alone when I commune with Allah," Aziz replied.

"Sure beats the hell out of the rat hole that you had in Islamic Cairo. It was a dump, and that was before you had it blown up." Sean did not try to hide his irritation. His short stay in Cairo was proving to be extremely dangerous. He had been on Egyptian soil for only a few minutes when his limousine was assaulted by a group of kamikaze motorcycle fanatics. After a day of calm they set off to look for Aziz, first trying the obvious spot; the hovel where Colin introduced Anna to the old man for the first time. Perhaps not surprisingly, the hovel had been booby-trapped. They figured out their dilemma in time to jump out the window and into the alley just as the roof of the second floor came crashing down, destroying the little apartment.

"Well, the people of Cairo have not been financially blessed by Allah. Tragedies occur all the time. Luckily no one upstairs was home at the time, so no dead." Aziz picked his glasses off the floor and pushed them onto the skeletal remains of his face. "Can I help you, gentlemen?" He asked calmly.

Colin stepped forward, holstering his weapon in an attempt to relieve some of the tension in the massive room. "I have some follow up questions for you, Aziz. Do you remember when I brought by the young lady from the FBI a few months ago? The one who had some questions regarding Aman?" Colin asked as he continued dabbing his neck with his handkerchief in a nervous gesture. The cool air permeating the room was slowly beginning to unglue his sweat-stained shirt from his body.

Aziz looked to the ceiling, appearing to ponder the question like an absent-minded professor. "A few months ago... I barely remember what I did hour ago. It is problem getting old. I don't recommend it."

"It beats the alternative." Sean interjected himself into the conversation.

"I take it you must be American friend of Colin's. Your rudeness gives you away. It is a distinct trait of all your people, no matter how hard you try to mask it."

Aziz turned his attention back towards Colin. "Now I remember, Colin. She also asked some questions about Aman's stepson."

"That's correct. We've had some issues come up recently that need clarification."

"Such as?" Aziz asked.

"I've recently learned that she didn't leave Egypt of her own free will. She was expelled from the country for some made-up excuse about a passport violation. It seemed pretty minor to me, and I was asked to look into it."

"What does this have to do with me, Colin?"

"Aziz, I know you have contacts in the Egyptian government. High ups. I heard a rumor that you asked that she be expelled. Do you want to tell me why?

"I don't know what you talking about," Aziz retorted.

"We're not here to play games, Aziz. I don't have time to fuck around. She told me all about it. She tried finding you again because she had some additional questions for you. Then she left the country abruptly. I had a little chat with our ambassador. He can be a real prick, by the way. He proceeded to tell me how our mutual friend in the government filed a personal complaint with the U.S. embassy. My question; is why would he even complain? She didn't bother anyone in your government. Why did you harass her?" Colin stepped towards the shriveled old man in a menacing fashion.

"She was causing trouble. She was following business associates of mine around city. Asking questions that had nothing to do with her. She is lucky one of my associates did not kill her."

"What was it about her investigation that made you nervous, Aziz?" Sean cut in.

"Don't play dumb with me you arrogant American. You know who she follow. I have no doubt that she told you that she follow Quasim. Quasim had contacts all over city. Don't pretend with me. I don't like games either. I have been playing them for too long as is."

Sean watched the old man's movements closely. He was sure Aziz was lying.. Before he arrived in Cairo, Sean had faxed Colin the after-action report Anna put together prior to disappearing in Las Vegas. Sean thought it would be a good idea for Colin to see it before he arrived. The report had been an eye opener for Colin, and had helped him to put together some of the pieces of his relationship with

235

Aziz that previously did not seem to fit. What had appeared as senility over the years, now looked to be a carefully choreographed plan to throw anyone with any curiosity off the trail.

Sean showed Colin that he had been duped by the old man for ten plus years. What appeared to Colin over the years as a mutual give-and-take of information was actually a one-way street. The old man had been hiding information, and most likely had someone murder Quasim in order to keep the trail cold. Sean and Colin were now trying to figure out why.

"What kind of games are you referring to, Aziz? The ones where Quasim's lackeys try to kill us by blowing us up with suicidal maniacs driving TNT laden bikes?" Colin asked with brazen sarcasm.

"Are we going to go through this again, Colin? How many times have I speak out against Quasim and others like him. I have spent my whole life trying to counter their disgusting destruction."

"And Aman?" Colin asked.

"Where is this leading, Colin? You know Aman and I have been friends for decades. I have not talked to him in many years. He has been busy with Zachariah's career. Aman is good man. How much money he has put back to this city fighting the murderers that run through streets?" He gestured dramatically towards the outer walls, and the stark poverty that lay in the alley below them.

"Let's just say I've had a religious awakening over the last few days, Aziz. I had a friendly discussion yesterday with your friend in the Egyptian government." Colin let the information sink in, waiting for a reaction. When the old man kept quiet he continued, "He was not happy with what you did with the information he gave you. I told him the trouble it could cause between our two governments if the truth came out. Your officials all claim to be pious observers of the Koran, but they are no different than ours. You threaten to cut off the hand that feeds them so they talk, just like ours do." The old man was shifting uncomfortably on the floor, his head looking everywhere except at the two

Americans standing above him. He took another pass on his opportunity to speak.

Colin continued in a quiet, matter of fact tone. "Aziz, he said he told you exactly when and where Sean was flying in to Cairo. He also said no one else in the government was told about the unannounced visit. That kind of narrows the list of suspects who could have ambushed the convoy. Wouldn't you agree?"

The old man continued to look around the room in furtive glances, his mind clearly attempting to make sense of the situation. After thirty seconds his head dropped in a gesture of defiance and his jaw locked tight. Blood began trickling out of his lower lip. The velvet voice of earlier was replaced with a bitter diatribe of a betrayed old man. "That bastard!" The words spat out of his mouth as quickly as he could fire them. "I knew I should have had him taken care of."

Sean's hand reflexively gripped his pistol tighter at the old man's change in tone. He injected himself into the conversation again. "Well, you missed your opportunity, and now you will have to pay the price. We know all about you, Aziz. Just make this easy on yourself and give us the final piece. What are you after? What are you and Aman up to?" Sean leaned towards him, his large frame towering over the kneeling man.

"You have no idea what you are up against. Aman is a great man, and his protégé will help bring about peace between Christians and Muslims for the first time in centuries."

"Peace through killing? I know it's your favorite modus operandi,"Sean shot back.

"As if that is different than what you have done through the centuries? Please do not give me any lectures. Not peace through killing, but peace on our terms. With Aman, your new President will have true believer giving him advice. They will not cave to Israel's every plea. I just be sure that Aman gets to that place where he can help change things. I know that bitch you sent over was after dirty information on my people. If I have to kill you to prevent you from finishing her work, it does not bother me. I

237

am too close to witnessing history. And besides, Allah will reward me." The old man stopped abruptly, realizing he had probably spoken too much.

Colin stepped back into the conversation, "What is your relationship with Aman? Is he a member of the Brotherhood of the Caliphate?"

The old man wiped his brow and began sweating despite the coolness of the massive room. "Does it matter? He is devout Muslim, a great man who has sacrificed his entire life by working in your godless country."

"You did not answer my question. Is he a member of the Brotherhood of the Caliphate?"

"Of course he is!" The old man spat it out in a frustrated tone. "All these men like Quasim and the rest of them, they do nothing but fight each other for the honor to be first in line to be screwed by U.S. and the Europeans." His arms flung around as if he was about to fall off a ledge, his voice hysterical as he continued. "The Muslim Brotherhood has brought nothing but pain to its people. I have worked my whole life trying to fix problems caused by the clash of our cultures."

"You are claiming your own little brotherhood just wants peace?" Sean asked.

"Someday, yes. But hear my words. There will be one final reckoning. It will be swift and violent, but aftermath will be peace." The bony finger wagged from side to side. The final words were said with supreme confidence.

"How did you first meet Aman?" Colin asked the question as an afterthought. He realized that they had never discussed it before.

The old man's face returned to serenity. He was glad to be done with the geo-political discussion.

"One of the others brought him into Brotherhood. Sometime in the 1950s. We became very close over the years. We shared passion for horses. In the early years he was always coming back to Egypt looking for stallions he could run in the States. I trained them for him."

"You trained his horses here, or in the U.S.?" Colin asked.

"Here, of course. Well, I went to States a few times to help him pick out American bred horses for breeding, but I lose interest. The best horses always come from here." His scrawny chest puffed up in pride.

Colin and Sean exchanged surprised glances. In his years of dealing with Aziz, Colin had never heard him mention visiting the United States. He was either misspeaking, confused, or accidentally saying something he had never admitted to previously.

Colin pressed the matter. "I didn't know you visited my country, Aziz. You should have said something earlier. When did you visit?" Colin returned to a friendly and harmless tone.

"Only once, and it was years earlier. I hardly remember it now."

***

Aziz waived his hand in a dismissive fashion. The feigned attempt at aloofness failed miserably, and he knew it. He looked at the two Americans standing in front of him and summoned all his strength to remain calm. He was too old to be playing these head games with them, he told himself. He knew he had already spoken too much. His attempt at lecturing them had been out of a great need to be heard. After years of hiding and suppressing his true mission, he had faltered ever so slightly and let his emotions have a voice. He chided himself for his impulsive outburst. It was the one time when he needed to be strongest, and he was failing. He now realized what he needed to do next.

Aziz resigned himself to his fate. He was so close to witnessing it; the beginning of a new period, but he would not see it after all. Trying to stay alive for a few more days would be childish, selfish, and may give them the opportunity to pry further. The fools did not have enough information to stop Aman's plan, and Aziz knew if he were dead the trail would go cold. His wrinkled face softened its hardened edges for his final acting job. He would have to watch from the heavens as history unfolded.

"Forgive me, Colin, but I am old and tired. Do you mind if I pour myself a cup of tea? My body is aching from its morning duty to Allah." Aziz's body creaked as he stood

239

up, and he motioned towards the corner of the room where a small, portable stove was set up on the only patch of tile in the vast room. A pot rested on top, simmering quietly and releasing its heat into a vent in the ceiling. Sean immediately made his way over to the corner first. A quick search found nothing of any danger.

"Would you like me to pour you some?" Sean asked, matching the suddenly subdued tone of the old man. The stove was giving off an intense heat. The old man must like his tea scalding hot, Sean thought.

Aziz shuffled over to the corner, motioning for Sean to step back, "No, my boy. There are some things I still do for myself. Not many, but this one of them." He waited for Sean to step back a few more feet to make sure he would have enough time to do the deed.

"Allah akbar." (God is great.) Aziz grabbed the kettle of scalding hot water, raised his head to the ceiling, and poured the entire pot of liquid fire down his throat and over his face. His eyes were aflame in agony, and the burning substance stifled his yell as it ravaged his vocal cords and singed his skin.

Even if his decrepit body could have survived the raw pain that was being inflicted on it, he would have been unable to ever speak again. It was a moot point as the searing liquid jolted his system, causing his weak heart to instantly go into cardiac arrest, as he knew it would. The blistering pain ravaged his body as the exploding of his chest overwhelmed the searing heat on his face.

The two Americans lunged for him in a panic, and began a wasted attempt at reviving him. The brief moment of excruciating pain was worth it to Aziz as he looked into his enemy's eyes and saw their looks of frustration through his scorched pupils. This was his final vision. His eyes closed, and his body succumbed to the self-inflicted wounds within seconds. His last thoughts were of how far they had advanced from their humble beginnings when they first began their visits to America. He prayed that Aman and Zachariah had the fortitude to finish the job.

Sean dropped the body in disgust and pushed it away from him as if it carried the plague. He now realized something that should have previously caught his attention. There were no glasses or mugs.

Chapter 37
May 1963

Flying dirt obscured the view through the binoculars for a brief second. Aman adjusted the focus as the seven horses burst out of the gate in a simultaneous flurry of hooves. His hands unconsciously shook from the blast of nature's fury, even though he was in his owners' box in the grandstands and unable to feel the horses' power. He waved off the waiter in the white coat with his right hand. No matter how many times he refused a mint julep, they continually badgered him on their next go around. Over indulgence in alcohol was just one of the many troubles this country had, he thought. He had no intention of joining the ranks of all these idiots.

A woman in the box beside him brushed up against his arm, knocking his binoculars askew for a few seconds. She profusely apologized as the whiskey in her hand splashed a few drops onto the wooden floor. Aman stared at her, and said nothing, but his icy glare left little doubt as to his thoughts. He adjusted his body so he would not come in contact with her again, and turned his attention back to the race. The horses were romping their way down the long backside of the track, and the massive crowd stood simultaneously to cheer on their chosen horse. Aman followed suit, bringing his binoculars back to bear on the track.

He silently cursed to himself. His horse was last and already losing ground with each stride. It was a six-furlong race, not even a full lap around the track, and was not a race meant to be won by being patient and trying to come from the back of the pack. The horses rounded first turn in pairs. The first two leaders were followed a few strides behind by the next two horses, and then the final pairing. Aman's horse was now four lengths behind the last pair, and his lone straggler was struggling mightily to keep up. They made their way around the final turn and headed towards the finish line. Aman sat his binoculars on his chair as they approached his seating area.

One of the horses in the final pairing suddenly exploded forward. His hind legs tore forward in a burst of energy that ignited the crowd to a pitched frenzy. It quickly zipped by the second pairing, and set its sights on the first pair. Could it catch up to them before the finish line? The chestnut stallion kicked into an even higher gear for the final sprint, peeling off the distance in incredible time. It tore between the two final horses, and broke the finish line a split second before them. Aman was impressed. He reached into his program to find out who owned the horse. His own stallion crossed the finish line last. When Aziz returned he would have to have a word with him. The race was secondary to their main objective, but he did not appreciate being completely embarrassed. It was unacceptable.

The crowd sat back down, so Aman took the opportunity to stand. He peered through his binoculars at the stables on the backside of the track. His left hand casually patted his slim green tie back into its rightful place. The breeze that tunneled through the covered grandstand eliminated any semblance of heat.

He focused his binoculars on the large pickup truck with the words "Sheik Stables" blazoned in gold across the side. Attached to the truck was a horse trailer with some special modifications. He watched the men moving around it, guarding it carefully. The trailer was designed by one of his mob connections in Las Vegas who did not ask questions. It was needed to haul cargo that was abnormally heavy, and the wheels were specially designed to support the additional bulk being loaded onto it. The men were finishing up their job from the previous evening. The trailer carried the gold that Aziz brought over from Cairo.

Aman assumed the gold was part of a horde that Aziz had come across during World War II, but his friend always refused to divulge the information. He heard rumors that Aziz smuggled some of his gold into Macao and sold it to the mysterious Dr. PJ Lobo, a wealthy recluse who made millions of dollars smuggling commodities between Hong Kong and Communist China. The Chinese price for gold was over fifty dollars an ounce, and Aziz could make millions with almost no risk. All Aman knew was that he was given a portion of the gold to do as he pleased, and that was all he wanted to know.

The gold would be melted down and used as additional financing for their ultimate goal. The revenue the casino generated would be more than enough for a normal gangster, but not for Aman. He had a lot of pockets to line, or wetting beaks, as some of the Italians around Las Vegas liked to put it. Bringing in the money was turning out to be the easy part however; Aziz's job in Cairo was proving to be more of a challenge. He had not had a chance to speak to Aziz one-on-one yet, and Aman prayed that he would soon be told a more concrete plan of how they were going to attack America and its minions.

The last few years had been hard on all of them. Aman hated America, but he resigned himself to the fact that he would probably be here for the rest of his life. Their friend and mentor Sayyid Qutb was rotting in prison. The socialist dictator Nasser was just waiting for the chance to execute him without causing a riot in the slums of Cairo. The thought of the leader of Egypt infuriated Aman. Nasser had risen to power after angry mobs rampaged through the city of Cairo ten years earlier. Nasser was assisted by many friends of Aman, and he had promised an Islamist government. Instead, he turned to the godless communists for assistance. Now all Aman could do was watch from an ocean away, and hope Nasser would be assassinated.

Aman watched the men close up the trailer and slam the bulky padlock down to seal it. The normal openings around the top where one would ordinarily see horses had been boarded up to prevent any nosy civilians from trying to peak in. He scanned the area around the trailer. Where was Aziz? He had not seen him yet. The idiot was supposed to be supervising the loading. A bony hand touched him daintily on the shoulder. Aman swung around. A large smile appeared under Aziz's thick glasses.

"Sorry about horse. He not handle the ocean trip. I afraid of that. Come. We talk," Aziz demanded.

Aman followed his superior out of the crowded grandstand, and they walked over to the stables for some privacy. Aziz sat on one of the bales of hay in the empty stall, his legs weary from a day of running about the track, supervising their smuggling operation and trying to get the horse ready. The horse's preparation suffered greatly due to his dual tasks, but it had to be done. As much as they both wanted to be successful, winning horse races paled in comparison to their ultimate goal. Aziz took a long drag from his cigarette and deposited the ashes carefully on the floor, crushing them with his foot. He immediately lit another one.

"How are things in Cairo? Are they as bad as what I'm hearing?" Aman asked as he lit his own cigarette.

"Yes, almost all brothers dead. Sayyid, as you know, is in jail. He will be killed soon. Nasser hate him, and our brethren in Muslim Brotherhood grow more impatient every day. They only help wretches of society. We should have killed leaders of Brotherhood. Their answer to everything is violence without thought to consequences. Even if they succeed, their own regime will not last. They do not see real enemy. Fighting each other get us nowhere good."

Aman fingered the buttons of his sport coat, shook it off, and hung it on a hook in the barn. His muscular physique was beginning to show its first signs of turning pudgy. The hours he spent in his offices in Las Vegas were catching up with him. "I understand their frustrations. You know I have struggled with our chosen path as well, Aziz. It is difficult even for me to come to grips with it sometimes."

Aziz switched to Arabic so there would be no misunderstanding as to their ultimate goal. "That is the price we have to pay. Our path is correct Aman. It is the most difficult, but it is correct. We both know it. The problem is that it provides no instant gratification for the hoodlums Sayyid counted on to terrorize those government officials. I was always concerned that his fiery rhetoric would bring us to this point. Yes, they certainly helped swell the ranks of our recruits, but most of those recruits chose the easy path offered by the Muslim Brotherhood. Even Sayyid seems to be siding with them from his prison cell. Aman, I am paying our few remaining members more and more money every day. I know money is not what drives them, but they can use it to keep their families content and happy. As long as their families are happy, they can do as they please. Our ranks may be small, but they have never been more dedicated."

"Good. If I have any excess funds I will send some back to you as an added precaution. Now, how is your search going? That is our only hope if we're going to succeed. Last time we spoke you told me we had some candidates. How are things progressing?" Aman asked nervously.

"Things are proving to be more difficult than I originally anticipated, but I believe they are our best hope." Aziz stood up before continuing, "The boys are finally showing the promise I saw in them. They are both staying with the doctor, and being examined and tested. They have both excelled in their schooling, and after a year under my control they still possess a strong resolve." Aziz's normally whispered tone was buoyant as he delivered the news.

"How did they become orphans?" Aman asked.

"The younger one's father was killed by the Israelis. At least this is what he claims. His mother had no money, no way to survive, and she turned to prostitution. She was knifed by her own pimp, and her son was kicked out of their apartment. Tossed into the streets. He hates everyone. He has a streak of volatility, but I have controlled him. He just needs to be pointed towards the target."

"And the other one?"

" He is even better. He is educated and is clearly of high intelligence. He is of mixed ancestry, which could be of great use to us if he makes it as far as we hope. His mother was European, French to be exact. She was killed during the brief scuffle for the Suez Canal. A bomb from an Israeli or American fighter jet went astray and destroyed their house when she was the only one home. His father is actually still alive, but he is a colonel in the Egyptian army. They were never married. The boy is a result of a one-night fling, and the woman hid the boy from the father. The man recently found out he has a son, and is trying desperately to get him back.

"I will not allow this to happen, of course. I'm already working on arrangements to have the father killed in the proper fashion. This will cement the son's loyalty to our cause. We found him wandering the streets right after his mother was killed, muttering about revenge. He was formulating a suicidal plan on the American Embassy. The child has a temper, but he is smart.

"How will you deal with his father?" Aman asked.

"I have found out through our channels that his father has additional duties besides just being a colonel. That is merely a cover. He runs dangerous missions into Israel and some of the other surrounding states, meeting with men willing to sell out their governments for money. He is a collector of information. It will be easy to make him vanish, and even easier to show the son who is to blame. I am already working on the story to feed him. We should be able to refocus his anger over the span of a few years. I will let you know more details at the appropriate time. For now, the doctor will have the final say, and then I will begin more intensive training for them." Aziz inhaled one final drag before dropping the butt of his second cigarette to the floor and smashing it out with his foot. "The American brands just do not compare to what I get at home." He pointed at the crushed pile of tobacco.

Aman breathed deeply, then flicked his own cigarette out the window onto the dirt path outside the stable. He was truly relieved to hear some good news from home, but he was exasperated with the reality of having to wait longer.

"You must continue to be vigilant for us, Aman. Your time will come." Aziz watched him carefully. Aman had been working undercover in the United States full time for over eight years now, and Aziz wondered if he was beginning to turn soft. It was always a danger. One could only hide among enemies for so long before unconsciously becoming like them. Aziz knew this from first hand experience. It almost happened to him during World War II.

246

A double life was hard, but Aman was the only one of their group with experience living in America. He was their only hope of keeping a presence in the country.

Aman straightened up and addressed his superior in a respectful tone. "I know. I am preparing the way as you ordered. Still, I feel like I'm not doing my part. I need to do more for the cause."

"Patience, patience, my friend." Aziz walked over and patted his friend on the back. He switched back to English for the remainder of the conversation. "I have idea, Aman. It will be five years before I return. Until then, you need to have party."

"Excuse me, sir. I do not know what you mean."

"Have a little American fun. Forget about your duties as Muslim. Drink and party with your American friends. They will then like you more. Sleep with their whores. Have fun. But just be prepared for our next meeting. After that, your life will be one purpose." Aziz stopped and then thought of one more thing. "I want you to be such degenerate American waste by time I come back, you will have to spend rest of your life praying to Allah for forgiveness."

Aman looked at him in a quizzical manner. "Aziz, I don't know if this is the best."

"Do it." The silky voice reverted into the tone of a commander. "Just be ready when I call." Aziz marched out of the stable to prepare for his journey home.

"As you wish," Aman whispered softly as the stable door slammed shut.

***

May 5, 1973

Aman adjusted his seersucker suit for the sixth time as the security guards of Churchill Downs parted the crowds so he could squeeze through the "owners only" entrance. He casually flashed his badge to the guard standing watch at the front of the paddock area. The guard acknowledged him with a brief nod before motioning Aman to pass. His day had been awful so far. His prized horse sliced to pieces by that fool of a stable boy; the same boy he was now under orders to raise in the U.S. as his own son. The horse had been carefully packed up and locked away before any inquest could be made. He reported the horse dead from a bacterial infection.

A record crowd of 134,476 had packed themselves in to watch the great Secretariat run a race. They were in a frenzy now that the Derby was less than two hours away. Aman no longer cared. He just wanted to finish his job and get the hell out of here. The track manager had already expressed his great sorrow at Desert Sheik's sudden death. He pleaded with Aman to stay, but said he understood if he wanted to leave.

Despite the cool day Aman was sweating profusely. His white shirt looked more like a towel as he gathered the last of his frayed nerves and walked around to the back of his stable where the truck with his horse's carcass was idling quietly. The congressman from New York waited patiently, sucking away on a cigarette as Aman approached. They shook hands.

"Congressman Rosenbaum, thank you for coming here today. It saves me a lot of time. I'm a busy man, and traveling this far from Las Vegas is difficult for me," Aman said. The congressman remained silent, and continued to nervously puff away.

"I trust you received my donation?" Aman asked.

Rosenbaum shook his head in the affirmative so Aman continued, "Oh, congratulations are also in order. I've heard you adopted a boy from Cairo," Aman said casually. His secret hand in the arrangement was unknown to the congressman.

Rosenbaum finally opened his mouth for the first time. The pitch of his voice reminded Aman of a woman's. "Yes, yes. Thank you for putting me in contact with that organization. My wife and I have been looking for a child to adopt. This is my way of giving back."

"How old is he?" Aman asked.

"Sixteen. He'll be arriving in the country next year with a small group of orphans. My wife will dote on him. As you know, we were never able to have children of our own. To be able to take a child off the streets of Cairo and give him hope is truly a blessing for us. Our government's immigration rules are truly awful. I've complained many times that we are killing thousands of young Arabs by not accepting more refugees. And the ones who don't die are taken by the extremists and twisted until they are handed a weapon and told to die for God. The organization that arranges these adoptions is truly doing God's work by bringing these orphans over, Aman," Rosenbaum replied as he glanced nervously at his watch. "I must get going though. My wife is waiting and she won't be friendly if we miss the big race." He dropped the cigarette and extended his hand in friendship.

Aman gripped it with fake enthusiasm. "Yes, I've heard good things about the man who brings in those young children. That is why I think I will adopt one sometime next year as well."

"Good. If you ever need any assistance from a lowly congressman like me, please ring me up. I will be happy to help out," Yohan said as he started to walk away.

"Thank you. I may do that," Aman said as he carefully watched the Jew for any sign of duplicity. Politicians were not to be trusted, but this one appeared on the fast track to power so Aman was cultivating the relationship. He decided to plant one more seed. "I want you to know I have already made a donation to your senate campaign as well. The government needs more people like you, who understand our two people must come together if we are ever going to stop the killing." Aman also hoped the man would be around long enough to be able to provide sensitive information when needed.

"Thank you. That is very generous of you. Now I must go. Thank you for the tickets. This place is truly beautiful." He gestured towards the racetrack. "My wife loves horse racing." Congressman Rosenbaum walked back towards the grandstand to watch the rest of the day's racing activities.

Aman glanced back at the stable boy shoveling hay and gave him a curt wave of acknowledgement. The boy was one of Aziz's handpicked warriors of God. Aziz planned to travel with the boy in the U.S. for six months before taking him to New York City to meet his new father. He turned

249

around and headed back to his stable where he found his nemesis for the day scrubbing the floor clean.

The teenager stopped when Aman appeared in the doorway. The look of submission from earlier that morning was replaced with a fierce stare. Aman was glad to see it. The boy had been rash and stupid, and deserved to be reprimanded. His spirit had clearly returned though, and he looked more determined than ever.

"Zachariah, are you ready to go and begin your new life?"

"Yes, sir." He stopped mopping, and stood fully erect to face his new mentor.

"We leave in a few hours. Your training will begin on the ride back. Go gather your belongings."

The boy hurried off. Aman made a mental note to have someone deliver the envelope of cash to Eddie Lauren. He would have to buy the reporter's silence now that his superiors had nixed the idea of disposing of him in a more permanent fashion. He headed back to the grandstand to meet Aziz for the first time that day.

Aman's look of disinterest stood in stark contrast to the massive crowd percolating with excitement around him. Secretariat, a horse thought by many to be on the verge of greatness, was less than an hour away from beginning his attempt at stardom. Aman gripped the wood railing in frustration, trying to control his craving for a cigarette and a mint julep. His years spent in the United States were like a cancer, slowly eating away at his core until there would one day be nothing left of his Muslim heritage. It was a race to save his own soul, he thought, and today would hopefully be the first notable step towards that redemption.

Aziz delivered on his promise. The two young boys he recruited so many years ago had now arrived in the U.S. with him as stable boys. They were teenagers though, after having spent the last eleven years under the tutelage of Aziz. Zachariah's father in the Egyptian military turned up murdered during the Six-Day War with Israel in 1967. It proved to be the final straw that pushed the boy over the edge. After Aziz revealed to Zachariah that his father's death was the result of a secret collaboration between American

250

agents and higher ups in the Egyptian government, Zachariah finally committed himself to the task of revenge. Zach's English was already flawless, and Aman was now ready to do his part. Zachariah was fifteen, and already a deep cover agent for them. The psychological toll had already begun to fray the teenagers mind, but the doctors assured them that he could be controlled.

The first week went smoothly. Aman thought that taking Zach back to Vegas and embedding him into American society would be simple. That was until a few hours earlier; when in a fit of pent up rage, Zachariah took a machete and butchered their horse into an unrecognizable bloody pulp. They had been more concerned that this type of behavior would manifest in Jamal, who had been a loose cannon in Cairo. By the time he was a young teenager Jamal had a blood lust that Aziz controlled by allowing him to butcher beggars who roamed the streets of Cairo at night. Now the boy was relaxed and staying out of trouble. Zachariah, however, was another issue.

Aziz spent the entire morning supervising the cleaning of Zach's butchery and formulating a lie about what happened to their horse. No one saw the horse's remains except the young reporter, and he would be paid off. Aman believed the reporter should have been killed, but Aziz overruled him.

The record crowd was the quietest it had been all day. The calm before the storm, Aman thought. For the first time he realized that raising Zachariah was going to be a challenge. All the theories he discussed with Aziz over the last several days about how to handle the transition, what type of schools to put Zach in, and what jobs would eventually allow Zach to wreck the most havoc were all shelved after this morning's episode. Hopefully the slaughtering of the horse would prove an anomaly, and not a harbinger of future control issues. This final thought pushed him over the edge. Aman gestured to one of the vendors and ordered two mint juleps while simultaneously saying a silent prayer, asking Allah for forgiveness. The cold, bitter liquid calmed his nerves. He took a seat and tried to relax. He reached into his pocket, grabbed a wad of dollars, and handed the unknown amount of money to his mistress, informing her to wager it all on Secretariat. He knew with his own horse dead there was no other competition for the massive red beast.

Aziz finally appeared in the owner's box at the same time Aman's mistress returned. Aman shooed her away, not caring whom she went to see as long as she stayed away for a while. Aziz frowned with annoyance at the site of the alcohol.

"I know I told you enjoy yourself, but do not do near me," Aziz commanded.

"This was your idea if my memory serves me correctly. These are my first ones of the day so relax. You haven't had to spend the majority of your life in this country." Aman was having as close to a middle age crisis as he would allow himself.

"Yes, yes. Do not think that I not understand the sacrifices you make for us, Aman. One question remain. Are you still prepared for this? This is most important phase now that boys finally make it here," Aziz said as he sat next to Aman on the metal folding chair that Aman's mistress previously occupied.

They were the only two people sitting. The rest of the massive crowd under the covered grandstand were all standing in their boxes, peering down, and waiting for the horses to saunter out from under the tunnel and onto the track.

"Of course I'm up for it," Aman replied in a hurt tone. He quickly moved on to the topic at hand. "And how is my new charge?"

"Sleeping. Finally. The doctor think Zachariah fine. He just need to blow off aggression. Unfortunately it was our horse. Better horse than person." Aziz ignored the whistles and hollering around him that preceded the call to the post. The horses appeared on the track, and the crowd's emotional level headed towards its pinnacle.

"Good to hear. The past twenty years have certainly been frustrating, but I feel reinvigorated now that I finally can at least see the beginnings of our journey," Aman said with true relief in his voice.

"Good. I know these years have been harder on you. Stuck here. In hiding. Practicing the thankless art of taquiyya. While we are across ocean fighting for Islam. I know you feel helpless, not being with your brothers. Now, I know you have Zachariah's schooling here all set up, but what about young Jamal? You have not told me a plan for him." Aziz was clearly more concerned about Jamal. He was a physical whirlwind of a teenager, already strong enough to kill most men. He needed discipline and an outlet for his rage. Aziz was extremely nervous about the plans for him. They would need to be ideally suited to his personality.

Aman waited a few seconds, a wry smile forming on his lips while he sipped his mint julep. His free hand smoothed the wide brown tie over his ever-expanding belly. For the hundredth time he silently made an empty promise that he would begin an exercise regime when he returned to Las Vegas. He quickly drowned out the hollow resolution with a final gulp, polishing off the last of his drink. The smell of mint lingered on his breath.

Aman's voice dropped to a whisper to match the low hissing of the crowd around them that was now gently singing "My Old Kentucky Home." The horses slowly meandered across the dirt floor of the track. The jockeys carefully scanned every buckle, strap, and harness one extra time, even though they knew everything was as it should be. Aman and Aziz now stood in unison with the crowd, Aman whispering conspiratorially in the shorter man's ear.

"He will be staying in New York City...with a Jew." Aman waited for the reaction.

Aziz's eyebrows arched slightly. The wheels of his mind clearly turning as he looked skyward and contemplated the choice. He was sure Aman was waiting for him to become angry. "That is curious. Either you have done most brilliant move possible or your time here makes you weak and traitor. Who is this Jew?"

"A friend of a friend in Las Vegas. The Jew is a friend of La Cosa Nostra in New York."

La Cosa Nostra, Aziz knew, was a popular name for the mob. "Go on," Aziz said. His eyes focused on the horses as they approached the starting gate, waiting for their

253

turn to step inside the metal contraption that would hurl them into the race.

Aman continued, "His name is Yohan Rosenbaum. He owns a chain of dry cleaning stores throughout New York City that have been utilized by La Cosa Nostra for several years to move money around. He is soon to be rewarded with a seat in the U.S. senate. They have it bought and paid for. He has been out to Vegas several times to meet with some of his friends. He sought me out at a party once and expressed remorse and guilt with what Israel was doing to our brothers. He feels like they should have never settled in Palestine, and that they used the sympathy the world felt for them after WWII to establish a state that should have been formed in Europe."

"Do you think he could be feeding you line? He could be spy for Mossad." Aziz chuckled at the irony of a dry cleaning business being used to launder money.

"I did some checking up on him through my sources and everything appears to be clean. I talked to him a few months ago and mentioned to him that I knew someone who was bringing some orphans to the United States and was looking to place them with families. He jumped at the opportunity. Apparently he and his wife are unable to have children of their own."

"So Jamal will join into Mafia? I do not like idea. I thought we agree they have legitimate careers? That is not the way to reach high level of American society," Aziz said in a tone that was not to be argued with.

The crowd now erupted in a roar as the metal gates released the horses onto the track. Aman leaned over the short man, and spoke into his ear. "No, definitely not. He will live with the Jew in Washington. I told you. He is already a congressman, and within two years will be a senator. He is going to sell his dry cleaning stores to his friends to manage for him. Our boy will live with him in Washington D.C. In a few years Jamal can enlist in the Army."

"Are you sure Jew will agree to send his foster child into army?" The thundering hooves reverberated throughout the metal grandstands as the traffic jam of horses shot by them in a blur. They looked up to see the horses fly by, while Aziz contemplated Aman's plan. It was crazy enough to be brilliant. They would launch their human missile right into the heart of power. He could release all his anger in the vicious training provided by the military. It would actually be a safe way to hide him until the appropriate time. The Americans were gun shy due to the slow bleeding they were experiencing with the Vietnam War. The protests that decimated support for the war were still echoing throughout the country. Aziz guessed that no future president would send soldiers into actual battle anytime soon.

"Yes, I lied to the Jew. Told him that the boy's father had been an Egyptian military officer. The father was killed running a secret operation. The Jew loved it. He agreed it would be a fitting tribute to the father, and of course Jamal will push for it. If the Jew changes his mind Jamal must be ordered to enlist anyway," Aman said with a confident tone.

"Good. I approve. It definitely not what I expected, which means our enemies will not suspect either. I have demand though."

They both fell silent as the horses completed their circuit around the track, and prepared for their stretch run. As Aman suspected, there was one horse quickly pulling away from the rest of the pack. The red-coated Secretariat came hurtling down the backstretch, kicking up dirt at an electrifying pace.

"Yes, Aziz?"

"I want you make sure he join the Marines. I have study American military. Marines rise the farthest after military service done. Plus, training regime should keep him calm for few years."

Secretariat passed their spot in a blur and zipped over the finish line. The crowd erupted as the time flashed on the board. The super horse eclipsed the two-minute mark, shattering the record for the fastest time in the race's history.

"I don't think that should be a problem. Come on, let's go. We have work to do back at the stables. Also, the Jew is here today. I got him tickets, and made some donations to his political campaigns. It will be your job to deliver Jamal to him and his wife in New York City in six months. I can't do it. I'm not supposed to know the boy. I cannot be seen with him," Aman said.

"You are full of secrets today my friend. Fine. I will. I guess it smart for me to make sure person we are entrusting our soldier to is capable man," Aziz replied. They scurried out of the box together, fighting their way through the hordes of people now milling about. They had their own Jewish Trojan Horse, Aziz realized. It only seemed fitting that they should use their enemy to get to their archenemy.

"The enemy of my enemy is my friend," Aziz mumbled to himself. He would never understand the personality types like Yohan. They reminded him of an antelope in the jungle, purposely showing itself to the lion trying to stalk it. He could at least respect the fighters among the Jews. There were plenty of them. He almost admired men like the ones in the Israeli army, who during the Six-Day War proved a brutal adversary. The compassionate and guilt ridden, which is what this Yohan sounded like, would be their doom. If the fool was going to offer his services, Aziz would gladly take him up on the offer. He only hoped that someday, if their boy did accomplish his goal, the Jew would still be alive so Jamal could turn on him and kill him too.

Part III
THE KILL

Chapter 38
Present Day

Aman's pudgy hands simultaneously hung up the phone and picked up a drink in one fluid motion. The Blair House may have been the home of the second most important man in Washington, but it possessed a first rate liquor selection to tap into. He dropped his large posterior into the luxurious leather chair, and tossed back another swig of top shelf gin. The mahogany paneled room was full of antiques, old books, and a few pictures of some of the better-known vice presidents. The room felt old to Aman, as if it belonged in another time period. The Americans were always trying to live off what they perceived to be their past accomplishments, and this room was a tribute to those misguided beliefs.

Until a few minutes earlier he felt like the fox guarding the proverbial hen house. Now he just hoped the farmer was not coming to get him with a shotgun after discovering the mistake. The young boy who called his cell phone was skittish and a mental wreck. He had broken every rule that Aziz had trained him to obey, but after the sixty-second conversation in their special code Aman could not blame him.

The old man was dead. It seemed impossible. Aziz had been frail and weak for years, but he also thrived off of that adversity, growing stronger from it instead of withering away. His young messenger, who was his only constant companion for the last several years, discovered Aziz's body on the second floor of the private area he kept for prayers.

The old man apparently took his own life by pouring boiling water all over himself. Aman shuddered at the incredible amount of pain it must have induced before he died. Aziz had always been the warrior. The boy apparently arrived at the building only to be caught and tied up by two strangers. He knew they were foreigners, which meant they were in all likelihood Americans. Aman rubbed his temple with his free hand, trying to massage away the headache that was rapidly engulfing his head. He dropped the drink on the table. It was doing more harm than good.

Looking around the room, he could not help but feel like a prisoner. Would they be coming to get him soon? *Impossible.* Aziz would never talk, and they purposefully kept the operation compartmentalized so no one would ever know the full logistics. Aziz did not even know what Zachariah was going to do with his new power once he took the oath of office. *Was it possible we left some part of the trail uncovered?* If so, could the Americans have extracted that information from Aziz to help them pick up the trail?

Pain gripped his entire chest and he grabbed for the bottle of ibuprofen next to him. He assumed the pain was caused by the excruciating tension he was under. They were only weeks away from accomplishing a goal that had taken years to materialize, and which he had come close to giving up on during numerous different occasions. Now that it was so close, every minute of his life seemed precariously too long, as if time was slowing down to snatch his ultimate goal from him right when it was within his grasp. He picked up the phone to place another call. Next to the phone was a handwritten list of several favors being requested by Zach's vice-president-elect, who was currently back in New York City tying up some loose ends before he assumed his primarily ceremonial office. As the mayor of New York he had been chosen for two reasons, to shore up the fringes of the party, and appease the East Coast establishment. This, combined with Zach's status as a senator from a west coast state, allowed their political dream team to pick off just enough purple states to seal the election. In addition to these assets the mayor of New York was also a spineless man with no true core values other than power, making him easy to manipulate.

Aman crumpled up the list of favors and threw it towards the nearest trashcan without a second thought. He punched in the phone number he knew by heart and called the one person who could find out who had been in Cairo trying to pull information from Aziz. The gravely voice on the other end was not happy with the request. He protested that he had already done enough for Aman over the years, and that he could get in trouble for asking the wrong questions. He told Aman he would not be much use to him if he got kicked off the Senate Intelligence Panel. A few minutes of arm-bending and some additional promises of assistance for his region finally persuaded the Jewish senator to agree to find out what he could. Aman hung up the telephone immediately and called Zach.

"Zach, we need to talk right away. I have some bad news. I'm coming over to see you right now, so stay put," he ordered.

"What is it? What has happened?" Zach asked hurriedly. He did not like surprises.

Aman shook his head in an exasperated fashion. The man had not changed in some facets. He could not just take a command lying down. He always was questioning orders.

"Just stay at the hotel. I'll be there as soon as possible." He punched the end button on his cell phone without waiting for a response. The sense of urgency propelled him out of the chair and towards the limousine idling outside in the circular driveway.

If there was one part of Aman's body that had not deteriorated over the years it was his eyes. They were as strong and penetrating as the day Zach first entered the United States that glorious May morning. Aman's stare was one of the few things Zach still feared. The piercing glare of Aman's two black bullets were currently focused on the bleach blonde hooker scurrying about the hotel suite, picking up random articles of clothing that were scattered throughout. Every few seconds their line of fire darted back to Zach, who was standing in the doorway of the bedroom with nothing on but an ivory silk robe with the hotel's initials on the left chest area. Zach kept his hands sheepishly tucked inside the front pockets, waiting for the situation to improve. The woman grabbed her large satchel and a fistful of money that had been strewn about the leather couch. Zach cringed as Aman furiously slammed the door behind her, just barely missing her posterior. The Secret Service would sneak her out the basement of the hotel.

Katie was a favorite of many of the congressmen and senators. Her only devotion was to money, which made her easy to control. She had no interest in publicity. If she did, she could have ratted out any of the hundreds of politicians with whom she did business. Yohan, who had partaken of her services until just a few years earlier when he attempted to be faithful to his wife, had suggested her to Aman. At least that was the excuse Yohan had told Aman. Zach guessed that he probably was slowly losing his manhood and did not want to admit it.

"Don't worry. She keeps her mouth shut. At least outside the bedroom," Zach said with a smirk. He lit a cigarette and inhaled the narcotic, letting the smoke coat his lungs. A cigarette was still the perfect ending to an evening of fornication. The politically correct crowd continued to try to eradicate smoking from every possible venue. The American populace could focus on the most insignificant problems sometimes, Zach thought as he flicked the first ash into an ashtray on a table. It was this short attention span that was so useful in the campaigns he ran over the years.

Now all that frivolous politicking was finally paying off. He was at a point he never thought he would actually reach. He could still vividly recall his arrival in the United States, hidden in plain sight as a stable hand for Aziz and his horse. The old man had been like a father to him while in Cairo, rescuing him when he was at his darkest point and showing him a way out of the black hole.

The streets of Cairo were a confusing place in the 1960s. The population was torn between Nasser's pseudo-socialistic regime, and the rising influence of the revolutionaries calling for a return to a pure Islamist state. There were thousands of children born after WWII who were forced to make a choice between these two extremes. Murders were commonplace throughout the city as Nasser used a brutal secret police to quell any descent. This only strengthened the resolve of the revolutionaries. It was a battle for the soul of Egypt, and the battle was still raging.

The battle for supremacy in the Muslim world went exactly as Aziz predicted. Both sides waged a guerilla war, however, the only true victor was the West. Aziz was a genius, a thinker way ahead of his time, as all the great ones were, Zach realized. Now he was about to fulfill Aziz's dream. With one stroke he would wipe the slate clean. He prayed every day that Aziz would live long enough to see the finale. The man saved him from ruin after the death of his parents. He tutored him on the hidden ways of the world and introduced him to the Brotherhood of the Caliphate, the secretive organization with a single- minded purpose to return Islam to its rightful place at the forefront of the world.

Zach had not spoken to Aziz since being left in Aman's care in 1973, but he knew what his teacher thought of Osama Bin Laden. Aziz would want nothing to do with him. Islam would never return to power as long as Muslims were trying to destroy each other. The proof of this fallacy could be found in the ten-year siege of Afghanistan. They conquered the Soviets, but at what cost? As soon as the war was over the mujahedin were at each other's throats, fighting for power and territory. The constant in-fighting left no one strong enough to unite all the factions of Islam. At the same time, the weakening of the Soviet Union only served to make America stronger. American power was simply too gargantuan to try to slowly bleed it dry. It had to be wiped out with one stroke, but only when the time was right. This required patience and fortitude, which most men lacked.

Zach still thought of those early teachings as the best days of his life. The thought of being worthy enough to assist Aziz in his grand struggle was an incredible feeling, Zach remembered, as if his destiny was laid out before him. When he mentioned his feelings to Aziz after a lecture the old man had smiled respectfully, and told him to be patient. All grand feelings would eventually pass and be replaced by the redundancy of everyday life. If one can fight through this

261

complacency, and the fire was still burning, Aziz explained, then he would be ready for the next step. Aziz used Zach's parents' death to cultivate his anger and despondency, and turned them into motivation.

Zach recalled when Aziz told him that in order to succeed he must be willing to purge himself of his identity and create a new one as a true Christian. He remembered the years of grueling teachings Aziz forced him to undergo. During that time he was taught everything about the West and America. By the time it was complete he felt like he no longer knew himself.

The training lasted until he was nearly fifteen. Zach was then informed that he would be sent to America for the rest of his life to fulfill his calling. He always knew that this was their ultimate plan, but it was still a depressing time. He did not want to leave Aziz, but the fire within him was ignited, and he was anxious to begin his quest to reassert Islam's supremacy. The decadency of the Americans reached staggering proportions by the time they were preparing to infiltrate him into the United States. The Vietnam War had been raging for several years. It was proving a political disaster, and showcasing once again their arrogance and continued determination to force their values on a helpless country.

He recalled the unusually warm night when Aziz told him for the first time they were leaving for America to meet up with another brother-in-arms. All the schooling and training he attacked with such vigor over the past several years would now be put to the test. He was to live with Aziz's counterpart in the United States. The cover story was perfectly forged, and Zach dutifully followed the teachings and instruction he received. It was time for his first step in a long journey.

Before leaving for America Zach was given the one item that would identify him as a true member of the Brotherhood of the Caliphate. In a small ritual attended by just a few confidants he received the small tattoo on his inner thigh, the symbol of the Caliphate. Aziz embraced him after the ceremony, telling him he was now a full-fledged member of their honored fraternity. The tattoo was seared into his skin, under the hair of his inner thigh. He was told to never show it to anyone until the time was right. Their journey commenced.

It started out horribly. He had never been outside Egypt, and the long boat ride across the Atlantic proved painful. He quickly discovered he hated the ocean, and spent much of his time in his own cabin vomiting as a storm rocked the massive steam liner they were riding. Aziz also neglected him on the ship, instead spending his time making sure the horse was comfortable, and tending to other projects from which Zach was excluded. By the time they arrived in New York harbor Zach was frustrated and depressed. The cultural shock of America only worsened his mood. He thought he knew all about the Americans. After all, he studied them intensely for years, but nothing could prepare him for his first encounter with the superpower.

The train ride through several states, as they made their way to Kentucky, opened his eyes to the scale of the task they were burdening themselves with. Despite the stories he heard about the disarray the country was in, he still saw nothing resembling the slums of Cairo. Could this seemingly invincible nation really be brought out of its arrogant state of mind? Seeing the country up close for the first time, he now realized why Aziz constantly expressed to him the enormity of their mission.

"Patience." He could still remember Aziz's silky voice repeating it over and over. "All empires are destroyed," Aziz had explained. "Look at ancient Rome. It once appeared invulnerable until it crumbled under the burden of its immorality. The Muslim Caliphate, which once possessed hegemony over all of the Middle East and Europe in the fourteenth century, was also destroyed. The corrupt eventually crumble under their own weight."

He remembered Aziz preaching that the original Caliphates were brought down by the Shia and Sunni rift that tore Islam apart. The Muslim world never recovered from this divide. Instead of focusing on their true enemies, Muslims spent the last few centuries tearing at each others' throats, while their true enemies established dominion over the entire world. Only someone with the forbearance to stalk his enemy, and carefully wait for that perfect moment, would be able to pull off a monumental task such as the destruction of the United States as a superpower.

Despite some of the American governments' poor decisions regarding war, it always managed to land on its feet. The sheer size of the country protected its soft underbelly. Zachariah had watched throughout the years as some of his enemies and friends in the government committed political suicide in their quest for money and power. It would be his job to instigate the first political genocide the country has ever seen. Only then will the rest of the world devour the carcass of America and look for a replacement to fill the void. The return of the Caliphate was the only entity powerful enough to fill such a vacuum. However, a person could not claim the lofty title of the Caliphate without humbling the West in a manner which has never been done before. That was Zach's purpose, mission, and destiny.

Zach's wondering mind returned to the moment. "Well, what is so important that you had to dash over here so quickly? I was about to look over the inauguration speech."

"Aziz is dead, Zach. His errand boy found his body. Luckily he called me immediately. I have trusted men taking care of the situation as we speak."

Zach stood dumbfounded, unable to accept the possibility that his savior was dead. The fond memories of just a few moments before were wiped away with the devastating news. He stared at the ceiling, refusing to acknowledge the truth of the old man's death. Zach's lower lip quivered. Just when it appeared as though he may cry, his face instead turned into a taut ball of anger. He steeled himself for the rest of the conversation. "What happened?" Zach demanded.

The intensity of the question shook Aman. "He killed himself. Apparently some of our friends in the U.S. government showed up to question him. I have Yohan trying to find out whom right now. We all know Aziz's health has deteriorated over the last several years. We both know how much he detests suicide. He must have felt they were on to something. He was probably afraid he would crack under

264

interrogation. It is the only thing that would cause him to take such a drastic course."

Zach stood motionless. The fire of the forgotten cigarette burnt his hand and he dropped it to the floor, wincing in pain. He stamped it out with his foot. "What is our next step?"

"Nothing. Continue on as normal. We have our scheduled walkthrough at FBI headquarters tomorrow. There you can announce your selection for commerce secretary. Hopefully by then Yohan will have some useful information for us. In the meantime, it is best we continue as if nothing has changed. If they had anything concrete on you I'm sure they would have already paid you a visit. I believe we are safe for the moment."

"Have you heard anything regarding our man in the White House?" Zach ran his hands through his hair, assessing the image of himself in the mirror above the fireplace.

"Yes, Mr. Gray has agreed that if we want to keep him as head of your security detail he is okay with it. Everything will be in place, just as we planned."

Zach smiled for the first time. At least things on this side of the ocean were going smoothly.

"I look forward to the reunion," Zach stated.

"Get some sleep. I'll be here tomorrow morning at seven a.m. sharp to pick you up." Aman opened the door to leave, but stepped back into the room one more time. "And don't call that whore again tonight. I don't care if you have used her before and trust her. Just go to bed." He slammed the door behind him. On the way out he gave strict instructions to the Secret Service agents to not let anyone into the suite without his permission.

Chapter 39

Alex stared at the dual computer screens in front of him, reading over the story for the third time. Anna stood behind him, crouching over his shoulder as she perused it as well. In a normal setting, having a beautiful woman like her breathing gently just a few inches away would have been quite enjoyable. The faint hint of her perfume would have been enough to throw all other thoughts out the window. In this case though, her sexuality was an afterthought, which spoke to the gravity of their mission.

They had spent the last few days cooped up inside the small cabin, trolling the Internet, and researching all the information that the CIA's database contained on Zach and his companions. Their search continued to yield nothing but the normal biographical information that everyone in America already knew about the incoming president and Aman Kazim.

They were still running into the same dead end. His life in the U.S. from age fifteen on was easily documented, but there was no record of his family or schooling in Cairo. As Anna discovered, even his birth records were unavailable. He was like a ghost in Cairo, with no documentation of his life until he appeared in the United States as a well-adjusted sixteen-year-old immigrant. He tore through his school lessons with ease while impressing every classmate and teacher who came in contact with him at Clark High School in Las Vegas. He was one of the top students in his class by the time he graduated high school, and his grades earned him a spot at Yale, the epitome of Ivy League schooling. His ascent toward fame continued at Yale as his prodigious ability in the classroom vaulted him towards the pinnacle.

After graduating in 1979 and finishing ninth in his class he returned to his home state of Nevada to run for Congress. A seat became vacant in his district at the perfect moment. The incumbent who held the seat the previous six years, and would have easily won re-election, decided to retire abruptly. An FBI report suggested that Aman greased the skids for his adoptive son, showering the congressman with gambling money and whores whenever he was in town. There were even rumors of a raunchy videotape locked away in a vault somewhere, but nothing could be verified. All that was known for sure was that the congressman from Nevada retired.

Aman's money machine and political influence in Las Vegas immediately made the Yale graduate a front-runner for the vacant seat. By 1986 Zach made it to the U.S. Senate, and in 1990 he finally got married. After all, Zach could not become a power player in Washington until he took a wife. No matter how much one ignored those wedding vows, Washington D.C. was about perception, not reality, and Zach slipped seamlessly in with the rest of the establishment.

Now Anna and Alex were on the trail of something new. Alex rocked back in his chair, gripped the table, and used it to balance himself while he waited for Anna to finish the story he had just shown her. He found it during a simple, open source Internet search after they received a mid-flight phone call from Sean Hill. Sean was over the Atlantic, returning to the States with Colin Archer in tow. Anna refused to divulge the conversation to Alex except for one fact. Sean had told her that Aziz admitted to being in the U.S., however Sean was under the impression it had been a long time ago. They knew Aziz had been a horse trainer in Egypt so Alex did some searches, but they all yielded nothing. Then he remembered what had once been merely an afterthought about Aman's biography. Back in the 1960s Aman raced some horses, but none of them achieved any notoriety. They had all run poorly, and after a few tries he left the business in the 1970s in order to focus all his energy on his burgeoning casino business.

The story Alex had just pulled off the Internet was an article from the Louisville Times dated May 5th, 1973. It was a short editorial handicapping the Kentucky Derby that was scheduled to run later that day. The writer, Eddie Lauren had picked a veritable unknown horse to win the race. He decided to pass on Secretariat, the overwhelming favorite, and pick a horse named Desert Sheik instead. Desert Sheik was an unknown entity, and had just arrived from Egypt a few weeks earlier. A syndicate called Sheik Stables owned the horse. There was a short biography on the horse, its racing pedigree, and its performances overseas, all of which had been impeccable.

Mr. Lauren believed that the horse was being disregarded by the handicappers because it had never raced in the United States. Below the article was a picture of the horse being walked to the track. The caption read *"Desert Sheik is escorted to the track by owner Aman Kazim for a morning workout five days before the big race."* A much slimmer version of Aman could be seen in the grainy black and white photo, gripping the reins of the horse and pulling the thoroughbred onto the early morning track.

She studied the photo intently, "Is this the only information on him regarding the race?"

"Yes, here is the rest of the information from that day. Specs on the other horses, names of trainers, owners, jockeys..." Alex gestured towards the second monitor, which showed the racing forum for that day. Aman's name was nowhere to be found. Only the name Sheik Stables was mentioned. He gestured towards the information on Desert Sheik's trainer. The name Aziz Al-Fasal stared back at them.

"If I were a betting man I would venture a guess that Aziz Al-Fasal is really Aziz A'zami. Maybe Aziz came into the U.S. on a passport with that name. But why hide this information? If he was Aman's trainer he must have had a much closer relationship with Aman than we previously thought. It appears that Aziz slipped up when he mentioned that he had been to the United States. If he snuck into the U.S. with the rest of the horse's entourage, then he must have had an important task to complete here. But what?" Anna asked.

"Did they ask, Aziz?"

"He's dead." As usual she went straight to the heart of the matter. She did not offer any more information, and Alex knew better than to ask.

"Aziz apparently killed himself in the middle of their questioning him." She leaned in closer to look into his

268

eyes. "He poured boiling water all over himself. Died of a heart attack."

Alex flinched at the thought of the horrific death. The man was either crazy or desperately trying to hide something. An idea flashed across his mind. Could that reporter still be alive? He started furiously typing on the keyboard.

"Is that reporter still alive by any chance?" Anna asked, her sudden flash of inspiration occurring almost simultaneously with Alex's.

"I'm already on it," Alex replied with excitement. The paper's website popped up on the screen. He clicked on the sports section, and there it was. Eddie Lauren was now the head columnist for the Louisville Times. "He's been promoted since 1974," Alex said in a matter of fact tone.

"It looks like we have something resembling a lead. I'll give Mr. Lauren a call. See if we can arrange an off-the-record interview. Keep on looking through that. See if you can find anything else useful. I have some travel arrangements to make for us." She stood up to leave.

"Us?" Alex asked with surprise.

"Yes, you lived in Louisville for a time, didn't you?"

"Uh-huh." Alex perked up. He was back in the game.

"Always a good idea to bring along a pair of eyes that have already seen the landscape. I don't think this should be too dangerous anyway." She broke a smile for the first time he could remember. "And, Alex?" Anna asked, and then waited until he looked her in the eyes.

"Yes?" He asked nervously.

"Good work." The simple statement of gratitude coming from a professional was the best compliment he could have hoped for. He turned his attention back to the dual monitors and continued studying the screens.

Chapter 40

Aman stared out the tinted glass of the limousine in disgust. There was a massive crowd lining the sidewalk in front of the J. Edgar Hoover building. *Why did every fucking event they went to turn into a circus?* They were going to tour the FBI building, then meet with Bret McMichael. The throng of people was an unusually large mix of gorgeous women, the normal political hacks, and a few families. Zach was not only the incoming president, but also a widower, and he brought out a different type of political crowd. A large percentage of them appeared to be delusional women, pretending they had a chance to be the next First Lady.

The limousine rolled to a stop on the curb. Aman would have preferred to go in the underground entrance, but Zach was insistent on mingling. He loved the adoration, even if he hated most of the people who screamed out their love for him. A pair of thong underwear fell harmlessly against the bulletproof glass, tossed from somewhere in the crowd. American women just did not know when to stop.

Zach chuckled softly. "They're the size I like," he said with a smirk, stretching his legs across the seat in front of him. They waited for the Secret Service to secure the area and create a corridor for them to move through.

Aman's cell phone vibrated. He looked at the luminescent dial. It was Yohan. *Finally.* Aman gestured to the Secret Service agent outside the window that they would need a few extra minutes.

"Yes?" Aman listened intently, pushing the phone as close to his ear as possible as he took in the precious information. Aman's eyebrows furrowed, "Yes, I understand the price." He then fell silent as the voice on the other end continued. "I told you, you'll get what you want," Aman whispered, but was interrupted by the caller again. "Yes, I won't ask for any more favors," Aman said in an exasperated tone. He leaned his head back and stared at the ceiling of the limousine as he rolled his eyes. *Fucking Jews.* No matter what the situation, they always find a way to make a buck out of it. Was Yohan talking this quietly, or was his hearing going bad along with every other part of his body? He made a mental note to have his hearing tested. He lowered his head, and Yohan finally stopped rambling. "You're sure? Okay. I truly appreciate this. I promise no one will find out it was you who leaked the information," Aman said in an annoyed tone. He shook his head from side to side and stared at Zach. He pointed at the phone and mouthed to Zach that the politician would not shut up. "Yes. I will see you at the inauguration. Goodbye." He flipped the phone down in finality and dialed another number by heart.

"Hello?" Solomon's voice answered after the first ring.

"Forget the woman. She's gone to ground. I have a new one for you. Sean Hill, FBI. Arriving today at 3. Howell air base. " Aman enunciated the words so there could be no mistake.

"Understood. Price remains the same," Solomon stated without hesitation.

"Agreed." Aman slammed the phone shut. After a few seconds, he bent the flip phone the wrong way until it snapped in two. He had no intention of using it again.

"I'm getting screwed by everyone today, Zach. But I think we may have solved our problem, or if nothing else, at least temporarily patched our leak. All we need is a few more days anyway."

Aman gestured to the Secret Service agent standing outside. The few minutes of being teased had caused the crowd to become frenzied with emotion. The door opened and Zach stepped out to the raucous cheers. His natural charm and magnetism kicked into gear. Aman rolled himself out of the plush seat and onto the pavement, falling in behind his adoptive son. *Just a few more minutes and we will be inside the five story metal building and away from these idiots.*

***

271

Northern Virginia

Solomon stretched his body across the cheap motel mattress and rubbed the two weeks of growth on his face. The new beard was already scratchy and annoying, but it was an absolute necessity. There were more spies from every country imaginable within a fifty mile radius of Washington D.C. than anywhere in the world, and they all had long memories. It was also the reason he spent the last two weeks moving among remote motels in Northern Virginia every night, instead of staying in D.C. It made for some extra driving, but he felt safer outside the city limits. Reaching underneath his pillow, he grabbed his FN Herstal 5.7mm pistol. He used the butt of the pistol to smash the face of the phone, rendering it useless. He then broke it in two.

The last couple weeks had proven difficult and frustrating. There had been a lot of money dangled in front of him to track down this woman, but he had come up empty. He contacted several people Aman trusted in the area with nothing to show for it. The woman was good at covering her tracks. After seeing the carnage she inflicted on Gregor and his men he admitted to himself that he was a little fearful about his current task. He promised himself he would not take any stupid chances. If he did find her, he would only take her out if the risk of hurting himself in the process was minimal. Fear was a useful emotion, as long one understood how to control it.

Now Aman had assigned him a new target, and there were less than six hours for him to put together a plan. Despite the dangerously short time frame he felt confident it could be done. Whoever this Sean Hill was, he could not be any more dangerous than the woman, and he was arriving on a military flight at a private air base. He knew the perfect location from where to watch the plane land. Solomon stepped out of bed and put on his earth tone outfit as he considered his options. The military planes that flew in to the base usually arrived at night in order to hide their approach, but this particular plane was not waiting. Whoever Sean Hill was, he was clearly confident that no one knew about his arrival. This was an edge that Solomon planned on exploiting to its maximum potential.

Ten minutes later he was suited up and ready. He wiped the motel room down; cleaning off any potential fingerprints he may have left. The large duffel bag of clothes would be deposited in the dumpster on the way out. The smaller bag contained the additional firepower of the Heckler & Koch MP5K sub-machine gun and a few extra magazines of ammunition. There was not enough time to formulate a quiet plan of action so he would keep it simple. He would utilize an aggressive strike with as many bullets fired as possible. This would give him the optimum chance for killing his prey, and then getting the hell away.

Chapter 41

Malcolm flung open the screen door of his walkout basement and hurled the tennis ball into his massive backyard as far as he could. His seventy-five pound golden retriever tore out of the house without hesitation and went bounding across the yard to retrieve his favorite toy. The CIA Director's estate sat in one of the few wooded areas left in Arlington, Virginia. His house was a good half-mile away from his closest neighbor. His right arm winced in pain. It was foolish to throw the toy as far as he did, but the violent motion did relieve a little stress, if only for the briefest moment. The shoulder injury was compliments of a Sudanese soldier during one of Malcolm's infiltrations into Northern Africa. Although the soldier received a much worse injury, the mission went awry and was not a good memory for him. That failed mission many years earlier seemed pretty simple compared to the current problem.

If Malcolm were a drinker he would have gone straight for the bottle. One of the many government attorneys who assisted the CIA had just left the house after a cantankerous discussion. Malcolm received the call from the

Congressional Oversight Committee the day before. The days of media speculation were coming to an end, and now he was being summoned to Capitol Hill for a question and answer session regarding President Gray's extracurricular investigation. There were rumors running all over town that the CIA assisted the FBI during its investigation in Egypt a few months earlier, and Congress was eager to give the CIA an opportunity to clear its name.

At least that was what the Senator from Illinois told him when he called Malcolm yesterday. Members of Congress rarely called him directly, and when they did, it meant only one thing. They felt they had a sure-fire case, and were eager to rub it in Malcolm's face while pretending to be fair-minded. Malcolm, however, knew better. Their investigation had always been fraught with danger, and now, just as President Gray feared, it appeared to be blowing up in their collective faces. His honey colored golden retriever came to a screeching halt next to him and deposited the slimy ball at his feet, oblivious to his master's contemplations.

After twenty years of service to his country it all appeared to be coming to an end. The last chapter of his career was going to be a rough one, and it may be the final straw that would end his own marriage, as well. It was already on very shaky ground. A job that required him to trust no one, and keep quiet about his successes did not mesh well with the vows of matrimony. When Malcolm combined this with his wife's personality, which was suspicious by nature, the combination proved toxic. Maria was currently visiting her parents in Arizona for an extended stay. This was for the best.

The last few weeks provided constant speculation about everything Malcolm had done for the past few months. His speeches, statements to the press, and travels were all receiving the full cavity body search that could only be delivered by an alerted press corps. What was anathema to the ordinary person was unbearable torture for a man like Malcolm, who spent most of his career before becoming CIA Director as an invisible agent, making his way through the labyrinth of terrorist networks in North Africa and the

Middle East.

Sammy sat down beside him, sensing the uneasiness of his master and trying to provide whatever comfort he could. Malcolm reached down, patted the dog on the head, and kicked the tennis ball over to him so he could continue licking it. The lawyer suggested coming clean about the operation. He suggested that Malcolm should claim it was the President's idea, and hang him out to dry along with the covert agent who went off the reservation. It would be the perfect way to make nice with Congress, and line himself up for a lucrative book deal after he resigned. Malcolm refused to even consider it. The President was an honorable man. He made hard choices, and stuck with them despite the fact that they were now unpopular.

The twenty-hour news cycle, which provided the CIA with a lot of free information, was a double-edged sword. It equated what was popular with what was the right thing to do. At that moment, Malcolm decided to plead the Fifth Amendment on every question. He would not allow the media or Congress to turn this into a spectacle like the Church Committee from the 1970s. That committee decimated the CIA's ability to do its job, and Malcolm would not allow it to happen again. If the only way to avoid another airing of the CIA's dirty laundry was for him to fall on his own sword, then that was the way it would be.

He was really looking forward to the anger this would incite from his interrogators. Plus, there was one other reason for hope. Brett McMichael had not called him yet to provide him an update on Sean Hill's trip to Egypt. There was still a slim chance that something might change over the next few days if either Sean or Anna discovered new information at the last second. Now that the game was exposed they were all in danger of going to jail. On the other hand, opening the investigation to daylight was sure to make Zachariah Hardin and Aman Kazim a little nervous. If there was some sort of nefarious plot underway, they were much more likely to make a mistake now that the media was about to focus on a story other than Zach's search to fill his cabinet positions.

Malcolm stepped back into the house, leaving

275

Sammy to gnaw away at the mushy tennis ball. The central alarm chirped as he shut the door. He walked up to the main floor to grab a bottle of water. As he took a sip his cell phone vibrated in his pocket. It was a text message instructing him to answer phone number eight. Anna was about to call him. Before the mission he purchased several special cell phones about which only Anna knew. Each one was to be used only once and then disposed of. They had already used four of them over the last several months.

Dashing into the master bedroom, he punched in the numbers for the combination on the safe and pulled out the phone. It began ringing a few seconds later. He listened intently as Anna gave him the rundown on what they had discovered. He wished her luck and hung up the phone, not wanting to know any more until they returned. They were about to make a trip to Louisville, KY and needed his assistance. He would have the secret CIA plane gassed up and ready to go. It was a glimmer of hope and it strengthened his resolve. He was really looking forward to dishing out the silent treatment to the Congressional Committee. He was not sure who despised silence more, Congress or his wife. He then dropped the phone on the floor and smashed it with his right foot.

Chapter 42

Solomon stood near the top of the enormous pine tree, completely invisible to anyone except a trained expert. He was a good half-mile from the military airbase, his car parked just off the side of the road on a hilltop. There was a jack and a spare tire lying beside the vehicle to give a false impression in case someone meandered off the road far enough to find the vehicle. He peered through a pair of French made Ugo Day & Night goggles. Straps secured the multi-functional goggles to his head, and allowed him to keep both hands free to balance himself near the top of the tree. A third lens protruded from the middle of the goggles, making him look like a Cyclops.

Solomon focused on the military C-130 cargo plane as it approached the runway. He had been sitting precariously in the tree for two hours, and had seen no other landings. He glanced at his watch. It was five after three. This must be it. The plane touched down safely on the tarmac that was protected by barbed wire and electrified fencing. The military preferred privacy. He could see a few guards scattered amongst the outskirts of the perimeter, meandering aimlessly. They would be easy targets if he had been after them. He slid the goggles up on top of his forehead and began cautiously descending the tree via the same route he ascended it. His original idea would have to be scrapped. The intense security detail at the airport posed too much of a risk. Solomon hurried back to the car and cleaned the area to make sure he left no traces he had been there.

Twenty minutes later he watched as the unmarked government vehicle pulled out of the secure airport and onto the open road. He gently pressed his foot on the accelerator, pushing the silver Mercury Sable out of the convenience store parking lot, and falling in behind them. He followed from a safe distance. They merged onto the freeway and Solomon followed suit. He was now within a few car lengths of the gold Ford Taurus, which seemed to be the U.S. government vehicle of choice. His target was moving along at a few miles above the posted speed limit on I-95 South in northern Virginia. Solomon had carefully chosen his rental vehicle for this mission. The area was teeming with government bureaucrats, and the ones who survived Washington D.C. long enough to attain a free car all seemed to drive either a Taurus, Sable, or some other standard American four door sedan. Solomon wanted to be sure that he blended in to his environment, just in case the driver of the other vehicle was being a little more alert than the average employee of Uncle Sam.

He took a quick glance through his binoculars. The idiots were not even driving in a vehicle with tinted windows. There were two men in the back seat. One was bald, and the other one was so tall that his head appeared to touch the top of the roof. The brief description that Aman provided him via a text message was enough for him to positively identify his targets. The orders were clear. Aman wanted everyone in the car dead.

Solomon eased off the gas pedal and switched into the slow lane just to be cautious. There was no need to get any closer. They would have to merge into the right lane once they arrived at their exit. Only then would he make his move. He double-checked the MP5K sub-machine gun lying on the passenger seat. The safety/fire selector switch was turned to the bottom setting. The weapon was set for full automatic fire. He patted his pocket and felt the reassuring bulge of his airplane ticket. A round trip flight to Belize leaving in two hours would have him on it. He had every intention of only completing the first leg of his journey.

Twenty-five nervous minutes later the vehicle he was tracking finally moved into the right lane, switching on its turn signal to indicate its intention to get off at the next exit. Solomon's gloved hands gripped the steering wheel, and he slowed down in unison with the vehicle. The highway sign announced that the Central Intelligence Agency was located off the next exit. Solomon chuckled to himself. The Americans really did not take their security seriously anymore. He doubted they had advertised the location of their secret agencies on street signs during World War II. The agency was just another government bureaucracy now. He would have to make his move quickly. He knew the CIA building was less than sixty minutes away once they exited the freeway, and he needed to act before they were within eyesight of the complex. There were too many cameras once they were within sight. His quarry slowed their speed even more. The exit was now just a few hundred feet away.

Solomon accelerated forward so no one could cut in between their two cars. As they merged onto the exit ramp the traffic light at the intersection turned yellow. It was the stroke of luck he was hoping for, and he pulled the MP5K closer to him and laid it across his stomach. He reached

278

underneath the visor and grabbed the ski mask he had stashed away and pulled it over his face. The Ford Taurus rolled gently to a stop, and he could clearly see the two occupants in the backseat. They appeared to be in a heated conversation. Solomon slammed the gas pedal down, accelerated forward, and swerved his vehicle in front of them, blocking their path.

***

Sean Hill's exhausted body could not take much more. The long flight back across the Atlantic in a stripped down C-130 Starlifter was miserable. The seating arrangements consisted of two tiny cots that could barely accommodate an average-sized person, much less his own tall figure. Now this idiot CIA officer wanted to blow the lid on their investigation. Colin's claim that he was not getting any phone reception on the plane appeared to be a hoax. The shouting match started as soon as they set foot on American soil, and continued unabated their entire journey.

"Fuck it. I'm not going to waste my breath with you anymore," Sean said. He stared out the front windshield as the driver gently rolled the vehicle to a stop at the end of the exit. He let out a guttural growl. He closed his eyes and wished for the pounding in his head to go away. The gunning of an engine percolated his senses for the briefest moment. Then the screeching sound of tires abruptly opened his eyes. His drained mind registered the car blocking their path, and exhaustion turned instantly to survival mode as the black clad figure in a ski mask threw open the door. The MP5K sub-machine in the assailant's two-handed grip began spitting a stream of bullets in their direction.

In the back of his mind, Sean realized that during the last thirty minutes he disobeyed every instinct ever burned into his psyche by his superiors. His hand instinctively reached into his sport coat in a last-ditch attempt to rescue himself from his own grotesque failure. The self-critique ended in a rain of bullets tearing into his chest until his vital organs were shredded from the excessive barrage. Colin and the driver both met the same fate.

***

Solomon continued firing away until the weapon

279

clicked to a stop, and the spent magazine dropped to the ground and clattered on the asphalt. He tossed the weapon into the stretch of tall grass that ran alongside the street. He had no intention of being caught, but if he was pulled over it was better not to have an empty automatic weapon in the passenger seat beside you. He jumped back into his car, tearing through the red light and crossing the intersection as stunned onlookers gawked at the carnage. He tore up the ramp and back onto the freeway in a mad dash to freedom.

Chapter 43

Anna stared out the window of the Gulfstream Aerospace G550 jet, gazing out at the muddy snake of the Ohio River that cut the landscape below them. The river marked the border between Kentucky and Indiana. The downtown landscape of Louisville, Kentucky stood below them. A bitter frost currently gripped the city. Malcolm insisted on them taking his own jet for the trip. The sleek, sharp angled plane was his pride and joy, and the Rolls Royce 157 Deutschland BR710 turbofans brought them to Kentucky in record time. The plane, which had its maiden flight in 1995, did not go onto the open market until 1997. At the time, Malcolm had just become CIA Director, and he was the first customer to receive the record-breaking plane. Malcolm had the plane sitting on the runway in Virginia for them, gassed up and ready to go. He was happy to do everything in his power to thumb his nose at the powers that be on Capitol Hill. Anna knew that Malcolm was expecting to be run out of town the following day, and she assumed he was determined to go out with a bang.

The plane touched down gently on the military runway that sat just east of Louisville International Airport. Alex sat across from her, sleeping quietly until the wheels finally hit the concrete. If he was calm enough to sleep through most of the flight maybe that was a sign that he was finally starting to come around, she thought. The plane taxied quickly and made its way across the open field. It came to a stop in one of the airplane hangars that sat just off the runway. The gargantuan hangar could handle a plane three times the size of the CIA Director's Gulfstream. The Ford Explorer Anna had requested was parked in the corner of the hangar. A Military Police Officer sat in the driver's seat, reading a sports magazine. Other than the vehicle, the hangar looked barren, and everything appeared to be in order for their arrival.

Anna had placed a call to the Louisville Times immediately after they had discovered their information regarding Aziz. She got a hold of Mr. Lauren at his desk as he was banging out an editorial about one of the local sports teams. Anna introduced herself as an FBI agent who needed to ask him some questions about Aman. Eddie Lauren sounded very hesitant and unsure of what to do, but after some prodding he agreed to meet her for a question-and-answer session. He did not have much on his plate the rest of the week, so they arranged to meet at Churchill Downs.

After talking with Anna he promised he would call his acquaintances at the track and arrange for them to be allowed in. The famous racetrack was closed for the winter so they would have plenty of privacy. As the lead sports reporter for the Times, Eddie could typically get access to the track whenever necessary. The grandstands were an excellent place for an off-the-record meeting, which Anna assured him it would be. There had been nothing veiled about her threat if he told anyone whom he was meeting.

Anna quickly descended the moving staircase that brushed up against the Gulfstream jet. Alex followed her in silence. He squeezed his coat tightly around himself as the freezer of the unregulated hangar replaced the climate-controlled warmth of the Gulfstream. The Military Police Officer stepped out of the Ford Explorer in silence, ushering Anna towards the driver's seat.

"You drive instead," Anna said as she pointed at Alex. She dismissed the MP, and they both climbed in to their seats. Alex yanked the gear shift into "drive" and cautiously edged the vehicle out of the hangar. There were plenty of signs to lead them off the base.

"That was simple. Obviously that guy wants nothing to do with us. Where to?" Alex asked as they approached the exit of the airbase. They were waved on through by a lone security guard.

"Do you know how to get to Churchill Downs from here?" Anna asked.

"Sure. We're not that far away. It's probably closed for the winter though."

"Well, that is where we will be conducting our interview with Mr. Lauren. He said he can get us in."

"Should be a good place for a discussion like ours," Alex replied. "Plenty of open space in the grandstand. Difficult place for anyone else to listen or bug."

"My thoughts precisely. Good to see you thinking through the scenario, Alex. Remember, when we meet this guy, you are to be seen and not heard. I'm not even going to introduce you. It's best if he thinks you are just some muscle I brought along to watch over me. I will ask the questions. Just keep an eye out for anything odd. There is always a chance this guy was, or still is, some sort of agent for Aman. I doubt it, but I wouldn't totally discount it."

Alex steered the SUV onto I-65 North, taking them towards downtown Louisville. At the outskirts of the city they merged onto an exit for I-264 West, known to locals as the Watterson Expressway. I-264 encircled the area, and provided easy access from one end of town to the other. The early afternoon traffic was sparse. Five minutes later they turned off the interstate at the Taylor Boulevard exit. The street was lined with one hundred-year-old houses in varying types of condition. A park sat on the opposite side of the street. It appeared abandoned due to the extreme cold. They hung a right onto Central Boulevard, and a few seconds later they could see the towering twin spires of Churchill Downs, jutting upwards into the frigid air. The place was a ghost town. Alex swung the SUV into the vacant parking lot and drove the vehicle all the way to the front gate.

They stepped cautiously out of the vehicle and casually strolled up to the lone man standing inside one of the glass enclosed ticket counters. The man appeared to be in his mid-seventies, and judging by the smile and his happy demeanor, he was probably a retiree who loved the racetrack and did his job for the pure enjoyment of it.

Anna stepped up to the booth and explained they were there to meet with Mr. Lauren. The elderly gentleman said they were early, but that Mr. Lauren did phone in the appointment. It was clearly nothing out of the ordinary to the old man, and he slid them two passes underneath the glass to attach to their coats. Anna waved off his attempt to explain the history of the track, so he grudgingly walked out of his booth, unlocked the gate, and allowed them in. The look of disappointment on his face was obvious, and Anna apologized, explaining they were extremely pressed for time. Her seductive smile served its purpose, and his disappointment vanished.

Anna took off at a brisk pace, passing the long line of betting windows that sat underneath the grandstands. They were currently boarded up for the winter. Their two sets of legs pounded the concrete, echoing throughout the massive walkway that ran underneath the length of the grandstands.

"Here it is. Section three-thirty. This is where he said to meet him." She said as she pointed towards the sign. They bounded up the stairs and pushed through the double doors that led to the open-air second level seating area. Anna scanned the area, analyzing potential problem spots, and exits if they were needed. The expansive track shimmered in the bright winter sun. The surroundings were like a cathedral, and the track seemed massive with no people or distractions to take away from its magnificence.

Corporate boxes with six metal folding chairs inside each one stretched the entire length of the level which they were standing. Anna and Alex waited beneath a covered area that partially shielded them from the elements. The local high rollers and corporations paid top dollar for the seats that enveloped them. The oval of the dirt track was manicured perfectly, despite that fact that no horse would run on it for several months. Two green wooden posts stood on either side of the track just below their vantage point, indicating the finish line was for most races. Alex glanced around at the quiet scene. He had visited Churchill Downs before, but only when throngs of people occupied the famous landmark.

They stood silently side by side in the cold air. Alex bounced up and down trying to stay warm until an icy glare from Anna caused him to stop. The gold plaque nailed to the wood of the box contained the name of a law firm etched across it, indicating the owner and his partners had the rights to the box whenever they so desired. Alex glanced at his watch. The meeting was scheduled to begin in five minutes.

As if on cue, the double doors below them swung open, and Eddie Lauren pushed through them with difficulty. Anna studied him carefully. It was definitely the same face from the newspaper photo, but thirty years later the face was pudgier, and the wild mop of hair from before had vanished. It was replaced with a receding hairline of honey brown hair, which he was trying desperately to hide with a bad comb-over. The weight gain on his face matched the rest of his middle-aged body. A set of perfectly round spectacles sat on his nose, giving him an absent-minded professor persona.

Eddie scanned the vast row of seats until he finally spotted the two of them standing almost directly above and behind him. He acknowledged them with a nod and slowly climbed the short flight of stairs. The man was either completely harmless or a very good actor. Anna guessed the former, but she was keeping an open mind. Eddie made it to their vantage point, breathing much heavier than he should have after such a short climb.

"Anna?" Eddie asked with a great deal of trepidation.

"Yes. Nice to meet you, Mr. Lauren." She extended her gloved hand. "This is my associate. He will be making sure we are not disturbed." She motioned for Alex to back away and he obliged, stepping into the box above them so Eddie could sit and chat with her more privately. Alex was still close enough to assist her if any problems arose, but Mr. Lauren reminded her of a scared animal. He would be much more afraid of them than they were of him.

"Please forgive me if I seem a little nervous, but it's

284

not everyday I get a call from the FBI asking me questions. You do understand?" The southern drawl of his voice was soothing and made him seem even more harmless.

"That's fine. I just have a few questions for you. Hopefully it will not take long," Anna replied. She guessed she would be using more carrot than stick for this conversation.

"Yes. You said you were interested in the 1973 Derby. Secretariat, of course. Probably the most famous horse in history. That was actually the first Derby I covered as a reporter," Eddie said with a hint of nostalgia.

"Correct, Mr. Lauren. I'm doing some research for the government, tracking down information on a man by the name of Aman Kazim. He was the owner of another horse that was scheduled to run in the Derby that day," Anna said. She wanted to get the conversation moving immediately.

"Of course. Desert Sheik. What a magnificent animal. It was a tragedy; that horse dying the day of the race like that," Eddie replied with true regret.

"Uh-huh. I have been assigned by the FBI to make sure Mr. Kazim is completely clean as far as his different business ventures go. Just routine stuff. As you may be aware of already, Mr. Kazim is an acquaintance of the man about to become president. We just want to be sure the new president does not get blindsided by something in one of his friends' past. He's already going to have enough on his plate to deal with, so we are performing in-depth background checks on his friends for him."

"I'm not sure how much I can be of assistance, but I will be happy to answer any questions you have."

"Good. I truly appreciate it. Now, did you ever actually meet Mr. Kazim during the time he was here for the Derby?" Anna lifted one leg and put it on the folding chair in front of her. Her elbow rested on her knee and her left hand supported her chin as if she was thinking deep thoughts. Her gloved hand was nestled warmly in her coat pocket, gripping a hidden pistol that was pointed directly at Eddie Lauren's stomach.

"Sure. That was the first year I was assigned to cover the Derby as a reporter. I got to meet all the owners

285

and most of the trainers," he replied.

"Did you find Mr. Kazim to be friendly?"

"He seemed a little standoffish, to be honest. He did not like to mingle with the rest of the owners. He tended to keep to himself. I was intrigued by his horse though, so I eventually got him chatting a little."

Anna reached into her pocket and extracted a copy of the short article Eddie had written many years earlier. She held it out to him before returning to her previous pose. He looked at the article and smiled in a distant way that suggested to Anna that it brought back both good and bad memories.

Eddie shook his head. "I see you have been doing a little research. When I told Aman I was writing an article picking his horse as a sleeper to win the race he became a lot friendlier. I think he just wanted someone to acknowledge the fact that he brought a good horse to the race."

"And did he?" Anna asked.

"Definitely! The horse was a dominant force in Europe. It won several huge races over there. We don't like to pay attention to horses from across the pond though."

"Do you really think the horse had a chance to win?"

"Absolutely. I would not have made the pick otherwise. I would have been a laughing stock if the horse flopped. Who knows, maybe the virus that killed that horse saved my career. Maybe I was young and arrogant at the time, but part of me still wishes Desert Sheik could have run in the race that day." Eddie nervously fiddled with his spectacles, adjusting them even though it was not necessary.

Anna studied him carefully. He was on edge, but that was to be expected. It is not every day that the government calls someone up to question him. He would probably be just as fidgety if the IRS showed up at his door.

"Did you ever get to meet Mr. Kazim's trainer?" She lifted her knee off the chair and stood up so she could pull her jacket tighter around her small frame. The covered grandstand was serving as a wind tunnel for the icy breeze funneling through it.

"No. Honestly, that was one thing I always thought

286

was strange. He went out of his way to keep his trainer away from me and the rest of the media. I had his name, but he kept a low profile. He made Aman seem like a showboat."

"Do you remember his name by any chance?" Anna asked. So far, she thought he was being very cooperative.

"His first name was Aziz. I cannot recall his last name. I saw him wandering around the track on a few occasions. I tried to ask some questions, but his people would not let me near him. He didn't seem to have any interest in talking to anyone," Eddie replied.

"Do you remember what he looked like? I know it has been a long time."

"He was a small guy. Skinny. He wore thick glasses with big black frames. The glasses looked like they were too big for him." Eddie stammered before regaining his composure. "He looked like he could have been a jockey himself."

It was the answer she wanted to hear, so she continued the conservation. "Mr. Lauren, we have reason to believe that Aziz was a terrorist, or at the least, a facilitator of terrorist activities in Cairo. We do not know if Mr. Kazim knew this or not, but we are trying to verify as much as possible. Can you think of anything else from that weekend that could help us? Any strange things that either one of them did that did not make sense at the time? Please think carefully. There could be a grave threat to the new president's life if Aziz has any friends left in this country." Anna thought it best to dangle the possibility that Zachariah's life could be in danger as a way to make him talk.

Eddie Lauren remained silent for an uncomfortable amount of time. He stared off once again into the empty space of seats behind Anna. Eddie avoided Alex's gaze, who was now watching the reporter with an intense look of his own. After a few moments Eddie turned his back to them and gazed out at the frozen dirt track and the empty grass infield, apparently grappling with some inner problem. The long silence told Anna that he was not a spy, and certainly not any type of operative for Aman. If he were an enemy, he would not have remained quiet for the past few minutes. He would have had a cover story ready to go. Instead, he was drawing too much attention to himself. She had the impression that he had something to say, but was scared to start talking.

"Mr. Lauren, I don't need to stress to you the consequences of lying to the federal government." She wanted to appear tough enough to scare him, but did not want to frighten him so badly that he would scurry into a hole, or worse yet, start asking for an attorney. She surely did not want to add kidnapping to her growing rap sheet either.

"There is one thing I have left out from that weekend," Eddie said as he continued to gaze upon the track. If he felt more comfortable talking while not looking directly at her Anna was fine with it. She was satisfied as long as his mouth kept moving.

"Okay. What have you got?" There was a hint of annoyance in her voice.

Mr. Lauren's voice went into cruise control, telling the story in a hurried fashion that suggested he wanted to distance himself from it as quickly as possible. "I ran into Mr. Kazim at a dinner for all the owners the Friday evening before the race. I told him that I was writing a short piece about his horse for the next day's paper, and that I was picking it to win. I told him I had followed the trail of his horse over the past several months." He swiveled his head for a moment to look back at Anna before continuing with the story. "The horse came from an incredible lineage. Its roots could be traced back to some of the finest desert horses from the early 1900s," Eddie continued as he turned towards the track again.

"I'm not interested in his abilities as a horse owner Mr. Lauren." The agitation in her voice came back.

"Well, I was," Eddie shot back. "We talked for fifteen minutes. He was impressed with how much I knew about his horse. I asked for an interview for the following day. If, by some reason, his horse would have pulled off a victory the pre-race interview with the owner combined with my bold prediction would have shot my career into the next stratosphere."

"Did he agree to meet with you?" Anna regained her interest.

"Yes. He told me to be at the stables the next morning at 3:30 and he would grant me the interview. He even agreed to show me the horse. I slept in my car that night because I was so afraid of oversleeping and missing the interview," Eddie said, and then stopped again.

Anna eyed him carefully. She noticed his breathing was now coming in quick, almost forced bursts, as if he was having to consciously make the effort to breathe. Was he going to pass out? His body went rigid, and he seemed to be willing himself to remain calm.

Eddie continued, "I don't know if I even slept that night I was so excited. I got up at three and found an all-night diner to serve me some coffee. Since I was already awake I decided to head on over to the stables a little early. It would give me some time to compose my thoughts and come up with a few additional questions for Aman. When I walked over to the backside of the track I made my way over to Aman's stable. It took me a little while to walk the distance. Aman paid extra for a separate stable away from all the others. When I made it to his stable the light was already on, and I remember being mad because I was hoping to beat him there. I walked up to the stable. I think the barn door was already open. Then I realized something strange was going on. There was someone grunting inside the stable. It sounded like someone was doing some sort of hard manual labor, which seemed odd to me, so I snuck closer to the door and I peeked around the corner to see what was going on." Eddie stopped again and his head dropped towards his chest. Another thirty seconds passed, then his head began shaking back and forth. He tried to focus and tell the story.

"What did you see, Mr. Lauren?" Anna asked in a soothing voice.

Eddie Lauren regained his composure as best he could. "Please understand, I've never told this story to anyone. It still freaks me out."

"Go on," Anna commanded. She wanted the information before he got cold feet.

"Aman's horse was lying in the middle of the barn.

It had slashes and stab wounds all over its body. The animal was covered in its own blood." Anna's stoic face hid the churning motors in her mind as she took in this completely unexpected piece of information. "Did Aman kill his own horse?" Anna proffered the question to him.

"No. One of his stable boys did! The boy was standing over the horse with a huge knife in his hand. The boy just kept on slashing away at the animal even though it was clearly dead. I was about to turn around and leave when Aman showed up and yelled at the boy."

The story was now getting interesting to Anna. Numerous questions and scenarios raced through her mind as she tried to decipher what this could possibly mean. "Why did you and Aman lie about his horse? The story was that it died from an infection."

Eddie was flustered, and he involuntarily shivered. "Aman was petrified that if word got out that one of his stable hands murdered a horse he would never be allowed to race in the U.S. again. Honestly, I understood his concern. He was already an outsider at the track, and he fought like hell to get his horse into the race in the first place." Eddie's breathing slowed as he finished the difficult story.

"Did you ever get the boy's name?" Anna asked.

"No, Aman said he was a troubled youth from the streets of Cairo. He wouldn't divulge anything more than that."

"So you just kept your mouth shut all these years out of the kindness of your heart?" Anna eyed him skeptically.

Eddie wilted under the glare. "I do receive a small package every few years with a large amount of cash in it. It's never addressed except with a note that says something to the effect of 'Thank you for your friendship and your silence. It will always be appreciated,'" Eddie said, reciting it from his memory as best he could.

"How much money does he send you?" Anna asked. Now she was fully engaged in the story.

"Roughly a thousand each time. Sometimes a little more. I really don't see the harm in what I did," Eddie

290

replied in a defensive tone.

"Did you help them get rid of the horse's body?"

"God, no! I stayed as far away from that stable and Aman as I possibly could after that morning. Ignorance is bliss. He called my home the day after the race to thank me for my cooperation. He assured me that I would be rewarded for my assistance in the matter. Oh, I do have a few items you might like to see." Eddie said it as an afterthought. He reached inside his winter jacket and yanked out a manila envelope.

Anna tensed for a brief second before relaxing again, letting go of the butt of the silenced pistol stashed inside her jacket.

Eddie saw the tense expression on her face and realized the danger he had put himself in. "Shit, sorry." His hand started shaking as he offered her the eight-by-ten envelope.

Anna took the envelope and tore it open. She pulled out several faded photographs and stared at them in silence. "Did you take these?" Anna asked. She remained outwardly calm as she analyzed the photos.

"Yeah, I took them the Friday night before the race. It was the only group photo I could get Aman to do. I told him I would need one if I was going to publish a follow-up article about him on Sunday, assuming his horse won the race, of course."

"Do you have the negatives?"

"No, one of Aman's bodyguards came by a few days after the race and picked up the negatives. Paid me very well for them. I had already developed these two photos. For some reason I wanted to hold on to a couple copies. He doesn't know they exist. No one does, as a matter of fact."

Anna studied the small group standing in front of the stable. She stared at Aman, his stoic face overseeing his little entourage. She immediately recognized Aziz A'zami, as well. He was sitting cross-legged on the ground. There was a look of irritation splashed across his face that suggested he did not want to be photographed. There were a few people in the photo whom she assumed were Aman's bodyguards, and several stable boys sitting on either side of

Aziz. Each one of the teenage boys had the same deadly look that Aziz was flashing for the camera.

"Which one of these boys killed Aman's horse?" Anna asked.

"This one." Eddie pointed to the smaller boy sitting to the right of Aziz.

Anna continued studying the photograph. The youthful face glaring into the camera's eye looked eerily familiar to her. She had spent too much time near him, and studied too many photos of him to be anything but absolutely positive about her assessment. She remained silent and reserved, but her finger pointed accusingly at the faded photograph. She traced her fingers over the images of the others in the photo, but continued to come back to the boy. The wild look in the teenager's eyes looked strikingly familiar to her. She had seen those eyes before. Anna felt like she could see the inner rage boiling behind the vicious stare. The face mocked her, seeming to say that she was too late and that he could not be stopped. The stable boy in the picture, the one who killed Aman's horse, was Zachariah Hardin, the next President of the United States.

Chapter 44
Naval Observatory, Washington D.C.

Zachariah Hardin paced back and forth across the room while he waited for Aman to finish up his phone call. He was now less than two weeks away from taking the oath of office. Each minute seemed laboriously long as he waited for his moment with destiny. Would it ever get here? He tuned out the feckless conversation Aman was having with the unknown person on the other end of the phone. It concerned arrangements for the numerous parties he would attend immediately after his swearing in. Zach could care less. He had no intention of staying at any of them for very long. He would have major issues to attend to as soon as he became president.

Aman had already taken the important call from their old friend less than an hour earlier. Jamal Mahmud was head of the Secret Service detail for President Gray, and he had officially received permission from his superiors to continue on in his position after the transfer of power. Jamal had asked for special permission to remain in place since he took over the position only two years earlier.

They were now waiting for Jamal to arrive to give them a quick briefing on the transfer of power. Aman closed his phone in annoyance at the same time someone knocked on the massive mahogany doors that sealed off the room.

"Enter!" Zachariah immediately barked the order. He was enjoying his newfound power.

Jamal strode into the room. His long, muscular frame strained every fiber in his navy blue suit. Jamal made his way towards his two co-conspirators. His toned body and shaved head made him look ten years younger than his real age of forty-three. Zachariah rushed towards him, and Aman pulled his obese body off the couch to greet him. How long had it been since they had last seen Jamal? Zachariah had lost count.

The two agents standing guard outside closed the door behind Jamal. Once the doors slammed shut a grin simultaneously burst across each man's face. The Brotherhood of the Caliphate's triumvirate was together again. They embraced each other in the center of the room. The group hug was thirty years in the making. Silent tears appeared on each man's face for the briefest of moments before being wiped away with joyous smiles. It was like a family reunion after years of separation. Jamal looked at both of them and placed one hand on each of their shoulders before speaking for the first time.

"My brothers, the pieces are in place. Our time has finally come." They had been separated for so many years that they had nothing to discuss but the specifics of their one mission in life that each had been working on from different angles. They were the ultimate co-conspirators, and had finally succeeded in sneaking inside the heart of their worst enemy.

"Everything went smoothly then?" Aman asked Jamal.

"Yes. I can continue on in my duties. Once the inauguration is finished, the transfer of the keys will occur, and we will be able to unleash our fury," Jamal said in a hushed tone.

Zachariah grasped Jamal in another huge bear hug. He was unable to contain the years of pent-up feelings that were now flooding out.

"I'm sorry. It has been so long..." Zachariah was overcome with emotion as he sat back down.

They sat in silence and enjoyed each other's company before Jamal gathered his wits and spoke to his friends. "Our patience has paid off, and now nothing can stop us," he said with finality.

Chapter 45

Alex sat quietly on the couch in the small cabin in Virginia, sipping bottled water and staring at the two photos side by side on the coffee table in front of him. The ride back from Louisville was unnerving. Anna spent the entire time studying the photo Eddie had given her, and re-reading all the background information they had gathered on Zachariah. She did not speak a word the entire flight.

Now that they were back, Alex finally understood why. She had spent the time composing an argument, and now Alex was the first juror to hear the case. The photo to his left was the one Eddie had given them. The photo to his right was one that Anna pulled from a national magazine that ran an article about Zachariah a few months earlier. The photo from the national magazine showed Zachariah at his graduation ceremony at Yale. Zachariah was huddled in the midst of a group of friends with the sun beating down on them. The sun was casting shadows in all the wrong places, and Zachariah's face was partially obscured. Anna had touched the photo up as best she could, and now Alex was studying her handy work.

"Well, I can't be a hundred percent certain, but they sure do look a lot a like. If I had to guess I would say it's the same person. Aren't there any photos of Zach from his high school years?"

"No. That in and of itself is highly suspicious. Nothing until his college years. I know that according to his official biography he came to the U.S. at the age of sixteen, so he only had two years of high school education in the U.S. Still, I would think there would at least be a few more photos of him with his new father, or hanging out with friends, or something to that effect. There is nothing though. I ran both photos through some comparison software we have on the system here, and it gives a ninety-five percent probability that these are the same person," Anna said as she pointed at the two photos.

"So, if this stable boy is Zachariah Hardin that means he arrived in the country illegally. That means the papers Aman produced to Immigration when he supposedly entered the country in 1974 are false." Alex said. He hesitated before asking the question that should logically come next. "So the incoming president is an illegal alien?" He asked incredulously. It was a lot to swallow.

Anna ignored the question as she continued to think. Why sneak him into the country illegally? If they put together the proper documents a year later to get him into the country, why didn't they just wait? What was the rush? She guessed it had something to do with Aziz. The fact that he came into the U.S. with Zach raised all sorts of red flags as far as she was concerned. Aziz never wanted to set foot on U.S. soil, and the fact that he arrived with Zach suggests there was a good reason for handling it this particular way.

She finally answered Alex's question, "Yes, he's an illegal, but we really have no concrete proof." She exhaled in frustration. The inauguration was just a week away. She felt tantalizingly close to something, but she could not nail it down. The ringing of the phone interrupted her thought process.

She grabbed the cordless receiver and answered in a

295

brusque tone, "Yes?" Anna listened intently. Her face turned ashen as she pressed the receiver harder to her ear. After a few minutes she hung up and continued staring at the floor of the cabin.

"What's the problem?" Alex asked softly, sensing the tension.

"Sean Hill is dead. Malcolm is coming out to see us now," she answered dejectedly before quickly disappearing into the back of the cabin. Alex returned to the photos and the reams of paper regarding Zachariah Hardin that were strewn about the table in front of him. For a second he thought he heard gentle sobbing coming from the back of the cabin before it abruptly ceased.

For the first time he felt the weight of an unknown pressure bearing down on him. Their research was quickly being replaced with real issues that would soon have to be confronted. What seemed like a crazy idea just a few days earlier now possessed a body of evidence mounting in its favor. A villain was appearing out of the midst, but they could not be sure how or what the real danger was. The fact that they could not grasp the full extent of the threat made it seem all the more omnipresent and sinister.

Chapter 46

Allan Gray was sitting up in bed and staring at the headline on the front page of the paper. The article was calling for his resignation despite the fact that he had only a few days left in office. The illegal investigation into Zachariah Hardin was now as big a story as the actual inauguration only days away. He downed the last of his whiskey on the rocks, and then pushed the buzzer for his butler to come in and remove the empty dishes. He did not want his wife to smell the alcohol in the glass. She had been eyeing him suspiciously lately, not trusting him as the front-page headlines grew worse and worse for him. Of course, her instincts were correct, he thought to himself. They almost always were when it came to his habits.

Allan's own people seemed to be ignoring him. Malcolm, the ungrateful prick, was stonewalling any time he asked him a question about their little investigation. The only solace Allan could take was that Malcolm treated the Senate Committee that called him in to testify even worse. The spectacle was downright hilarious, as Malcolm basically spit in their collective face. He refused to answer any of their questions, and he stormed out halfway through the session before being forced to come back in.

Then the news of the shootout on the freeway and the death of Sean Hill dropped the President into complete despair. There appeared to be nothing left to do. Mr. Hill's trip to Egypt was their last hope at discovering something, and Malcolm told him that nothing of any use appeared to have come out of the trip. Malcolm then vanished, and Allan could not get him to answer any of his phones. It appeared he had gone into hiding. Allan was sure that Malcolm was probably utilizing a safely valve that no one knew about to use as an escape.

Allan Gray closed his eyes, his head pounding from the stress. The thought of suicide crossed his mind for the first time in his life before being quickly dispelled. Never, he told himself, would he do that to his family. There were still a few more days left. He just hoped Malcolm was working the case, and not vanishing from the face of the earth. It would all be over in less than a week. It was the only thing that kept him going.

Chapter 47

Aman flopped into the back of the limousine, exhausted and ready to get some sleep. Zach climbed in after him dressed in his tuxedo. He was still full of vigor and vitality, despite spending the last several hours hobnobbing and shaking hands with the largest donors to his campaign. The final thank you banquet before the upcoming inauguration was a way to give the party faithful a chance to mingle with the legend himself. The posh affair in the ballroom of the Hilton contained the normal cast of celebrities. Aman was grateful that Zach finally showed restraint and never disappeared into the bathroom with one of the constant stream of starlets who approached him at different intervals throughout the evening. His pending mission seemed to finally accomplish what Aman could not; Zach was finally focused on the task and nothing else.

Zach kicked off his shoes and propped his feet up on the seat in front of him. "Hell of a party, Aman. Those asses probably won't like me as much in a few days."

The deliberate understatement annoyed Aman. "Forget about them, Zach. They are cowards. They're the reason this country is so weak and decrepit. Did you get the itinerary from your publicist earlier today?"

"Yes, it looks fine. Timing this thing should not be a problem. The handover of the codes will be done right after I take the oath of office. When we get to the White House, disappearing for a while should be simple. Then Jamal will prove his worth. Are you still flying to Cairo?" Zach asked with a small amount of trepidation. He was hoping Aman would stay and see it through to the end with them. Zach knew it was foolish and selfish, but he no longer cared.

"Yes. I will leave sometime within the next three days. I've purchased tickets on several different flights, just to be safe." He laid a meaty palm on Zach's knee and patted it gently like a parent comforting a child. "You don't need me to finish the job, Zach. Once this is over you will have done something that all the armies of the world over the last thousand years have failed to do. You will single-handedly bring the West to its knees. You will be the Caliphate and the Madhi, all rolled into one. Just follow the escape route Jamal has for you, and you will be able to vanish amidst all the confusion. If you don't make it, someone else needs to be able to tell the world who you were, and why you did it. Now that Aziz is gone, that task falls to me."

Aman stared out at the silhouette of the Jefferson Memorial as their limousine made its way through the empty, late night streets of Washington D.C. He felt a pang of disgust about how soft he had allowed himself to become over the past thirty years. He never thought he would have the opportunity to return to Cairo permanently, so he just accepted the American lifestyle. Now that a new life was so close at hand, the debauchery of his last thirty years was once again becoming grotesque to him. A bemused smile appeared across his face. *Maybe I am not as weak and corrupted as I thought I was.*

Zach seemed to read his thoughts, "Aman, the end is almost near. Have you thought about that? We may never see each other again after tomorrow." Zach stared out the window with a reflective gaze.

"Of course I have. But stick to the plan. Jamal has been in the White House for years. He knows all its secret escape routes. Do not panic, and you may very well survive. Then we can meet again in Cairo and take our rightful places at the forefront of Islam." Aman's taciturn face conveyed the seriousness of his remark.

"And Jamal?" Zachariah asked.

"Jamal has to stay. He will die. He will die the most glorious death one could imagine."

"What about Mr. Gray's investigation? Anything we should be concerned with?" Zach asked.

"No. The woman is nowhere to be found, but we killed two of her accomplices. They are too late. Besides, Mr. Gray already seemed like a paranoid maniac to the press, and this story only confirms what most of them already believe. There have even been rumors that Gray has started drinking again. Most of the country already thinks he has a vendetta against you, and now he wants to finish the war he started. It's Nixon on steroids, if you will," Aman pronounced proudly. He would have to have someone leak that phrase. The Americans loved to coat everything in a sports analogy.

"Back to the main job. Do you have a final list of targets for me?" Zachariah asked.

"Yes, we can discuss those when we get back to the hotel." Aman pulled a cigar from the interior of his sport coat and lit it. The aroma of tobacco filled his lungs, soothing his nerves. He was anxious to return to Cairo. He was tired of being in D.C., and exhausted with his double life now that he was so close to being able to shred his false identity. Aman looked at his watch and willed the hands of the clock to move faster. They were enticingly close to restoring the world's proper order.

Chapter 48

Malcolm maneuvered the massive Chevy Suburban through the narrow, graveled path towards the cabin that he could not see, but knew was there. The black SUV handled surprisingly well considering the amount of protective armor it contained. The dense forest around him made him feel slightly claustrophobic; most of the trees in the area were pines and thus never lost their leaves. This kept the private cabin hidden during all times of the year.

The entrance off the main road was concealed flawlessly, and they had very few problems over the years with anyone accidentally finding it. A few kids and one hunter once ventured too close, and they were politely warned off the premises, but nothing else. The drive out to the cabin provided Malcolm with some much-needed time to think. The situation was rapidly deteriorating, but Anna's request to see him indicated there was a glimmer of hope.

That was excellent news since the rest of his world seemed to be falling apart. His testimony before Congress would certainly lead to his dismissal as soon as the new administration took office, and the news that Sean Hill and Colin Archer were both gunned down in broad daylight by a man wielding an Uzi threw a pall over everything.

Bret McMichael had already called to vent his frustration over losing one of his best men. Malcolm felt terrible about Sean, but one of his own men died, as well. Mr. McMichael still seemed determined to find a way to extract his own ass from the fire that was raging all around them. By some miracle the FBI Director was still managing to avoid being targeted by the media, and Malcolm was beginning to have his suspicions why that was the case. It did not matter anyway. There was no longer a middle ground to be staked out. It would either be complete vindication, or he would have to make a dash for a little island he owned that no one knew about. Besides, he trusted Anna's instincts and was very curious why she had called him out here.

No one knew where he was. It felt good to actually be behind the wheel of the vehicle for once. He couldn't remember the last time he drove himself anywhere. Only his two bodyguards, who were sitting quietly in the backseat with anxious looks on their faces, knew he left his house. They did not like the idea of their boss driving, but he insisted. His tone told them to tread carefully. When he told them they were headed to a CIA safe house they seemed to feel better, and grudgingly acceded to his wishes.

The gravel road finally ended in a small clearing, and the rustic façade of the cabin suddenly appeared in front of them as they emerged from the maze of the forest. Another black Suburban, identical to Malcolm's, sat next to the cabin. He pulled up behind it, and cautiously stepped out. He stretched his legs, paying careful attention to his right one, which was forever scarred thanks to one of his dalliances with shady characters in the Horn of Africa.

His guards immediately jumped out and surveyed the area, scanning for trouble even though they knew there was nothing to worry about. "Triple-check everything, and then look again" was their modus operandi, regardless of

301

how secure they felt. Malcolm breathed in the frigid air. It felt invigorating after several hours inside the metal cocoon of the SUV.

"Let's go," Malcolm ordered, and they made their way towards the cabin. A massive deck encircled the entire structure. As they approached, Anna appeared from the side of the house. She must have been standing on the back deck when they pulled up. The intense look on her face told Malcolm that she was still in full mission mode. It was good to see somebody had not given up yet.

Malcolm followed Anna around to the back of the deck. She strode over to the back door of the cabin and yanked it open. Alex joined them on the deck, clutching a packet in his hands. Malcolm's hand came up in protest like a traffic cop bringing a vehicle to a halt.

"Malcolm, he assisted with the research. As of matter fact, he discovered the piece of intel that got the investigation jump-started again. I told you I was going to involve him. We had no choice."

"Okay, Okay. I know. Still hard to get over. My life is in your hands already." Malcolm grudgingly accepted the logic. There was no one left to trust but Anna, and he would have to let her do it her way. Malcolm waived his bodyguards away, and they headed towards the front of the cabin to stand their lonely vigil.

Five minutes later, Malcolm was cupping the steaming mug of decaf coffee with both hands, and looking out at the rushing river below as he filled them in on the latest happenings in Washington D.C. Zach's inauguration was now just days away, and his swelling organization had now fully taken over the Capitol with their zeal and excitement. There seemed to be nothing out of the ordinary going on. Malcolm offered to brief the incoming President on the latest intelligence coming in from around the globe, but was patently refused.

He was forced to listen to a five-minute diatribe from Zach about how he was going to fix all the problems that Malcolm had helped cause. The first order of business would be a withdrawal of all U.S. military personnel from the Middle East as quickly as possible. Zach assured

302

Malcolm that he would not back away from his campaign promises as past presidents had so cavalierly done. His reiteration of this commitment when he toured the FBI building a few days earlier was sparking unrest in several countries throughout the Middle East. Malcolm was concerned that the entire region would be sucked into a war within the next few months if they were not careful to protect their allies.

The news of Sean Hill and Colin Archer made the situation worse. The killer's car was found abandoned in the long-term parking lot of a D.C. airport. They really did not expect to find anything, but they searched it thoroughly and no fingerprints turned up. The car was a rental vehicle that had been stolen. This pointed to the seriousness of Sean's assassin. He had gone out of his way to track down someone in a rental vehicle, and then steal it. The police wasted half a day trying to find out who rented it, and later tracked down the unlucky business traveler who was stranded at his hotel after discovering his rental car had been stolen in the middle of the night.

The frightened computer salesman sat nervously for an hour while the police questioned him. He was eventually absolved of any wrongdoing. The fact that he reported the vehicle stolen probably demonstrated his innocence, Malcolm suggested sarcastically as he and Anna paced back and forth across the deck. The little wrinkle of stealing the rental vehicle wasted just enough of the police's time for the assassin to get a much needed head start. They were now going to need a lucky break if they were going to successfully track down the unknown enemy. Malcolm assumed the killer to already be out of the country.

"How did your little session before Congress go?" Anna knew the answer, but wanted to hear Malcolm's take on the charade he was forced to sit through.

Malcolm gave her a quick summary. The session had started with him taking his seat. He acknowledged his name, and then proceeded to sit quietly while senators peppered him with every imaginable question regarding the leaks that were slowly dripping out to the press over the past few weeks. After each question he quietly declined to answer. His silence allowed each senator on the committee to provide his or her own little soliloquy to fill the void, each one trying to out do the others with their patriotism and incredible respect for minorities.

They all acted shocked and dismayed that the first minority to run the CIA could launch such a shameful investigation against an immigrant Christian from the Middle East. The hand-wringing and grandstanding lasted several hours. It finally came to an end as Yohan Rosenbaum, the senior Senator from New York, gave an impassioned speech about how proud he was of his own adoptive son, who was Muslim, served in the military, and was currently a member of the Secret Service.

Malcolm took his arms off the railing of the deck, "Enough with what I've been doing. I have been wasting my time as you can see. I know you didn't drag me out here unless you have discovered something very useful."

Anna motioned for Alex to step forward. She quickly and methodically began outlining their discovery and their excursion to Louisville. Every so often she allowed Alex to fill in gaps she left out, or show one of the photos that Mr. Lauren provided to them.

The different possibilities danced around in Malcolm's head. One question begged an answer. Why did they feel the need to sneak him into the country illegally? The logical answer at first seemed to be that there must be something in his past that would have prevented him from being granted a visa the legal way. But he was still a teenager when they snuck him in. He made a mental note to find out if the U.S. was even accepting visas from Egypt at that time. Maybe they would have had to have waited too long for the acceptance? That made sense. God knows the U.S. government dragged its feet on stuff like that. He suddenly realized Anna and Alex had finished talking, and were waiting for a response.

"So Mr. Hardin is technically in this country illegally," Malcolm said. "It makes for an interesting story, but he could fight that as a smear campaign against him. The country would not want to be put through a fight like that, and frankly neither would I. It could severely weaken the power of the president. The question is why? The membership in the Brotherhood of the Caliphate is what is disturbing. As you said, it appeared to be a very small and benign group, but if he is a member he must be a Muslim. I could care less about his religion, except for the fact that he has always claimed to be a Christian. Why lie?" The cold air Malcolm exhaled gave his ponderings a physical quality.

Anna cut in. "I agree. There are a lot of little lies and discrepancies that, if they stood alone, would be nothing of significance. But there are so many of them that I know there must be something there. Maybe he felt like his religion would be an impediment to success, but I just feel something else is not right. I got an email that Sean sent on the plane ride back, detailing their interview with the old man. The way he killed himself...." The chill in the air gave her cheeks a reddish hue that belied her serious tone, "I'm just afraid that we won't know until it's too late."

"Oh shit," Alex muttered under his breath as he stared at the bundle of papers in his hand. He quickly flipped through the stack until he found the name he was looking for. His finger traced the unknown path he was chasing down the page.

"What is it?" Anna asked. She watched Alex as he rushed inside the cabin. He motioned hurriedly for them to follow. Whatever it was, he was still staring intently, trying to confirm his initial surprise.

"I'm fucking freezing anyway. Why we didn't have this discussion inside, I don't know," Malcolm said as he gently pushed Anna toward the cabin so they could find out what caught the newbie's attention.

Ten minutes later Anna and Malcolm passed the pieces of information back and forth between them. Alex sat quietly and waited for a response. It was yet another coincidence to pile on top of the previous ones.

Alex had listened closely to Malcolm's recollections of his last few days even though most of it was useless information for him. His questioning before the Senate Intelligence clowns was just another example of how out of touch politicians were with the world of intelligence. When Malcolm first mentioned Yohan's comments Alex did not pay close attention. Senator Rosenbaum was simply doing his best to pander to the masses with his speech. However, when Malcolm mentioned the first name of the Senator's adoptive son Alex went tearing through the stack of information that Mr. Lauren had provided to them. The old photo the reporter had of Aman, Aziz, and his stable hands had a few of the names written on the back of it. Scribbled in messy cursive was the name Jamal, and right beside it was written, "stable boy," seeming to confirm that one of the stable boys was named Jamal. It was the same first name as the Senator's adoptive son.

"Shit," Malcolm uttered as he stared at the evidence. There were thousands of Muslim men with the same first name. Normally Malcolm would have guessed the chances of the boy in this old photo being the same person adopted by Yohan as slim at best. He realized for the first time that they may have been looking at the investigation through a prism that was too narrow.

"Could they both have been snuck into the country illegally?" Anna asked the same question that was going through Malcolm's mind.

"We never even considered a second accomplice. Does the Senator have any connections with Zach or Aman?" Malcolm looked at Anna for an answer. She was the field agent involved in the investigation from the beginning, and he knew she possessed the most knowledge about Zachariah Hardin.

"Yes." She kicked the kitchen chair in frustration. "Of course! He co-sponsored the bill with Zach in the mid-nineties that led to the constitutional amendment."

"Do we know how, or when the Senator first adopted Jamal?" Alex chimed in. He was continuing to wait patiently and choose his moments. They both had a much better view of the big picture, and he wanted to make sure they both hashed out their thoughts before he jumped into the conversation.

"No. But I'm sure as hell going to find out. I need to make a few discreet calls around town." The cell phone appeared out of Malcolm's jacket before he even finished his sentence. He grabbed a cinnamon apple energy bar out of the

306

bowl on the table, and stepped outside for some privacy.

"Let's see what information we can pull up about his adoptive son." Anna gestured towards the upstairs that held the computer that provided remote access to the CIA's database. "We should have intelligence stored on all Secret Service personnel."

Ten minutes later the file was pulled up on the flat screen monitors. Alex peered over her shoulder. On the left hand side of the monitor was a recent photo of Jamal in the typical garb of a Secret Service agent; dark suit, sunglasses, small earpiece with the mini-phone cord just visible snaking around his right ear. The biography to the right of the photo said he was born on March 5, 1958 in Egypt. His mother abandoned him on the streets at the age of five, and from there he was taken to an orphanage where he spent several years in anonymity before heading to the States.

He was part of a group of children that was taken to the U.S. for adoption. The rich philanthropist who helped the children remains anonymous. The wealthy man from Cairo apparently spent years as an orphan on the streets himself, and liked to arrange for the orphans to live with good families in the U.S. who could not have children of their own.

"The rich philanthropist could easily be Aman. The timing dove tails perfectly." Anna voiced her thoughts out loud before continuing to scroll the cursor down the page. They sat in silence as they scanned the information together.

The Senator adopted the boy in 1974 at the age of fifteen. He spent three years in high school in D.C. before joining the Marines only a few years after the end of the Vietnam War. Jamal spent ten years in the military, traveling to some of the most dangerous locales in the world including Beirut, Saudi Arabia, and the demilitarized zone between North and South Korea.

His service in the military put him on the fast track to becoming a Secret Service agent, where he has remained for the last twelve years. He was finally awarded for his service and joined the presidential detail four years earlier. Last year he moved even further up the ladder and became one of the few agents on the president's personal protection

307

team. One of the other agents in the protection detail was forced to retire early, and Jamal was first in line for the promotion. Normal procedure was for the president's personal guards to be switched out once a new occupant enters the White House. However, because Jamal was just promoted, he had been allowed to stay on. The biography highlighted a small article that appeared in one of the Washington newspapers discussing the unusual event. Other than the article, the prolonged extension did not seem to be creating any stir within the Secret Service. Jamal's service records were impeccable, and the dossier included nothing but glowing reports about his career in both the military and Secret Service.

Malcolm appeared in the doorway of the tiny room. "I made some calls. Yohan adopted Jamal sometime in early 1974. The Senator had all the proper papers, so nothing was made of it. My source seems to think Jamal may have been considered a war refugee after the Six-Day War in 1967. He is checking another angle for me, but I bet it's going to be a dead end. I think we should pay a little visit to the Senator. Have a little friendly chat with him." The sarcastic tone suggested Malcolm would pepper the Senator with questions that would make him squirm.

Malcolm stood over the two of them and began scanning the biography on the computer screen, as well. The printer on the table was whirling away, printing off copies of the information for each of them to review.

"Looks like your source has the same info the agency has. I was thinking the same thing as far as a visit. Put him on the spot and see if we can get him to talk. I don't think it will be too difficult." Anna's understatement was not lost on her two compatriots.

Chapter 49

The morning streaks of the sun ricocheted off, and around the Washington Monument, sending rays of sunlight in all directions. The top of the monument was just visible from Jamal Mahmud's residence. The sunrise lit up his penthouse apartment at 20th and L Streets, crashing through his balcony and engulfing his kitchen in a ball of light. The brightness did not faze Jamal as he lay prostrate on his balcony, bowing towards the heavens and praying for strength.

He obtained the apartment thanks to some strings his father was able to pull. It was just one example of many why this country was so corrupt, he thought to himself. One is nothing without money in America. Things were about to change though. He chanted prayers quietly to himself. The beads of sweat formed on his temples and ran down his naked chest to his running shorts, before overflowing onto the prayer rug. His morning ritual of pushups and crunches caused him to sweat profusely, so he had stepped out into the cold January morning to pray and cool down.

The blinding morning sun only served to heighten his prayerfulness and focus. There were now only a few days left until they would make their move. This would be one of the last times he prayed on this balcony overlooking a city whose orders from on high brought so much pain and misery to his fellow brothers in the Middle East. That pain would now be returned to their enemy in spades. The fact that such an American cliché floated through his mind only served to anger him more, and he responded with ever more fervent chanting.

Thirty minutes later his body was spent, and he stepped inside to fix something to eat. He sat at his oval kitchen table, nibbling on a breakfast of scrambled eggs, toast, and protein bars. The itinerary for the next few days was sprawled across the table in front of him, and he studied it closely. This would be his only day off before the inauguration, and he was expected to put to memory every last detail of how the inauguration, transfer of power, and late night revelry would go down. The chances of making their mission a success would be dependent on him finding the perfect moment to separate Zach from his entourage for a short period after he was sworn in. Once he found that moment he would tell Aman so the diversion could be launched.

After eating he began to meticulously disassemble and then reassemble the Mark 23Mod0.45 caliber pistol that was lying on the chair beside him. It was a holdover from his days in the Special Forces, and he could not let go of the weapon. The Secret Service frowned on the different weapon, but accepted it due to his outstanding marksmanship with it. He now felt a new excitement forming in him. It was the same feeling he used to get as a Marine when he knew there would be an opportunity to kill. In his more than forty years on earth Jamal Mahmud never experienced lust for a woman, and refused to have sex despite many opportunities. His only desire was a blood lust, and it was beginning to form in him again as his expectations mounted. He was anxiously looking forward to the day when the thrill of this long, silent hunt would finally morph into the ecstasy of the kill.

His mind wandered from the detailed plans in front of him. The Secret Service was ideal for keeping him disciplined, alert, and in shape, but the Marines and Special Forces had given him opportunities to kill. The Secret Service, on the other hand, had honed his skills to perfection, but never gave him the opportunity to use them. During his stint in the military he traveled the world, and could disappear into the slums of a foreign city to satisfy his blood lust by disposing of some worthless retch.

His current job required constant discipline and attention to detail, but never an opportunity to utilize his killing skills. His Muslim brothers around the world could kill the infidel at random while he was continuously forced to lay low. There were times he felt like he was frittering his life away while others received all the glory. Now the years of training and patience appeared to have come to fruition at the perfect moment. Maybe Allah was watching down on them as Aman had assured him would happen all those years ago when they first arrived in America.

He would never forget that day at the racetrack, when Aman and Aziz explained that he would be going to live with a Jew in New York City. The adolescent tantrum he threw was monumental, and he stewed for hours as they told him the plan. He would cry like a baby and then curse them vehemently all within a short time span. Maybe he should have killed someone in order to attract their attention? It would have been one better than Zach's butchering of Aman's race horse, and it may have scared them enough to change their plans. But he could never bring himself to disobey Aziz. The old man meant too much to him.

Aziz continuously drummed into him that they were taking a different approach; one that would take a long time, and would often seem pointless and frustrating. However, it was the only way to reach their ultimate goal. Their brothers around the world sacrificed long-term progress for instant gratification. It felt temporarily satisfying, but they always ended up back in the same spot. Jamal stood up from the kitchen table and stared out the window at the magnificent view. He needed to kill. It was time. It would not endanger their mission, and thirty years of patience was enough. The Jewish parasite that he pretended to love had survived long enough. His death would have to suffice for now.

Chapter 50

Alex cautiously turned the midnight blue Chevrolet Suburban onto the tree-lined street of Summit Place, a ritzy neighborhood in northern Washington D.C. They were just a short drive away from Rock Creek Park, Embassy Row, and the Kennedy Center. Summit Place looked like it belonged in a travel magazine. The streets were immaculate. Every tree, shrub, and flower was trimmed to perfection, and the streetlights provided just enough of a glow that one would think he was following the path to heaven on earth. A long line of two-story early 1900s solid brick homes ran down both sides of the street. Each one of them had a small front yard that led to a sidewalk where all the neighbors could enjoy a leisurely stroll. The brutal January night kept everyone indoors. Wafts of smoke could be seen from a few chimneys, indicating a toasty fire was blazing.

Alex, Anna, and Malcolm left the cabin immediately after their decision to pay a visit to the senator, and they cut thirty minutes off of the normal three-hour drive. Alex manned the steering wheel while Malcolm spent half the trip punching away on his cell phone, trying feverishly to locate Senator Rosenbaum. The senator's underlings continued to blow Malcolm off. They were still agitated with Malcolm's lack of cooperation at the hearing, and were not in an accommodating mood.

"The Senator will be back in a moment. The Senator is in a meeting. The Senator is out to lunch." The constant stream of lies were grating on Malcolm's nerves. Yohan was clearly trying to avoid him. Malcolm tried one final lie, telling one of the kool-aid drinking interns he was ready to come clean and talk frankly with the Senator. Even that did not get him anywhere. It was clear that if they were going to speak with Yohan, they would have to just show up.

It was easy to track down his address. Malcolm gave his bodyguards the night off, despite their protests. He did not want them losing their jobs on his account, and he did not want anyone else brought into this mess. Alex slowed the vehicle to a crawl, and they made their way cautiously down the street. Anna and Malcolm both stared out the tinted windows, trying to read addresses as best they could from the light provided by the street lamps.

"There. Stop the car," Anna demanded quietly. She looked for a few more seconds before confirming it. "Yep. That's it. The lights are on. It looks like we won't have to drag him away from a whore." Anna's brusque tone let the two men in the car know she was going into interrogation mode.

Malcolm ignored the comment about the senator's sexual proclivities. Just about every politician in town had sex with someone other than his wife on a regular basis. It happened so often he no longer cared. He just accepted it, and tried to deal with the ones who were the least corrupt.

"Okay, let's go. If you think you see any trouble, Alex, remember to just lay on the horn. Let's go Anna," Malcolm said. He stepped out of the front passenger seat, and Anna fell in behind him.

Alex watched silently as they made their way past the perfectly manicured lawn, and up to the front porch. Reflexively reaching inside his coat, he touched the butt of his pistol for a small amount of reassurance. His palms were sweaty, despite the freezing temperatures outside, so he turned off the heat in the SUV. The weapon now felt like it belonged as part of his normal attire, and he was much more comfortable with it on his person. The cabin they had spent so much time in over the last week also had a hidden gun range in the basement, and when they were not doing research, Anna tutored him on the art of the pistol. After firing thousands of boxes of ammunition he was developing into a decent shot, at least in the sterile environment of the range.

Alex watched as what appeared to be a butler opened the door, and gave them both a once over that suggested the Senator had no interest in visitors at 10:15 p.m. on a Thursday night. He watched the conversation closely. He did not need to hear what was being said to know that the butler was vehemently protesting. The butler was fighting against two very stubborn individuals who were clearly not going to be denied. The body language of the three individuals relayed the pace and topic of conversation just as well as if he would have been standing there next to them.

After five minutes the butler disappeared inside the Victorian home. Anna slid her foot inside the door to prevent it from closing on them. The butler reappeared a few minutes later, and more heated words were exchanged until the old man's shoulders sagged, indicating his defeat. He unceremoniously pulled open the door the rest of the way,

313

and allowed them to walk in. Alex was sure it was the rudest greeting anyone had ever received at the Senator's house. Now that Malcolm and Anna were inside the two-story residence Alex turned his attention back to the street, scanning the area for anything that seemed out of the ordinary. The ritzy subdivision yawned back at him. The one person who was walking his dog stepped back into the warm confines of his home, leaving the tree-lined street deserted.

***

The butler led Anna and Malcolm through the main room of the house. It was decorated lavishly, and was probably a room strictly for show, Anna thought. All the items looked too pricey to risk being damaged. They took a left down a long narrow hallway. The butler glanced behind him to make sure they were still following. His suspicious glare left no doubt that they were on his territory, and he would be protecting it like a nervous dog. He stopped at the last door, and motioned for them to enter, closing the door behind them so they could talk in private with his boss.

Senator Yohan Rosenbaum was seated in a tall leather chair, legs crossed, reading a newspaper. There were no bare walls. The four sides of the room were bookshelves from floor to ceiling. The shelves were filled with antique books from every great writer imaginable. Anna felt like she was in a library from the 1800s. If only the Senator had a pipe in his mouth he would be the perfect grandfather, ready to tell his grandkids a bedtime story before shooing them off to bed. The paper came down, revealing an annoyed look on the haggard face. He folded his copy of the New York Times carefully and methodically, set it down, and took a cautious sip of the black coffee sitting next to him.

Yohan coughed violently before speaking. "You have a lot of nerve coming here, Malcolm. After that shit you pulled in front of my committee." Yohan was not in an accommodating mood. He set the coffee down as Anna and Malcolm stepped forward.

Malcolm took a seat on the leather sofa while Anna remained standing just a few feet away. Now that she was closer she could smell the coffee. It was Irish. Good, she thought, a little alcohol in him would make him more likely

314

to have a loose tongue.

A phony smile appeared on Malcolm's face. "Yes, Senator. I felt bad about that. I thought I would drop by tonight and try to clear the air. Off the record, of course," Malcolm said. He let his body slip into the comfortable couch. His normal ramrod posture gave way to a more casual and relaxed form, as if they were two friends about to engage in some friendly banter.

"Don't give me that bull, Malcolm. I've been around this city too long. Whatever the hell you are trying to pull here I won't help. You tied your own noose the other day, and I'll be damned if I want any part of trying to help you weasel your way out of it." The raspy voice of the Senator suggested he may be coming down with a cold. "If you're lucky you'll just be run out of town. Our new President has a long memory, and my guess is you could soon be facing an indictment from a special prosecutor." He gave Anna a sideways glance, followed by a leering smile that gave away what his thought pattern was at the moment. "I see you brought along your enforcer to do your dirty work for you."

"I didn't think you could get it up anymore," Anna retorted. The matter-of-fact statement caused the man to wilt in his chair. Men were so easy, she thought, in so many ways.

Yohan pretended to ignore the comment. "Enough of the fun and games. You have five minutes to beg me to ask the new President to take it easy on you, Malcolm. Get it over with so I can tell you 'no' and go to bed," Yohan said in an exasperated tone.

"That's not what I want, Yohan. I just have a few questions for you. Some loose ends I would like to clear up." Malcolm's voice remained care free and light.

"Aboutwhat?" The Senator straightened his rickety body as best he could.

"Your stepson, Jamal." Malcolm waited carefully for the reaction.

"What does he have to do with anything?" The arrogance from a few minutes earlier was now washed away, leaving only a very confused look. What could they possibly

315

want with the boy? Yohan was a typical parent and still thought of his son as a young child. He never would have thought parenting would be so rewarding. They learned to be more tolerant through one another, and Yohan loved Jamal as much as he would have loved a biological son. Jamal was obedient, intelligent, and dedicated to his adoptive parents. He was the one thing left for Yohan and his wife to cling to. Otherwise, they would have divorced years earlier. Jamal was the reason he pushed for the Israeli-Palestinian reconciliation as hard as he did. Surely there were many more like Jamal, just waiting for the chance to be heard, instead of having a belt full of explosives strapped around their bodies.

"You seem quite proud of him. Tell me again. Where did you adopt him from?" Malcolm asked. He continued to purposely flaunt an arrogant persona.

"What is this about? You couldn't bring down Aman so now you want to go after another Muslim? My boy spent way too many years in the Marines, spilling blood for this country to have you come after him." The Senator was still confused by the line of questioning. His boy's career was impeccable. He was a Boy Scout. He would never even consider jaywalking.

Anna re-entered the conservation. "He has served his…" She paused, allowing the next word to linger for a second longer than necessary. "…adopted country valiantly, Senator. When you spoke so proudly of him at the Senate hearing we were both impressed and wanted to know more. We were confused by one item though. We never could figure out how he got into the country. We know he arrived when he was fifteen, supposedly with a group of orphans from Egypt." Anna was not in the mood to waste time dancing around the topic.

The Senator returned to his look of frustration. "Yes. You know how he ended up here. His arrival here is well documented for anyone who wants to check. He was part of one of the groups that the anonymous Egyptian donor brought over. He rescued kids from the streets of Cairo, then used his contacts in the U.S. to bring as many over as Immigration would allow so they could be adopted in the

316

U.S. He never would reveal himself to the public though. Quite a recluse from what I understand. An honorable man though. The Muslims and Israelis would be much better off if there were more like him," Yohan said, stifling a yawn. He took Jamal off the streets and raised him to be a man. His conscience was clean.

If the boy had one flaw it was that he could be overly aggressive sometimes. He pummeled a few kids that made disparaging and racist remarks during his senior year in high school. By then he had reached his full height, and his dedication to the weight room during football season gave him a physique that could do a lot of damage when put in to motion. Yohan was scared when Jamal first said he wanted to join the Marines. He could never bring himself to fully trust the military experience, but it seemed to have done some good for his boy.

Anna watched Yohan carefully. She could tell he was trying to make sense of what they wanted. Suddenly she saw the perfect item out of the corner of her eye. She walked briskly around Yohan to the massive mahogany bookshelves behind him, and grabbed a gold-encrusted picture frame. She stared at the picture resting in front of the collection of first edition Hemingways. It was undoubtedly the same boy. The discovery thrilled and petrified her at the same time. She turned around to catch the two men staring at her, both with the same quizzical look plastered over their faces. Malcolm's changed to a smile as he saw the framed photograph in her hands. She handed it to Yohan in silence. He stared at it incredulously.

"That is your son?" Anna asked the rhetorical question.

"Of course it is." He gingerly sat his adoptive son's high school senior picture on the small table beside him. The pride in his voice was evident. Anna extracted the envelope from her purse, handing it to him to open.

"Have a look," she said to him softly.

The Senator silently obeyed. If they were about to show him some photo of him running around town with a young blonde then they were trying to blackmail the wrong man. He came clean to his wife years earlier. He would not

317

have lasted very long otherwise. Her knowledge of his affairs gave her a certain amount of power over him that she relished, and she used that power whenever it became necessary. Her job was to always keep quiet so he could remain at his powerful posts and continue his rise in his party. His wrinkled fingers fumbled twice before pulling out the photograph. He stared at it for a moment, carefully studying the faces. Aman was easily recognizable. The man has certainly fattened up, Yohan thought to himself. Another face caught him completely by surprise. The Senator stopped fidgeting as he stared at it, trying to make sure his eyes were not deceiving him. He reached for his glasses. He needed confirmation before he said another word.

It was unequivocally Jamal. His adoptive son was seated at the bottom right of the photo with the same forced smile he always gave whenever he was upset or frustrated, but did not want to admit what was causing him the anxiety. The photo appeared to have been taken around the time Yohan adopted him. He grabbed his drink and swallowed a large gulp, barely noticing the scorching alcohol as it coated his throat and steadied his nerves. He looked up at his uninvited guests and found them both watching him carefully, waiting for his reaction. What was going on? Jamal never mentioned that he knew Aman, yet it seemed clear from this photo they knew each other. Was it coincidence? Were these two CIA nuts trying to blackmail him in some way?

"Where was this photo taken?" Yohan asked meekly. He knew the answer.

"At the Kentucky Derby. May of 1973," Anna answered as she continued to eye the Senator carefully. The sustained silence and questioning look on his face suggested he was taken by surprise by the photo. If he was feigning fear he could pass any lie detector test ever invented.

"In America? That can't be right. He didn't come in until November 1973, and he was brought in on a boat with a small group of orphans, not..." Yohan looked down at the photo again, hoping it would change. The serious looks of Aman and Jamal continued to stare at him from the photo, almost as if they were mocking him and his naivety.

318

"This can't be a real photo. Someone is playing a game with me." The Senator's defense was weak and he knew it. "How did you get this photo?" Yohan asked in a more urgent tone. "I have to know." The Senator's hands were trembling at the realization that Jamal lied to him from the moment he walked into his house. Why? The unknown reason haunted him. He doubted the answer would alleviate his fears.

"We stumbled across the photo during our investigation. Your son was not a part of the investigation, I assure you," Anna said, revealing a piece of the puzzle to keep the Senator talking.

"What?" Yohan looked to the CIA Director for confirmation.

"Senator, this photo recently came to light during our investigation into the President-Elect. I was not aware of its existence at the time of my testimony to your committee. We weren't sure that this was your son in the photo until you identified him for us just now. He is a late entry into our investigation. If you will look at the photo closely please," Malcolm said calmly. Years of experience in the field taught him how to be commanding and quiet at the same time. It was an art form few could master. "Look at the other kid in the photograph. Does he look familiar?" Malcolm asked.

Yohan looked at the kid. He appeared to be about the same age as Jamal, except much skinnier and several inches shorter, although he could not be sure of the height since he was sitting cross legged on the ground. The boy looked harmless except for his eyes, which conveyed a savage intensity. Yohan studied the photo again, "I don't think so," he said honestly. The face was familiar, but he could not quite place it.

"It's Zachariah Hardin, your President-Elect," Anna spit out the statement in a sharp tone.

The Senator studied the kid's face intently. Yes, he had to admit it was possible. He squinted, putting the photo near his face as if it was a treasure map and he was looking for the "x" that marked the spot. Zachariah's eyes gave him away. He possessed the same stare Aman had in the photo. It was as if it were a learned trait. He looked up at his two late

319

night intruders, and found their two sets of eyes following his every move. His gaze returned to the photo. Yes, he decided, it was almost assuredly Zach. Jamal grew up with the President-Elect? He never mentioned knowing him. For the first time in his life he felt estranged from Jamal. His adoptive son appeared to be hiding a huge portion of his life from him for some unknown reason.

"You said this was taken in May of 1973?" A vile feeling was creeping into Yohan's stomach, and he was beginning to feel the life he knew slip away. He was petrified to find out any more information, but he knew he must push on for his own sanity.

"Correct," Anna answered. She could see the wheels in motion as the Senator's thought process showed on his face. She thought it best to let him express his concerns out loud without any prompting. It was like teaching a child. If one can fool a child into thinking he discovered the answer on his own then he will become even more interested in the subject, and the teacher's job is that much easier.

***

The Senator focused as he thought back to that day at the track. Aman had been despondent over his horse's sudden death earlier that morning. He remembered the day vividly because it was his first face-to-face meeting with the Egyptian. It was several months later that he met with the frail man who represented the children and arranged the adoption. He was always grateful to Aman for connecting him to Aziz.

His forehead furrowed as he tried to recall all the important details of that day. Had Aman already adopted Zach by that time? No, because he talked about his desire to adopt his own boy from a similar group. Aman supposedly adopted Zach sometime in 1974. The Senator stared at the photo one last time. This photo meant that Zach was in the U.S. a year earlier than anyone knew.

"Good Lord. Zach entered this country illegally," Yohan muttered to himself before downing the last of his coffee. "But why?" He looked to them for an answer.

"We're not sure. The fact that he appears to know your son, combined with them now reuniting at the White House of all places tells me that something is amiss. It seems that Aman has been orchestrating this from the beginning. As to why, we don't know. But the facts point to nothing good," Anna said. She stopped for a few seconds to let Yohan continue to soak in the newfound information. "Senator, do you know if your son is a member of an organization known as the Brotherhood of the Caliphate?" Anna asked.

"I've never heard of it."

Malcolm entered the conversation, providing a quick rundown on the organization. Eventually they discussed Zach's tattoo, which Malcolm explained was the way members identified each other after years of separation.

"Do you know if Jamal has a tattoo? On his inner thigh?" Malcolm asked. "It would be two green Arabic symbols, with a slash through them. It stands for Caliphate Creation."

"Yes, yes. I remember a few times accidentally seeing him getting ready in the morning for school. He told me that it was something he got when he was on the streets of Cairo. It was a way for the young orphans to form a kind of family for themselves. If this brotherhood was as benign as you say it was what then is your concern?" He stopped momentarily before realizing what this meant.. "Zach is a Muslim," Yohan said it as a statement and not a question. A Muslim who lied about his true beliefs, and was now literally days away from taking the oath of office to be the president, Yohan thought.

"Senator, what is your son's specific position with the Secret Service? I know he's on the President's personal security detail, but what is his exact job?" Malcolm asked.

"He guards the man in control of the nuclear codes." The Senator's face was now ashen. The military man who controlled the nuclear football was never more than a few feet away from the president. The man's job was to always be prepared with the nuclear codes so the president could launch a strike if it ever became necessary.

Three sets of eyes now flicked back and forth in the room, all of them afraid to acknowledge out loud the danger. Two illegal immigrants, both Muslim, who lied to those closest to them for years were now about to gain control of the most extensive arsenal of nuclear weapons the world has ever known.

"I think we have a problem." Malcolm's baritone voice shattered the silence.

Chapter 51

Alex stared at the luminescent digital clock in the dashboard for the fifth time in a minute. It finally rolled over to twelve a.m. His first stakeout started off with an air of excitement, but after nearly two hours of waiting for Malcolm and Anna he had become bored and tired. He stifled a yawn, sipped a Diet Coke, and forced himself into an alert state of mind. He knew this was a part of his eventual job and something he would have to learn to do. He feared the moment his concentration would lapse would be the time when something serious happened. He could not afford any mistakes. The lights were still on in the Senator's house, and every once in a while he could see shadows moving about through the closed shades. A few snowflakes started to flutter through the lights that lined the street.

Glancing at the passenger side mirror, Alex saw a hint of motion on the sidewalk. It was approaching from the backside of the vehicle, along the south end of the street. He squinted, trying to see what it was. A few seconds later he could make out the silhouette of a tall man, jogging down the sidewalk. Alex involuntarily tensed. He grasped his weapon in preparation. It was a little late and extremely cold for a jogger, but there were all types of hard-core fanatics when it came to exercise. He knew because he was often one of them. The man grew larger and larger in the mirror. He was at least six foot two, maybe taller. His physique suggested this was not his first midnight run. A large Washington Redskins hoodie hung over his head, obscuring the man's face except for a pair of lips that were pursed in concentration. His pace slowed as he jogged closer to the truck, but he continued on his way, throwing a furtive glance at the Senator's home before continuing down the street.

Alex exhaled loudly. He cursed himself as he realized he had spent the last twenty seconds holding his breath in anticipation. The jogger made a right hand turn at the next cross street, and disappeared from Alex's line of sight. Five uneventful minutes later the front door opened and Malcolm and Anna stepped out of the house with solemn looks on their faces. Alex watched intently for any sort of inkling to how the meeting went. He was surprised to see the Senator himself appear in the doorway behind them. The three exchanged some unknown words, and each shook Yohan's hand with what looked like true feeling. The Senator shut the door, and Malcolm and Anna both walked quickly towards Alex. He turned the key and the SUV's engine roared to life.

***

Jamal's mind raced in lockstep with his feet as they pounded the concrete sidewalk. He decided to circle the neighborhood one more circuit to see if the Chevrolet Suburban was still parked in front of his father's house. The Suburban's presence could only mean something bad. He had scanned the license plate, committing it to memory. He would run it through the database at work tomorrow to find out to whom it belonged. He gave a silent prayer to Allah that their plan had not been compromised. He knew that kind of vehicle all too well. It was the favorite vehicle of the Secret Service, as well as numerous other government officials.

When he ran by it earlier he studied it carefully. Jamal noticed many of the tiny characteristics that only a trained agent like himself could recognize. He knew it possessed more safety features and accessories than anything someone can buy at a car dealership. The government tags and extra safety features suggested it was either FBI or CIA. Neither one was good for him. He slowed down for a brief moment as he completed his circle, and came back around to his parent's street. His hand reached inside the extra-large hooded sweatshirt and maneuvered the safety of his silenced Mark 23 pistol, preparing for action.

His breathing slowed when he noticed the vehicle was gone. He picked up the pace until he was almost sprinting down the lighted street. He slowed to a walk as he strode up the walkway and used his key to let himself inside the spacious two-and-a-half story home in which he grew up. The silence of the antique living room yawned at him. The house was quiet.

A clatter came from the kitchen where he found his father's servant stacking some plates in the sink. The servant looked up and gestured at Jamal's familiar face, indicating that his father was in his study. Jamal extracted the weapon and thanked him with a silent whistle of death. The bullet lodged in the butler's heart, killing him instantly. Jamal stepped forward to catch the limp body. He dropped it gently on the cold, white tile of the kitchen floor. He had nothing against the servant, but there could be no going back now. No witnesses. It was the only way. No one would cut him any deals for only killing his target. Anyone in the home would have to suffer the same fate.

He walked purposefully up the winding staircase to the second floor. He yanked the door open and fired two more bullets in quick succession, instantly killing the sleeping form of his mother. She uttered one quick grunt of protest before falling silent.

He quickly descended the staircase. He assumed his father would probably be drunk at this late hour. Only alcohol could keep him up past ten anymore. Jamal stopped at the end of the hallway and pushed the door of the study open without knocking. Yohan sat slumped in his favorite reading chair, a spilled drink staining the Oriental rug in front of him. He appeared oblivious to it. They both stared at each other in silence.

Jamal looked at the dejected old man who raised him with surprise. There was a look on his adoptive father's face that he had never seen before. It was the look of a disappointed parent. His father had always been extremely

324

proud of him. He knew the look because he vividly remembered seeing it on the parents of some of his friends when he was growing up. In that instant he realized that Yohan knew something. Jamal reached down to hug his father before sitting on the leather couch. Yohan ignored the embrace, and stared at his son with a blank stare.

"Why?" The slurred word came out in an accusatory manner.

Jamal decided it would be best to play dumb for at least a few minutes. "What are you talking about father? I just stopped in to say hello. I was out for my nightly jog." He tried to keep his voice as normal as possible.

The Senator's hand fumbled for the end table beside him, searching furtively for his drink before he remembered that he had dropped it on the floor in front of him. "You lied to me. All these years. What are you up to?" Yohan's voice was raised as high as it could go without actually yelling.

"Don't bother trying to get James' attention father. You're wasting your breath. I killed him," Jamal said with no empathy. He felt liberated. The façade of pretending to like this place was now completely dropped. For at least what he assumed would be the final days of his life, he could show his true nature.

The Senator stared at him, studying every feature of Jamal as if he were looking at him for the first time. In a sense, he was, Yohan thought to himself. He was gazing at the real Jamal, a cold-blooded murderer. There was no longer any kindness in his face, only malice and hatred. The Senator sensed his son was reveling in the freedom, as if an invisible weight had been lifted off of his broad shoulders. He looked like some of the senators or presidents who passed through Washington before, and when they finally realized their time was done, began speaking their minds without thought of repercussions or elections. It was liberation of the mind and soul.

Yohan's eyes now focused on the silenced pistol in Jamal's hand for the first time.

Sensing the thought, Jamal tucked the weapon back inside his sweatshirt, and stepped forward. He originally planned to

325

spend some time bragging about what he was on the verge of accomplishing, but the sight of the SUV parked outside changed his plans. He would have to be satisfied with a death and not a taunting.

"Where is Helen?" Yohan blurted out the question as the bulky figure of his adoptive son stood over him.

"She's dead. I have waited a long time for this. I was hoping to tell you more, but circumstances have changed. Who was here a few minutes ago?" His log of an arm reached out and grabbed Yohan by the throat.

The Senator choked, spitting out his words with venom that matched Jamal's. "You bastard! She loved you as if you were her true son. Why?" He implored again since he had still not received his answer. "You know Zach. You have known him since he was a child, but have kept it a secret from everyone. What are you up to?" Yohan hissed in an accusatory manner.

Jamal ignored the decrepit old drunk and continued his interrogation, "Answer my question! Who just left? You are about to die, that I can assure you, but it can be quick and painless or it can be excruciating." He tightened his grip around his father's neck. Yohan wheezed, fighting to breathe as his arms and legs flailed helplessly about. He tried in vain to get up from the chair and free himself from the large man's grip.

"Go to hell," the Senator's voice was already weak from the pressure being applied.

"You can precede me." Jamal lightened his grip ever so slightly, allowing more oxygen to flow to the Senator's brain. He decided to partially answer the man's question.

"Yes, you are correct. I have known Zach for years. We are soldiers. Soldiers in the same war that will soon reach its climax. And when the dust settles from the new holocaust that we are about to unleash a new leader will arise from the ashes. The first true Caliphate in centuries." With that final statement Jamal brought both hands to bear on the man's neck, choking him until the body went limp and the eyes rolled back in a final surrender to his brute force.

326

Chapter 52

Alex wrenched the wheel of the vehicle into a sharp U-turn as he cursed to himself. He ignored the blaring horn of the vehicle he cut off.

"Hurry!" She demanded, "I bet that jogger was Jamal." Anna braced herself to keep the sharp pitch of the vehicle from throwing her into the door.

How could I have been so stupid? Alex continued his self-examination. A few minutes earlier everything had seemed to finally be turning their way. Anna and Malcolm had just finished giving him a rundown of their conversation. It took some time, but after the self-loathing finally ended Yohan agreed to find out what he could. He was scheduled to meet with Zach sometime before the inauguration, and he promised to cautiously probe for clues.

They all agreed that it was now too late to do anything but catch Zach or Jamal in an act of treason. With only seventy-two hours to go before the inauguration they could not bring forward charges claiming the president was not a legal citizen. They would look like sore losers in the political game, trying desperately to strike back at the incoming president.

Only after Anna brought up the imposing size of the Senator's son did the image of the jogger come back to Alex. The bulky physique, the cruel mouth peeking out from underneath the hood of the sweatshirt, and the single glance he tossed in the direction of the Yohan's house all came flooding back.

"Another lesson, Alex. Observe your surroundings. Always keep an eye out for anything unusual. It sounds pretty stupid and basic, but you should have noticed him immediately. Joggers are pretty common in this area, but not at midnight when it's fifteen degrees outside." Anna's instructions were forceful, but not condescending.

Five minutes later they jerked to a stop a block away from the house. Anna bounded out of the car and up the street, keeping her upper body hunched forward as she ran through the neighbor's yards in order to avoid the lighted sidewalks. Malcolm ordered him to keep the engine idling, just in case they needed to make a quick escape. They both watched as she vanished through the unlocked front door of the Senator's home. Ten long minutes later she reappeared, crossing the expanse of lawns in less than a minute. As soon as she shut the car door they roared off, getting as far away from the area as possible.

"He's dead, strangled to death." Anna's voice was calm and cool.

Malcolm nodded knowingly. He already accepted this outcome as the most likely scenario. He ordered silence until they arrived back at his house in Arlington. As they sped out of the neighborhood they could hear the distant whining of police sirens.

They pulled into Malcolm's massive attached garage forty minutes later. The garage door closed behind them before Alex had time to shut off the engine.

"Don't worry, Anna. The wife is not home. She's at her parents, probably putting together some divorce papers as we speak," Malcolm added mischievously as they simultaneously climbed out of the vehicle.

He flicked on the lights in the kitchen and started pouring steaming cups of coffee from the pot one of his bodyguards had already brewed for him. Sammy the golden retriever, appeared from one of the bedrooms and slinked back and forth among the trio, looking for attention. After a few hopeless minutes the dog plopped down on a spot near the glass door to continue his surveillance of the backyard. Anna stood behind the island in the middle of the kitchen and waited for the go ahead to speak. Malcolm took a sip and then motioned to her to begin.

"You were right, Malcolm. The jogger must have been Jamal. I found the Senator in the library where we talked with him. He was lying on the floor dead. His neck was crushed. It was completely limp, snapped like a twig." She made a motion with her hands like she was breaking a stick. "I found the butler and his wife dead as well. Each one killed with a bullet through the chest. I wiped down the area you sat in and everything I touched, so there should not be any prints from us, but this could be trouble. I'm sure he noticed Alex parked on the street, and now he has a way to give the police a lead once one of the neighbors discovers the bodies. This complicates matters. We could easily become the prime suspects in a murder investigation, and to top it off, they even have a motive for us after the dressing down he gave you at that special session of the Senate Intelligence Committee."

Anna placed her mug on the granite countertop with too much force, sending a small amount of the scalding liquid over the rim and onto her hand. "Any ideas?" She bristled slightly from the burn and waited for her boss's response.

"I think it's time to bring President Gray into this." Malcolm stood with his back to them, staring out the bay window of his kitchen into the darkness of his yard. The moon provided the only light. It threw shadows through the trees, allowing him to catch glimpses of the rabbits at which his dog was intently staring.

"Have you talked to him within the last few days?" Anna asked.

"No. I wanted to wait and see how things developed. I also wanted to inoculate him from the pariah I've become. He's in deep enough as it is. He needs to know now though. I hope he sees the same danger that we see. There's always a chance he will get cold feet and cut his losses. I wouldn't blame him. Our little investigation has cost him every ounce of credibility he had left after his defeat."

"What can he do for us now? He only has a few days left in office," Alex tossed out the question.

"Malcolm, remember what Yohan said? There are rumors floating around town that he's started hitting the bottle again. I know how cruel the Washington gossip scene can be, but what if it's true? He may rat us out. It would be a great opportunity for him to make good with the Washington press before he leaves office. It may even save his speaking career," Anna said with a hint of sarcasm mixed with angst. She did not trust any politician in the D.C. area.

"Never," Malcolm shot back at his officer with a

deadly look. "He has his flaws, but he would never do that. He's a patriot, regardless of the shit that has been heaped on him the past few years. He took a massive risk to even approve this operation in the first place. He would not turn his back on us now. I couldn't imagine it."

Malcolm's certainty trailed off for a moment as he began ticking through the possibilities. If Allan Gray was on the bottle that could be trouble. The last thing he needed with this fiasco was involving someone who was not completely clear-headed. He turned around to face them. The clock on the microwave read 2:12 a.m. He had an idea. It could help allay his fears, and now would be the perfect time to find out if there was a potential problem. He excused himself and made his way to his private office. It was time to place a call to the White House.

Chapter 53

Zachariah Hardin fumbled around in the dark, his cell phone was attached to his ear by his left shoulder as he groped in vain for his pants. The leggy blonde rolled out of bed and was experiencing the same problem on her side of the hotel suite. Zach finally found the light switch and smacked it in disgust.

"Yeah? Hold on, okay?" He put the phone down on the bed table, and tossed the girl her thong. "Here! Now get the hell out. I've got a job to do," Zach said as he shoved her out of the room naked, a ball of clothes hiding her nude body.

"Get her out of here!" Zach groused to the Secret Service agent on duty outside his suite. He slammed the door shut without even looking to see which agent it was, and rammed the deadbolt through the door so he would not be disturbed.

He swept up the phone off the table. "Sorry. What is it?" The late night call from Aman worried him. He listened carefully for fifteen minutes. The adrenaline surged through his body as Aman ran through the story as quickly as possible. "Okay." Zach said, trying to remain as calm as possible. It was not good news. "Yes, I understand. Okay, he's as good as finished. Forty-eight hours. They can't stop it now."

Zach shut the phone, a look of disbelief etched across his face. The CIA Director was hot on their trail. How they put the pieces together, he did not know, but Aman had received an urgent call from Jamal, who told him of the night's events. He wanted to curse Jamal for his inability to control his blood lust. However, were it not for his ghoulish visit to his father, he would have never seen Malcolm's van parked outside.

Jamal ran a trace on the license plate through his government channels after killing his father and confirmed his suspicions. Allah must be watching out for them. There was no other way to explain it. Jamal's loss of control was actually helping them. If he had not gone over there who knows what would have happened? Now they could go on offense. Aman was already placing calls to some friendly reporters.

Zach walked into the bathroom to shower. In a few hours he would hold an impromptu news conference where he would announce that Malcolm Ray would not be continuing in his job once his administration took over. It would be for the best. The man clearly had a personal agenda against him, and they could not possibly have a good working relationship in an environment like that. Zachariah smirked as he thought about the statements he would soon be making. He loved playing the press for fools.

***

The White House

Allan Gray was dreaming. His re-election campaign had been victorious, and he was basking in the adulation from the press when a distant rapping on a door startled him. He opened his eyes and was back in his reality, a one-term president. The knocking continued.

"Mr. President. Please wake up. There's an urgent

331

call for you." It was the voice of one of his Secret Service detail maintaining the night watch outside his bedroom door. After a few seconds Allan's clouded mind came into focus, and he realized the knocking was real.

"Come in," the President yelled out. He rolled his legs over onto the floor, trying not to disturb the sleeping form of his wife.

A head with closely cropped blonde hair cautiously peeked in. "Sorry to disturb you, sir. You have a call from the CIA Director. He's insistent on talking to you."

Allan stood up. "I'll take it in the Oval Office. Jack, right?" He took a stab at the agent's name. There were so many new faces these past few months he was losing track.

"Yes, sir. I'll call down and tell them you will take it."

Allan hurriedly threw on the clothes that were on the floor below him. He kissed his sleeping wife on the cheek, and followed Jack through the White House living quarters and over to the West Wing of the mansion. He was granted the privacy he requested. Allan plopped into the massive leather chair that was the closest thing to a throne that America would ever have. There was nothing to see outside the long window behind his chair except outlines of trees and shrubs on the White House lawn.

"This is President Gray," he said with more authority than he felt.

"Mr. President. How are you doing this morning?" Malcolm refused to be the first person to break the formal tone the President set. He was pretty sure President Gray was not going to abandon them, but he wanted to be sure before divulging what they discovered.

"You tell me, Malcolm. Its four-thirty in the morning and my body is a little off kilter. I sure hope you drug me out of bed to tell me something important. And when I say important I'm referring to only one item." The President swiveled in his chair, and grasped for the steaming cup of coffee that had been placed on the desk before he even walked into the room. *I will definitely miss the efficiency of this place.*

"Yes, sir. I have good news. Well, at least of a sort.

332

It appears our hunch is correct. Only it is even worse than we thought. I have one question before I continue, sir. I'm sorry to ask this, but are you having problems with your drinking?" Malcolm hated to ask, but felt it was a necessity.

The President stiffened in his chair, "Of course not. Now, tell me everything." It was the first true command he had given Malcolm in the last three months.

He listened intently as Malcolm relayed everything that transpired over the past week. He left nothing out. The tattoo on the President-Elect's leg, the discovery of the Brotherhood of the Caliphate, and the trip to Louisville, were all told in rapid-fire succession. Then came the photo, which revealed Aman, Zach, Jamal, and Aziz as co-conspirators in some unknown plot that appeared on the edge of fruition. Malcolm told him for the first time that the murder of Sean Hill was tied directly to their investigation. He spoke about Sean's confrontation with Aziz, and the horrific suicide he witnessed. Finally, he told him of their visit to Yohan just a few hours earlier, and Yohan's subsequent murder by his adoptive son.

When Malcolm finished Allan sat silently, holding the White House telephone as if he were unsure what to do with it. His mind whirled a million different ways, unsure of how to react to the news. He long ago accepted his fate as a president who would be talked about the way Nixon, Johnson, and Grant were discussed; either with a ting of hatred or sympathy, but nothing else.

Allan's emotions now ran the gauntlet of extremes. His natural tendency towards cockiness was creeping back out of the coffin he had buried it in a few weeks earlier. The realization that they were right in their assumptions all along was frightening because now he was being forced to actually play his hand. He realized that with legitimate proof they would have to do something to catch the conspirators in the act.

"Sir, are you there?" Malcolm interrupted his thought process.

"Sorry, Malcolm. Just taking it all in. I still can't believe we were right." He turned back towards his desk so he could jot some notes on a pad emblazoned with the

Presidential seal.

"Are you with us?" Malcolm asked meekly, unsure of what President Gray was thinking. He was one of the few men in the world Malcolm had trouble reading sometimes. Every time Malcolm thought he had President Gray figured out he did something completely out of character. As far as Malcolm was concerned helping them made perfect sense. There was nothing left to lose, and the President already had come along this far with them. Would he be frightened off at the last possible second?

"Yes, sorry, Malcolm. I'm still just a little shocked that we appear to have been proven correct. I do agree with you. We can't possibly break this to the press now. With less than three days to the inauguration we have to literally catch him in the act of something treasonous. What do you need me to do?"

Malcolm breathed a sigh of relief and told Allan what he needed. The President quickly agreed and they parted voices amicably, each one of them excited, but both in dire need of sleep.

***

"We are good. It's a go," Malcolm said as he re-entered the kitchen. Alex and Anna were both sitting silently on their bar stools, waiting anxiously for his return.

"Now what?" Alex asked.

"We get some sleep. The guest rooms are down the hall. You can argue over who gets the one with the bigger bed."

"What about Aman?" Anna asked.

"He's staying at Blair House over at the Naval Observatory. It's normally the vice-presidential residence. You and I will go see him before noon. I want to get to bed though and at least get a few hours of sleep tonight," Malcolm said.

"What about me?" Alex chimed in.

"You stay here until we get back. We'll decide on our next step after we confront Aman and see how that goes. We'll see if we can cut some sort of deal with them to get Zach to resign as soon as possible. If he doesn't go for it, which I think will be the case, then we'll have to try another route. We will keep our options open until we see how Aman reacts to our threat." Malcolm yawned and left the kitchen without another word. They could hear his footsteps trudging up the cedar wood staircase that led to the second floor. The conversation was apparently over.

They followed Malcolm's lead and silently exited the kitchen and headed off to bed. Neither one of them bothered to even look at which bed they were acquiring. Everyone was exhausted and did not care. Alex shut his door, yanked the covers off, and flopped onto his bed without taking off his clothes. For a moment he thought that if this were a movie he would be making love to the beautiful woman in the room next door before going off to save the world. The comical thought was never completed as his eyes shut and his exhaustion finally overpowered his fear.

Chapter 54

Alex nearly fell out of bed as his confused body tried to remember where it was. He moved his head in a few semi-circles to take in his surroundings. After a few seconds he finally remembered that he was in Malcolm's house. His right arm automatically reached behind him to feel for the pistol tucked underneath his pillow. Was this the life of a spy? The feeling of complete paranoia appeared to be turning into a staple in his life.

He raised his arms towards the ceiling and let out a long, drawn out yawn. The silk sheets were magnificent. He still felt tired, but it was a different kind of exhaustion; the kind that overtakes one's body when he or she sleeps too much. He glanced at the alarm clock. The luminescent dial read 11:16 a.m. "Shit," he mumbled to himself as he rolled out of bed.

After hitting the bathroom and splashing cold water on his face he found his way back into the cavernous kitchen. Sitting on the counter was a single sheet of white paper that stood out from the dark cherry wood that dominated the kitchen. Alex squinted as he walked in front of the huge bay window. The winter sun blasted its rays across the entire room. The message was simple. *"We are gone for the day. We have a meeting. Stay in the house and rest. We will be back by 7."* It was signed A & M.

Alex crumpled up the paper in annoyance. They had left him out of their plans. He knew they were doing something dangerous, and as an amateur he would do nothing but create additional headaches, but he still wanted to contribute. It made him even angrier that in his gut he felt relieved that they left him out of the mess this time. He avoided danger without having to put up a false sense of bravado.

"Anybody else here?" Alex yelled out as loud as he could. No one answered. The bodyguards must have gone with Anna and Malcolm. He grabbed a bottled water from the fridge and sucked half of it down before looking out the window again. Sammy was circling the backyard in a frenzied pattern, chasing after an animal Alex could not see. The scene reminded him that he had not had much exercise over the past week. He may as well make the most of his free time. A jog in the frigid air would be just the thing to wake up his body. He slugged back the last half of his water and went to search for some sweats to run in.

***

Jamal gripped the binoculars in surprise as he watched the tall man hustle down the front stairs of the CIA Director's house and break into a quick jog. The last twelve hours had been a whirlwind of activity. After he informed Aman that the CIA Director was onto them, Zach retaliated with the early morning press conference where he unceremoniously fired Malcolm Ray. The speech to the media was sizzling, and he did not mince words with how displeased he was with Malcolm's performance, and the lack of integrity shown by the Agency over the last few months. As Aman anticipated, Malcolm's sudden dismissal brought about an angry phone call from Mr. Ray.

Tracking down Malcolm's address was a simple

matter for Jamal. He staked out a spot in the woods early in the morning, and waited for dawn. The press conference caused a flurry of activity, and he hoped it would pull the CIA Director out of the safe confines of his home. When the black Chevrolet Suburban shot out of the driveway on cue he began making his preparations for their return. He had maneuvered in his burrowed hole as best he could while organizing the mini-arsenal of weapons that lay on the ground beside him. It would be a quick death, which was more than the Director deserved, but time was of the essence. There was the larger picture to keep in mind, and petty squabbles with Malcolm Ray would have to be dealt with quickly and precisely.

Now, a few hours later, Jamal was putting the finishing touches on his little trap when the slam of the front door startled him. He grabbed his binoculars and saw a man exit through front door of the house. Jamal followed him as he broke into a light jog. *Was this guy an idiot?* What was he doing stepping foot outside the armed palace of the Director? He adjusted the binoculars to get a more focused view. The trees surrounding him were chopping his viewing time into tiny segments, and he wanted to be sure. He watched a few seconds longer before making up his mind. It was definitely the man who had been sitting in the driver's seat of the car parked outside his dad's house.

He slowly maneuvered out of his hiding place, and moved from tree to tree as quietly as possible. The fresh snow from the previous evening cushioned the noise his feet were making. The jogger did not even glance into the woods once. Not that he would have been able to see anything. The jogger was either extremely arrogant or an idiot. Jamal's senses were in full motion now, and he felt like he was back in the Special Forces again. He always felt at peace when he was stalking someone. It was a power trip. The hunted had no idea what was about to hit them. After twenty minutes Jamal made his way to the edge of the street and found a suitable striking point to wait for the man to complete his circuit around the street.

***

Alex's chest heaved as his body struggled to filter

337

the cold January air. He was almost back to the house. He decided he would try his best to enjoy the day of safety. He would let the professionals deal with the wackos today. He had an uneasy feeling about what they were walking into though. Before heading out for his run he flicked on the monstrous plasma TV in the living room to find every cable news network blaring the same story in constant repetition. The President-Elect called an impromptu press conference this morning where he fired Malcolm.

No wonder they left so early in the morning. Alex continued trying to formulate what their next step might be. Malcolm seemed to have something up his proverbial sleeve. He had discussed it with President Gray in the wee hours of the morning, however Alex would have to wait to find out what it was. He rounded the bend in the street, and Malcolm's giant wooden palace came into view. Fifty yards from the house he picked up his pace, determined to finish strong. The dense forest of trees stood just a few feet away. He suddenly heard a burst of motion from the forest, like a rabbit darting from its hiding place. Before he knew it his feet were swept out from under him. He started to yell as he began to fall to the ground.

***

The yell was cut off as Jamal's meaty paw pounded the man's head onto the cold, frozen earth beside the road, knocking him unconscious. He quickly dragged the man's body into the woods like a lion hiding his massacred prey, and then ran six minutes up the street to retrieve his pickup truck. He had left it parked in the next driveway, which happened to be a mile down the road. A flash of his federal badge was all it took for the neighbor to agree to let him park it there. The constant string of feds was a way of life for the closest neighbor of the CIA Director. Jamal drove back, loaded Alex's limp body into the back, and covered it with a tarp. Before leaving he quickly disassembled his trap, and gathered up his arsenal of weapons. The death of Malcolm Ray would have to wait.

Chapter 55

Anna stared out the backseat window as they drove up Massachusetts Avenue. They were passing through Embassy Row, where every building was the home of a country's ambassador. The homes were a slew of different styles; the size of each home often times corresponding to the country's power and influence. She gazed with amusement to her left as they passed the Egyptian embassy. It was a three-story cream-colored brownstone home built at the beginning of the twentieth century. A little further up the road was the Brazilian embassy, a three-story glass building, which stood on concrete stilts. Its contemporary construction the exact opposite of the last block of buildings they passed.

Two blocks further and on their right was a building that looked like an old warehouse that was no longer in use. There was no sign indicating which country it belonged to, and frankly she did not blame them. She would not want to take credit for the dilapidated structure either. Finally, they were almost to their destination. The last building they passed was the massive compound belonging to Great Britain.

A long, tall, wrought iron fence was the first signal that they were approaching the vice-presidential residence. The fence was on their left, and it ran until it disappeared around a bend further up the street. It encircled the acreage of the Naval Observatory, and was the first line of defense for the massive compound, which sat at the top of a hill on the southeast side of the estate. She exchanged a weary look with Malcolm as they pulled up to the main entrance of the U.S. Naval Observatory. There was no going back now. She knew that once they passed through those gates, if they were wrong, they would either be dead or going to jail for a long time.

Malcolm's bodyguard deftly eased the bulk of the armored SUV around the circular driveway and up to the gated entryway of the U.S. Naval Observatory grounds at the corner of 34th Street and Massachusetts Avenue. A three-foot tall, thick metal wall protruded from the concrete driveway, blocking the entrance. It was used to stop anyone from trying to careen onto the grounds. The wall vanished into its hideout in the ground as they slowly crept up to the guarded entrance. The guard waived them through with a cursory glance. He had been expecting them.

They started up the concrete driveway. The normal cornucopia of flowers that surrounded the driveway was absent due to the frigid temperatures. They stopped at the top of the hill and parked the vehicle in the massive circular driveway that sat in front of the century-old, white brick Victorian home that served as the vice-president's residence. At the moment, it was Aman's base of operations for the final few days of the world's oldest peaceful transition of power. A lone Secret Service agent stood at the covered entrance, watching them like a sentinel. Malcolm stepped out of the back of his personal vehicle, and Anna followed close behind him. He felt relaxed and could not suppress a slight smile. Anna retained the role of the taciturn field officer. The purse slung over her right shoulder contained all the trappings that a beautiful woman would carry with her to work, and one deadly weapon that looked completely out of place.

The morning had progressed perfectly for them up to that point. One of Malcolm's bodyguards woke them up early to show them the press conference that was underway. The perfect excuse to make a call to the President-Elect's inner circle was dropped right into their lap. Malcolm immediately seized the phone while the press conference was still going on. Zach Hardin looked even more haughty and self-confident than usual as he spent fifteen straight minutes listing a litany of abuses that Malcolm and the CIA perpetrated against him.

After twenty minutes of being shepherded from one aide to the next Malcolm finally got Aman on the line, and began vigorously complaining about not being given prior knowledge of his dismissal. He even impressed himself with his feigned anger. Aman played the role of the perfect statesman and presidential confidante. He agreed to meet with Malcolm to see if they could come to some sort of mutual arrangement. Aman expressed a desire to put the situation to rest as quickly as possible. The last thing they needed was a distraction that created animosity between the administration and the CIA. There had been enough bickering within Mr. Gray's administration which had been running the show for the last four years, and Aman wanted Zach to start off on a positive note.

The agent's right hand shot up as if he were a bored traffic cop, indicating for them to stay on the front steps. He spoke in muffled tones into the lapel of his sport coat, and after receiving a response they could not hear he turned to them and said, "You were supposed to come alone." The agitation in his voice was evident.

"She's in our Operations Department. I have a few other items I need to discuss with the President's aid. Some loose ends they need to know about before I get the hell out of this town." Malcolm continued to play the part of the disgruntled employee.

"All weapons stay outside." The black holes of the agent's sunglasses turned towards Anna. She offered the purse without a fight. He extracted the weapon, promising to give it back to her when they left. "You can go in. Aman is in the den at the back," the agent said as he smoothly opened the door for them. He placed the pilfered weapon inside his navy blue sport coat. They eagerly hurried through the proffered door.

The huge house was silent until the sound of motion came from the back, right-hand corner. President Gray's vice president had already moved out of the house, and only those items that were a permanent fixture of the Naval Observatory still remained. It looked more like a tourist attraction at the current moment than a home. They followed the sound of the noise to the back of the house. They soon found the door leading to the den, and entered without knocking.

Aman was standing with his back to them. He was bent over an L-shaped oak desk, shuffling through a disheveled stack of papers. He appeared to be looking for something. "Have a seat. I'll be with you in just a second," Aman said. He seemed to find what he was looking for a few

341

seconds later and held up a single sheet of paper like it was the final clue to a puzzle. He turned to face them. The look of shock on his face only lasted a split second, but they both recognized it. The stare focused on Anna.

"Excuse me, I'm feeling a little tired. I need to sit down." His large frame maneuvered around the desk and plopped down in the comfortable chair. She was the woman from Las Vegas, he silently thought. The woman Zach tried so desperately to seduce. His fears were realized. She was a spy after all. If she was with Malcolm, he assumed she must work for the CIA, as well.

"Feel better?" Malcolm looked on in disgust at the fat Arab. He could barely fit in his chair. The two armrests looked to be under a great deal of pressure from his bulge. They may need a shoehorn to get him out of the chair, Malcolm thought. Aman reminded Malcolm of the decadent sheiks who ran Saudi Arabia, who preached Islam by day and hosted orgies by night.

"Yes, thank you. I'm sorry about this morning Malcolm, but it was Zach's idea. He insisted on cutting you loose immediately. The little illegal investigation that you ran for President Gray didn't seem to be coming to a halt, and he thought this was the only way to get your attention. As usual he was correct." Aman's voice beamed with pride for his protégé.

"Yes, I guess I should have figured that you wouldn't keep me on. How goes the transition of power?" Malcolm asked flippantly. He looked casually around the room until his eyes fell on an open side door that led into the huge kitchen. On the floor of the kitchen were several huge suitcases lined up and ready to go.

"Busy, but no complaints. It will all be over in a few days," Aman spoke with assurance.

"Of course. I hope Zach is not nervous about his inauguration speech." Malcolm was enjoying the pathetic attempt at small talk they were both making. It was clear that Aman was edgy. Whether it was simply the pressure of being in power or something else, he intended to find out in due course.

Aman's patience quickly ran down to empty.

342

"What the fuck do you want, Malcolm? I haven't got all day. Do you want to work out some sort of deal so we don't hang you with an indictment in a few weeks?" His eyes flicked back and forth between Malcolm and Anna, looking for a reaction from either one of them. They could not possibly know enough to stop them now, especially this late in the game.

Malcolm simply shrugged his shoulders. Aman thought the CIA Director was enjoying himself too much. The antics suggested one of two extremes. He either thought Malcolm had pushed himself to the limit and was going down in flames, or he had pulled off a last second miracle. Aman would have felt much more comfortable were it not for the fact that Malcolm had paid a visit to their Jewish friend the previous night.

Aman continued, "I see your little game. You beg me for a meeting and then pretend that you are doing me a favor by coming to see me? All I can promise is that I will have a talk with Zach for you. We may be able to work out a deal where we don't press serious charges. We have more pressing matters to deal with, and we don't want the distraction. We have a war to end." Aman began stacking the papers on the desk into several neat piles. "Who is the woman?" He tossed out the line as if she were not in the room.

"This is one of my best people in our Operations Department. Her name is Marilyn." Malcolm chose to use her code name from the mission. At Malcolm's heeding she grudgingly stepped forward and shook Aman's hand. Malcolm continued, "She has been working on a few very important projects for me; projects that I think Zach needs to consider continuing after I'm gone. I thought perhaps we could cut a deal, as you suggested before. My final operation gets to stay afloat and I promise to keep my mouth shut, at least for a while," Malcolm replied as the mischievous grin reappeared. The time was almost right. He was looking forward to Aman's reaction.

"That doesn't sound like a fair deal to me. The last time I checked, you were the one looking at some jail time. You spooks are all the same. You think you are above the

343

law. Considering your last investigation was against Zach, I'm curious to find out what you think you have that is important enough to warrant this clearly imbalanced trade." Aman was now watching them closely. The woman stepped forward, accepting a manila envelope from Malcolm that appeared from the inside of his brown tweed blazer. She extracted a photo and placed it on the table in front of Aman.

"Feel free to keep that copy, Aman. I have several others stashed away in case of theft or damage," Anna said matter-of-factly.

Aman picked up the picture and held it with just his thumb and pointer finger like it was on fire and about to burn his fingers. The symbol was quite recognizable. He would know since he had one on his leg, as well. He gently laid the photo down, his eyes blazing unrestrained hatred at them as his breathing became more pronounced. "What are you trying to pull with this?" The friendly campaign manager quickly revealed a fiery temperament.

"You know what that is, don't you? And don't play games." As she talked Malcolm moved to close and lock the side door to prevent any unwanted guests from entering.

"Of course. You're a CIA agent running an illegal operation inside the country. You are also the whore that Zach was obsessed with in Las Vegas. I should have known his dick would eventually get him into trouble. I was concerned from the beginning when he started talking about a new girl he wanted to get his hands on. I should have known it was trouble when he refused to say where he met you. If you don't mind, how did you meet him?"

Anna laughed, "You should have kept him away from the strip clubs. The man has a problem. All it took was one dance, and I had him hooked." She reveled in taunting him. The Washington grapevine was full of stories of Aman warning his protégé to stay away from the seedy side of Las Vegas, but all the warnings were to no avail. Zach thought that because he was widowed he had carte blanche when it came to his sexual dalliances.

"Back to her original question, Aman. What is the photo of?" Malcolm was annoyed with the tangent their conversation had taken. She was already revealing more than

344

she should.

"Why don't you tell me? It's just a hairy leg with a tattoo as far as I can see. It looks like some Arabic symbols to me, but I haven't studied the language in years. It doesn't mean anything to me."

Anna ignored the obvious lie, and extracted another photo from the envelope and laid it on the table. Aman looked at the youthful version of himself in the old black and white photo, standing with pride, while surrounded by his loyal entourage. His two holy warriors seated below him. Where did this come from? And most importantly, how could they have found a copy of it? He tried to fidget in his chair, but the expanse of his body rubbed against the armrests, making it difficult to move. His eyes roamed back and forth between the two photos. He watched out of the corner of his eye as Malcolm paced around the perimeter of the room, closing the wooden blinds so they could no longer see the expansive, lush green fields of the acreage encircling them.

The silence in the room was an entity unto itself. Beads of sweat began to form on Aman's temple. He could use a drink. They were still waiting patiently for his response. His right hand suddenly balled into a fist and came thrashing down onto the solid wood of the desk.

"The reporter," Aman muttered under his breath. The son of a bitch must have horded some extra copies of those photos. I knew they should have let me kill him, he thought to himself. Now that mistake was haunting him at the worst possible moment. He finally looked up to see they were both staring at him. There was nowhere to run. He was trapped.

"Very good, Aman. We found the reporter. Or should I say Marilyn did. You should have killed him when you had the chance. Zach is a member of the Brotherhood of the Caliphate. The hairy leg in the photo belongs to Zach and the tattoo is the symbol of your little brotherhood. You brought Zach into this country illegally, which makes him an illegitimate candidate, and thus barred from holding any political office in this country." Malcolm's authoritative voice spoke the words with precision.

"These photos are fakes. I'm going to have you arrested." The words were hollow and uncertain. Aman grabbed for his cell phone, but Anna was ready. She brought her hand down in one quick and violent motion, cracking his arm. He yelped in pain.

"Come on, Aman. You can't seriously think you were going to get away with that," she said as she scooped up the phone and dropped it into her purse.

Aman tried desperately to think of a way to bargain his way out of the situation, but nothing seemed feasible. He would keep his mouth shut and see what they offered. Jamal had been left out of the conversation up to that point so he could only hope they did not discover him, as well.

Malcolm cut into the conversation. "Our offer is this, Aman. No games. We can keep this out of the press on one condition. Zach has to resign within two months of taking office. The stress of his wife's death a few months ago, and a heart condition that somehow was missed during his physical exams. That will be the story. We will let him disappear quietly into private life, and he can spend his remaining years giving speeches for a hundred thousand a pop."

"And if I refuse?"

"Then we go public with the story within a few days. We have several copies of the photographs stashed in numerous locations in case of a problem. Even if the story is treated as an expose at the National Enquirer for a while, it will eventually attract enough attention and reporters. Like flies on crap. People will start digging around and asking unpleasant questions. It may take a few months, maybe even a year, but eventually it will catch up to him."

Aman played along, pretending to grapple with a decision. Inside he was thrilled. They did not appear to know the full extent of his operation.

"I obviously cannot make any promises. I will need to run it by Zachariah." He pushed himself out of his chair. "Now if you don't mind. I need to touch base with him. I will have an answer for you very shortly." Aman opened his palm in a silent gesture to have his phone returned to him.

Malcolm laughed heartily. It was a laugh that

relayed how ridiculous the whole conversation was. They all knew the score, yet no one was willing to admit it. "Oh, by the way, there is one other part of the deal. The new head of his security detail, Jamal Mahmud, must resign as well," Malcolm said as he stared at the fat Egyptian. The time for games was over.

Aman looked around in panic. The self-assuredness that had returned for a few brief moments was once again replaced by the look of a cornered animal about to be slaughtered. "Never. You're too late. You cannot stop us." The venomous words spilled out in a low hiss. "We have won, and you will not live long enough to see the glorious return." The cryptic warnings were accompanied by a pounding on one of the doors.

Malcolm rushed towards Aman, getting the melon of a head in a chokehold just as a voice yelled out from behind the door, "Secret Service!" The door swung open and the agent stepped cautiously into view, his pistol sweeping the room in a professional manner. "Everyone, put your hands up!"

Anna stood behind the agent and out of his view. She acted instinctively, and her right leg flashed upward, cracking the agent across the elbow and wounding his arm. The weapon clattered to the ground, and he let out a guttural growl of anger after being taken off guard. The agent immediately reached for the throwing knife tucked around his calf, but Anna thrust her right arm down in a lightning fast motion, catching him on the back of the neck, and rendering him unconscious.

She performed a thorough sweep of the house. It was empty except for the three of them. She found some rope in a closet in the kitchen, and noticed the same row of suitcases. After retrieving her pistol from the agent's sport coat, she bound and gagged him, then tossed the remainder of the rope to Malcolm. He pushed Aman's squat figure back into the chair and tied him down. Aman writhed in fury, trying to free himself from his bonds.

"Well, if we were not fugitives before we are now. I don't know what the penalty is for assaulting a Secret Service agent, but I doubt it's just a slap on the wrist," Anna

347

said.

Aman screamed once before Malcolm slapped him across the face, "Shut up. We have some more questions for you," Malcolm said as he looked in Aman's eyes. He saw the glazed look of a man who had lost all control. He doubted he would be able to get much information out of him.

"You and your President are excellent at torturing people. This should be enjoyable for you." Aman's spittle landed on the desk in front of him, covering his papers and an oversized note holder crammed with telephone messages in a small shower.

"What is with the luggage, Aman? Going somewhere?" Anna kicked open the side door that led to the kitchen, revealing the pricey designer luggage on the floor.

"You are wasting your time. Just kill me and get it over with. I will tell nothing."

Anna ignored the comment. She picked up the stack of papers on the desk and began flipping through them. Malcolm pushed the note holder out of the way, moving it closer to Aman, and picked up a stack of envelopes to look through, as well.

"Here we are." She raised the packet in triumph. It was buried under a list of donors from Zach's campaign. "One ticket to Cairo that leaves this evening," she said, waving the ticket in the air to mock Aman. "Aren't you going to stick around to watch your protégé take the oath of office?"

"I have more important things to tend to. My work here is finished. I have done what I have been called to do." Aman spoke with a sense of true satisfaction. It was a completely honest statement.

"For the Brotherhood?" Malcolm asked.

Anna suddenly had an idea. She took the unconscious agent's throwing knife, wheeled Aman's chair so he faced the wall, and grabbed one of his legs. She roughly cut out two large swaths of the beige fabric. He sat frozen while she did it, petrified she was about to cut off his genitals. She roughly tore off the remaining shreds of his pants, tossing the remnants to the side like a child discarding

348

wrapping paper on Christmas morning. She ignored the grotesque waistline and grasped his inner leg, trying to view it. He squirmed in annoyance now that the knife had been put down. It was there. She knew it would be. The two Arabic K's with the green slash through them stared back at her. It was the same tattoo that was on Zach's inner thigh. Malcolm looked on from a few feet away. He knew what she was doing.

"Do you want to tell me what they stand for, or do I get to really cause you some pain?" She stepped away from him. She grasped the knife, flipping it playfully around in her hand while she circled around to the other side of the desk so she could stand beside Malcolm.

***

Aman smiled at her. In her exuberant wrenching of his pants she accidentally loosened his binds just enough to allow him to make the attempt. He willed himself to do it.

"Well?" She asked him.

"Of course. It stands for Khalifah Khilahah. It means Caliphate creation." Aman leaned back in his chair as if he was debating what else to say. It was the only solution and he knew it. There was no one else from whom they could extract information, and with only forty-eight hours until the inauguration they would not be able to stop it. He was their last hope to prove anything. If he was dead they had nothing. Aman acted on this reassuring thought before he could change his mind.

Without warning his upper body suddenly came throttling forward, his head slamming into the pointed note holder resting on the desk in front of him. It tore into his left eye, piercing through his brain in a white hot flash of pain. Blood flowed out over the desk. His job was complete. Aman's slumped body twitched horridly in the throes of death as Malcolm and Anna watched in helpless shock.

Chapter 56

Alex opened his eyes to nothing but a black void. *Am I dead?* The pain that shot through his wrists told him 'no.' After a few seconds he adjusted to the disorientation of not being able to see, and realized the blackness was caused by a piece of cloth that was tied tightly around his head. As his senses became more attuned he began to feel pain in different areas. The vice grip of the rope that bound his wrists to the metal chair and the tightly bound cloth squeezing his temples were accompanied by more rope that secured his ankles to the chair. The professionally tied knots began to hurt more as he slowly awakened and remembered what had happened.

He had no idea how long he had been unconscious. His head throbbed from the blow he took from the unknown assailant. The silence of the room provided no clues as to where he could be. The black void was silent torture, and it was beginning to make him claustrophobic. He began sweating profusely. The panic quickly began to bubble up, and his chest heaved as his breathing became more erratic. What the hell had he gotten himself into?

A thunderclap smashed across his face, knocking him and his chair to the floor with a thud. In a perverse way it felt good. It was the first sign that he was not lying in a ditch or buried alive somewhere. Two strong hands grasped the back of the chair and pulled him back up as if the chair were empty and not occupied by a two hundred pound man.

"Who is there?" Alex suddenly remembered that still being alive meant he could actually speak and not just sit there like a mute. Another smack to the face answered his question. This one was not quite as intense as the first since he still remained upright. "Whoever you are, I think you have the wrong guy," Alex said as he gasped feebly, trying to catch his breath.

"Hah," an amused voice replied. "I don't have the wrong guy. You are in league with the CIA Director and that woman. I know it is so. Do not try to bluff me."

"What are you talking…" Alex tried to intervene.

"You clearly know what they know, or at least most of it. I have seen you with them. I'm not going to fool around so I will tell you this once," the stranger said in a staccato burst of words.

"I don't know what this…" Alex tried to horn in on his speech.

"Enough! Say another word and I will break a finger in two. I will not lie. I don't have time to play any games or fool around. Either talk now and tell me everything you know, and perhaps I'll let you live. I cannot guarantee it, but you will at least have a chance. If you don't talk now you will talk very soon afterwards, and then you will die a horrible death. And you will have caused yourself a great deal of excruciating pain for no reason besides your foolish pride. I will give you ten minutes while I prepare. After that, there will be no bargaining and no remorse." Jamal stood up and went about making the necessary preparations.

Alex tried to speak but was immediately cut off by another slap across the face. He was confused and disorientated by the lack of chitchat. He was not even being given some sort of bargain. It was an all or nothing proposition. Alex's body was now drenched in sweat. He could feel his clothes becoming heavier from the dampness created by his own body. He twitched and fiddled with his arms in a pointless attempt to free himself. He heard a small chuckle from across the room. Whoever it was, he seemed to be enjoying his power. Alex made up his mind and steeled his body for the pain that his decision would bring down on him.

Jamal munched on pita bread and hummus while he cleaned up the room. It was a habit he could not break, even as he was preparing to launch an inquisition. He picked up a few pieces of trash that were strewn about the cheap linoleum floor of his little safe house on the Virginia side of the Potomac. The mortgage on it had been paid by a few of his co-workers in the Secret Service who used it for a variety of reasons. There had been many a mistress brought to the secluded home, and all his colleagues paid him for the privilege to use the house. The money was helpful, but

Jamal found the home more useful because of the power that it gave him over his co-workers. He had even used the house to entrap the former head of President Gray's Secret Service detail, forcing the man into an early retirement. This allowed Jamal to take over the man's post.

After a few more minutes of silence from his prisoner it was clear that the hard way had been chosen. Well, he did warn him. He needed to crack Alex Bryce, at least that was the name on his driver's license, as quickly as possible. It was almost midnight, and there were just a few hours left before he would have to go back to work. The White House was a mess as the two transition teams milled about the people's mansion. One of the teams was moving items in with a gleeful pleasure, while the other was morbidly packing up its belongings and preparing to exit the national stage.

Jamal picked up the chair with Alex in it, and dragged him into the next room. There was nothing in the room except a specially designed piece of wood that Jamal had constructed himself. This was his first opportunity to use his special device. It resembled a giant wooden table turned upside down, except it had no legs and covered almost the entire floor. The outer edges of the wood contraption stood three feet off the ground and were coated with a sticky substance. Overall, it looked quite harmless, and by itself, it was.

Jamal lifted Alex and the chair over the top of it and dragged him into the middle of the wood contraption. Alex sat quietly, conserving his energy for the unknown pain that would soon begin. Jamal went back into the kitchen and retrieved the drum full of insects and an acetylene torch. The little farm he cultivated in the backyard was finally going to be put to use. He took off the lid and peered into the drum. The entire inside of it was alive with thousands of crawling cockroaches.

Jamal sat the drum next to Alex and unsheathed a large hunting knife from its scabbard. He gently brushed the knife down Alex's leg. The razor sharp blade clipped many of the hairs on his leg. Alex tensed his body, preparing for the pain. Jamal expertly sliced into his calf, cutting a wound approximately an inch long. He probed the knife inside until blood began to drip onto the floor. He then repeated the exact same act to Alex's other leg. The wounds were mild gashes that, if treated quickly, would simply require several stitches. Satisfied with his work, he put the knife away and fired off his final warning to Alex.

"Those may seem like minor wounds, but if you don't immediately begin telling me everything you know you will soon be wracked with unimaginable pain. This is an old form of torture that was used in the fourteenth century in Egypt. It was developed by a religious emir named Shaykhun who used it to kill one of his rivals."

Jamal paused for a few seconds to give him another chance to capitulate. He then continued, "In a few minutes I will let cockroaches loose right next to each of your wounds. The wounds are just large enough for the cockroaches to crawl inside you. I will then tape a metal cap around the wound and use this handy torch to apply the heat to the metal cap." He flicked the button of the acetylene torch so Alex could listen to the low hiss of the flame. "The cockroaches are hungry and they do not like the heat so they will continue to burrow deeper inside you. You will soon have a few hundred of them inside your legs, feeding on your muscles, and causing you immense pain. If for some reason you still will not talk after this first round I will begin cutting wounds higher up on your body until you talk. Shaykhun actually bored holes into his prisoner's head, and allowed the insects to eat their way into the man's brain. For both of our sakes, I hope you don't allow it to come to that. It will waste my time, and you will suffer perhaps the worst death any American spy has ever experienced."

"You are a sick man," Alex spat the words out angrily and began fighting desperately to free himself. His binds felt even tighter now. He could hear the man begin to move about and make whatever preparations were necessary for such a horrid job. "This must be something you learned from Aman."

Jamal's face lit up with a big smile that Alex could not see. "Yes, that is right. I have learned a great deal from him." Jamal went about his work. He deposited the first handful of cockroaches near the wound and they immediately began darting inside.

"Now please continue telling me what you know about Aman and Zachariah." Jamal took another handful and dumped them in the pool of blood under the other leg. He quickly discovered that if he inserted a few directly into the wound, the rest of them would follow suit, like hyenas being led to a carcass.

Once the appropriate amount of cockroaches had crawled inside Alex's leg Jamal covered the lid of the drum, and wrapped both wounds tightly with duct tape and a metal cylinder. He fired up the acetylene torch. The blue hiss of the flame alerted Alex to what was happening. Jamal held the flame right up against the metal. A few of the insects scampered out from underneath the cylinder, but once the heat of the flame hit the metal no more appeared. They were burrowing themselves deep into Alex's legs, looking for another way out.

**

Alex felt the first twinge of pain in his legs. Then it consumed him. His legs were on fire, literally and figuratively. The heat from the torch that continued to singe him was nothing compared to the fire that was raging inside his legs. He thrashed about as much as his bindings would allow, but that only seemed to make the pain worse. Beads of sweat from his forehead quickly morphed into a miniature waterfall spilling down his face and splashing onto the floor.

Should I talk? He did not think he could hold out. If his legs hurt this bad what would it feel like when the crazed lunatic opened a wound in his chest or in his head? Maybe he should lie. He assumed the monster would know if he were. The fiery pain now shot through one of his feet and he let out a scream of pain.

"Feel better? No one can hear you. Think how much better you will feel if you just tell me what you know. I can uncover this wound and the roaches will find their way out. Or I can take the metal cap off and allow more in. Then they can continue to eat you alive until they find another opening they can escape from. It is your choice." His torturer shut off the torch.

Alex felt like his head was on the verge of exploding. Every pain sensor in his body cried out for mercy. He could now hear his own sweat hitting the floor. Or was that his blood? Did it really matter? From somewhere in the distance a telephone began ringing. After five rings he heard movement.

"I will be back in a few minutes. Then I will open up another cut for you," the voice said.

The pain continued to tick upward in intensity. Every time he thought it could not get worse he learned how wrong he was. He could hear the muffled voice in the background, but could not understand any words. Alex continued to try to wrench his hands free until his head was racked with another burst of raw pain. Unable to take it anymore his body shut down, and his head slumped forward.

Jamal re-entered the room to find Alex passed out. He yanked the metal cylinders off his legs, cut the bindings, and carried the unconscious body into a bedroom. He dropped the limp body on the bed, and re-tied his appendages to the four corner posts. The cockroaches began poking their antennae out of the two wounds and making their escape. Jamal needed him alive for the moment. They may need this Alex as a bargaining tool now.

Chapter 57

Anna stared blankly out of the tinted window of the SUV at the thin layer of snow that surrounded the Washington Monument. It was Inauguration Day, and a beautiful, crisp January morning greeted them. The police were out in force setting up barricades all over the city in preparation for the momentous occasion. Malcolm sat at the other end of the backseat, composing his own thoughts. They looked like an unhappy married couple who had just had a knock-down drag-out fight only to discover they had nowhere else to go, and so were attempting to create as much space between one another as possible. In reality they were both loners, the kind who were self-reliant and preferred to do things themselves. It was this similar characteristic that made them the best at what they did. It was also the reason they needed to be left alone with their thoughts before the final confrontation.

The last forty-eight hours brought nothing but bad news. Aman's suicide left them with nothing. A confession from him would have gone a long way towards being able to take their case to the current President, the FBI, or someone who may be able to assist them. They were forced to leave Aman's body inside the vice-president's residence. They smuggled the unconscious Secret Service agent out in the back of their car. He was currently drugged up and unconscious at Malcolm's house. He would sleep for another twenty-four hours at least.

In addition to this, they discovered that Alex had disappeared when they returned to Malcolm's house. Their first thought was that he had turned on them, but no federal agents ever showed up to arrest them. The other option was just as bad. He must have been kidnapped by one of Aman's men. Anna assumed the most likely candidate was Jamal. After all, he had seen Alex in the car the night they visited the Senator. He must have found out whom the car belonged to and staked them out.

Their vehicle slowly turned into the White House driveway. She watched carefully for anything out of the ordinary that might suggest they were about to be arrested. A Secret Service agent armed with a submachine gun waved them through the final security stop, and motioned for them to continue to the North Portico of the White House. It was time for Malcolm to deliver President Gray's final PDB (Presidential Daily Brief) in person. This was a lucky gift from Zachariah Hardin, who made the firing of the CIA Director effective immediately after the inauguration. This gave Malcolm an excuse to visit the White House one more time.

Anna felt on edge as she stepped out of the SUV. The door was opened by one of the White House staff. It was her first visit to the White House, and she felt like she

356

was heading into the den of an enemy instead of the home of the leader of the free world. The hand written speech she found when they riffled through Aman's belongings came back to her now.

"Before today, the world was divided into two houses, the House of Islam where Muslim law solves all problems, and the House of War, which is ruled by the West. With the return of the one true Caliphate and Mahdi, and the destruction and humbling of his enemies the world is now forced to submit to Muslim rule or face annihilation. The Great Satan made its choice. It is now a vassal of the new Caliphate. Now the rest of the world's citizens must choose sides."

The chilling declaration stood at the forefront of her thoughts as she and Malcolm crossed the threshold into the White House. They were at the mercy of President Gray now.

Chapter 58

Zachariah Hardin stood quietly in front of his bathroom mirror and methodically shaved his face. The razor slid harmlessly over his flat chin, cutting off the stubble that had accumulated during the night. The dark circles under his eyes were evidence of his lack of sleep. He was glad he called the makeup artist. He would need to be spruced up in order to be presentable to the cameras. He carefully pushed a stray piece of his jet back hair back into place. A little extra gel ensured it would not fall down again. He was jumpy and nervous. This was to be expected of someone about to become the leader of the free world, but his fear was of a different sort now. Every knock on the door could be a group of federal agents coming to snatch him away and make him disappear just as he was reaching his goal.

Twenty-four hours earlier he brimmed with

confidence. Now he just wanted to hold off his adversaries a little longer so he could have his victory. No matter how close his enemies were, he knew that time was on his side. Aman had never called him to inform him that he arrived back in Egypt, and Zach spent a fruitless hour trying to reach him at several different locations. After all the dead ends he had Jamal escort him to the Naval Observatory in the middle of the night, where they discovered the awful scene. Aman was dead of what was surely a self-inflicted wound, and his Secret Service agent was nowhere to be found. Jamal cleaned up the mess. The brutal death had to be kept quiet until after the inauguration. Afterwards it would not matter anyway. The city was already abuzz with the discovery of Senator Rosenbaum's body at his home, and Zach could not afford any more distractions.

He glanced at his cell phone to check the time. Jamal should be arriving at the White House within the hour. He was likely checking the parade route and security arrangements for the inauguration address on the steps of the Capitol at that moment. His real duties, however, would not begin until the speech was over. There were a whole slew of agents who would make sure the short trip from the steps of the Capitol to the White House would go off without a hitch. Once Zach and his entourage made it to the White House all the parties would commence and Jamal and his team would take over security, and more importantly, the nuclear codes.

It would be somewhere in the White House where they would make their move. For the first time he allowed himself to mentally picture the scene that would make him infamous to the majority of the world, but an instant idol to another group. They would disappear into a room with the Military Officer carrying the nuclear football. Jamal would dispose of the man, and then, with the codes in their hands, they would unleash the nuclear arsenal of the United States on itself.

The first nuclear missile would explode in the atmosphere. It would be an EMP (electro-magnetic pulse) weapon, and it would render everything that relied on electricity in the continental U.S. worthless. The entire mainland would be thrust into the Stone Age. Then he would launch as many nuclear missiles as possible, and turn the country into a radioactive wasteland. He would become the ultimate agent of influence, as the CIA Director would say, as he would turn the country's most devastating weapons on itself. Zach thought of the only other agent of influence to have wormed his way so close to presidential power. He had been a vice-president at the beginning of the twentieth century. The man was a Soviet spy, but that was just before the advent of nuclear weapons, and the president at the time quietly removed him from the ticket after their first four years in office, thus preventing him from doing any damage. This time would be different.

Zach set the razor down and looked at his reflection with satisfaction. The punishment of the U.S. was a long time coming. Sheik Osama would be a mere pauper compared to him once the missiles were launched. It still seemed like a dream to Zach, but now it was about to become something even better; a nightmare for the United States. He hoped to live and make his way back to the Middle East in triumph, but it really did not matter. Martyrdom could be the best possible thing for him. He would never be as popular, or more reviled than he would be in the next few hours and days. Why not go out on top? He picked his razor back up and began meticulously shaving a few missed spots. He needed to hurry. The makeup artist would be arriving shortly.

Chapter 59

"That is certainly one hell of a story. Unfortunately, I believe every word of it," President Gray said as his eyes shifted back and forth between Anna and Malcolm, looking for some kind of deception on their part. He knew it was not there, but he felt obligated to pursue all possibilities.

He tossed the front page of the Washington Times in their direction and motioned towards the article discussing the death of Senator Rosenbaum. "I thought that smelled of you. When you wanted to personally give me my final PDB I knew the game was still alive. Any idea why Aman's death has not showed up on the news yet?" The President took a large bite from a cinnamon donut and sat it back down on his desk.

"My guess would be that either Zach or Jamal found the scene and secretly cleaned it up. There would be no way to explain it to the press without generating all sorts of uncomfortable questions," Malcolm said. He sipped his bottled water and ignored the proffered paper. He had already read the article three times at his house and memorized every piece of information he thought could be useful.

President Gray stood up and paced the room. They were all racked with tension and nerves. They were making decisions that could soon land them in jail if their instincts were wrong.

"Still no sign of the amateur?" The President was referring to Alex.

"No. I would presume he is dead. We can only hope he has not divulged any information to his kidnappers. Have any police or FBI been asking questions about Malcolm and I?" Anna asked the president in a clinical tone, keeping all emotions for her vanished colleague in check.

"Not that I'm aware of. I'd steer clear of Jamal if I were you though. He was supposed to arrive here an hour before you did. He is probably walking the grounds now to make sure everything is in order for the transfer of power. By the way Malcolm, Zach called me this morning and wanted me to inform you that you are not welcome at the inauguration." He smiled at his CIA Director. He knew Malcolm would not care, but it was fun to needle him a little. A little levity right now was the only thing keeping him from losing his cool.

Malcolm returned the smile with one of his own. "That will work well for what we have in mind. Now my no-show will be expected. Just make sure you casually mention to some members of the press what happened. Once the reason for my vanishing act is out in the open I won't be missed. Everybody knows I'm on his shit list anyway. They will quickly lose interest in me."

"I will have a talk with them. Now what did you have in mind? I need to get going in a few minutes. My wife and I have to meet with the President-Elect in thirty minutes so we can head over to the Capitol together."

"Can you hide us out somewhere in the White House?" Malcolm asked. "We have to be here when Zach first arrives. Our guess is that they're going to activate their plan immediately. If we can catch them in the act we may be able to keep ourselves from receiving life sentences at the federal pen."

President Gray stared blankly at the wall. The White House was teeming with people, and it seemed like everywhere he walked there was someone in his way. An idea popped into his mind. It would be a tight fit for a few hours, but it was the one room where they would not be disturbed.

Ten minutes later the three of them were standing amongst a sea of suitcases in the Lincoln Bedroom of the White House. Guests of the sitting president typically used the room, but today it served as the moving room. The first couple's belongings were in a holding pattern until the next day when they were scheduled to be picked up, but for now the room was the world's swankiest storage facility. The green and brown floral patterned carpet could only be seen in spots thanks to the piles of luggage. They maneuvered around the bags to get to the cherry wood furniture upholstered in a milky white ivory fabric.

Anna glanced at the wall and noticed a signed copy of Lincoln's Gettysburg Address. She thought it was very fitting for the moment upon which they were closing in on. Lincoln once possessed the same absolute certainty that what he was doing was best for the nation, and he was forced to tear the country apart with a brutal civil war. Were their own instincts as on target as Lincoln's, or were they recklessly pursuing a selfish path more similar to Jefferson Davis? President Gray interrupted her thoughts.

"You can stay here until the President-Elect arrives. This is all my stuff so you probably won't be disturbed. If

361

someone does come in you can just hide behind one of the piles of luggage until they leave." It was a ridiculous sounding statement, but it was true. "The movers aren't scheduled to pick it up until tomorrow. Too much going on today," President Gray said with a smirk on his face. He was proud of his joke.

"Thanks. It will work perfectly. Did you get our weapons back?" Malcolm asked. President Gray pointed to the cabinet behind the love seat. I had my secretary stick them in there. Don't worry, she will keep her mouth shut. She likes the incoming guy less than we do." He stepped over a few bags and headed towards the door. "Now I need to get going. I have an inauguration to attend." The lock of the door clicked loudly into place as he left the room.

"Everything okay, sir?" Malcolm and Anna heard an unknown voice in the hallway.

"Yes, fine, Brian. The wife thought she left a personal item that she needed in one of the bags. Damned if I can find it amongst all that crap!"

They heard the President's deft lie from the other side of the wall, and traded smiles. President Gray always worked best in spontaneous moments.

"The limo is ready to take you to the Capitol," they heard the agent say as the sound of a door being opened was immediately followed by the President's footsteps leading the way towards the North Portico.

***

President Gray could see the columns of the portico through the exterior glass doors as he made his way down the elaborate hallway. Another Secret Service agent joined him so that he would be covered on both sides when he stepped outside. A service door suddenly opened in front of them and Jamal stepped out into the hallway, nearly bumping into the President.

"Sorry, sir." The icy glare flashed for a moment, showing the briefest sign of disrespect. President Gray returned it with a knowing look. He was tempted to make a stupid comment, but he kept his mouth shut and continued his trek towards the waiting limo.

"Mr. President?" Jamal spoke to the back of President Gray.

"Yes, Jamal?" He swiveled his body around to face the traitor. Jamal's chiseled figure was an intimidating figure in the hallway.

"Just wanted to check one thing, sir. I noticed that Director Ray was on the guest list this morning. Do I need to escort him out, or has he already left?"

"No, he's gone. I just showed him out myself," the President said tersely, not waiting for a response. The White House doors closed behind him, and he stepped outside. He saluted the ever-present Marine, and the door of the limo slammed shut behind him. He watched the figure of Jamal disappear into the White House. He felt like he was leaving the White House to an enemy. As the motorcade pulled into the street for the short trip to the Capitol he suddenly realized that he would never step foot inside the People's Mansion again. His wife gripped his hand, sensing his sorrow.

Chapter 60

The massive crowd surrounding the Capitol Building extended well into the Mall and past the museums that stood on both sides of the street. The twenty-degree temperature, combined with the light snow covering the ground, allowed the early afternoon sun to reflect off the snow, lighting up the area like a bright summer day. It was as close to perfect as one could expect when the temperature was as low as it was.

The crowd sat in rapt silence. Only the press, who experienced this every few years, continued milling about. All eyes were focused upwards at the steps of the Capitol. The stoic figure of Zachariah Hardin stepped into view behind the clear, bulletproof glass that surrounded the two administrations; one group standing down from power, and the other coming forward to take history by the throat. Zachariah was dressed in a full-length coat and classic dark suit, a grey sweater vest, and green tie completing the ensemble.

The black robed figure of the Chief Justice of the Supreme Court stepped forward with Zachariah and offered the Bible for his right hand. He placed his hand reverently on it, and recited the words that all his predecessors spoke over the years and centuries before him. He spoke the Oath of the Presidency authoritatively. The cold air gave tangible life to the passion and precision of his words. Once Zachariah finished, the military band immediately began playing. A sea of hands came forward to offer congratulations. The last hand offered was the now-former President. Mr. Gray grabbed Zachariah's hand and squeezed it as hard as he could. The offer of congratulations was friendly, but it was at odds with the piercing stare. For a moment Zachariah thought the man was about to do something crazy. Allan finally released his grip and took his seat. With the sea of hands now parted Zachariah stepped to the front of the podium. The crowd waived their hands enthusiastically and thousands of camera shudders flickered in unison. He acknowledged the clamoring crowd, and after calming them down with some hand gestures he launched into his inauguration address.

***

Inside the White House Malcolm and Anna lay flat on their stomachs on the floor, watching the speech on a small television that sat on the dresser. The TV was muted so as not to attract any unwanted attention. It was just as well. Neither of them wanted to listen to the man on the television. Because Anna had never been inside the White House before that day Malcolm spent a great deal of time giving her a rundown of the schematics of the mansion, and discussing possible opportunities where they could hope to catch Zachariah Hardin in a treasonous act. He drew a rough diagram on a piece of White House stationary and told her to memorize it. The whole exercise was surreal. They were drawing up plans for a potential guerilla attack inside the confines of the White House.

"So you think these two areas are the most likely spots?" Anna pointed to two different rooms that were circled on the handwritten diagram.

"Yes, I think they make the most sense. The Situation Room would be ideal in normal circumstances, but I don't see how he could possibly come up with an excuse to go in there in the middle of all these parties. Unless, of course, he wants to disappear for a while with one of his harem." Malcolm threw in the sarcastic remark as an afterthought.

Anna started field stripping her pistol, making sure there were no obvious defects. She wanted to be ready when the unthinkable happened. After satisfying herself she slammed a magazine into the butt of the weapon and stowed it away inside her oversized purse.

"Anything else you can think of that I need to know?" She looked inside her purse again to make sure the extra magazines were where they should be.

"No, I think we're good. We just sit tight for now. President Gray told me that from the way Zachariah had spoken to him he got the impression that Mr. Hardin wants to take his time strolling down the street and shaking hands since he sees himself as a real man of the people. Sometimes it's hard for me to see him as a real danger. He sounds and acts too much like a true politician."

Anna picked up the remote control and started flipping through the channels in a desperate attempt to find something else to watch besides the inauguration speech. She was about to give up when she stopped at one of the twenty-four hour news networks. Zachariah Hardin was continuing to give his passionate address, but below his dashing figure a news scroll flashed across the bottom of the monitor.

"*BREAKING NEWS,*" the familiar headline blared. "*MULTIPLE EXPLOSIONS ROCK GOVERNMENT BUILDINGS IN CAIRO. AMERICAN EMBASSY ALSO STRUCK. EYE WITNESSES CLAIM TO HAVE SEEN SUICIDE BOMBERS AT SEVERAL LOCATIONS.*"

"Malcolm, Look!" Anna's urgent tone brought Malcolm's attention to the television, and they both read the

365

scrolling headline in shock.

"Could this have been part of Aman's plan?" Anna remained calm and composed.

"It's possible. Let's just sit tight and see what happens. Aman was supposed to be heading back to Cairo, but that doesn't prove anything."

Despite the lack of proof Malcolm's gut told him that somehow the incident was connected to Zachariah. Aman, Jamal, Zachariah, and Aziz were all from Cairo. The Brotherhood of the Caliphate had its roots in the city, as well. Every move they made seemed to originate from the ancient city. He grabbed his cell phone and called in to Langley on one of the encrypted lines. His deputy picked up on the first ring, but refused to divulge any information. Malcolm had technically been fired thirty minutes earlier, and his deputy was in command for now. The Deputy Director apologized profusely, but the new administration specifically forbade any contact with Malcolm Ray.

On the steps of the Capitol President Zachariah Hardin finished his speech and soaked in the thunderous applause from the crowd. Anna thought it was the perfect elixir for his ego. She continued to watch even though she found the charade disgusting. Zachariah Hardin stepped away from the podium to more congratulatory handshakes and hugs. The military band started up again, and the sea of dignitaries began to split up. They would take different routes back to the White House for the celebrations that would soon follow.

***

Inside his limousine Zachariah Hardin struggled with a range of emotions beginning to well up inside of him. The power he felt while standing on the podium was intoxicating. His newly minted National Security Advisor rudely interrupted his thoughts. The impish, Ivy League educated man received his job due to party loyalty rather than any knowledge of foreign affairs. He grabbed Zachariah by the arm and yelled, "What the hell is that?" He pointed frantically at the small television mounted in the limo.

The new secretaries of Defense and State, both of whom served in previous administrations, remained calm as they watched the carnage unfold in Cairo.

"Shut the fuck up, Larry," The Defense Secretary demanded as he closely scrutinized the television. He adjusted the monitor so he could see what was happening.

The Defense Secretary was a long time military man whose strong national defense credentials made him an easy choice for his new role. Zach spent much of his campaign dropping not-so-subtle hints that he would appoint him as his secretary of defense if he were elected. It helped to shore up the fear of many of the independents that Zach would be a president who was weak on defense. He was also the only member of his cabinet from the opposite political party.

"Mr. President, this looks bad. A government friendly with the U.S. has been attacked along with our embassy. The first reports are saying the embassy is mostly rubble. We probably have hundreds of people dead. I suggest you head straight back to the White House to make a speech condemning this barbaric act. Once there, we can try to collect as much information as possible and decide on a course of action." The baritone voice of the Defense Secretary was calm and level.

Zach looked around at the rest of the group who all nodded their approval. "Okay. Let's move. John?" Zach rolled down the window on the limousine door.

"Yes, sir?" One of his Secret Service agents who were walking beside the slow moving vehicle leaned down to take the order.

"Get us back to the White House immediately. We will have to skip the parade," Zach's voice sounded disappointed. He spent the last few minutes in the limo feigning interest in continuing the parade. The plan was working flawlessly, and the sooner he could get back inside the White House to meet up with Jamal the better.

"Yes, sir," The agent began barking instructions into his earpiece.

The limousine picked up speed and raced down the street as a rowdy crowd suddenly fell silent. People looked at one another with quizzical expressions on their faces. The news slowly began to filter through the crowd. Some of the

367

spectators began running hysterically to call families. A large portion of the crowd began to make their way towards the White House to show solidarity with their new Commander in Chief.

Chapter 61

"Several sources at two of the buildings where the bombs exploded reported hearing the suicide bombers yell, 'Khalifah, Khilahah.' The blonde reporter struggled to get the phrase out. "We have been told this means Caliphate Creation. Back to you Mike." She finished her statement to the viewing crowd back home in the U.S. Anna noticed that the reporter was standing on an unknown street in Cairo, just a few blocks from the American embassy. A swirling mass of people could be seen darting behind her.

"Do you know what that could mean, Rachael?" The anchorman for the twenty-four hour news network asked from the safe confines of his New York City studio. Anna put the TV on mute and looked at Malcolm.

"Now that is no coincidence," Malcolm spoke with a stern voice. He began his ritual of making sure his pistol was ready to go. Each one stashed extra clips of ammunition in every pocket they had. They both looked back to the television as nervous reporters breathlessly described the situation. The view on the television was a shot from above of the Presidential limousine as it raced towards the White House at a dangerously high speed. Anna's face flashed back and forth between anger and tension, each one trying to establish its dominance. She felt odd. Their quest, which seemed so far fetched and ridiculous, was now coming to a conclusion. She could easily be dead within the hour, yet she felt an inner peace that seemed out of place in the midst of all the chaos around her.

***

The limousine came to a violent stop in front of the

368

East Portico of the White House. Zachariah Hardin stepped out, flanked on both sides by Secret Service agents. He did not acknowledge the cameras that stood nearby. Jamal met him at the entrance and ushered him inside. His national security team followed on his heels. The podium in the East Room was set up per Zachariah's instructions, and he strode purposefully down the Cross Hall towards the room. The cameras were ready, and the feeds to the networks were rolling. For the second time in less than an hour he stepped to a podium to address the American people.

"My fellow Americans. What should have been a glorious day for our country has been wrecked by crazed madmen." He stared into the camera and continued. "A series of terrorist attacks have been launched in Cairo. They have struck our friends in the Egyptian government and our own embassy, most likely killing hundreds. This barbarianism will not stand. America and Egypt will rise from this tragedy together, and we will hunt down the people responsible for this carnage. I have cancelled all inauguration celebrations until further notice. I am sorry, but I need to confer with my Cabinet so we can immediately begin the process of hunting down these common criminals. I can assure you I do not fear these monsters who glorify murder. I promise to provide you with every shred of information I am allowed to. Please keep your televisions on and pray for the victims. We will have more information to you as soon as possible. May God bless you, and may God bless America."

The anchorman appeared back on the screen and the odd soliloquy came to an end. The reporters in the room began shouting questions even though they were no longer on a live feed. The strange speech had the Washington establishment befuddled.

"No questions," Jamal yelled as he and another agent immediately took Zachariah under their protection, and headed off towards the situation room. The Military Officer carrying the nuclear football trailed close behind.

Chapter 62

Zachariah took the offered bottle of water from one of his underlings, and strode down the hallway. He was now minutes away from his destiny. He barked out orders as they passed different rooms that were filled with his friends, benefactors, and colleagues. They were all still milling about with dazed looks on their faces. Jamal stayed close to him. He glanced back to make sure the Military Officer was still near. He was right behind them. Jamal spoke feverishly into his headset, and instructed other agents around the building to get all unnecessary personnel out of the building.

"Where is the Defense Secretary?" Zach asked.

"He's already in the Situation Room sir. He's waiting for you," Jamal responded.

They reverted back to silence. Two more turns and Zach, Jamal, and the Military Officer came upon the secure stairwell that led to the Situation Room below ground. Jamal issued more instructions to another agent to remain at the top of the stairs.

"No one is allowed down after us unless the President personally requests it," Jamal barked. As a precaution he called in a second agent to guard the stairwell. They headed down into the sub-level of the White House with no one left to stop them.

"Hand me a weapon." The sinister tone of Zachariah's voice was unmasked as soon as the door closed behind them. They stopped halfway down the stairwell. Jamal quickly, but calmly extracted a Walter PPK from the inside of his sport coat, threaded the silencer onto it, and handed it to the President.

The Military Officer stood dumbfounded on the step above them, his eyes registering a scene that his mind told him was absolutely impossible. He tried to comprehend what was happening, but his words stumbled out of his mouth. "Sir, what is this... I mean, what's going on?" He watched in horror as the President swiveled the weapon until its black hole pointed at the officer's chest.

"You are sure you know how to operate the codes?" Zach asked Jamal one last time. He was about to reach the point of no return.

"Absolutely positive my Caliphate. Kill this man." Jamal said it with disdain, as if the Military Officer's life meant nothing to him. Zach put two shots into the man's chest. Jamal then picked up the black suitcase that would provide them with instant immortality, and they bounded down the stairs. A few more deaths to dish out in the Situation Room, and then they could deal the U.S. a blow from which it would never recover.

Chapter 63

"Okay, they should almost be in the Situation Room by now. Let's go," Malcolm said tersely.

They watched Zach's second speech from the Lincoln bedroom and waited patiently for a few more minutes. They needed perfect timing. He had to be caught in the act. Nothing else would suffice. It was the only way anyone would believe it. Anna stepped cautiously out the door and peered down the empty hallway. She pushed the door open and motioned for Malcolm to take the lead. They still kept their weapons holstered and hidden. It was risky, but they would have to catch any Secret Service agents off guard. They had no desire to initiate a firefight. They were severely outgunned, and it would probably get them killed.

The first guard was stationed at the elevator that would take them from the living quarters down to the main floor of the West Wing. Malcolm stepped around the corner and into the man's view, Anna trailing right behind him. Malcolm saw the suspicious look on the man's face.

"Call down and tell the President I'm on my way down. He just called for us," Malcolm said with authority as they both strode right up to the guard. An agent's first instinct was always to follow orders without question, and he hesitated for just a second. Anna's elbow flashed forward, catching him in the jaw, followed immediately by a chop to the neck from Malcolm which rendered him unconscious.

***

The guns fired simultaneously and the bodies of presidential advisors crashed to the floor. The advisors had been in the process of putting together briefing papers for the new President. That very man was now spraying them with bullets. The National Security Advisor screeched like a wounded animal when Zach's shot rammed him in the chest. The searing pain in his chest quickly ended with a perfectly placed bullet from Jamal's weapon. The man's head exploded, sending particles of blood and brain all over the long boardroom table which sat in the middle of the small room.

"Have you lost your mind, sir?" The Secretary of State said in horror as he stared at the body of the Secretary of Defense that lay crumpled in the corner. The body twitched slightly as blood oozed onto the dirty carpet. He was still alive for now.

"What is this?" Tears began to stream down the Secretary of State's face. He sat frozen in place, completely baffled by a scene that was impossible for him to accept, but was occurring nonetheless. His years of service to his country brought him into many stressful and dangerous situations, but the shock of the carnage that lay before him left him immobile with fear. His body's only reaction was to cry.

"What have you done?" He wailed again in a fit of anguish. He sat frozen while Jamal and Zachariah moved to the back of the room, and began meticulously making their preparations.

Jamal turned to face the Secretary of State. The cold, uncaring face sneered before he leveled his weapon and fired. The shot landed right between the eyes. The limp body dropped to the floor, ending the hysterical screams in mid-sentence.

"What I have been training to do all my life," Jamal replied to the dead body. "I knew I should have done all the shooting. They were making too much noise." He stuffed the weapon down the front of his pants, and then stepped back into the corridor to retrieve the black suitcase with the nuclear codes. When he re-entered the room Zach was laughing.

"The place is soundproof, you idiot. Besides, we didn't want one of them having time to trigger an alarm. I'm sure there is one here," Zach said as he suppressed a button on the weapon, dropping the empty magazine onto the floor.

He took the briefcase from Jamal, and walked to the head of the table at the far end of the room. He stole a look at the Presidential Seal nailed to the wall directly behind him, flipped it the bird, and then sat the nuclear football on the table. He was going to enjoy this. He yanked out the codes that he had received just a few hours earlier, and began readying the launch sequence. It would take less than thirty minutes to set the destruction in motion.

A flicker of movement in the corner of the room caught their attention. The Secretary of Defense's meaty hand stretched upwards and reached for the red button hidden underneath the end of the table. The button would summon additional help in case of a sudden medical emergency. The room, which was used for such stressful situations, had induced a few heart attacks and fainting spells over the years, all of which had been kept out of the press. The emergency button had to be there to summon help immediately.

Jamal saw the hand reach out, and yanked his pistol out of his waistline. He had been watching Zach intently, giving him instructions as he went through the sequence, punching in codes that would send nuclear tipped missiles into the heart of Los Angeles, Las Vegas, San Francisco, St. Louis, Nashville, and other major cities. It would be a nuclear umbrella of death that would blanket the entire country, killing tens of millions and destroying the United States as a world power. Jamal pulled the trigger. He ended the Secretary of Defense's life just as the hand pressed down on the emergency button.

Chapter 64

There are moments in history when the balance of world power hinges on a minor change or split second decision. A slight alteration of a battle plan that may seem miniscule at first, but can allow the other side time to adjust, and what looks like a resounding defeat morphs quickly into a decisive victory, or vice versa. History is replete with such scenarios, and the truly great world leaders and military commanders recognize them and learn from them. Malcolm and Anna did not know this was happening to them. All they saw as they stepped into the corridor were five Secret Service agents approximately forty yards away with their backs towards them. Agents were racing towards the stairwell that led down to the Situation Room. This lucky turn of events gave them a free run across the hallway and over to the stairs that led to the basement.

"Stop! No one else is allowed down," the lone guard left to watch the entrance yelled with authority.

"The President called for us." Malcolm blurted out the words as he simultaneously reached into his jacket and whipped out his pistol, crashing it into the agent's head and shattering the earpiece he used to communicate with his fellow agents. The man grunted in anger, shocked by the violent attack. Anna followed the pistol whip with a knee to the groin, then an elbow to the head. The burly guard finally slumped to the ground unconscious.

"You ready?" Malcolm asked.

They stood in silence for a few brief seconds. She pulled out her pistol, leaving the silencer in the bag. Subtlety and surprise were no longer part of the plan. She made sure all her extra magazines were in her pockets before nodding affirmatively. Malcolm gave her a quick explanation of where the stairs led and how the Situation Room was laid out. He had visited the room on several occasions during the war with the Taliban.

"You stay low. I'll stay high," Malcolm said. He pushed the door open and they proceeded cautiously down the stairwell. As they neared the end of the stairwell they saw the body of the Military Officer strewn awkwardly about the staircase. They cautiously continued the remainder of their descent. The dead body was the final confirmation of their worst nightmare.

Malcolm led the way with Anna following closely behind him. Their weapons scanned the empty space for targets, but found nothing at which to shoot. They reached the bottom without incident and stopped. Both of their backs pushed firmly against the wall. Malcolm poked his head cautiously around the corner. The six agents who preceded them down the steps were bunched up around the door that led into the Situation Room.

Malcolm had assumed they would hold their meeting in the video teleconferencing room directly behind the main meeting area, but he appeared to be wrong. He could see the door propped slightly open. Jamal appeared to be having a serious discussion with the agents in the doorway. The group looked unorganized and confused. They were huddled together and all facing Jamal. They were easy targets.

Malcolm turned back and gave a hand signal to Anna indicating the number of agents in the hallway. They were a blessing and a curse. They provided the duo with cover for their final approach, but he knew they would have to kill many of them in the fog of war they were about to enter. Anna indicated her readiness, and they threw themselves into the open corridor with their weapons raised.

Chapter 65

It was the flash of the guns reflecting off the cheap ceiling lights that first caught Jamal's attention. His eyes bulged when he saw the two people appear at the opposite end of the hallway. Malcolm and Anna fired simultaneously. The noise reverberated throughout the hallway, amplified by the metal walls. One of the agents yelped in pain as a bullet tore into his shoulder.

"Intruders! Kill them now!" Jamal screamed.

One of the agents pushed the door open in an attempt to get into the Situation Room and hide from the fusillade of bullets that were exploding everywhere. Jamal threw his shoulder into the other side of the bulletproof door, resisting it.

A second agent now applied pressure to the door, as well, and it finally flew open. Jamal jumped back out of the way. His only duty was to protect Zach long enough to complete the firing sequence. The two agents looked at the bloodied bodies in the room in stunned surprise. Jamal repeatedly squeezed his trigger, pumping one of the agents with four shots. The lifeless body thudded to the floor.

The second agent looked at Jamal, and then turned towards the hallway. Two of his four friends lay motionless on the floor behind him, and the other two were bringing their weapons around to fire amidst a pool of their own blood. Their hands held loose grips on their pistols. They were wounded and fading fast. As the agent turned around to assist his colleagues Jamal fired into his back, and then retreated to the other side of the room to watch over Zachariah.

Anna and Malcolm approached the open doorway. Malcolm had worked in some of the dirtiest and dangerous countries in the world doing things he would never tell a soul, but none of them even remotely compared to this. He was slaughtering Secret Service agents.

The man in the doorway still did not drop his weapon despite Anna's screams to throw it to the floor. Malcolm slammed a new magazine into his weapon and regretfully blasted away, striking the agent from the front as Jamal's shot simultaneously hit him from behind. They both got low to the ground and jumped through the open door, using the massive table in the middle of the room to shield as much of their bodies as possible. Both of them were on one knee, their clothes soaked from the blood of the Secret Service agents.

"Drop the weapon, Jamal. It's over!" Malcolm's

voice boomed. Jamal replied with several wild gunshots that blasted into the table, sending chipped fragments flying. Anna winced as one of the bullets grazed her arm. Jamal now positioned his body directly in front of Zach, who was still furiously working the nuclear football. It was taking longer than anticipated. The color-coded bar turned from red to green.

"Almost there!" Zach said fiercely to Jamal.

Jamal grabbed Zach's gun off the table just as his own ran dry, and pumped several more wild shots towards the two figures now hunched behind the other end of the long conference table.

"Anna, unload your clip and keep him occupied for a second!"

Anna immediately lifted herself back onto one knee, exposing her upper torso, and began firing off several errant shots. Jamal steadied his weapon and fired, catching her in the right shoulder. The showdown gave Malcolm just enough time. He swung his left leg underneath the table as if he were a soccer player looking to make a particularly dirty sweep of an opposing player. He caught several of the chairs with his leg and pushed them out of the way. The underside was now much less cluttered and provided him a better opening. At the same time his leg swept the chairs, he unloaded the empty magazine and rammed another one into place just as the view under the table opened.

He fired off most of the chamber. A few of the bullets splintered the wood of the two remaining chairs, but the last several bullets found their mark. They slammed into Jamal's legs and he buckled, dropping to the floor and exposing Zachariah.

Malcolm emptied the last of the magazine into Zachariah. The President collapsed to the floor, dragging the nuclear football with him. Malcolm quickly installed a fresh magazine, raised himself up off the floor, and fired two shots into Jamal's chest. He then began making his way towards the two traitors.

"Stay put, Anna," he commanded to his wounded partner.

Malcolm turned his attention to Zachariah Hardin.

377

The President was breathing erratically. His hand reached out in a vain attempt to push the final button that would bring him to glory and martyrdom. Malcolm scooped up the briefcase and sat it on the table. He needed to get someone down here who knew how to properly handle it. He stepped on Zach's shoulder, pinning him to the ground.

"Find out what they did with Alex." Anna's raspy and weakened voice floated across the room to him. She was slumped on the floor and about to pass out.

"Where is Alex Bryce? He vanished yesterday," Malcolm demanded as he stood over the dying President.

"You are just like all the other Americans. Too weak to do what is necessary," Zachariah said as he foamed at the mouth like a rabid dog.

"Where is he?" Malcolm stepped down on Zach's shoulder with more force.

"He is at Jamal's house. He should still be alive. Unlike you," Zachariah said with a venomous tone.

Malcolm shot him in the head execution style. As far as he was concerned, it was the least vile thing he had done that day. He picked up the phone on the table and rang the Vice-President. Or President rather, Malcolm mentally corrected himself. The man had been waiting patiently upstairs for his instructions from Zach. After several minutes Malcolm finally reached him, and ordered him down to the Situation Room. He told him to bring in the medical team that was always on call at the White House.

***

"Oh, my God."

Malcolm turned around when he heard the New York accent of Zach's running mate. The new President was standing in the doorway, unable to mutter anything else. The air seemed to be sucked out of his lungs. He dashed for the corner and threw up in the garbage can, his whole body heaving in convulsions. His Secret Service agent stepped through the doorway right behind him with a look of shock that was becoming commonplace to Malcolm.

"Make sure the President is okay." He emphasized the word President to the agent who nodded his understanding. "After he reinstates me as CIA Director we have a story to concoct," Malcolm said with authority. He walked over to Anna and knelt down beside her. She opened her eyes. They sat in silence as a group of doctors swarmed into the basement to administer help to the wounded. Anna and Malcolm exchanged smiles of congratulations tempered with the knowledge that this was only a battle in a long and deadly war.

EPILOGUE

The successive explosions echoed throughout the underground firing range. After a final thirty seconds of continually squeezing the trigger Alex Bryce stopped and put the pistol on the wooden table in front of him. The ejected shell casings tinkled quietly on the concrete floor before coming to a rest. The basement was now eerily silent after thirty minutes of shooting practice. Alex used his right foot to sweep away the empty shell casings on the ground before taking off his ear protectors and setting them beside the pistol. He flipped a switch, and a hydraulic pole in the ceiling hissed softly as it brought the silhouetted target of a human up to his face. Alex took the target off the pole, limped over to his chair, and began studying his handiwork.

"Not bad. You're getting better." The familiar voice of Anna Starks spoke authoritatively from the stairwell behind him.

Alex swiveled around to look at his superior. He stood back up and smiled. He had not seen her since she appeared at Jamal's house to cut him free of his bindings, and he had not been in a proper state of mind to discuss anything then. Alex had to undergo minor surgery on his legs, and had spent the last few weeks under the care of an Agency doctor. Malcolm had decided to ship him back to the cabin to recuperate.

"Don't move. I'll come to you," Anna said as she hurriedly covered the distance between them. They had a long embrace before separating. "How are the legs?" Anna asked.

"Better. The doctor said it will take a month or so for the muscles to heal, but I should be a hundred percent after that," Alex replied. The reminder of his ordeal caused him to feel woozy so he sat back down. "Enough about me. What happened at the White House?" Alex asked. "I've been following the news from here, but I'm assuming everything in those stories was planted by Malcolm."

Anna picked up the empty pistol and squinted down the target sights before putting it back on the table. "We were right, Alex. We caught Zach as he was trying to launch nuclear missiles on U.S. cities. Malcolm shot them both dead. I wasn't much help," she said as she motioned to her bandaged shoulder. "We'll fill you in on the details later."

Alex nodded solemnly. He assumed there must have been a nasty shootout in the White House. The press reports announced that a gas leak in the Situation Room killed the President, some Secret Service agents, and several members of the president's Cabinet. "How long do you think you can keep that story going?" Alex asked.

"I'm not sure. We will just have to wait and see. My guess is not very long. There are too many people who witnessed the carnage. Some of the families of the agents are skeptical, as well. They d'dn't like having to wait to see the bodies of their loved ones. Eventually we will probably have to tell at least some version of the truth of what happened. For now, though, all the witnesses, including the President, are in agreement to keep it quiet."

"What about me?" Alex asked with some trepidation.

"As far as the rest of the world is concerned you are dead. It was the only way to clean up the mess in Las Vegas. Your ex-wife was informed."

Alex looked vacantly through the holes in the silhouetted target before dropping it to the floor. "I guess that makes sense. I don't have any siblings and my parents died a few years ago. Still seems a little harsh though. What about my job?"

"You're going to work with me. Our job is not finished yet. I haven't told you the full story."

"Okay. What now?" Alex said nervously. He was no longer surprised by anything.

"Jamal escaped. After Malcolm shot him we didn't check him closely because we assumed he was dead. The doctors swarmed the room, and Jamal's body was immediately taken away to a secret morgue with some of the other agents who were killed. The ambulance never made it to the morgue. It was found abandoned a few hours later. The driver was dead. We found a discarded bulletproof vest and a thin plastic covering that contained packets of animal blood. Apparently the blood that Malcolm saw oozing from Jamal's chest actually came from this plastic covering that he wore over the vest. In our hurry to scrub the room clean we royally screwed up."

"Where is Jamal now?" Alex asked with a slightly menacing tone. Now that he knew his torturer was alive his blood pressure began to rise. Alex knew it was foolish, but he hoped they would be going after the crazed lunatic.

"Somewhere in the Caribbean, I think. I've spent the last week looking into Aman's operations. He owned a boat that he kept off the coast of Miami. The boat disappeared from its mooring a few days ago. We tracked down several people who gave descriptions of someone who sounds very similar to Jamal," Anna replied.

"Why is he going to the Caribbean?"

"We think he's going after Solomon."

"Solomon? Aman's head of security?" Alex asked with surprise.

"Yeah. We found a stolen rental car in an airport garage a few weeks back. It was the same car used in the assassination of Sean and Colin. We went through airport surveillance at Dulles and found images of Solomon catching a plane to Belize. We think Solomon has money stashed somewhere in the Caribbean."

"Is Jamal after his money, or wanting to kill him to keep him quiet?" Alex asked.

Anna smiled knowingly. Alex was proving to be a quick learner. She was beginning to think he would make an excellent partner. "We're not sure. Maybe both. Solomon certainly has secrets in his head, and he has money hidden away. Jamal is going to need money to escape."

"When do we start?" Alex asked with a hint of impatience.

"I'm leaving for Belize tomorrow to try to pick up the trail. You are going to have a month of intensive training by a top operations man, and then you will be meeting up with me."

"I thought you were the top operations man!" Alex said sarcastically.

"Not anymore. We have a new guy. His name is Malcolm Ray."

"What! They fired Malcolm?" Alex could not believe he was fired after what he had endured.

"Not at all. He is going to voluntarily resign so he can take over as Deputy Director of Operations. His old DDO is now the head of the CIA. Malcolm decided being the Director involved too much paperwork. His first job as DDO will be personally training you."

Anna pushed a fresh magazine into the butt of the pistol and placed it back on the table. "Better keep practicing. Malcolm is a difficult person to please." Anna embraced him one more time and gave him a light kiss on the cheek. "Hurry up and get better. I'll see you soon." She moved quickly across the basement and up the stairs.

Alex watched the remarkable woman leave. All words seemed pointless. How could you thank someone who had saved your life so many times? Alex did not think it was possible so he watched her leave in silence. He suppressed his emotions and picked up the pistol. He needed more practice. The unknown future that now lay before him was exciting and terrifying at the same time. He could not fathom a guess as to what lay ahead, but he knew his fate, whether good or bad, was forever entwined with Ms. Starks.

END

Acknowledgements

First of all, I would like to thank my parents. They have worked hard for thirty years to provide me with all the tools I need to succeed in life, and I could not ask for better parents.

I would also like to thank my good friends Kevin and Phil for humoring me by reading the poorly written first drafts, and being kind enough not to say anything.

A special thanks is in order for my wife Angie, and my Uncle Bruce, who both spent an untold number of hours reading the manuscript, editing it, and providing me with helpful insights and constructive criticisms.

Following is an excerpt from the sequel to Agent of Influence. It is scheduled for release in late 2014.

One Single Warrior
Volume II in the Agent of Influence Series
By
Russell Hamilton

"When the time of triumph comes, with good fortune from both worlds as our companion, then by one single warrior on foot a king may be stricken with terror, though he own more than a hundred thousand horsemen." Ismaili Poet.

Chapter 1

A rickety ceiling fan clicked slowly away, tossing the slightest of breezes into the otherwise humid room. It sputtered in its final throes as the slowing blades struggled to wipe out the rancid smell of death below. Flies circled the two naked corpses. A man's slender body sat strewn akimbo in a bamboo chair, his shaggy black hair partially obscuring the sharply defined jaw line.

Sweat perspiring down his muscled chest, the assassin, naked himself except for gloved hands, stepped to the side of the chair, placed a pistol against the limp head and fired one shot with the dead victim's .45 caliber Glock 21 into the right temple, and in the process obscuring the execution shot he made only minutes earlier with his own 9mm weapon. The second shot travelled the same flight path as the first so that there was just one entrance wound to go with the larger exit wound. This made it resemble a self-inflicted coup de grace. Blood and brain matter sprayed onto the dead hooker's corpse sitting on the bed.

He wiped the gun down as an added precaution and laid it loosely in the dead man's hands. The scene of betrayal, murder, and suicide appeared obvious. The assassin took two steps back and tried to examine the scene with a clinical eye. It would be an open and shut case for the local police, and they would have no desire to investigate further when a favorite prostitute of a drug lord was butchered and left with the telltale warning of the cartel. Move the bodies and move on with their lives would be the path of least resistance.

His primal instincts flared as he turned his focus on the woman. She had claimed to be from Columbia, but her shoulder length hair was dyed bleach blonde, a stark contrast to her mahogany skin tone. The bleached hair reminded him of a vain American woman, and this thought gave him additional pleasure when he crushed her larynx. Satisfied with his handy work he stepped into the rudimentary shower just off the bedroom to rinse off. He scrubbed vigorously until the blood of his victims was washed clean from his matted chest hair and legs. It mixed with the dirt and grime near the shower's floor drain before descending into the rusty pipes below. He dried off, put on gym shorts and a tank top, and stepped from the dilapidated one story bungalow out into the muggy night.

The neighborhood of shacks was quiet except for a few yapping dogs. The smell of salt water and the lapping of waves reminded him of how close the ocean was. The banker provided him with the correct information. It took a few weeks, his target was no novice after all, but the assassin was the perfect killing machine. A man whose ancestors were the original assassins, hired to kill neighboring sultans and then rewarded with gardens of milk, honey, and whores. Almost all of their victims were fellow Muslims, a point lost on the ignorant and unwashed, and the assassin hoped to follow in their footsteps. His mentor, a man named Aziz taught him patience, and cunning, but it had been his mortal enemy that turned him into a remorseless killing machine. Now that training had tied up a loose end before it could fray into something dangerous and unforeseen.

Despite being well over six feet tall he slinked smoothly and calmly through back yards, thickets of palm trees, mounds of junk cars, and pounds of debris scattered around the neighborhood until he came upon the wharf filled with fishing boats in various degrees of disrepair. He stalked to the end of the pier, climbed into his gleaming yacht, and generously paid the locals for standing watch over it. Within five minutes he was in the open ocean.

Unable to control it, his mind's eye returned to the carnage of the tiny apartment. It was not the death that disturbed him, but the sex. It was his first time. Why he raped the hooker before crushing her larynx he was not sure. Forty two years as a virgin certainly made one curious, but it was not so much that as the need to guilt himself into an act that only made him even angrier. He spent his entire life controlling that anger, channeling it to the appropriate place and time before striking a death blow to his enemies. He was that rare breed that the angrier they got, the better his performance. This made him a lethal killer when he was in the Special Forces and it was why his superiors silently put up with the rumors from his teammates that he went on one man killing raids when they were on assignments in various third world hell holes.

Even the best of killers can only last in the Special Forces for so long and his bosses were more than content to shuffle him along to his cozy job as a Secret Service agent before he screwed up. He now had an additional sin to atone for and he would not fail this time.

Chapter 2
May, 2005
Ambergis Caye, Belize

It seemed an odd place for a cemetery, but on such a small island you must make do with every inch of available land. Anna unfurled her blanket, dropping it underneath the shade of a large palm tree. The pristine white beach prickled her toes as the late afternoon sun scorched the coarse sand.

"Drink miss?" a young island boy in crisp white shorts magically appeared.

"No thanks." She motioned for him to leave. She picked this spot because it was close to the graveyard that took up a part of the beach and she did not think the zealous cabana boys would bother her.

"Here. Take this and leave me alone. I need some sun." She extracted some Belizean dollars from her beach bag and stuck them forcefully into his hand.

Anna Starks sat on the blanket, stretched her bronzed legs, and took in her surroundings. She soaked in the familiar sights and sounds from the last few weeks of reconnaissance. A block to her right a group of local boys raced barefoot up and down a basketball court that was as much sand as concrete. To the left groups of tourists baked in the sun. Books dangled loosely from wet fingertips, while others sat in a zombie-like state soaking in the Caribbean heat with fins and snorkels resting beside them. Most of the sun worshipers held scuba certifications and spent their mornings diving the world's second largest barrier reef that was a five minute boat ride from any of the hotel docks on the tiny island.

The young boy scurried off to harass other tourists. Anna fiddled with her striped Ella Moss Portofino cover up that helped to hide her slim figure, tied her black hair into a ponytail, and put on a ball cap to shade her facial features from prying eyes. She slid on a pair of fashionable, oversized sunglasses and lay on her back, the sunglasses hiding her methodical scanning of the beach.

An hour into her vigil the banker appeared for his daily swim. *Right on time.* He dropped his personal effects onto a folding beach chair and walked purposefully into the ocean. She studied his pale white, lithe frame as it glinted off the water. He swam freestyle furiously for twenty minutes before exiting the ocean. He was breathing heavily as he plopped onto his chair and closed his eyes.

Anna quickly stood and rolled up the towel, stuffing it in her over-sized beach bag. She felt around the bottom of the bag until she touched the two silenced Sig Sauer pistols sitting at the bottom. *An advantage of being an*

387

agent and a woman was that you could carry huge bags around with all sorts of deadly goodies and blend right in. She recited her mentor's line again. No man could carry a bag with enough room for a silenced pistol, much less two, and not draw unwanted attention.

Exchanging flip flops for Adidas running shoes she trudged through the sand, walking in the opposite direction of where the banker was napping. She circled the cemetery and came up to the dusty street running alongside the beach, taking a seat on a bench in front of the basketball court. *Keep La Isla Bonita clean.* Anna read the words on the garbage can as she pondered her course of action one more time. Would this banker have the information she needed? Two weeks of cautious inquires around the island and using her self as an old-fashioned honey trap had left this banker as her only possible target. *Can he lead me to Solomon before his previous employer caught up with him?*

Solomon murdered two of her colleagues in broad daylight on a cold January day in Washington D.C. just a few months ago and then fled the country. He previously worked for a man named Aman Kazim, a Las Vegas casino owner whose massive tentacles stretched to D.C. where he curried favor with anyone willing to take his handouts or his whores, the most pliable and weak taking both. Aman's power and influence got his adopted son, Zachariah Hardin, elected President of the United States. They were both dead now, but their accomplice, an even deadlier foe was still on the loose. As sick as it made her she was ready to let Solomon go in exchange for certain intel, but first she had to find him. He could not spill his guts if he was already gutted.

The banker appeared again on cue, scurrying up the beach and onto the street. *Twenty minute nap and now back to his office for a little overtime. He has forgotten the danger of a predictable routine.* Fiddling in her bag she extracted a disposable camera and started a leisurely stroll. She proceeded south on Great Barrier Reef Drive, the main street of the tiny "city" of San Pedro, the only city on the 25-mile island just off the coast of Belize. The streets were in fact nothing but dirt roads that were barely bigger than alleyways in America. The only vehicles that traversed them were government pickup trucks and golf carts hauling locals or lazy visitors.

She stopped at a tiny tourist trap and pretended to ponder entering it. An old woman standing just inside the creaky, white-washed wood building smiled a toothless smile and beckoned her to come inside.

"No thank you," Anna said sweetly before continuing onward. She heard the crunch of footsteps on the dirt road approaching behind her and she picked up her pace. She walked past numerous little cafes, gift shops, and businesses and all the buildings were in a similar state of poor condition with weather-beaten wood, peeling white paint, and numerous boarded up windows. San Pedro had the appearance of a shanty town and a rough neighborhood but it was actually quite safe. The town was solely dependent upon the tourists and the feeling of danger which accompanied your first visit quickly vanished after a day on the island.

Anna could see the two-story building several blocks further down that housed the Catholic school on the island. Just past the school you literally ran into an eight foot chain link fence and just beyond it the tiny airport consisting of cracked concrete and scattered splotches of weeds that was just big enough to accommodate a constant stream of puddle jumpers. She glanced at her watch and hurried down the street, putting on a show for the banker she knew was rapidly approaching. *Does he recognize me?*

Stopping at the next intersection she glanced up at the façade of the building. *Alliance Bank.* Out of the corner of her eye she spotted Alex Bryce, her assistant for the moment casually reading a newspaper on a bench. He would make sure they were not disturbed. The two story wood building was in slightly better condition than the surrounding ones but still looked nothing like what you would imagine the typical Caribbean bank would be. Anna tried the door and found it locked, as she knew she would since most businesses on the island typically closed early on Friday. She put her face to the glass, peered inside, and waited.

The shuffle of shoes behind her stopped. A throat cleared. "Can I help you?"

Chapter 3

"Anna! It truly is good to see you again. You are lucky I like to work late on Fridays. It's one of my habits from the States that I haven't been able to shake," Joseph Barnes said enthusiastically as he dropped his towel on the floor and plopped into his orthopedic back chair. His computer booted up quickly. His desk was pristine, an oasis of calm amidst the rest of the building which looked unusually messy and cluttered for a bank.

"This is your cubicle? I must admit that the way you talked at dinner a few nights ago I was expecting something a little...classier?" Anna pointed disapprovingly at his desk which was against one of the exterior walls of the building, sitting opposite the vacant teller stations. The bank did not look very secure, as everything was made of wood. *Nothing in here that will stop a bullet.*

"Snobbery from a beach bum hiding out in the Caribbean? I love it. Sorry, but this is it. San Pedro is a very safe town. Don't need any fancy buildings here. The money is secure. That's all that matters." Joseph pinched his water flecked t-shirt, flapping it in an attempt to dry it. The chilled air of the bank made goose bumps visible up and down his arms.

"Now, what can I help you with? You decide you want to purchase something on the island or has my charm finally caught up with you and you want to sleep with me? I know you cannot afford the real estate prices here so I am hoping for the latter!"

"As stimulating as our conservation was the other night I will have to pass." Anna reached into her beach bag and tossed an ID badge on the table.

"Shit," Joseph muttered.

"Sorry for the deception but I'm actually FBI and I have a few questions for you regarding a murder investigation." The silenced Sig Sauer pistol appeared in her right hand and she dropped the beach bag on the floor.

Joseph tensed, staring at the weapon intently. A Caribbean banker knew his clientele preferred anonymity for a variety of reasons both legitimate and not so.

"Well, this is definitely a surprise. I can assure you neither I nor any of my clients have killed anyone," he responded airily. His hands moved slowly towards the keyboard positioned underneath his desk.

"That being said, since when do FBI agents question potential witnesses at the point of a gun?"

"Keep your hands visible please," Anna said sharply as she scooped up the badge and dropped it back into her bag.

"Do you really think a fake badge is going to make me talk? Who are you really? CIA? DEA? Or some other new alphabet soup agency the U.S. government spits out every year?"

"The badge is a joke, but I'm hoping the real gun may get your attention." She ignored his second question, pointed at the floor beneath his desk, and discharged a single bullet, splintering the wood.

Joseph jumped, the wheels of his chair ramming against the wall.

Anna reached into the pocket of her swimsuit cover and dropped a surveillance photo on the desk.

"Seen this man recently?"

He cautiously rolled his chair forward; straining his neck as if afraid the item may jump up and bite him. "Doesn't look familiar to me," he replied confidently.

"Look closer," Anna demanded. She motioned with her pistol.

He inched his chair towards her to hover over the picture, his right hand reaching to grasp it. In a flash his left hand grabbed the framed picture on his desk, flinging it at her while at the same time springing forward over his desk like an eel coming out of its hole in the coral reef that was just blocks away. His left hand grabbed her right, holding the

391

pistol towards the ceiling as they rolled in a heap towards the floor.

The simple feint bought him a few seconds as they tumbled backwards. Anna recovered her composure as her back touched the floor. Utilizing his momentum she brought her knee up in a short, rapid fire burst, delivering a blow to his groin as they bounced up off the floor in a flurry of motion. The line of defense did its trick and he let out a short cry of pain, releasing his grip slightly. Anna was outweighed by thirty pounds in any struggle she was involved in but a strike to the groin along with her judo skills, and lightness on her feet equalized most fights.

Patience. Wait for your opportunity. All four hands locked together, as if they were an uncoordinated couple attempting to dance. Bending her knees she swung her right leg in a quick circular motion. He arced backward, avoiding the blow but it loosened his grip on her unarmed hand, partially freeing her from the awkward wrestling match. He grunted in frustration, throwing a quick punch that landed on her shoulder.

Her knees buckled as she dropped towards the floor once more, the banker now mounting his assault as he continued trying mightily to wrench the pistol out of her grasp. Sensing weakness he rose up to his full height for better leverage, striking downward with another punch, this one launching towards her jaw. Anna inhaled, arching her back downwards until she touched the hardwood floor to avoid the knockout punch. His torso now exposed ever so briefly she used the floor as a launching pad, her legs springing forward, counterclockwise, and drilling him squarely in the chest. He crashed into the floor, his head cracking the ground as she was simultaneously flung upward by the momentum until she landed on top of him like a lover straddling her man. He let out a short scream, the blow to the head stunning him for a moment as his torso was sandwiched between the floor and Anna's legs now wrapped around him in a vicious squeeze.

Chapter 4

As his eyes came into focus, Anna, a silenced Sig Sauer pistol in each hand, applied downward pressure on each of his shoulders. He squirmed in pain.

"Never thought you'd be straddled by a woman quite this way, huh? Make a move and you get a bullet in each shoulder. Got it?"

"How the hell did you...," Joseph stared at the second pistol that was now in her left hand and his eyes then moved towards the beach bag askew on the floor beside them.

"You never reached in that bag unless...You grabbed it during our little tumble onto the floor?" Joseph stared at her in disbelief and pondered if it was possible that he was actually knocked unconscious.

"Who the hell are you?" The acrobatic move still did not seem possible to him.

"I ask the questions. Don't f with me and you will live. You can trust me there. I'm tired of killing people. I just want some answers."

"Now, where is Solomon?" She thought it best to get right to the point. Her partner was waiting for her.

"I don't know what you are talking about," Joseph said indignantly. He barely finished the sentence before the silenced pistol loosed a bullet through his right shoulder and lodged in the wood plank floor.

"Argh. You little bitch! Ow!" He screamed as she now applied pressure to the wound.

"Where?" Anna demanded.

"What does it matter to you? He's small potatoes. Just a former enforcer for the Columbian drug lords!"

"He also is wanted for killing agents of the FBI and CIA on US soil who were friends of mine."

"You're lying."

"Think so? He is also wanted for aiding and abetting two terrorists." It was a new threat that tended to work well. Drug dealers were often ignored by the authorities due to time and money constraints. Terrorists used the bolder ones to move money around. Threaten a small fry in the market and they sometimes got nervous.

Joseph looked unsure of himself for the first time as he realized the potential enormity of the situation. It made more sense than a DEA agent looking for a drug suspect. She was taking too many risks with her assault on him for something so minor. The wheels of justice in the islands of the Caribbean were still lax and greased by bribes. You could easily find yourself in jail if you made the wrong provincial governor angry. Many islands had vastly improved in order to attract more foreign money, but the threat was still there, especially for outsiders so it would not make sense for her to run that risk unless Solomon was in deep. He made a quick decision.

"I helped him transfer some money into Mexico. He was looking to hook up with one of the cartels there. Drug wars are starting to turn nasty. It's the new Columbia."

"That's better. Why did he choose you to do the transfers?"

"We're a small bank. Off most people's maps. He liked that. Plus I know the ropes around here," he said with a hint of pride.

"You're former life as a DEA agent probably helps to?"

"How the hell did you know?" The smirk of pride vanished quickly.

She ignored the question and continued her pursuit. "Where in Mexico did he go?"

"Merida."

"When did he leave Belize?"

"Two weeks ago. At least that is when he said he was leaving"

Ten minutes later she had used the password he gave her to get all the information on Solomon's banking activities off his computer as well as the name of a realtor he gave to Solomon. Joseph was unconscious on the floor, his wound bound as best she could for the moment. She would call in the robbery to the police shortly. She shot out the cameras, wiped down any surface she touched, and took some cash to make the robbery look a little more real. She cautiously stepped out into the dusty, deserted road, the late afternoon soon baking the rows of dilapidated buildings.

She was one step closer to her goal. *Can I get to him before Jamal?* Solomon was morally bankrupt, a former spy, and a former bodyguard for drug lords and terrorists, but he was almost certainly being hunted by an even more dangerous creature; the former secret service agent/Navy Seal/now terrorist known as Jamal. A beast of a man who in their last encounter not only almost ended Anna's life, but nearly succeeded in unleashing nuclear Armageddon on the United States. A seasoned veteran at just a shade past thirty years old Anna had survived longer than most in the dirty business of espionage, and there were few things left that scared her. Jamal fit nicely into that small category.

TO BE CONTINUED....